Theirs was a world of explosive passions ignited by one radiant moment of desire. . . .

SVETLANA OZEROVA—A rebellious beauty, she would turn her back on tradition to face the future in her enemy's arms.

MA LI-CHUN—He risked his life to save a kidnapped foreign beauty only to find himself exiled, banished from his own people and from the woman he loved.

VLADIMIR PANOV—An elegant man and a demanding lover, he became a bitter and unforgiving husband, willing to destroy his marriage to regain his pride.

RAISSA OZEROVA—Her provocative beauty marred in adolescence, she sought comfort in her passion for her sister's husband that, once unleashed, threatened to destroy them all.

SONYA OZEROVA—A proud Russian matriarch, she ached for revenge against the Chinese bandit who rescued her daughter—until she learned the shocking secret that forever bound her family's destiny to his.

LEGACY OF AMBER

LEGACY OF AMBER

Alla Crone

Originally published by Dell.

Copyright © 1985, 2004 by Alla Crone

ISBN: 978-1-5040-3029-8

Distributed in 2016 by Open Road Distribution
180 Maiden Lane
New York, NY 10038
www.openroadmedia.com

ACKNOWLEDGMENTS

I wish to express my appreciation to the staffs of the Hoover Institution at the University of Stanford and the Russian Museum of Culture in San Francisco for their gracious assistance in my research.

I also want to thank my friend Mah-li Wang Shaw for going over the Chinese part of this book.

I owe special thanks to my editor, Susan Reu, for her suggestions, meticulous editing, and moral support during the progress of this work.

DEDICATION

To my friend Valerie Herr,
who inspired this work

Upon such sacrifices, my Cordelia,
The gods themselves throw incense.

Shakespeare, *King Lear:* Act V, Scene 3

AUTHOR'S NOTE

The Chinese bandits in Manchuria were called *hunghutzu,* but to retain authenticity throughout the book, I have used the Russian version of the word: *hunhuz* (singular) and *hunhuzy* (plural).

The origin of the Chinese bandits dates back to the seventeenth century, when the followers of the fallen Ming dynasty, unwilling to surrender to the new Tai-Ching rulers, escaped into the Manchurian taiga, from which they raided government posts and settlements. In time the political faction disappeared and the ranks of *hunhuzy* were replaced by adventurers and ordinary criminals.

As the years went by, *hunhuzy* played an important role in Manchuria. The local population occasionally required protection from the arbitrary rule of government bureaucrats, and the army, unable to control these functionaries, sometimes hired whole bands of *hunhuzy* into their service and bestowed a high army rank on the head of the group.

In rural areas however, there were feuding *hunhuzy* groups who controlled their own territories, and villagers regularly paid the local bandits to protect them from rival bands.

Some of the warlords in China were said to have

come from the ranks of the *hunhuzy,* and legend has it that the great Manchurian warlord, Marshal Chang Tso-lin, may have had his start among them, after his older brother was executed as a bandit.

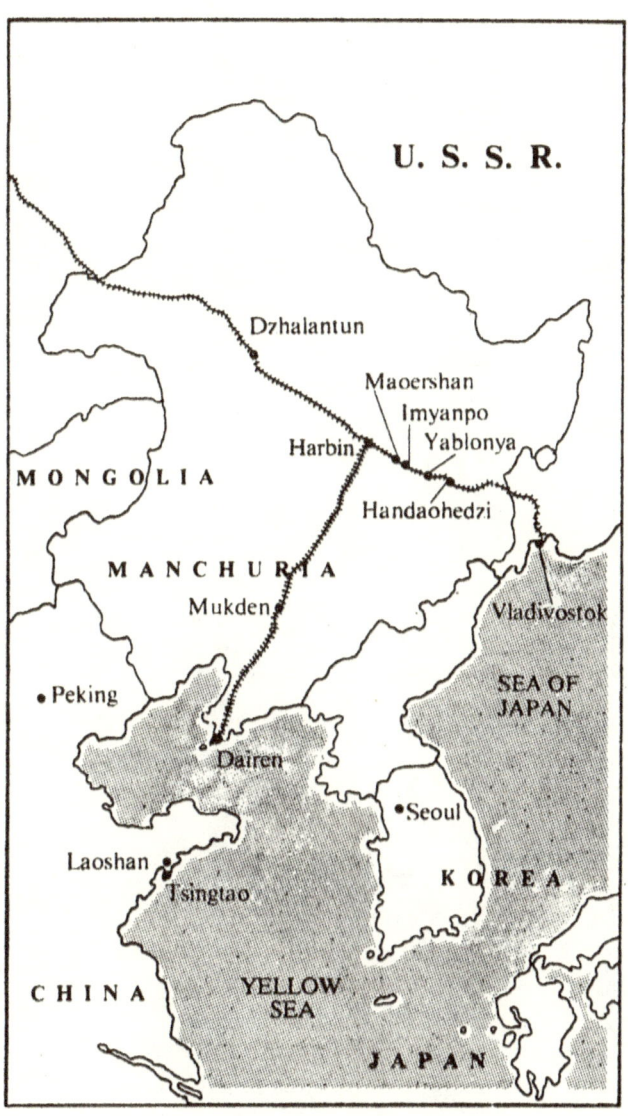

PART ONE

The Interlude

Prologue

Across the virgin land of eastern Manchuria, over its fast rivers and majestic mountain ranges, an echo of gunfire rumbled in the summer of 1900. Deep in the lush taiga, so dense it was called Shu-Hai—Forest Sea—the aura of human travail pervaded one of the hidden enclaves of the Chinese *hunhuzy* bandits. Their chieftain, Ma Fu-li, a feared Manchu giant of a man, was raging in grief over the loss of a long-awaited son, whose stillborn appearance into the world had also taken his mother.

To vent his anger against fate, and to avenge the capture and execution of three of his most trusted lieutenants, he had embarked on a looting rampage of peaceful villages. He didn't touch the hamlets in the territory that he controlled, for he levied a regular sum on the villagers in return for his protection from other feuding *hunhuzy* factions. But he raided the neighboring area under the control of a rival chieftain, Mao De-lu, where he looted, and sometimes kidnapped a wealthy merchant for ransom.

On this hot August day a convoy of fifteen horsemen moved silently through the forest. Dressed in faded blue cotton pants tied around their ankles with strips of cloth, and high-buttoned belted white shirts, they carried carbines and large-caliber rifles slung across their shoulders. Their stubby, shaggy-legged horses trotted rhythmically along a familiar path.

17

At the head of the column was Ma Fu-li himself. His rugged, suntanned face betrayed no emotion, except for an occasional flashing glint in his black eyes. With his sight and hearing honed by years of living in the forest, he knew the music of the taiga, and was alert to the rustling sounds in the underbrush, the sudden grating call of a woodpecker perched atop a cedar branch, the ominous snapping of a twig.

At the edge of the forest Ma Fu-li raised his hand to halt his column. With narrowed eyes he studied the land. It was early morning. The sun had not yet risen above the towering peaks that surrounded the small valley floor. A few tall patches of grass rose through the scattered puffs of morning fog that hung suspended near a meandering creek. The moist air was filled with the scent of cedars and pines and the dew-covered freshness of awakening wildflowers.

But the tranquil serenity of the valley was lost on Ma Fu-li. The scene of the execution, branded on his brain, was vivid in his mind's eye. Like a fugitive he had hidden in the tall grass and watched his three men made a spectacle of as they were beheaded before the villagers, a lesson for the unwary. He was proud of them, for they had not begged for their lives, but had submitted to the executioner in silence.

Now, as he sat in his saddle, tightening the reins of his impatient horse, his gaze traveled to the left of the creek, where a cluster of clay *fanzas* with thatched roofs huddled together like lost children in this mountain range. The small hamlet was inhabited by Chinese farmers and hunters. There was one exception: at the edge of the village was the house of a Russian engineer, Oleg Rotov, and Ma Fu-li's eyes now rested on this *fanza*.

He was pleased. His scouts had given him accurate reports. Set slightly apart, Rotov's *fanza* was larger and newer than the rest of the dwellings in the village. Ma Fu-li's mouth pressed into a thin line. The Russians were fools to have sent a well-paid engineer to live in a remote Chinese village in the heart of *hunhuzy* domain. The reason for this had developed a few years back, when China signed a contract with the Russo-Chinese Bank to build the Chinese Eastern Railway to connect the Trans-Siberian Railroad with Vladivostok. Shortly afterward a team of Russian engineers had come from Moscow to build the town of Harbin, which would administer the right-of-way area of the railroad, and to oversee the construction of the railway east and west of Harbin. And so Oleg Rotov had appeared in this remote hamlet with his young wife, Anya, and was provided with supplies and a new *fanza*.

The construction of the railroad had been progressing well, until a few weeks ago when the Boxer Rebellion had spread into Manchuria. Ma Fu-li had been well informed about the destruction wrought by the Boxers on the railroad and about the July attack on the city of Harbin. Russian women and children had been evacuated both from Harbin and the hamlets along the railroad track, but the Rotovs must have thought themselves safe in an entirely Chinese village. And so they had been, until today. Ma Fu-li's lips twisted in an ironic smile.

Railroad company employees were paid in gold rubles. They were rich. Thus, Rotov's *fanza* would be the richest in the hamlet, and the first to be raided. Besides, Ma Fu-li reasoned, the men of the hamlet would have already gone on their hunt and Oleg Rotov to his work, leaving only defenseless women and children to contend with during the band's looting of the village.

With a firm forward sweep of his hand Ma Ful-li motioned his men to follow him; then he pressed his black *u-li*, his shoes, into the sides of his horse, and the animal began to trot.

Ma Fu-li had no way of knowing that Oleg Rotov was still in his *fanza*. Tall and broad-shouldered with thick eyebrows that shaded clear hazel eyes, Oleg was pacing the floor nervously while a neighbor tended his wife in childbirth. His erect posture and the proud tilt of his head suggested the aristocratic background of someone reared in the palaces of St. Petersburg, in spite of his modest birth in the Eastern Siberian town of Khabarovsk. Educated in Moscow, Oleg had a keen intellect and had attracted the attention of his superiors, and when engineers were selected for the new venture in Manchuria, he was chosen to go along with his married colleague, Nikolai Ozerov.

The two men had watched the building of Harbin together, and when Oleg married Anya, a Buryat girl of Siberian-Mongolian origin who had come from Chita to work in the railway-company kitchens, she and Nikolai's wife, Sonya, became close friends. The two couples were inseparable until Oleg was transferred some one hundred miles east of Harbin. Now he surveyed the land there for the stretch of railroad to be built from Harbin to Vladivostok.

The villagers had accepted Oleg and Anya with warmth and respect, and had given them a large two-room *fanza* near the creek. It had been a year now since they had moved, and although there existed an ever-present danger of *hunhuzy* raids, Oleg was relieved that in the time they had lived in this hamlet, he had had no occasion to use his loaded Mauser rifle for anything more than a hunt.

When Anya went into labor, he rushed to a neighbor for help, but with no midwife in the village he could only pray that the baby would come quickly. After twenty-four hours of suffering and no relief in sight, Anya was weakening, and Oleg cursed himself for not having taken her to Harbin and left her in the good hands of the Ozerovs.

As dawn broke on the second day, Oleg, who had gone sleepless for thirty-six hours, stood swaying on his feet from dizziness, but he refused to leave Anya's bedside. A steady humming had started in his ears, and when at last the lusty cry of a newborn infant suddenly registered in his brain, he wasn't sure he had heard it until the neighbor rose from her knees and said, "You have a son! Here, sit on this taboret and hold him. I must clean up Anya. She's bleeding too much." She spoke slowly, enunciating each word carefully, and although Oleg had learned the local Chinese dialect, he had difficulty understanding her this morning. He accepted the small bundle and lowered himself wearily onto the stool. The tiny body squirmed inside the moist blanket, and as Oleg looked down at his wife, a faint smile illuminated Anya's pale face. "We'll call him Gennady, after your father."

Her last word was drowned by the crack of a rifle shot outside their *fanza*. In the frozen moment that followed, the Chinese woman's eyes locked with Oleg's. Then she jumped. "The *hunhuzy!* My boy is alone in my *fanza!*"

Before Oleg could stop her, she was out the door and running. With the child in his arms, he bent over his wife, watching Anya's eyelids flutter in semiconsciousness, the bloodstain on the sheet spreading rapidly. Oleg panicked. Bandits or not, he had to run for help before Anya bled to death. The *hunhuzy* wouldn't touch her. He had heard that they didn't harm women—and surely not one in Anya's condition. Placing his son gently by Anya's side, he grabbed his rifle and ran out.

At the edge of the village the *hunhuzy* had grouped together.

They watched a woman dash out of Rotov's *fanza* and flee down the road. Ma Fu-li fired his carbine to scare her, not to kill, for killing women arbitrarily was not his custom.

But it was quite another matter when Rotov himself appeared at the door. His patrician bearing and pointed rifle looked threatening, and Ma Fu-li's reaction was instantaneous. Seconds later Rotov lay sprawled on the ground, face down, motionless, but still clutching his rifle. Ma Fu-li took no chances; he shot the fallen man again to make sure he was dead. Then he turned to his men.

"Go to work!"

The bandits needed no prompting. They quickly scattered through the hamlet like rolling gravel.

Ma Fu-li dismounted and headed for Rotov's *fanza*. As he reached the door, a Buryat woman staggered out and fell upon Rotov's prostrate body. Her long, high-pitched shriek clawed at the air, echoing into the hills. Ma Fu-li frowned. He hated hysterics. He was reminded of his own mother, who had whined and wept over his father's grave for days, when he was still a boy in the *hunhuzy* village.

He moved abruptly to go in, but suddenly the woman jumped from the ground and threw herself at him. Before Ma Fu-li could get over his surprise, she had raked his face with her fingernails.

With one violent thrust he flung the small woman aside and watched as she fell back on top of Rotov and lay still. Too bad. He hadn't meant to hurt her, but it was intolerable to have his men see him being scratched by a woman. He touched the blood on his cheek, then turned and entered the *fanza*.

It was dark and quiet inside. Ma Fu-li paid no attention to the rumpled bedding on the k'ang, but swept the room with a

practiced eye. The added luxury of a wooden floor did not
escape his notice as he took in the combination of Chinese and
Russian furnishings: a tall wardrobe stood against one wall, a
cedar chest near it with brass fittings; two straight-backed ebony chairs with carved dragons on the arms seemed out of
place by the side of a crude wooden table in the center of the
fanza; in the right corner of the room a few small icons were
clustered on a triangular ledge covered with a white cloth
cross-stitched in vivid colors.

Ma Fu-li looked into the adjoining kitchen area and there,
leaning against the large cooking caldron, he found what he
was looking for: two sacks of grain and flour. He dragged
them into the main room and was about to leave, when he
noticed a lacquered box on top of a square table that stood by
the side of the k'ang. He dropped the sacks and picked up the
box. It was small and oblong, with a brightly painted picture
on its lid. Curious, Ma Fu-li studied it. It showed a Russian
youth with a rounded haircut and a loose, side-buttoned shirt
astride a humped and winged horse flying above a village with
onion-domed churches. Eager for loot, Ma Fu-li opened the
box but found only a piece of amber on a gold chain and a
letter written in Russian. Disappointed, he pursed his lips and
pulled out the necklace to examine it. Ma Fu-li remembered
his mother once saying that amber to the Russians was like
jade to the Chinese. He studied now the milky yellow stone,
then shrugged, and after dropping it back in the box, threw it
into one of the sacks.

He was about to leave, when out of a corner of his eye he
caught a movement in the k'ang bedding. Instantly alert, he
stood rigid for a few seconds, watching. Then he heard a faint
sound, followed by an infant's lusty cry.

In one swift move he threw the covers aside and stared at
the blood-soaked sheet and a howling baby kicking at its
wrappings. Mesmerized, he watched for a few moments, then
unwrapped the blanket.

A boy-child!

Ma Fu-li straightened. The child's father—and probably the
mother too—lay dead outside, and he, Ma Fu-li, had caused
the newborn to be orphaned. His heart quickened.

The helpless baby was his for the taking.

Why not?

It was a sign from the gods, who had taken his own son and now were offering him another. The child's mother was a Buryat, and the boy, when dressed in Chinese clothing, might pass for his own son.

Ma Fu-li's hands trembled as he rewrapped the infant and lifted him in his arms. He had never handled a fragile baby before, and surely that was why his arms shook as he carried the child in one arm and dragged the sacks of grain and flour with the other. At the door he paused and looked down at the tiny face. Held in the warmth of a human arm, the infant smacked its tiny bud mouth in the primeval search for its mother's breast. Ma Fu-li chuckled. Surely the gods were giving him a sign of approval, for, cradled in his arms, the baby had stopped crying.

Outside, the bandits had already mounted their horses with their loot—grain and flour, clothing for the winter, and what ammunition they could find. Now, silently, they waited for him. He looked down at the two bodies on the ground. The Buryat woman still lay on her back as she had fallen, her eyes now half-open and sightless. Ma Fu-li looked down the road. Two girls stood against the clay wall of their *fanza,* immobilized by fear. A few female heads peeked out the doors and quickly vanished again.

Ma Fu-li skirted the two bodies on the ground and, passing the sacks to another bandit, mounted his horse without a word. The rest of the *hunhuzy* eyed the infant surreptitiously but none dared say anything. Trotting behind him single file, the band headed for the forest.

The sun had risen above the towering mountains, slanting its rays into the valley, shrouding firs and cedars with a golden veil. The remaining dew sparkled on the grass and the evaporating droplets carried the fragrance of fresh greens into the air. Wild joy surged through Ma Fu-li. The gods were kind. He had a son! He would make him a mighty *hunhuz,* he would send him to school to learn to read and write not only in Chinese but in Russian as well. He would make him a powerful warlord, his fame would spread through the country, and he would be feared and respected. He would call him Li-chun.

So the chieftain *hunhuz* Ma Fu-li planned and dreamed and rejoiced.

Chapter One

On a clear March evening in 1922 the strains of the "Skaters' Waltz" echoed across the block-long HOTKS skating rink, to spill over into the hushed side streets of Harbin. The initials stood for Harbin Organization of Tennis and Skating Sport, which was particularly popular among the younger generation of the city. The snowbanks around the rink were still hard with ice, and there was no sign of the approaching spring. Naked branches of a tall elm that rose out of the snow showed no buds, and clumps of trees behind the high wooden fence spread their branches across the moonlit sky like filaments of an intricate web.

The entrance to the rink was from the Bolshoi Prospekt, and on each side of it stood two houses. The smaller of the two was called the *teplushka,* the warming hut. Inside, a large coal-burning stove was centered in the room, and the wood-planked floor was deeply grooved by the steel-bladed skates. Here the chilled skaters rubbed the stiffness out of their hands over the stove or stamped their feet as the cold numbness gave way to the pain of returning circulation. On the other side of the entrance was a small clubhouse where paying members could warm themselves with a little more comfort and leisure than in the *teplushka.*

But the cold air was no deterrent to the crowd of skaters filling the rink this Sunday night, for the brass band played only on Sundays and holidays. Completely enclosed in a shell-like wooden structure in one corner of the rink, the musicians sat around an iron stove, its glowing coals coloring their faces pink, as they played waltzes, polkas, or tangos, the music floating out on waves of warm air that escaped through a single window.

Singles, or couples with arms and hands crisscrossed, glided in rhythmic steps along the outer circle, careful not to bump into beginners, who pushed wooden sled-chairs for balance. The center of the rink was reserved for figure skaters and dancing couples.

Among the latter were Svetlana Ozerova and Vladimir Panov. Held in the firm embrace of her fiancé, Svetlana kept her eyes closed, surrendering to the dizzying sensation of the whirling dance, secure in the knowledge that Vladimir's expert guidance would keep her from falling. Dressed in a rabbit-fur jacket and a heavy brown skirt that flared around her ankles, a tasseled white scarf wrapped around her neck, Svetlana knew that many eyes were on her.

"Dreaming, my dear?" Vladimir whispered in her ear, and startled, she looked into the hazel eyes of the tall young man she was soon to marry.

"I love to waltz with my eyes closed," she said, smiling, "and I know you'll keep me from falling."

"But you're preventing me from looking deep into your eyes and reading their secrets," Vladimir said. "I wish they would play 'Dark Eyes' tonight, and rename it 'Gray Eyes' in your honor."

Svetlana felt a flush of pleasure rise to her cheeks. At eighteen she was conscious of her blond beauty and the startling effect of her contrasting dark lashes rimming her gray eyes. The debonair Vladimir had spoken of that effect often enough!

Someone tapped her on the shoulder. Still waltzing, she turned slightly to see her former classmate, Nina Serova, bundled in a white squirrel coat, grinning maliciously. "Watch out, you lovebirds, that you don't bump into someone. You narrowly missed me!"

Svetlana looked down at the short, plump girl. *Are you being righteous or jealous?* she thought, but aloud said, "Don't worry, Vladimir is an expert dancer and he wouldn't be that careless."

Nina's eyelids fluttered and she skated away. Svetlana had no doubt that she was the envy of all her classmates at having captured the most eligible bachelor in town, a man sought after by many matchmaking mothers. Seven years her senior, he had received his engineering degree in Liège, Belgium, and then returned to Harbin to take a well-paying position in the Chinese Eastern Railway Company. So, when he began to court Svetlana, she was not only flattered by the attentions of this mature man whose polished manners carried an aura of St. Petersburg salons, but had promptly fallen in love with him. His parents had been born in Kazan, and Vladimir's father, Arseny Panov, who was an architect for commercial buildings and a deacon at St. Nicholas Cathedral, had instilled in him a religious piety that was highly praised by the older generation.

They had met a year earlier at the Zhelsob, the Railway Club, during a dance where Svetlana, always in demand with her rapidly developing soprano voice, had been asked to sing a couple of Tchaikovsky's songs. For a year now she had been studying in the First Harbin Music School, and she was considered one of its star pupils. Because the school was patterned after the conservatories in Russia, Svetlana's parents felt she would not only get excellent training there, but a fine musical education as well.

That night at the Zhelsob club, Svetlana had blushed at the look of unconcealed admiration in the eyes of the twenty-four-year-old engineer when they were introduced. From then on it had been a whirlwind courtship of seeing moving pictures at the Oriant Theater on Novotorgovaya Street where Rudolph Valentino fanned her romantic imagination; of walks through the Pitomnik, the arboretum near Modyagowskaya Street; of summer dances at the Zhelsob club; or of winter excursions to the other side of the Sungari River, where they laughed giddily as they rode sleds down the ice hill of the hunting lodge. A fairy-tale year it was, in spite of the frequent presence of Raissa, her loquacious, brown-haired sister, who was sixteen now, dimpled and kittenish, but still seemingly unable to understand that the young affianced couple wanted privacy.

Tonight was no exception. When Vladimir had come to pick up Svetlana, Raissa had grabbed her skates, kissed her mother, and gone along. Although Svetlana chafed inwardly, she would never tell Raissa that her presence was annoying, nor would she mention it to her mother, who also seemed unconcerned by her older daughter's need for privacy. Vladimir accepted the situation without complaint, and Svetlana could only wonder whether his good manners prevented him from showing his displeasure or whether he truly didn't mind Raissa's presence and incessant chatter.

Right now, though, Svetlana relished her privacy in Vladimir's arms, the kind of privacy one can create in the midst of strangers. Raissa had never mastered the intricate figure-skating steps and so was off somewhere on the outskirts of the rink.

Assured of his expert maneuvering, Svetlana relaxed against Vladimir's muscular shoulder. Although she worried that his fitted broadcloth jacket was not warm enough, she was nevertheless proud that he was stylishly dressed and could afford a fur-lined cap. He wore it now with its earflaps jauntily tied on top, so much more elegant than the wool-knit caps with pompons. Still, she fretted, and she'd pulled him twice into the *teplushka*, where she made sure that his angora scarf, which her mother had knitted for him, was well wrapped around his neck, and his thick brown hair tucked inside his cap.

As they twirled on the ice, the ruffled night breeze bit into their faces, but knowing his penchant for style, Svetlana dared not suggest that he cover his ears. It was the same with the patent leather shoes he wore to the dances in winter. In spite of the snow and temperatures of thirty below, he customarily walked her home the five blocks from Zhelsob club without putting on his galoshes. What's more, the last time he brought her home, he had kept her in front of the picket fence talking as if the cold did not matter, as if his thin-soled shoes were immune to the snow. And she, caught up in their discussion of her singing lessons, had forgotten the cold, too.

When she had told him about the long hours she spent studying her singing, he'd asked with genuine surprise, "Do you think it is all worth it, Svetlana?"

"Is what worth it?"

"Your time, your hard work, your dreams of a future that may never be? Fame and fortune are elusive, you know."

"Why, Vladimir!" she had cried then. "That's a pessimistic viewpoint. Without challenge there is nothing in life but boredom."

"Not at all. There are more realistic challenges for a woman. Failure to achieve so ambitious a goal might prove devastating for you."

"Why particularly for a woman? Do you disapprove of my wanting a singing career?"

"I meant that for a woman in our world today, there are always greater obstacles to overcome," Vladimir had said evasively after a moment's pause. "Remember, air castles don't last long."

"I intend to build a solid foundation first. That's why I'm spending so many hours in voice training."

"But to what purpose? You have a natural gift, sufficiently developed to sing Tchaikovsky songs for your family and friends."

Svetlana had rephrased her question. "Do you object, then, to my training my voice?"

Vladimir had lifted her chin with his gloved hand. "I'm only trying to shield you from future disappointments."

And with that he'd kissed her on the forehead and left. She had stood in the foyer of their house that night for a long time, confused and alarmed. A slight shiver had rippled down her back and arms. What had he really meant? Would he object to her singing professionally? Surely not. She shook her head to chase the thought away. Silly it was to read something into his words that wasn't there. He simply thought her young and impetuous and was trying to protect her from future hurts.

Now, safe in his arms, Svetlana forgot her dismay at their differing views. She felt a surge of exultation as she caught the envious glances of the other girls. Hadn't she captured the handsomest bachelor in Harbin? How delightful it was to open the door when he came to call with his arms full of roses or Mars candies—the best in town. Her elegant, dashing fiancé, always immaculately dressed, always proper. Even his

kisses were gentle and patient, surely intended not to shock
her with premature passion. Though grateful for his consider-
ation, she really did wish sometimes for a spontaneous embrace, one that would take her breath away and do to her
some of the things the heroines experienced in the romantic
novels she read.

But, skimming effortlessly over the smooth ice, she kept
reminding herself she was a lucky girl. She should be ashamed
now for resenting her own sister's presence. After all, Raissa
was only sixteen and what could she know about the thrills of
being engaged?

After the waltz ended, Svetlana turned her foot inward to
cut into the ice and break to a stop, but her Snow Maiden
skate with its curled tip caught in a groove and twisted her
ankle. Her shoulder jerked sideways, and before Vladimir
could steady her, she had slipped and bumped into someone
behind her. There was a woman's cry and a thud as the other
skater fell. Her right foot raised in the air, Svetlana fought for
balance, tottering and clutching at Vladimir's arm. Unable to
hold on, with an instant reflex she brought her foot down.

She felt her skate land on something soft, heard a scream
pierce the silence that was still ringing with the final strains of
the waltz. She jerked her foot up quickly, lost her balance, and
fell sideways over the legs of the fallen skater.

Vladimir, barely able to retain his own balance, bent over
and pulled her up. Then they both looked at the fallen skater,
and Svetlana stared in horror at her sister's bloodied, terrified
face and heard Vladimir's shocked cry: "Raissa! My God!"

As he tried to lift the screaming girl, she fought him, blood
dripping on the ice and instantly freezing into shiny dark
globs.

"Raissa, Raechka! I am so sorry! I didn't see you!" Svetlana
cried. She tried to staunch the flow of blood from the girl's
jaw with a handkerchief, but Raissa shrieked.

"It hurts! Don't touch me! I'm bleeding!"

Other skaters crowded around them. "Let's get her to the
club," one said, and someone else replied: "Here, I'll help you!
I've got her shoulders, you take her legs."

Holding back tears, Svetlana leaned on Vladimir's arm.
There was so much blood, she could not tell in the dark how

badly Raissa had been hurt. How could this have happened? Where had Raissa come from? No matter. Raissa was hurt, and it was she, her sister, who had done it. Her fault. *Oh, God, don't let it be serious!*

After the two men had lifted Raissa in their arms and started toward the club, Svetlana turned to Vladimir, but he was beside Raissa, his eyes riveted to her bloody face. *What's going to happen to Raissa's face?* Svetlana bit her lip, tears welling in her eyes, dropping unheeded onto her fur jacket.

They carried Raissa up the few steps to the club and, once inside the warm room, lowered her gently on one of the wooden benches. Someone had recognized a doctor skating in the rink, and brought him in. After examining the girl's face and dabbing it with a wet gauze, the doctor looked up at Svetlana. "We must take her to the hospital. The cut needs stitches."

Distraught by the sight of her sister's injury, perspiring in her fur jacket, which she had forgotten to take off, Svetlana felt faint and staggered back, lowering herself into a wooden chair.

Vladimir's insistent voice sounded as though from a distance: "Svetlana, we should go with Raissa. The doctor insists we take the sleigh to *Tsentralnaya Bolnitsa*, immediately."

Raissa clung to Vladimir's arm throughout the seven-block downhill ride to the hospital. Once inside, she wouldn't let go of his hand until he disengaged himself gently and told her that he could not go into the operating room with her.

Then at last he turned to Svetlana. "The doctor said that the injury looks worse than it really is." He sat down beside her and patted her shoulder. "What's a little scar on her jaw? As a matter of fact, it may add character to her face."

"I'm so sorry it happened," she said, still distraught. "I didn't see her! She was supposed to stay in the outer circle for regular skaters." *Why did she break the rules?* Svetlana wanted to say, but checked herself. "Why did she skate directly across?"

Vladimir shrugged. "Who knows? Maybe she wanted to show that she was good enough to figure-skate, and didn't realize the danger. Too bad it had to be you who bumped her."

"Oh, I feel so guilty about it. What will Mother and Papa say?"

Vladimir smiled absentmindedly and patted her hand. "Don't fret about it, darling. Raissa is young and her skin is healthy. Before you know it, the cut will heal and the whole incident will be forgotten."

Somehow, he didn't sound convincing. Svetlana fell silent, dreading to see her sister's injured face and accusing eyes.

Ten blocks away, inside a one-story stone house on Tsentralnaya Street, their mother stood by the window of their dining room and waited for her daughters to come home. At forty-one Sonya Ozerova was still shapely, though slightly on the plump side. Her once blond hair was now streaked with silver and neatly pulled back into a heavy chignon at the nape of her neck. Dressed in a simple beige wool dress, a warm angora shawl around her shoulders, she was smiling, absorbed in her thoughts. How pleased she was that her two girls were such good friends, for Svetlana's engagement, instead of separating them, seemed to have drawn them closer together. How fortunate that Vladimir liked the gregarious Raissa. Another couple of years and maybe he would find her a husband too. He was a religious young man, that one, a regular churchgoer, and a loyal son of his parents.

Sonya sighed. She wasn't entirely comfortable with the fact that her daughter's future in-laws were so deep into their religion, for although she herself believed in God and attended church regularly, she was not as involved in the church as they were. Well, she would surely find something else in common with them. There was much to be done in the next few months before the wedding.

She turned to look at her husband. Nikolai was sitting in the small alcove off the spacious dining room, wearing a red silk smoking jacket and reading a newspaper. Still handsome at forty-seven, he wore a gold-rimmed pince-nez and had a trace of silver in his ash-colored hair that only added character to his rugged good looks. He adored her. He had lost his parents long ago, and his only brother had died of diphtheria in adolescence, so when he married Sonya, he had poured all his affection onto her. "My little *ponchik,*" he called her, and at first, sensitive about her rounded figure, she had taken offense.

"But, darling," Nikolai had said, "you know how I adore those wonderful jellied doughnuts! Everything in them reminds me of you: the delicious sugar on the outside, and the softness of the dough, and the most important of all, the delicate sweetness inside—my favorite raspberry jam! Now how can you tell me it doesn't describe you perfectly?"

She had to laugh of course, and since then the endearment had stuck. Now he lifted his head and looked at her over his pince-nez.

"Don't stand by the window, *ponchik,*" he said. "In spite of the double frames it is still drafty there and I don't want you to catch cold."

"I thought I might hear the girls coming home," she said. Turning back toward the window, she peered through the frosty panes once more.

Tonight the moon was high and the snow in the square across the street so bright, she suddenly thought of the white nights in St. Petersburg she had heard so much about when she was growing up in Moscow. But all the glory of her homeland was in the past. Expatriates all, they had to live an illusion that Harbin was a part of St. Petersburg or Moscow, and that a corner of every Russian's hometown was woven lovingly into the tapestry of this city—this safe haven outside their country's boundaries.

With a sigh Sonya crossed the room and, slipping down beside Nikolai on the long curved sofa, looked at the newspaper he was reading. It was the *Svyet,* whose editorial policy was slanted toward Ataman Semenov and the Japanese. She frowned. That Cossack Semenov. Rumors abounded about him. Sponsored by the Japanese, he was the leader of the White movement against the Bolsheviks. A true patriot, some said. A self-seeking, brutal dictator of unspeakable atrocities, others countered.

She tapped her finger on the paper. "I don't understand, dear, why you have to read a newspaper that is so far to the right. You know very well how biased it is."

Nikolai peered at her affectionately over the top of his

pince-nez. "You don't seem to mind my reading the *Novosti Zhizni*, which is to the far left!"

Sonya pursed her lips. "I don't see why you have to read three papers. The *Zarya* is the best of all; it has everything in it, including gossip and satires, and it's fun to read. It doesn't make you feel that someone else's opinion is being shoved down your throat."

Nikolai folded the paper and turned to look at his wife. "Well, you see, my dear, after reading all three papers, I can form my own opinions on world affairs, and I like to see what the various political factions say about our life here. But whatever they print, we mustn't forget what a good life we have. Harbin is not built on our native soil, but it *is* the old Russia that we lost, and it is here, it *exists!*"

He paused, seemingly abashed by the passion of his words, then went on: "Remember how we worried that the Soviets would take over our railroad? Thank God that General Khorvat had the courage to turn it over to the Chinese government before his retirement. But you know, even though he was an excellent director, I feel that Ostroumov is now an equally brilliant administrator. No, we have nothing to complain about. Usually we are not even aware that we live under the Chinese laws now."

Nikolai narrowed his eyes, hesitated, then added, "You know, *ponchik,* I am a little disturbed by your leftist leanings. It's rather farfetched to blame the tsar for your parents' unfortunate deaths, don't you think?"

Sonya swallowed hard. She didn't like being reminded of the remote and painful past. It all seemed so long ago. She had met Nikolai in Moscow, in 1897, when she was only seventeen, fresh out of the gymnasium, a bewildered and lonely girl who had been orphaned a year earlier in the tragic Khodynka Fair incident. It had happened during the tsar's coronation festivities, when the stands at the Khodynka Field collapsed and her parents, who had gone to see the fair, were trampled to death. Frightened and grieving, she had married Nikolai not so much out of love as out of gratitude to someone who cared for her and was kind and helpful.

How excited she had been when her young engineer husband was ordered to the remote land of Manchuria, where he was to help build the Chinese Eastern Railway that would shorten the Trans-Siberian by some three hundred miles! They would live in Harbin, he told her, a town built and still being expanded by the Russians in the area of extraterritorial rights that Russia had acquired along the railroad.

How exotic and adventurous it had sounded to her then, and how dreadful it turned out to be. But she didn't know, couldn't dream, at the time, what was in store for them.

Now, sitting beside her husband on the couch, she was aware that Nikolai was waiting for her answer. She lifted her brows and shrugged.

"We're all influenced by events in our personal lives," she said slowly. "Show me one person who can look at his life in a detached manner, and I'll name you a saint. And my leanings are not so much to the left, as they are for democracy. I try to keep my political sympathies to myself, darling, so let's not quarrel over it."

He reached over and touched her cheek with the back of his hand. "Nonetheless, *ponchik*, personal tragedies shouldn't be blamed on the government. And I'm afraid that's exactly what you're doing."

Sonya leaned back on one of the many pillows on the sofa and ran her finger over the Chinese half-moon embroidery on the turquoise silk upholstery. Nikolai was right, and she knew it. But how could one be objective after all that had happened? She sighed and thought about the past. After they had come to Manchuria with Nikolai's colleague, Oleg Rotov, she was delighted when he had married the Buryat Anya, thus providing her with a woman friend. The cheerful, diminutive Anya with her ingenuous smile had a bottomless reservoir of love, which she poured unchecked on those whose lives she touched. Deprived of her parents, Sonya had cherished the Rotovs' friendship.

Those were difficult years for them all. Harbin was still in its infancy, and life was primitive amid the constant construction and expansion of the city limits. When Sonya had a miscarriage, Anya nursed her tenderly, and after Sonya recovered, they became very close. Although others complained that there was nothing in Harbin but mud, sand, and dust, the two young women didn't mind. Enamored of everything Chinese, they spent hours together embroidering oriental designs on pillows, buying silks and threads from peddlers, or shopping in the newly opened Chinese store, Tun Shin-lun.

Sonya had wept when the Rotovs were transferred to a remote village. In parting, the young women exchanged gifts. Sonya gave Anya a piece of amber on a gold chain, a necklace that had belonged to her mother, who had told her that for many centuries amber was considered to possess curative value. She had also told her that in Greek mythology amber was formed out of the congealed tears of Phaethon's sisters, who had been turned to poplars while weeping over his death. Sonya had shed many tears after her parents' deaths, and because she had cherished the necklace, she wanted Anya to have it. In turn Anya gave Sonya all the pillows she had embroidered, and after her tragic death that collection of her handiwork was all Sonya had to remember Anya by. The alcove off their dining room had become a sort of shrine to her memory, the only room in the house now that had a Chinese decor.

Picking up a round burgundy silk pillow with ruffled edges, she leaned her chin on the top, smiling as she remembered how Anya had struggled with the intricate white chrysanthemums she embroidered on it. Despite her efforts one flower had come out slightly lopsided.

"I hope you no longer feel bitter about the Rotovs' deaths, *ponchik,*" Nikolai said quietly, his glance traveling from her face to the pillow she was hugging. "You haven't mentioned them in a long time."

"I'm not sure I'll ever get over the bitterness, Nikolai, but at least I'm trying not to feed on it. The way they died was dreadful. And ever since we have had children of our own, I worry about what the villagers told you—or rather, what they avoided telling you."

Nikolai sighed. "You can't let go of that, can you? I've told you over and over again what they said."

Sonya closed her eyes in an effort to shut out the painful memories, but instead they rose again to mock her in vivid detail. The Rotovs hadn't even had the dignity of death at the hands of the Boxers, who hated all Europeans, but had to meet an ignominious death from the *hunhuzy* bandits. An il-

logical guilt had gripped Sonya for years. During the Boxer
Rebellion she had been evacuated to Khabarovsk with other
women and children, but pregnant Anya Rotova remained
with her husband in the Chinese hamlet in spite of the destruction the Boxers had done to the railroad—burying rails,
chopping down telegraph posts, stealing wires, burning down
station buildings and dwellings. Sonya had her own worries at
the time. She agonized over Nikolai's safety that fateful week
of July thirteenth when the Boxers attacked Harbin. For a
whole week the Cossack detachments repulsed them until on
July twenty-first Russian ships appeared with reinforcements
on the River Sungari, and the violence was over.

What a relief it was to learn that the Rotovs' village had not
been touched—and then what a shock to hear of their deaths
a few weeks later! When the news reached them, Nikolai had
asked for the bodies, but the villagers explained that because it
was summertime, they had already buried the Rotovs in a
common grave outside the village.

Suddenly, Sonya was choking. She opened her eyes and
looked at Nikolai. "I know what they said!" she cried. "They
told you that a tall *hunhuz* shot Oleg and that Anya bled to
death in childbirth. But what about the newborn infant? They
refused to say how it died. The *hunhuz* must have done something so dreadful to the baby that the villagers dared not tell
us."

"Why do you want to know the gory details, Sonya? It's
best we don't."

"But my imagination won't let me rest! I'd rather know the
worst and learn to bury it, than conjure up a torture scene."

Through the years her intense hatred of the tall *hunhuz*
killer had magnified, then spread to encompass everything
even remotely connected with the *hunhuzy.* That hatred had
become an obsession that she could not overcome because of
the Rotovs' unavenged deaths.

Nikolai reached over and put his arms around his wife.
"Ponchik, why don't you release their souls to rest?"

Sonya pushed away and looked at her husband. Puzzled by
his last words, she asked, "What do you mean? I'm not holding their souls."

"Oh, yes, you are. By allowing your imagination to run

wild, you surround their souls with horror and disturb their peace. Let go!"

Sonya shuddered, musing on this idea. "Perhaps you're right. I realize that. We have much to be thankful for."

She leaned her head against Nikolai's shoulder and closed her eyes. Yes, there was much to be thankful for. As the years went by after the death of the Rotovs, the Ozerovs' life had assumed a comfortable pattern, and even the 1904 Russo-Japanese war—although alarmingly close—did not involve them except to make them aware that the Japanese were now entrenched in the southern part of Manchuria. When the 1914 World War broke out, followed by internal revolt in Russia, it all seemed remote to the residents of Harbin, who shrugged and said that it was yet another attempt at revolution and would be quickly crushed like the one in 1905.

Not until Tsar Nicholas II abdicated in March of 1917 did they realize that something major had happened in Russia. "Well," they said, "the Provisional Government under Alexander Kerensky will hold things together until the war is over and then the internal problems will be resolved." But then came the October 1917 Revolution, the tsar and his family were placed under arrest, and the atmosphere of contentment in Harbin began to change. When in July of 1918 the tsar and his family were brutally murdered in a cellar of Ipatiev House in a remote town of Yekaterinburg in Siberia, and Lenin and his Bolsheviks were firmly in power, the shock wave in Harbin spread rapidly, leaving a pall of doom over the city.

There was no going back to Russia, but the fact that they were now stateless, without a country, did not sink in until the influx of refugees, bedraggled, exhausted, and hungry, flooded the city. The grief on their faces was as eloquent as the tragic stories they told, and after listening to them, the Russians in Harbin realized that they were the privileged few who had escaped the horrors of the revolution.

Yes, Sonya realized now, she should count her blessings. She stirred and listened. The muffled sounds of horse's hooves and the squeaking of a sleigh's unvarnished blades outside were unmistakable. Who would be coming down their way this time of night in a sleigh? Curious, she went to the window. The sleigh stopped in front of the house, and moments later the front door burst open, letting in a gust of frosty air.

Sonya watched in horror as Svetlana and Vladimir half carried Raissa into the parlor. Raissa's head was heavily bandaged; blood seeped through, coloring the gauze with a crimson stain.

In one second Nikolai was beside his daughter, helping to lower her on the divan. "What happened?"

As Svetlana tried to tell her parents about the accident, Raissa began to sob. Not until she was given valerian drops and made comfortable in her bed was anyone able to finish the story.

"How deep was the cut?" Sonya asked. "What did the doctor say?"

Vladimir answered for Svetlana. "He said that it required quite a few stitches, and that there would be a scar, but he said it was impossible to tell at this stage how much it will show."

Svetlana looked at her fiancé with tenderness, grateful to him beyond words for having spared her the necessity of telling her mother the possible extent of Raissa's injury. When all was told, her parents did not blame her for the accident. But in their silence, in the stunned glances that passed between them, did there hang an unspoken accusation that she, Svetlana, was responsible for her young sister's possible disfigurement for life?

Chapter Two

Raissa's recovery was slow. A restless, disobedient patient, she seemed determined to shadow her sister's life with permanent guilt. Where before she had dogged her sister's footsteps, now . . . was it Svetlana's imagination, or did her sister studiously avoid her? When the bandages came off, the red, puffed welt along her jawline revealed that Raissa was one of the people who form keloids, those thick, ungainly scars that do not fade with time.

When the wound had sufficiently healed, she returned to school, but at home Raissa continued to avoid her sister. Svetlana endured the silent accusation and was grateful that Vladimir took on the role of an older brother, trying to cheer Raissa by reading to her some of Sasha Chyorny's tales, those hilarious stories about soldiers' misadventures in the Imperial army.

As time went on Svetlana tried not to show her own hurt. The family did not go out of their way to make her feel blameless. But what else could she have done? Over and over she relived that moment when she had balanced on one leg trying to regain her,footing. Why, oh, why, had Raissa been skating in an area where she shouldn't have been?

No one made her feel better. Not even Vladimir. And she especially wanted reassurance from Vladimir—wasn't he her fiancé? Perhaps he wasn't even aware that she needed to be reassured.

Her parents avoided the subject entirely, yet Svetlana suspected that they secretly accused her of carelessness.

Raissa's sullen attitude had brought gloom to the household, and so as soon as the school year was over, Sonya announced that she was taking her two daughters on their yearly vacation. This time, she said, she had chosen Maoershan.

Svetlana sighed. Her mother then, had not yet overcome her fear of the *hunhuzy*. Never fond of the resorts west of Harbin where the terrain was not as spectacular as in the high mountains and thick forests of the east, Sonya kept selecting places closer and closer to the city, hoping irrationally that perhaps the *hunhuzy* wouldn't risk coming this close to Harbin, in spite of isolated cases of kidnapping in the city itself. Svetlana's earliest recollection was of Yablonya, a resort whose name was derived from the profusion of its apple orchards, which, when the trees were in bloom, caused the illusion that the whole village was wrapped in a white cloud. But this large resort was located too close to where the Rotovs had died, and the following year Sonya chose Imyanpo, a little closer to Harbin. Here was a huge park with a picturesque bridge suspended over the river, colorful flower beds, scattered benches, a restaurant overlooking the river, and croquet and tennis courts, all carefully planned to provide the vacationer with rest and recreation. Nonetheless, Sonya had been restless all that summer, and in subsequent years had tried other resorts; once she took the girls to Laoshan, a rugged mountain resort twenty-five miles inland from the picturesque port of Tsingtao. But it was a long journey by train and boat and they had never gone back.

So, this year she was going to try Maoershan, Svetlana thought, not even a hundred miles east of Harbin. Well, at least there was no boredom in variety, and the fresh mountain air would be welcome after the late-spring dust storms that blew over the city from the Gobi Desert, covering the sidewalks with a gritty film and forcing pedestrians to protect their noses and mouths from the sandy onslaught.

In the past Sonya and the two girls had spent every summer away from Harbin, with Nikolai joining them twice for a few days. This year their plans were the same with one difference: Vladimir promised to spend two weeks with them early in July. Svetlana's excitement grew as she thought of the walks she and Vladimir would take along the trails in the seclusion of flowered valleys and embracing forests.

"I may persuade Mother to come with me," he told Sonya as they were saying good-bye. "She doesn't like to leave Father alone for any length of time, but she might come along for a couple of weeks."

Sonya smiled. "We'd be delighted to have Vera with us. Besides, it would be an excellent opportunity for Svetlana and her future mother-in-law to get to know each other better."

Vladimir bent over Sonya's hand and kissed it lightly. "I'm sure Mother already loves Svetlana," he said with a smile, adding, "Who wouldn't?"

They took the train to Maoershan and moved into a spacious cottage rented from a local Russian resident.

Built above the river, the four-room dacha was light and cheerful, smelling of fresh paint and carbolic soap. The two bedrooms were furnished with brass beds, chintz bedspreads, starched lace curtains. There were also a massive oak wardrobe, a nightstand, and a dressing table. The dining room doubled as a sitting room; a square table and chairs stood in the center of the room, a plush upholstered sofa and matching armchairs nestled in one corner. At the back of the cottage a small kitchen and a screened porch wrapped around two sides of the dacha, overlooking the river Maoershan.

The owner, Ivan Ezhov, a stocky, middle-aged man with a silky bronze beard, greeted them at the door, and after showing them the house, he took them to the garden ablaze with flowers. Then he turned to the girls.

"While your mother is resting, would you like me to show you around the resort?" he asked.

Eager to explore the area, Svetlana readily agreed and was pleasantly surprised when Raissa joined her. In the last few days before their departure from Harbin, Raissa seemed more relaxed and friendlier to her sister. Svetlana took her hand, and the sisters followed Ezhov outside.

They stood near a cluster of whitewashed cottages built on

a steep hill east of the river. Below them was the railroad, and beyond—a settlement where Russian railway employees lived, as well as local residents who made a living selling grape wine, honey from their apiaries, and strawberries from their patches. Farther still, a Chinese hamlet of clay *fanzas* huddled on the shore of the river where it curved west.

Ezhov turned and, looking north, pointed to a mountain with a spectacular vertical cliff. "There's our pride," he said. "We call it Sugar Head, and it's at least one thousand meters high. Doesn't it look close?" He waited for Svetlana and Raissa to nod and then laughed. "Everyone thinks so, yet it's seven versts from here! But what seven versts! There are almost daily excursions to climb Sugar Head because the approach to it snakes through the taiga and is very exciting. Several small bridges cross the river, and the most beautiful of all is called the Devil's Bridge. You must join that excursion while you are here and make the climb."

Svetlana gave a small laugh. "We're not exactly fond of mountain climbing, Mr. Ezhov," she said.

Ezhov shrugged. "You don't have to climb it. There's a Buddhist monastery at the base of Sugar Head and the monks are very hospitable." He paused, then chuckled. "If you go, they'll show you an icon of St. Nicholas. Amazing how the Chinese revere our saint!"

Svetlana listened in fascination. She'd love to take the trip and see the monastery. Perhaps when Vladimir joined them, he would take her there, for she knew that without him her mother would never let her go deep into the taiga, even if she were to join an excursion.

"Do you organize these tours to the mountain?" Raissa asked, looking curiously at Sugar Head, now veiled by a bluish haze.

"No, I don't," Ezhov replied. "I'm too busy with my bees, but there is someone going there almost every day. As a matter of fact"—he turned and pointed down to the Russian settlement—"we have a hotel here, the Kavkaz, where many visitors stay, especially during our hunting season. You could ask there."

On the way back to their cottage Svetlana breathed deeply of the pure air filled with fragrances from the blooming flowers, the freshness of pine sap, and the moist grass beneath her feet. How good was the world, she thought. Raissa seemed finally to have buried her resentment and they were friends again; Vladimir would be joining her soon and they would go on long walks and talk and kiss and plan their future together. Vladimir's mother would come, too, and although a formidable woman, she seemed to approve of Svetlana; it wouldn't be difficult to win her over completely in these magnificent surroundings where everyone was relaxed and happy. As for her own mother, surely in this lovely resort crowded with vacationers, she would overcome her fear and sadness. Svetlana tilted her head toward the blue and sunny sky and laughed without apparent reason.

Ezhov and Raissa looked at her in surprise, and Svetlana was embarrassed. "I love your village, Mr. Ezhov," she hastened to explain, "and I know we shall have a wonderful vacation! Thank you for showing us around."

As the two girls started up the hill, Raissa threw her sister a sidelong glance. "What made you laugh, Svetlana? I think Mr. Ezhov thought you were laughing at him."

"Don't be silly, Raissa. I told him how happy I was here. You can't help but feel exhilarated in this beautiful place. Look around you."

But Raissa shrugged and went ahead. Something had spoiled the mood. Svetlana sighed. Their temperaments were so different, she wondered if she would ever understand her sister. But then, Raissa was only sixteen. She couldn't possibly understand how her older sister felt. Perhaps someday she would know the same happiness.

Two weeks later Vladimir arrived with his mother, Vera Panova, and Svetlana was struck anew by Vladimir's good looks, his carefully groomed appearance, and his obvious pleasure at seeing her. His mother hugged her and Svetlana felt smothered in her embrace, overpowered by a superabundance of Guerlain's L'Heure Bleue fragrance. For a large woman her face was birdlike and pinched, her small chin blending imperceptibly into a thick neck. Small brown eyes darted from side to side, taking everything in.

The Ozerov women greeted Vladimir and Vera with warmth. They had prepared two rooms for them in a neighboring cottage, and when Vera entered, she sniffed at the air, which she claimed was musty, and immediately opened all the windows. "To let in the fresh air," she said to Sonya. "These rooms will be fine for two weeks," she added, flicking a bit of dust off a bureau top. "I wish we could stay longer, but my Vladimir has to return to work, and as for me, there's my husband. Arseny has never been good at staying by himself. He says he doesn't like our cook's cooking." Vera laughed, her ample bosom straining against her cotton print dress. "Silly of him to think that I do the cooking. I only supervise."

Though Sonya listened patiently, Svetlana guessed that she did not find the woman very endearing. Ah, well, she thought, the important thing was for her and Vladimir to be happy, and the rest would take care of itself.

The next few days were exciting, if not entirely relaxed. Svetlana listened in amazement as Vera admonished her for wearing such frivolous attire, hinting broadly that she should wear something more demure and appropriate for a young lady of consequence. What was so frivolous about a summer dress that was only a little shorter than the ones worn in the city? But Sonya nodded her agreement, then whispered to her daughter: "Humor her, my dear. It's smart to get your future mother-in-law on your side."

Svetlana shrugged and changed obediently into a modest cream-colored batiste dress. This minor annoyance was offset, however, by the pleasure of the lovely walks she took with Vladimir. She held hands with him, waiting for his kisses that came in the wooded glen or by the rippling brook at the foot of a cliff, and although she was a little disappointed that his embraces were restrained, she was glad for the privacy the forest afforded them. Fortunately, Raissa did not want to go with them on these long walks; she disappeared into the village near the railroad tracks where she joined boys her own age for a swim in the river or watched them play *lapta* with a large bat and a tennis ball.

In the evenings they ate together at the large dining table, enjoying marinated mushrooms that had been picked in the nearby forest and prepared for them by Ezhov's wife as a

special treat. For dessert there were huge bowls of fresh strawberries or raspberries with cream, and tea with honey.

The weather remained warm and sunny, and Svetlana
wished the vacation could last forever. Then suddenly, one
morning, they awoke to an electrical storm and a relentless
downpour. Thunder reverberated in the mountains, and lightning sparked and crackled as if bouncing on metal. For two
days the rain poured down in torrents, and on the third day
the river overflowed its banks. The freed waters rushed at the
Chinese hamlet, sending the villagers scampering for safety,
their children and bundles on their backs. Sheltered by those
on higher ground, the villagers watched in horror as their
hamlet drowned in the turbulent river.

On the fourth day, as abruptly as it had started, the storm
ended. When the sun came out, it dried the wet leaves quickly
of their prismatic glitter, leaving the grass, refreshed and
bathed by the heavens' downpour, to steam with moisture and
perfume the air with blended fragrances. Dragonflies feasted
on tobacco plants, colorful butterflies hovered over the last
blossoms of lavender-pink rhododendrons, and sparrows busily pecked at the ground in search of food.

It was a pastoral scene, an inviting one. It beckoned the
vacationers of Maoershan to come outdoors. Svetlana and
Vladimir were the first out, leaving Raissa and the two mothers still asleep in their cottages. They were eager to enjoy the
beauty of the forest again, to walk and embrace in their favorite glen. But the scene that greeted them, unfolding as they
watched, stunned them.

The burgeoning river rushed its waters, carrying broken
twigs, household items, and dead animals, and swirling past
large tree trunks on the valley floor. It also circled the roof of
one *fanza* that seemed to jut out farther from the rest of the
hamlet, and on it was an old Chinese woman. Surrounded by
angry water on all sides, she sat in the center of the thatched
roof. Svetlana and Vladimir rushed down the hill.

At the edge of the river a crowd of both Chinese and Russians had already gathered. They shouted and gesticulated,
quarreling over the best way to rescue the old woman.
Svetlana held on to Vladimir's hand, mesmerized by the sight.
The old woman hadn't moved since they first saw her; she sat

quietly, resignation written into the age-old wisdom etched on her pathetic face.

"What are they going to do, Vladimir?" Svetlana asked. He pulled his hand out of hers and turned to a blond Russian youth standing nearby.

"How deep is the water here?" Vladimir asked.

"It's probably over our heads," the boy replied. "But it's no good swimming out to her. No one could make it across that current."

Vladimir narrowed his eyes and studied the terrain. Svetlana followed his glance. A few paces from where they stood, an old oak shaded the bank. It leaned slightly into the river, its leaves shaking in the breeze over the fast-moving water below. Vladimir walked over to the tree, then turned and looked across to where the Chinese woman was still sitting. Then he turned to the youth.

"How many men can you get together?" he asked.

The boy shrugged and pointed to a group of young men nearby. "About a dozen, I guess." Then he looked at Vladimir suspiciously. "Why do you ask? If you think we're going to swim across, you are out of your mind."

Vladimir raised his hand. "Hear me out. See this tree? Get me a thick rope, and I'll show you what I plan to do. In the meantime all of you hurry up and change into swimming suits and get back here."

In a few minutes the youth returned with a rope and handed it to Vladimir. The rest of the group, their curiosity now aroused, scattered, and soon they were back in their swimsuits and crowding around Vladimir.

He wrapped the rope around the trunk of the tree and tied a secure knot. Then he circled the rope around his waist. This done, he motioned to the blond youth. "We'll make a human chain. I'll show you how."

Twelve young men stood waiting.

Svetlana watched her fiancé with pride. The boys were no more than sixteen or seventeen years old, and they looked up to Vladimir with a mixture of doubt and respect, watching his movements and half ready to obey. Vladimir raised his left arm and showed them how to crisscross their arms and grasp each other's shoulders. With his other arm he circled the trunk of the tree.

"Now," he ordered, "all of you come over here and form a line, and then move into the water until the last man reaches the old woman."

Fascinated, the youths quickly obeyed, joining the row and pushing into the river. As the human chain progressed, fighting the dragging current, the stress on Vladimir increased and he spread his feet for better leverage. Svetlana could see his tensed shoulder muscles ripple and knew the pull was tremendous.

For a moment resentment welled within her. Why should he have subjected himself to such a test of physical endurance when he could have joined the wading row and let a younger man take the brunt of the anchor? But as soon as she thought that, she was ashamed. Vladimir was older and stronger than the boys, and she was proud of him.

A sudden commotion in the water drew her attention away from Vladimir. One of the youths had lost his balance and his head went under for a few seconds. Coughing and rasping, the lad struggled to surface. The supporting arms that held his shoulder on both sides pulled him upright. *How clever, this human chain,* Svetlana thought. He was wise, her Vladimir. She glanced indulgently at him. He was watching the water intently, his upper arm shaking from strain as he coaxed and encouraged the young men to keep the line as straight as possible.

Another few minutes, and the first youth reached the roof of the *fanza*. How fortunate that the river was narrow at this point, no more than ten yards wide.

"Don't let go!" Vladimir called, and the last boy waved back in acknowledgment. With his free arm the boy reached for the Chinese woman's hand and started to pull her toward him. But the woman resisted; her face collapsed into a myriad of wrinkles, and she began to cry and shake her head.

By now the crowd of spectators on shore had increased, and shouts of advice carried across the river. Svetlana moved closer to Vladimir and touched his shoulder lightly. "Can I help?" she asked timidly.

Vladimir nodded without taking his eyes off the human

chain. "Go down to the edge of the river and wait. Then help the woman when they bring her ashore."

Svetlana turned and started down the slope. She felt good about being a part of the rescue, and at the water's edge she watched the drama that was taking place across the river. The woman was visibly shaking now, pointing to the water, making eloquent signs about her inability to swim. Exasperated, the boy grabbed her hand again and jerked her toward him; she lost her balance and tumbled into the water. In the splash that followed she thrashed and coughed and, with a high-pitched "Ai-yeee!" clawed at the boy's shoulders and neck, dragging him down.

With one swing of his hand he slapped her face and in the next move grabbed her around the neck before she could go under. With the crook of his elbow under her chin, he tilted her face upward and tried to pull her away from the submerged *fanza*.

The human chain started to move toward the shore. The young man linked with Vladimir stepped back, transferring the arm of the next man in the chain onto Vladimir's shoulder. Svetlana watched with alarm. How long would Vladimir hold out? The young men were relieved one by one, but still he stood there, resisting the pull.

When the last youth had stepped out of water and hawled the terrified woman ashore, Svetlana grabbed her shaking arm and helped her stand up. Gently, she pushed the wet strands of hair off the woman's face and wiped it with a handkerchief.

Where moments before only the young Russian men were participating in the drama, now Chinese men and women crowded around the rescued woman and took over from Svetlana. Relieved, she rushed to Vladimir and helped untie the cord that bound him to the tree. "I'm so proud of you, darling," she whispered, and was rewarded with his pleased smile.

"That was the only thing to do, Svetlana," he said, and then turned to the young men who were cheering and slapping one another on the back.

"Good work, men, thanks," he said. "Any of you speak Chinese?" And when he received a nod, he added: "Better tell that woman to stay with her family next time."

The crowd guffawed, Vladimir waved, and linking his arm through Svetlana's, he started uphill toward their cottage.

"You did what?" screamed Vladimir's mother, crossing herself several times. "Watch now that you don't get a hernia from all that strain. Why didn't you get one of those boys to take the brunt?"

Vladimir colored. "I'm not that old, Mama. Besides, I knew exactly how to do it, so it was natural for me to be the anchor man."

"What do you mean, you knew exactly how to do it? When have you done it before?"

"I haven't, but I saw it done several years ago, and I remembered that it worked."

Svetlana listened in silence, afraid to interfere in a mother-and-son dispute, eager to come to Vladimir's defense and say how proud she was of his performance, yet afraid to antagonize her future mother-in-law. She turned to look at her mother.

Sonya was clasping and unclasping her hands. "And all this for a mere Chinese peasant who hadn't the sense to follow her relatives when the flood started," she said, her voice shaking with emotion.

Shocked and embarrassed, Svetlana said, "Someone had to rescue the poor woman, Mama. She was alone and helpless."

Sonya frowned. "Where were her relatives, then? Why hadn't they taken her with them?"

Vera straightened her shoulders and raised her chin. "Maybe she didn't have any relatives. My son would rescue anyone who was in distress, Sonya. That was not the point I was trying to make. I'm only concerned over his straining himself. I would hate to have him hurt, especially before the wedding."

Vladimir patted his mother on her arm. "Don't worry, Mama. It's all over now. I'm none the worse for it all."

At a loss as to how to end this awkward conversation, Svetlana turned toward the door and collided with her sister.

"I hear I missed all the excitement down by the river," Raissa said, smiling up at Vladimir. "I guess congratulations are in order. You must be a hero among the Chinese by now."

Vladimir looked at her with a half smile, then said, "I really don't care about the praise. The woman had to be rescued, and we did it because we were first on the scene."

Several times in the next few days Svetlana lured her fiancé away from her family into the seclusion of the forest glen where they collected flowers and talked.

Not until after he had gone back to Harbin did the thought occur to her that although he went with her willingly enough, it was she who initiated the embraces each time they were alone. For a worldly man of twenty-five he was shy indeed. She thought of their conversations during those long quiet walks, and how glad she was to have had them, for she had learned more in a few days about the man she was soon to marry than she had in the preceding months of their courtship in Harbin, where they always seemed to be surrounded by people.

From those talks a picture had emerged of a man dedicated to his work and career—disciplined, deeply religious, and proud of his background. She would have to be more careful, she thought, with her liberal ideas on religion, her family's easy approach to the church and its customs. Since early childhood she had been steeped in the Russian Orthodox traditions with an easy symbiotic relationship between the Church and their daily lives, not at all with the rigidity she now sensed in Vladimir. She shifted uncomfortably thinking about it. His was a kind of rigidity that made religion seem an overbearing symbol that stood for everything proper and good; a blind obedience without question or compromise.

Svetlana was troubled. Might this cause dissension in their marriage? Would he expect her to join the church sisterhood and follow in his mother's devout footsteps? Nonsense. He would have said so long ago, and she was surely imagining things. The time of the wedding was drawing near, and she must be having the usual prenuptial jitters.

Just before he left, he had taken her in his arms and held her close against his chest for a few tender moments. Then he had lifted her chin and kissed her slowly and deeply. After he'd released her and taken her hand to kiss, he had looked at her from under his brows, his hazel eyes clear and direct.

"My dear, we shall be married soon," he had said. "You will be my lovely wife." He leaned closer to her and whispered: "I'll be so proud of you! I can hardly wait!"

A shiver had raced down her spine. How she yearned for more such embraces! To cover her excitement Svetlana had pulled her hand out of his and reached up to touch a shock of hair on his forehead. "And I am proud of you, Vladimir," she'd said, a vague apprehension intruding strangely into their embrace.

"I'll do my best to be a good wife to you," she had said, and thought her voice sounded hollow. Quickly, she'd smiled and added: "I mean it shouldn't be difficult at all, darling, should it?"

Vladimir did not smile, only nodded. "Of course not, my dear. We think along the same lines of what constitutes a good marriage, and any minor differences we have will not be hard to iron out."

She had wondered if he were referring to her singing ambition, but thought it best not to bring it up right then.

He had looked at her carefully, then said, "We have the same religion, the same friends, and we care what those friends think of us."

Now, picking flowers two weeks later, Svetlana suddenly remembered his last words, and reflecting on them, she thought it a strange thing to have said. She shook her head to chase away these unanswered puzzles, wondering if thoughts of the responsibilities of being married were overwhelming her, for after all, she was only eighteen. Raising her head to the blue, sparkling sky, she smiled, remembering his last, deep kiss. Silly to worry about anything.

But back in the cottage she found her mother sitting on the porch, rocking purposefully in her chair. She didn't look up at Svetlana as she walked in—a bad sign, Svetlana knew—but continued to stare at the floor.

"What is the matter, Mama?" she asked. "Has Raissa done something wrong?"

Sonya shook her head.

"Then what is it?" Svetlana persisted. "You should be outside, the sky is clear and the day is beautiful. It's too warm to sit on the porch."

Slowly Sonya's eyes came around and fastened on Svetlana.
She grasped her daughter's hands and held them tightly. "Oh,
Svetik," she said, reverting to Svetlana's childhood nickname,
"the anxiety is coming back. It's an obsession with me, I
know, but I can't help it. That day . . . that Chinese woman
on the roof of her flooded home . . . it all started again. I
keep thinking of how Vladimir didn't hesitate a moment to
help the Chinese woman, and yet no one came to the Rotovs'
rescue, and they died. Where is justice?"

Svetlana freed her hands and clasped her mother's shoulders. "Mama! We've been through all this before. Please don't
dwell on it again. It's been twenty-two years since they died.
How long are you going to brood over it?"

"I don't know. I thought I was over it, but now that I've
been reminded of it here, I'm full of fears again. We're vaca-
tioning near the taiga, and *hunhuzy* are hiding in there. I
know it. I heard just yesterday that they've been stealing bolts
from the railroad near here and the railway guards have been
shooting at them without much success."

"What has that to do with the Rotovs' deaths, Mama?"

"Don't you see? The *hunhuzy* are everywhere in these forests, and they can come near Maoershan and kidnap for ransom. Now that Vladimir is gone, don't you go far into the
forest alone, do you hear?"

Svetlana straightened slowly and sighed. The cloudless day
that had promised to be so lovely was suddenly overcast with
her mother's chronic foreboding.

"Don't worry, Mama, I never go beyond the closest glen. It
would be foolish of me. You better watch Raissa. She is the
impetuous one."

"Raissa doesn't like the taiga," Sonya replied. "She stays
near the hotel with other young people. No. I'm not afraid for
her, she doesn't like to be alone. But you—you are the
dreamer in our family, so you be careful on your solitary
walks."

"I will, Mama."

For her midmorning meal Svetlana ate a bowl of strawberries with cream, a piece of fragrant sesame bread thickly covered with liver pâté, then drank a cup of chocolate and afterward went for a walk. Mindful of her mother's anxiety, she

was determined to obey her. Besides, as she told Sonya, she
never did venture beyond the first glen in the forest, always
within earshot of the village. It was so beautiful there, so full
of sweet memories of her walks with Vladimir, that she
wanted to savor and remember their conversations and kisses
again.

In spite of the warm sun the taiga was always cool in the
shade of the giant firs. She picked up her peach-colored knitted shawl and headed toward the forest.

Chapter Three

Svetlana walked slowly along the narrow path toward the taiga. On the way she stopped long enough to pick a bouquet of field flowers for her mother. They would cheer her up. Sonya loved flowers and every morning freshened arrangements in all the rooms of the cottage.

Clutching a few daisies and forget-me-nots, Svetlana smelled their delicate fragrance and looked up into the shining sky. The day was beautiful—clear, shimmering, warm. There was no wind and the only movement in the air was a rushing swallow, and a butterfly darting out of her way. She waved good-morning to the bird and watched it dive into the woods.

And the sun—oh, the sun! It caressed and it kissed with the tenderness reserved for humans. Enveloped in the glorious shower of sunlight, Svetlana luxuriated in its embrace. When she entered the forest, cool air washed over her, and after a short walk over the shaded path, she reached the clearing. Once there, she closed her eyes to relive Vladimir's recent presence, for in that same verdant glen they would sit on the grass and kiss and talk of their future. And now, as she stood encircled by the trees, protected from the curious eyes of other vacationers, a boundless joy welled within her. She threw open her arms and twirled, then looked up to the tops of the pines that seemed to meet the sky. Ah, to be a bird and to fly up there right now, see the world, and sing from those treetops! She laughed at her silly notion; but she could sing, though, couldn't she? And why not? She was alone, no one would hear her. Exuberant, she burst into a song, choosing the opening chorus from Tchaikovsky's *Eugene Onegin*. It was so fitting, she thought. The singing peasant girls, cheerful and carefree, must have been strolling on Tatiana's estate through a pastoral scene similar to the one she was enjoying now.

It was glorious. Unhampered by human structures, the air carried her powerful soprano through the trees, bouncing it from their branches and echoing it back to vibrate in her ears. And as she sang, Svetlana began to sway from side to side to the waltzlike rhythm of the lilting melody and then, closing her eyes again, started to whirl. This was how it would have felt if Vladimir were here, holding her around the waist, circling on the green velvet of grass until she would lean against him from dizziness.

Dizziness was wheeling in her head now as she finished her song and smiled. The sky tilted, the treetops whirled, and the flower-dotted grass rose to meet her. She let herself fall, her legs buckling under, her body floating down, down, to meet the soft, cool grass.

For a few moments she lay quietly, then raised her arms and put them behind her head. The colorful carpet beneath her was soft, so soft! How wonderful to be able to give in to the delicious sensation of floating with the brilliant sky above, no disapproving parental eyes to break the spell. The only sounds she heard now were the birds in their orchestration of chirps and trills.

And as she lay there thinking of Vladimir and venturing to open her mind to the private fantasies about married love and those secret mysteries that were awaiting her, there came into her communion with the sky and the grass and the birds, another sound. Distant it was and probably imagined. She raised herself on one elbow and listened. A faint, ever so faint, yet unmistakable barking of a dog. Svetlana sat up abruptly. It must be lunchtime. She must go back, but she would keep her delightful tryst private. There was something deliciously tantalizing about the seclusion of this charming place, and she did not regret having acted with such abandon.

Quickly, she picked up the flowers she had thrown down, brushed off her skirt, and headed into the forest along a narrow path toward the sound of the barking dog.

She walked briskly this time. No need to linger further and annoy her mother. She would scold her for being gone this long, but if her mother could see how peaceful it was in the forest, how much cooler in the darkened arbor of the ancient trees, she would understand her reluctance to leave.

Although the dog had stopped barking, Svetlana continued to walk toward the faded sound, her mind drifting to Harbin, wondering where Vladimir was at that moment, hoping she had made a good impression on her future mother-in-law, and secretly glad that the formidable Madame Panova had returned to the city with her son.

A fallen tree trunk loomed across her path, and Svetlana came upon it so abruptly, she nearly stumbled. Strange. It hadn't been there on her way in. How could such a big tree have fallen without her hearing the noise? But even as she thought about it, she realized why: she had been whirling and singing out there in the glen, so how could she have heard it? She shrugged, and without dwelling on the puzzle, stepped over the trunk and went on.

When she had entered the forest earlier, it had been alive with sounds: a chorus of twittering birds, a squirrel racing up a tree or rustling the ferns by the side of her path, a soft breeze sighing around the huge tree trunks. But now the forest had become silent. It was only a short distance from Maoershan to the glen, yet now as she walked, she found herself still in the woods. Perplexed, she stopped and for the first time tried to orient herself. She had walked this path with Vladimir so many times, surely she would recognize something along the way—a bush, a small clearing, perhaps even a tree? She looked about her, turned around. By now she should be near the edge of the forest, where the trees were sparse and the sun filtered through them onto the thinning underbrush. Instead, the ferns were thick and high, the trees dense. Nothing looked familiar. She peered ahead but could see little beyond a few yards.

She took a closer look around her. The smooth and well-trodden path had disappeared and instead the ground was covered with moss and pine needles. The air was damp and smelled of resin. Had she taken a wrong path? But there was only one trail into the forest and the same one out. How could she have taken the wrong one?

Suddenly, the answer came. She had twirled too much, and in her giddy abandon she had paid no attention to the familiar landmarks of the glen and had entered the forest on the wrong side. She had gone east instead of west to Maoershan. How far had she walked? How foolish to have forgotten her wrist-watch.

Resolutely, she turned around and started back, but after a few steps the path unexpectedly split into a fork. She had not noticed the other branch before. Which one had she walked on? She tried to remember. And as she stood there wondering, an awareness of something amiss came over her. She raised her head and listened. Silence. A palpable silence, secretive, untested. It wrapped itself around her, trapping her like a gigantic web.

The truth edged itself into her mind. She was lost. Where was she? She looked up. The trees above her formed a thick roof and she could not see the sun to orient herself, but then what good would that do when it was midday and the sun was high? She took a few tentative steps on the right branch of the fork but the path ended abruptly against the base of a huge pine. She retraced her steps hurriedly and started on the other path.

A dog barked again. She paused to listen. The same dog, only now it sounded closer. What was a dog doing so deep in the forest? A hunter? A peasant searching for the priceless ginseng root? Whoever it was, she needed help to get out of the forest. Placing her hands to her mouth, she called: "A-oo!"

Her voice echoed far into the forest, and sure that whoever was with the dog would hear her, she trilled the "A-oo!" in a cadence, listening until it died down. The barking increased, and suddenly apprehension surfaced. What was she doing, inviting a stranger to find her? Who was with that dog? Surely not the *hunhuzy;* they wouldn't be this close to Maoershan. But then, how far had she gone into the taiga? She had lost track of distance and time. How foolish, how utterly irrespon-

sible, of her to be this careless. But now there was nothing to
do but stand still and wait for whoever would find her. All her
mother's fears began to surface in her mind.

She shivered. The palms of her hands grew moist and she
rubbed them together. Then she hugged herself to keep from
trembling. Her heart pounded. Dreadful not to see the
stranger, or know who it was.

Another few moments, and out of the rustling underbrush a
full-grown husky burst forth, stopped abruptly a few feet in
front of her, and barked hysterically.

Svetlana stood still, fists clenched, every muscle rigid. A
high fern behind the dog moved suddenly, and a man
emerged. With a curt order in Chinese he silenced the dog and
then looked at Svetlana. Tall and erect, he was dressed in
black, baggy pants tied at the ankles and a high-collared
belted shirt, and he carried a rifle over his shoulder. Svetlana's
heart skipped a beat. A *hunhuz?* But although he spoke to the
dog in Chinese, and wore Chinese clothes, his face bore traces
of mixed blood. He was strikingly handsome. There was
something patrician in the shape of his head, in the aquiline
nose, and the smooth curve of his chin. Surprisingly, his black
hair had reddish highlights, and although his dark eyes
seemed slightly tilted, there was a Caucasian look in them.
Right now they were studying her with intelligence and curiosity. Incredibly, his eyes sparkled with a touch of humor, not
menace, and as she stood there looking at him, the moment of
terror passed. Whoever he was, her fear abated.

The young *hunhuz* stood riveted to the ground. He was Li-
chun, the twenty-two-year-old son of the band's chieftain, Ma
Fu-li, and he had been on a routine scouting mission around
his father's territory when he came upon the girl. He stared at
her. She was beautiful. He had never seen one so beautiful or
so delicate before. What in the world was she doing alone this
deep in the forest?

When, earlier that morning, he had left the bandit enclave
hidden deep in the taiga and started on his rounds through the
forest, he ignored his dog's barking. He had learned to recognize variations in the urgency of the animal's bark, and at first
it was but an idle threat to a passing squirrel. But as he pene-

trated deeper into the taiga, the barking changed and he knew at once that a stranger was near.

It was his duty then to find the trespasser—a distasteful job, for most of the time it turned out to be a bandit from a rival band, and the primitive court the bandit would face in Ma Fu-li's *fanza* was something he did not wish to dwell on. Yet he dared not disobey his father's orders, for disobedience to the chief of the band was punishable by death. Li-chun had difficulty coming to terms with this because he had been educated in a Russian school, and the last four years—since his return to the taiga—had not been easy for him. He felt neither Russian nor Chinese, for although he had been raised since infancy by a Chinese woman, he'd spent his school years with a Russian family.

His memory of his early childhood was vague. He remembered pungent smells of cooking garlic, cabbages, and ginger; also, dry garlic hung from the ceiling of his *fanza* as protection against infection and illness. He had been cared for by a woman he called Aunt Hsu, who nursed his colds and coughs with a mixture of garlic juice and honey and allowed him to run wild in the village. When other children began to point to his face and tease him because he looked different, he would slosh through mud and cow dung, chasing them as they ran squealing to their own *fanzas*. He asked his father about it after he went to live with him in the forest, and Ma Fu-li explained that Li-chun's mother had been part Buryat, part Russian, but refused to answer any more questions, and Li-chun understood that it was not a subject to be discussed.

When he was ten years old, his father took him to the village of Handaohedzi farther east. Here Ma Fu-li had made arrangements with a Russian farmer, Mitrofan Karpov, to take Li-chun in for the school years so that he could go to a Russian school. It would never occur to Li-chun to ask why he was singled out instead of being sent back to the Chinese village where he had grown up with other bandits' children. One of the first rules he had learned was unquestioning obedience to the head of the band, and so he listened silently as his father guaranteed that in return, Mitrofan Karpov's village would be free from bandits' raids. Li-chun saw Karpov's hesitation and reluctance to agree, yet he knew that the Russian feared Ma Fu-li's reprisals.

Li-chun missed his father and yearned for the taiga, but as the months slipped by he thought of the forest less and less. The Karpovs were a boisterous family with two sons, Vanka and Mitka, who were about his age. In the beginning the family were cool toward him, but soon the boys became friendly and Li-chun felt welcome despite the villagers' suspicious attitude toward him.

The only Chinese boy in a Russian school, he was frequently teased, and although his skin was light, he nonetheless knew that he looked different from other boys. When they called him *phazan* for the first time, he asked his teacher what it meant and she said that it was a Russian word for *pheasant*. It went back to the times of the Manchu dynasty, she explained, when the Russians had first met Chinese government officials, who wore the image of the phoenix bird on their clothes, and the Cossacks thought it was a pheasant. After that they had taken to using *phazan* as a nickname for all Chinese. Yet Li-chun earned his classmates respect by never betraying his tormentors' names to the teacher.

He spent the summer months with his father in the forest, where Ma Fu-li taught him how to hunt and survive in the taiga. He missed his Russian family but dared not tell this to his father. After all, he *was* Chinese, and it would not do to admit that he preferred his Russian friends to those he had played with during his early years in a Chinese village.

In Handaohedzi the Karpovs treated him as one of their own. Never mind that other Russians in the village avoided him, for he understood eventually that it was not because he was Chinese, but because his father was a bandit, and although this knowledge hurt, Li-chun did not take it personally. With his Buryat features he felt even more an outcast in the Chinese village. Here, he only regretted that he had to wear his blue, high-collared shirt with a black, quilted winter jacket and pants that set him apart from the rest of the children, and he had come to hate his pointed *u-li* shoes, so different from the leather ones the Russian boys wore, for his were made of rawhide and felt, thickly inner-lined with grass to keep him warm in winter, cool in summer.

Vanka and Mitka's parents were hardworking people who had little time to spend with the boys except to give them chores: cleaning out the chicken pen, milking the cow in the shed, kneading the bread, or turning the ice cream. But they were kind, and he had learned to love this Russian family, though in doing so he felt guilty and disloyal to his father.

At times Li-chun heard the Karpovs discuss the fall of the Ch'ing Manchu dynasty in 1911 and the establishment of a republic by Dr. Sun Yat-sen, who, they said with regret, had resigned after only two months in office. They worried that the regional warlords, instead of strengthening the new government, had instead fought one another for a larger piece of the land, and then set up their own rule. Listening to the Karpovs, Li-chun wondered why his father wanted him to attend a Russian school instead of learning his own history better.

Eventually, his father explained that he wanted him to study Russian in order to have the advantage over his adversaries when he himself became the mighty chieftain of a band. After all, he pointed out, Russia was their neighbor, and since the building of the Chinese Eastern Railway through Manchuria, a large number of Russians had populated the country. In dealing with them he should know their language and history.

Li-chun had decided then that he would learn everything he could, and that after his schooling was finished he would ask his father to let him go to Harbin, where many Russians lived. Secretly, he didn't want to become a chieftain as his father wished, for he had no taste for looting and killing; far better to deal with the Russians through the trade in furs or wild game.

As an adolescent on leave from school he had paid scant attention to his father's bandit activities, but when, a couple of months before his eighteenth birthday, he left Handaohedzi for good, Li-chun found himself questioning the rigid rules of his father's disciplined band, as well as the unwritten laws of the taiga itself. Although he dared not voice his doubts, he did win one minor victory. After living among the Russians for so many years, he hated wearing a queue, and his father, grudgingly, allowed him to cut it off. Subtly, he rebelled against other things. Trained to handle a gun, he nonetheless avoided using it, and rarely joined the band on routine raids on villages. Although his father robbed only the wealthy and never disgraced women, Li-chun hated pillaging and terrorizing the villagers and knew his father was disappointed in him.

"I want you to be more than a chieftain of a band, my son," Ma Fu-li told him soon after he came home from school. "You should become a great warlord like the Old Marshal, Chang Tso-lin. His older brother was a bandit, and I heard that the marshal, too, lived among the bandits once, and then became a fearless leader. He should be your model."

Li-chun seized the opportunity to broach the subject of his leaving his father's enclave. "Yes, honored Father," he said, "I bow to your wise judgment. Perhaps I could start by enlisting in the great Chang Tso-lin's army."

Ma Fu-li puffed on his opium pipe, squinted at Li-chun, and nodded. "Yes, I approve. But first, you must live with me and learn more of the ways of the taiga and the laws of our band. Obedience and discipline have always been our first rules, and your future success will depend on that."

And so Li-chun had no alternative but to yield. Today, on this beautiful sunny morning, he left his father resting in the large *fanza* where he lived with several of his most trusted lieutenants, surrounded by faithful dogs and an arsenal of weapons.

As a rule Li-chun enjoyed these scouting rounds, for they were peaceful and, for the most part, uneventful, giving him a chance to be alone and dwell on his secret desire to become a legitimate son of his country. This morning, however, his dog was restless, barking nervously and urging him on.

Deep in thought, he was startled by the echo of "A-oo!" He recognized the Russian call—he had heard it often enough in the Russian village. This one was powerful and of bell-like clarity, but what startled him the most was that it was a woman's voice.

He hastened his steps and on reaching a small cluster of ferns, watched the dog suddenly growl and rush forward. Li-chun followed, spread the bushes and stepped out into a clearing.

He had expected to see a lost peasant woman whom he would scold for wandering so far from her village. But what he saw instead took his breath away. An angel stood before him. Surely it was an angel in human disguise, one of the many blond ones he had seen in picture books in his Russian school. Only this angel was tall and willowy and wrapped in a gossamer cloud of some exquisite fabric.

Yes, she was beautiful, this Russian girl. She had a vibrant face with a clear, innocent look. The Russian girls in the village where he had lived were robust and red-cheeked, not pale and slender like this one. Her hair was pulled straight back into a single thick braid, and it was the color of wheat at harvest when it turned golden. The high forehead was smooth, and the perfectly shaped, small nose ended high above full lips, now slightly open and quivering. But it wasn't her nose or the mouth that really startled him. What dominated the lustrous face were her remarkable eyes. He had never seen such eyes in his whole life. They were gray and huge. Most astonishing of all, however, was that those gray eyes in that pale face were rimmed with the thickest and longest dark lashes he had ever seen. And now those eyes were opened wide and staring at him with unconcealed terror.

Yet he was reluctant to speak and break the magic of this encounter. And magic it was in this dark forest now, for it did things to him like speeding his heart and moving his mouth into a tentative smile. He continued to look at her, and as he looked, he saw that the stark fear in her eyes dissolved in their deep pools and curiosity rose to fill them.

Then the girl spoke. Pointing to her mouth and shaking her head, she said, *"Putunda.* I don't understand Chinese." She pointed in various directions, and asked, "Maoershan?"

Li-chun smiled broadly. "Don't worry, I speak Russian," he said, and was pleased to see her startled reaction. "Maoershan is that way," he added, pointing to the west. "You're a long way from it."

The girl clasped her hands and shook her head. "I had no idea I'd strayed so far. Please help me find my way back!"

There was nothing more he would have liked to do than lead her quietly out of the forest and back to Maoershan, but he knew he could not.

"I'll be glad to show you the way to Maoershan, but not

right away," he said carefully, and watched the color drain from her face.

"What do you mean, not right away?"

"I must first take you to my father. You see, you have crossed the boundaries of his territory and our law is such that I, as a scout, must bring to him anyone I meet in the forest."

A flicker of fear flashed in the gray eyes. "Are you—are you a *hunhuz?*"

Li-chun did not answer immediately. He hated the word. Among themselves the bandits never used it. It meant "red beard," and they resented the deprecating nickname.

"My father is the chieftain of the band that controls this area. I must take you to him."

The girl's voice rose. "Then you are kidnapping me?"

Li-chun shook his head. "I'm obeying my father's rules, that's all."

"But your father doesn't know that you found me. You can take me back to Maoershan and no one would learn that you had seen me."

"I can't do that. I couldn't lie to my father." He spread his arms. "I'm a poor liar. He would know I wasn't telling the truth and that I had seen someone. He must have heard the dog barking. Please don't worry. All I have to do is explain what happened and then I shall take you back to the edge of the forest. From there you'll find your own way to Maoershan."

The girl shrank from him, fear clearly intensified in those magnificent eyes.

"Come on," he coaxed, offering her his hand, but she did not move.

"Don't be afraid. No harm will come to you, I promise. You'll be home before dark tonight."

Li-chun was growing impatient. It was time to go. He held his hand out and waited until the girl moved forward hesitantly, reluctantly, and slipped her hand into his. It was soft and cold, and he fought a wild impulse to put his arm around her to reassure her.

To hide his reaction he pulled her roughly behind him and moved back through the thicket of ferns and onto a narrow path that led to the main bandit *fanza.*

Chapter Four

It took them a long time to reach the enclave. Svetlana tried to pocket her fear despite the tension and suspense. She had to think of this as an exciting adventure, and how lucky to have encountered a friendly *hunhuz* who not only spoke excellent Russian, but had also promised that no harm would come to her. Still, doubt persisted. What if his father turned out to be not as friendly as this young man? But then, what could she do now except blame herself for not having heeded her mother's warning? Childish behavior, that's what it was.

Intent on her thoughts, she hadn't been watching where the bandit was leading her, and it wasn't until she stumbled over a root and he caught her around the waist, that she looked at him again. His arm was firm yet gentle as he helped her regain her balance, but after he released her, she felt a sudden chill. Pulling her shawl closer around her shoulders, she asked: "What's your name?"

"Ma Li-chun," he answered quietly. "And yours?"

"Svetlana Ozerova," she replied, giving him a sidelong glance. *Ma Li-chun,* she thought, *a Chinese name.* She studied him surreptitiously. "What's your father's name?"

He hesitated a second, then said, "Ma Fu-li."

"You look different from . . ." she said, and didn't know how to finish her thought without offending him. There was something about the look in his eyes that definitely did not seem entirely Chinese.

"My mother was half Russian, half Buryat," he answered, obviously guessing the rest of her sentence.

Svetlana waited for further explanation, but he did not elaborate, and she did not pursue the subject.

Another chill waved over her body. The forest had become more dense, and it was impossible to tell how low the sun had sunk. The trail was twisting, tortuous, overgrown with burdocks, frequently running through thick underbrush. Suddenly, Li-chun took her hand and pulled her off the path into the ferns. Frightened, Svetlana resisted.

"Why are we leaving the trail?" she asked.

"Because it leads to nowhere. A secret path begins farther on. It's to keep trespassers from finding my father's *fanza.*"

The dog, which had followed them closely behind, now rushed forward and moments later was lapping at a brook that meandered along their path. A few more steps, and they emerged onto a tiny glade. Moss-covered logs lay rotting against the tall firs that surrounded the meadow. For the first time the sun filtered down upon them in deeply slanted shafts; with a sinking feeling Svetlana realized that it was already late afternoon, the air now damp and cold. Her mother must be beside herself with worry. She paused, but Li-chun pulled her on.

"We must keep going. It isn't too much farther."

Reluctantly, she followed him back into the darkness of the surrounding taiga.

There was something mysterious about this *hunhuz,* but his laconic sentences discouraged any questions. And she so wanted to question him! Perhaps, if she knew where he came from, just who he was, her apprehension and fear of the unknown would not trouble her so. Then another fear surfaced.

"Aren't there wild animals this deep in the taiga?" she asked, bracing herself for the answer.

"Not here," Li-chun said. "Wild beasts shy away from humans. The tiger favors caves on higher ground, usually near an oak grove where he can hunt boar. We're safer here in the thickets of pines and cedars."

This was the longest speech he had yet made, as if he felt

more at ease speaking about animals than about himself. She
wanted to ask about the black bear, but no animal loomed as
frighteningly to her right now as the prospect of facing the
hunhuzy enclave. She concentrated on the underbrush before
them. Grapevine intertwined with ferns, its sharp branches
catching her skirt, and she had to stop and pull the twigs out
of the fabric. They were no longer following a trail but tram-
pling over wet leaves and moss.

Suddenly the hand that was clasping her wrist tightened,
and a moment later Li-chun pulled her out into a large clearing.

Svetlana stopped in amazement. She hadn't expected to
come upon habitation so suddenly without hearing any
sounds of human life. To her left stood the largest *fanza* she
had ever seen. Made of wood and covered with a thatched
roof, it blended into the surrounding trees. *A perfect camou-
flage,* she thought. In the center of the clearing several men
busily piled kindling under a trestle from which hung a large
cauldron. They moved with speed and stealth on their soft
u-li, dressed in the same drab blue cotton pants and high-
collared shirts as Li-chun wore.

Now they raised their heads, staring at Svetlana. *I'm a trespasser,* she thought. *How hostile they look.* Without thinking
she clutched at Li-chun's arm, but he ignored her gesture,
pulling her forward without looking at the men, who had now
returned to their chores. As she and Li-chun walked past
them, she noticed that their narrowly slit eyes were following
her steps.

At the *fanza* she stopped, but Li-chun resolutely pulled her
in. Immediately, an overpowering odor of something stifling
and sickening assaulted her before she had time to adjust to
the darkness inside. As she tried to identify the smell, she
discerned at least a dozen men lounging on the k'ang (the
elevated floor she had heard about) puffing on long, thin pipes.
Opium, she thought in dismay, looking at the men. She had
heard, of course, of the poppy fields that the Chinese cultivated and the profitable opium market that flourished, but
still, she was revolted by the sight. And as she looked, her
attention was drawn to a large *hunhuz* reclining slightly apart
from the rest of the men. He was dressed in a white high-

collared shirt and black pants, and Svetlana guessed him to be the head of the band. It was toward him that Li-chun now moved.

With hands joined together he bowed and said something quietly, pointing to Svetlana without so much as a glance in her direction. This deprecating gesture, so at odds with the polite *hunhuz* who had led her to this camp, alerted Svetlana to danger, and her apprehension grew. The older man raised himself slowly on one elbow. His shiny black hair was pulled tightly into a queue, and the exposed high forehead was marred by a crescent scar. In one hand he held his long pipe and its attached metal bowl burner, and with the other he stirred the pipe's opening with a tiny metal stick, inhaling the opium with half-closed eyes. He studied Svetlana, sweeping over her with a measured, unhurried appraisal. This deliberate scrutiny made her tremble in spite of her valiant attempt to appear unafraid. She had heard it said that the *hunhuzy* respected fortitude and courage in their captives, and she was determined not to show her anxiety.

The large man's glance now settled on Li-chun as he asked him a short question. His voice was deep and loud. Li-chun shook his head in reply and began to speak in short, staccato phrases. His baritone was soft, but as he talked, the big man's face clouded. Slowly, he placed his pipe by his side, then slipped off the k'ang and stood towering above Li-chun. *My God*, Svetlana thought with a shock, *a giant! He must be well over six feet tall!* His face was broad, his skin toughened by outdoor life. In spite of her fear she couldn't help but notice the difference between father and son, one so rugged and fearsome, the other patrician and soft-spoken.

Suddenly, the older man barked something at his son, and for the first time Li-chun's eyes darted briefly in Svetlana's direction. Bowing rather stiffly, he spoke again. The large man shouted and pointed to the back of the *fanza*. After bowing again, Li-chun turned, motioning Svetlana to follow him outside.

The other men in the *fanza* had ignored the heated exchange, as if unaware of what was going on.

Once out in the open, Li-chun led Svetlana to the side and

around the far end of the *fanza*. There he stopped and looked at her, something in his face warning her of danger.

"I told my father that you were in his territory because you were lost."

"Then why was he so angry?"

"Because I told him that I had promised to take you back to Maoershan today."

"And that was wrong?"

Li-chun's answer was oblique. "You're now my father's responsibility."

"What has that to do with your taking me back to Maoershan?"

"It was wrong of me to promise you something without asking my father's permission first."

Svetlana's hands shook so badly that she clenched them into fists. "I don't understand. Why do you need to ask his permission to take me back? I have done nothing wrong."

Li-chun held his head high, but his eyes studied the tips of her shoes. "My father has greater experience in life than I. He is wise and has good reasons behind his decisions."

"I don't understand what you're trying to tell me!" Svetlana's voice shook. She could not control its rising pitch. "We're wasting time and it's getting late. Can we please go back to Maoershan now?"

Li-chun shook his head. "Not today."

"What do you mean, 'not today'?"

"As I told you, my father is a wise man and he said that I made a foolish promise. You've seen yourself how long it took us to come here, and it's too late to go back now. We shall never reach Maoershan before dark."

"You mean you're going to keep me a prisoner here overnight?"

"Not a prisoner. A guest."

Svetlana clasped her hands against her mouth. "My mother will be so worried! She'll call the police."

Li-chun didn't answer. With narrowed eyes he motioned her to follow him through a side door. She stepped into a small enclosure where large pipes from the main room in the *fanza* protruded from the wall, connecting to a large cauldron that stood in the center of the dirt floor.

Li-chun pointed to a pile of straw in the corner. "I am sorry we can't offer you anything more comfortable to sleep on than that, but we're not accustomed to accommodating women. The only strangers here are our prisoners. You're the first woman to see this camp."

Svetlana looked at the straw in dismay, then turned to Li-chun. "Am I to stay here all night alone?"

A flush rose to Li-chun's face. "You'll be well guarded, I promise you. And now, you must be hungry. I shall bring you food. It may not please your tastes, but it's what we eat."

Svetlana squirmed at his words. He had said "guarded," not "protected." That meant she was truly his prisoner, and he was too polite or too ashamed to say so, after having promised her earlier that he would take her right back to Maoer-shan. Why hadn't he done it at once when she wanted him to take her out of the forest? Was he *so* afraid of his father that he wouldn't chance his anger? She would never understand these Chinese.

She looked at him in resignation. "I *am* hungry."

When Li-chun left without a word and she was alone in the semidarkness of the small enclosure, all Svetlana's bravado suddenly evaporated. What was to become of her? Li-chun's father's reaction had seemed out of proportion to such a small infraction of his rules. But then she was probably just over-wrought, imagining all sorts of dangers. All Li-chun had said was that his father had ordered him to keep her in the camp overnight. It was for her own good, after all; why build up imaginary threats?

Temporarily calmed, she looked up at the small opening above the pile of straw. It was covered with yellow oilpaper and served as the only window in the tiny room. Well, at least she had a place to herself. She smiled ruefully at this small consolation, then sat down on top of the straw. It felt soft and she realized just how tired she was.

As weariness began to seep in, Li-chun came back carrying a low table that looked more like a stool, and on it were a tin plate, cups with food, and chopsticks.

Svetlana shook her head. "I don't know how to use the chopsticks!"

Li-chun gave her one of his rare smiles. "I shall teach you. It is not difficult."

He lowered the table to the floor. Although really hungry now, Svetlana looked at the food before her in dismay: thinly sliced pieces of dried salted fish, hot red peppers fried in oil, a half-full cup of horseradish, and a small bowl of steaming white rice.

Before she could say anything, Li-chun placed the chopsticks in her hand and showed her how to use her thumb and the first two fingers to manipulate one of the chopsticks with greater ease. Then he pointed to the food. "Try to pick up a piece of fish," he said.

Her first attempt failed. Svetlana could not narrow the chopsticks enough to grasp the slice of fish. Patiently, Li-chun took her hand again and, holding it firmly in his own, guided it to the food. Uncanny how every time he touched her, she felt warmed and soothed. His presence took the edge off her growing anxiety.

"Please eat," Li-chun said, nodding again toward the plate. Svetlana tried, and after a few more unsuccessful efforts, she was finally able to carry the food to her mouth. She was afraid to tell him that nothing tasted good to her, that the fish was too heavily salted and the red pepper burned her throat. She didn't touch the horseradish but ate most of the rice.

After she'd finished, Li-chun picked up the little table. "I'll bring you some tea, towels, and a blanket," he said.

When he returned, he smoothed the straw on the pile and spread one of the towels on top, folding the other into a pillow. Then he turned to Svetlana and handed her a blanket.

"I hope you will sleep tonight. This is the best I can offer," he said.

She couldn't tell from the tone of his voice whether he was angry or not.

"If—if you need to go out during the night"—he hesitated, and looked away in embarrassment—"you will have to use the —the outdoor accommodation." He pointed vaguely toward the bushes.

Svetlana was mortified. "I hope the morning will come soon, and that you will take me home immediately," she said, unable to keep the indignation out of her voice.

Li-chun turned slowly to face her. "Please remember that you're not an invited guest here. Though comforts are missing it is not through our oversight."

This time Svetlana detected a note of suppressed anger in his words, and the fear returned, permeating her tiny cell.

"Thank you for whatever you are able to do for me," she whispered, trying to keep her voice steady. "Is it possible to have a candle and matches for the night? It's going to be so dark in here!"

Without a word Li-chun disappeared, returning a few minutes later with a small candle stub and matches. "We don't have many of these in the camp, so please use it sparingly."

Another moment, and Svetlana was alone. It was already so dark in the room that she could barely discern the outlines of the cauldron, the pipes that led back into the main room, and another pipe that rose up to the roof. As she raised her head to follow its outline, she saw that there was no ceiling, only the rafters beneath the thatched roof and a wooden post supporting it. The walls were black with smut, and shaggy clusters of soot hung from the rafters. As she looked, a small dark shadow detached itself from the roof and dived past her. She screamed. Almost instantly the door opened and Li-chun appeared, his dark silhouette outlined against the dusk outside.

"There's something flying in here!" she said, her voice shaking.

"It's only a bat," Li-chun said calmly, and opening the door, waved a towel above his head. When the bat flew out, Li-chun dropped the towel and left, closing the door firmly behind him. Svetlana was alone once again.

Slowly she lay down on the straw and covered herself with the blanket. Weariness and hope for a brighter tomorrow struggled with her fear.

Trying to analyze the day's events, she decided that given his background, Li-chun couldn't have been more polite or considerate. What more could she expect from a *hunhuz* anyway? He was bound by his rules and he had behaved in a kind, if reserved, manner. That his father had become angry was unfortunate, but then, what did she know about their customs and laws? To her it seemed natural for Li-chun to have promised to take her back immediately, but evidently he had to ask his father's permission first. No one had hurt or threatened her, so why wouldn't the anxiety go away? It smoldered and nagged and taunted. Her mother's fear of the *hunhuzy* must have worked itself into her subconscious, and now, in the darkness of the taiga night, it surfaced to play on her nerves at random. She shut her eyes tightly to rid her mind of these intruders.

Her poor mother. She must be frantic by now, and the search parties would be starting to look for her in the early-morning hours. Li-chun was on her side, Svetlana was sure of that, despite his momentary anger at her indignation. Solicitous and thoughtful, tomorrow he would surely guide her swiftly toward Maoershan.

Chapter Five

In the morning Svetlana was awakened by the smell of cooking. Although she had slept through the night, she was still tired, and her muscles ached. No matter. She was going home today and there would be plenty of time to rest after she got back to the dacha. She squirmed. There was going to be a lot of explaining to do to satisfy her mother. She would tell her how sorry she was and promise not to go alone into the forest again. She pushed the thought to the back of her mind. First things first. Slipping off the makeshift bed, she looked at her dress in dismay: wrinkled, smudged with dirt, and covered with bits of straw. She tried to brush them off without much success, then touched her hair, smoothing it with her hands and pushing the loose strands off her face. That done, she opened the door and looked out.

Somewhere in the back horses neighed and dogs barked, silenced sporadically by sharp human commands. In the middle of the clearing several men were stirring something in a tin pot hanging from a trestle over a small fire. She sniffed. The odor of garlic filled the air, but the smell of boiling cabbage was a welcome one, for hunger pangs were adding to her discomfort.

She stepped out and nearly colhded with Li-chun, who seemed to be waiting for her by the door.

"Good morning," he said politely. "I hope you were not too uncomfortable during the night."

"I managed under the circumstances," she said with a shrug, determined not to give him the satisfaction of knowing that she had slept through the night. Then she added, "I would like to wash my hands and face."

Li-chun nodded. "Yes, of course. We have a washstand at the back of the *fanza*. Please follow me."

Although the washing facilities consisted of a pan of water atop a taboret and a bar of coarse soap, Svetlana was grateful for the chance to refresh herself.

"When you're through, please go back to your room and I shall bring you something to eat."

"I don't want to eat," Svetlana lied. "I don't want to stay here one minute longer than necessary!"

Li-chun raised his head, looking into her eyes for a moment, then lowered his gaze to a point somewhere in front of his *u-li*. Was he angry, perhaps? She remembered his doing that when she had asked him why he needed his father's permission to take her back to Maoershan. Foolish of her to antagonize the one man in the camp who seemed to be on her side.

"I mean I'm anxious to go home," she hastened to explain, but Li-chun shook his head. "You have to eat first. The way is long, and it is wiser to start without hunger. Please wait. I shall bring you food."

She walked slowly back to her room, trying to ignore the sidelong glances of the few men scattered about the yard. When Li-chun returned with the small table and cups of food, she realized how truly hungry she was. There was tea, steaming cabbage with black mushrooms, and a bowl of millet.

"I'll come back in a little while," he said, and left her to struggle with the chopsticks alone.

After a few abortive tries she managed to finish most of the food, then walked out the door. Li-chun was pacing the ground outside.

Her shawl wrapped tightly around her shoulders, Svetlana felt comfortable in spite of the early-morning chill, and the anticipation of leaving the camp and heading back to Maoer-

shan was now uppermost in her mind. Li-chun, who was looking in the opposite direction, did not see her approach.

She touched his arm. "I'm ready to leave now," she said.

He hesitated for a long moment, then shook his head. "We
have to wait until my father gives you permission to leave.
He's in the back checking our horses. Come with me, we'll
wait in the *fanza.*"

Svetlana was stunned. "What do you mean? Why do I need
his permission to leave? Yesterday he wouldn't let us go back
because it was too late and he said to wait until this morning.
Why do you have to ask him again?"

"Because my father told me so."

The answer was curt and final and Svetlana knew instinctively that it would be futile to ask any more questions. Reluctantly she followed him into the *fanza.*

This time she studied the empty dwelling. Here, too, the
room was black from smoke, and shaggy clusters of soot dan-
gled from the rafters. The k'ang on which the men had been
lounging the previous night now stood empty. She had never
seen one before, and she studied it curiously. It stretched the
whole width of the room, and looked like a masonry platform.
She judged it to be no more than two feet high and about six
feet deep. She remembered that a friend's Chinese cook had
once described its purpose: this was where the pipes from the
cauldron were hidden to serve as a heating element for the
whole *fanza* and to create a warm sleeping area at night. It
was covered with a layer of felt and a length of straw mat on
top.

To the right of the k'ang a life-size image of an idol, garishly
painted on a large sheet of paper, hung on one wall. She
turned to Li-chun. "Who is that?" she asked.

He seemed reluctant to answer, and then said: "Huang-ti,
our first great ruler."

Svetlana studied the expression on Huang-ti's face. It was
calm and majestic, and she only wished that Li-chun's father
were that serene. In front of the image stood a narrow black
lacquered table with two red candles in tin holders and a wide
urn with ashes where three incense sticks emitted a peculiar
odor, their red tips glowing in the semidarkness.

On the wall behind the k'ang at least two dozen guns hung

from wooden pegs. In contrast to the sooty room they were clean and shining, their muzzles plugged with pieces of red cloth. Svetlana remembered someone telling her once that when the bandits prepared to shoot, they pulled the red cloth out of the muzzle and held it in their mouths, and this was how they'd earned the nickname of "red beards"—*hunhuzy.*

"Li-chun!"

The sharp command was unmistakable, and Svetlana wheeled to face Li-chun's father, who had entered the *fanza* behind them. He was alone. Li-chun bowed and stood aside to let his father pass. Ma Fu-li walked slowly by without looking at them, then sat down on the k'ang. Svetlana was struck anew by his large size. It wasn't that he was fat, but rather large-boned and broad-shouldered. He asked Li-chun a question and when the younger man answered, a lively dialogue ensued. From the tone of his voice Svetlana gathered that Li-chun was arguing about something. If only she could understand what they were saying! Suddenly, Ma Fu-li fell silent and for the first time looked at her. Svetlana squirmed inwardly under his scrutiny. After several long seconds he said something to Li-chun.

"My father wants to know your father's name and what he does," Li-chun translated.

"My father's name is Nikolai Ozerov and he is an engineer with the railway company in Harbin."

"Is your father with you in Maoershan?" Li-chun continued to translate.

"No, he's in Harbin."

Father and son exchanged a few more words, and suddenly Svetlana noticed that Li-chun's face had grown dark, and a vessel begun to pulse in his neck. He said something else but met with an obvious curt dismissal from Ma Fu-li, who grew red in the face and seemed to have difficulty breathing.

Li-chun turned to Svetlana. "Come," he said, motioning her to follow him, and walked out of the *fanza.*

Relieved to be free of the chief bandit's intimidating presence, she walked briskly beside Li-chun. The day before she had carefully noted the side of the forest from which they had emerged, and so she now headed in that direction, but Li-chun stopped her.

"What's the matter?" she asked, looking around. Everywhere, men were working, some chopping wood, others stacking it in neat piles against the side of the *fanza*. Two or three squatted by a tin pot hanging above a fire, stirring something that looked like millet.

"We must talk," Li-chun said. "There's a small meadow behind those trees." He pointed to the opposite side of the clearing. "Follow me."

It was a lovely spot, where nature's whimsy had cleared the ground of underbrush, fashioned a green carpet of grass, and walled it with silver spruce. The blue dome of the sunny sky served as the ceiling, its brilliance pouring light into the enclosure. In this pastoral spot fenced off from the rest of the bandits, Li-chun told her that his father had decided to keep her in the camp for ransom.

For a few seconds Svetlana could not speak, refusing to believe what she had just heard. Then her throat closed and nausea rose from her stomach. When she finally found her voice, she cried, "You tricked me! You promised! Oh, please, please, take me home!"

Li-chun nodded glumly. "I told my father I would lose face for breaking my promise, but he said *he* would lose face even more if—if he allowed you to leave."

"Why would he lose face?"

"Because it would be a sign of weakness for him to let you go." Li-chun paused and looked away.

Exasperated, Svetlana cried, "I don't understand! What are you talking about?"

When Li-chun looked at her, she saw embarrassment and pain in his eyes. "You see," he said quietly, "my father is responsible for the welfare of all his men, and your being here is a ready-made chance for profit. He doesn't want to pass it up because when your ransom is paid, it will be divided among all of us."

"I see," Svetlana said, her voice shaking. "You make it sound as if you were discussing a piece of merchandise." She swallowed, then added bitterly, "You all benefit from the bounty."

"Please understand that I can't go against my father's will. I'll do my best to make you as comfortable as possible. I promise you that much. I have already asked to guard you myself while we wait for the ransom to be paid."

This was too much. "I thought the *hunhuzy* kept their word," she said, her voice shaking with anger. "I—I thought you said that no harm will come to me."

"And that is quite true. You will not be hurt. I shall see to that."

"Just like you saw to my coming here, saying I could leave the next day, and to my sleeping on the straw with a bat in that dreadful place?" she waved toward the small room where she had spent the night and saw with satisfaction that Li-chun flushed.

"I told you yesterday that you were not an invited guest here. You trespassed on our land. If I were you, I wouldn't complain to my father. He doesn't like to be accused of anything, and if you anger him, he can make you more . . . uncomfortable."

The veiled threat was clear, and Svetlana's anger turned to apprehension. "Very well," she said as calmly as she could, "as long as I'm your hostage, I'll keep silent."

Li-chun gave her a sad smile. "You need not be silent. You can tell me if there is anything you need. I'll do my best to help you."

Suddenly, Svetlana was overwhelmed by the enormity of her situation. "Oh, what am I going to do?" she cried, wringing her hands. "What's going to happen to me? I'm so frightened. Oh, God, I can't even speak your language."

Li-chun frowned and grabbed both her wrists. "Get hold of yourself, Svetlana," he said sternly, and in spite of her anguish, she was startled. It was the first time he had called her by name and, incongruously, she felt relieved. Something in the familiar sound of her name made her feel not so alone. As he released her wrists, she nodded.

"I'll try. But I'm so frightened," she said again, "so terribly frightened. I've heard stories that *hunhuzy* cut off their victim's finger or ear to speed up the ransom money."

The moment she'd said it, she was terrified. What had made her blurt this out? Was it because he didn't look wholly Chinese and spoke Russian so well? She shouldn't—she mustn't —forget that he was, after all, a *hunhuz*.

"I can promise you on my head," Li-chun said, and his voice shook with emotion, "that this will never happen to you."

Svetlana's lips quivered so much she was afraid to speak. The whole world was crashing around her and she did not know how to cope.

In danger and alone as she was, there was only one hope. One small hope. Li-chun. And she wasn't even sure if she could trust him, but then, what alternative did she have? Without thinking she grasped his hand in hers and whispered through tears, "Please, oh, please, help me!"

Chapter Six

One day. Two days. Three. Then a week, and yet another. Waiting, not knowing what was going on at home, was torture. Svetlana missed her family dreadfully, could hardly bear to think of her mother and the agony she must be suffering. No. It wouldn't do to dwell on it and become even more upset than she already was. She needed all her willpower to push these thoughts away, to concentrate on how to endure and survive in her predicament.

Why was it taking so long to pay the ransom? Could it be that the message hadn't reached her mother? But Li-chun assured her that one of his father's men had personally taken the message to Maoershan. If what he said was true, then why the delay?

Svetlana fretted. Maybe Ma Fu-li had asked too much and her parents didn't have the money. Li-chun said no, his father was being reasonable in his demands; but her woman's intuition was stronger than the logic of Li-chun's words.

Li-chun.

She had come to depend upon him. He was always there, bringing her food. fresh straw for her bed, aware of her needs. In spite of Li-chun's assurances that she had nothing to fear, the surly bandits who gave her stealthy glances terrified her. She couldn't help remembering now her mother's words that her friend, Anya Rotova, had died because of the *hunhuzy* raid on their village. In spite of the common knowledge that the bandits did not rape, there were stories about women who were mistreated and mutilated if the ransom wasn't paid on time.

Although she realized as the days went on that the *hunhuzy* continued to ignore her, she still avoided walking across the clearing and kept close to her side of the *fanza*. There was nothing to do but accept the situation for the time being, and be glad it wasn't worse. The straw bedding was not too uncomfortable, the food—plentiful and not too bad. The boiled cabbage with black mushrooms was delicious, and she was getting used to the millet. But the soya bean cake had a strange, unpleasant flavor, and after she refused to eat it, Li-chun brought her snipe and an occasional partridge as a welcome substitute for her evening meal. She had seen the partridges brought live and fluttering into the camp and asked Li-chun how they managed to catch them.

"Our hunters never waste ammunition on partridges," he said. "They trap them in a net."

"How do they manage that?"

"They sway a white cloth screen in front of them, and the partridges, wary of the moving object, back away and eventually fall into the net."

Svetlana listened in fascination. Gradually she began to seek Li-chun out, for she found him comforting and patient in answering her questions. And she had many. She had noticed, for instance, that when he took her on daily walks in the woods, he never did so openly, but motioned her surreptitiously to follow him to the side of the *fanza* near her small sleeping space, where no *hunhuz*, he told her, was allowed to pass. "No women are ever allowed in our camp," he said the first time she asked him about it. "This is why we have excellent discipline and obedience among my father's men."

"Do you mean that if women were allowed to cook and clean for you, the discipline would disappear?"

"I mean that women could cause dissent among the men," Li-chun answered evasively. "And that's why no man here dares to talk with you."

"Yet your father is not afraid to let me go into the woods by myself. What if I decided to run away?"

"You couldn't get very far without getting lost, and we would find you anyway. My father lets you walk near the camp because he wants people to know that he's fair and humane in his treatment of . . ." Li-chun didn't finish the sentence and moved on.

"Of his captives, right?" Svetlana finished for him, and when Li-chun didn't answer, she asked, "Then why are you going along with me?"

Li-chun hesitated. They had just reached an area in the woods where the trees were not so dense, the sun warmed the air, and the ground was covered with silvery ferns. Lacy they were and delicate, and taken by their beauty, Svetlana paused and sat down on a tree stump. Li-chun stopped, and as she looked up at him waiting for an answer, she was struck anew by his handsomeness, by the lightness of his skin color and the line of his cheekbone, which seemed distinctly Russian. For a moment in the clear afternoon light, that seemed to overpower his Oriental features.

With a half-Buryat, half-Russian mother and a Chinese father, there should be little Russian blood in him, yet something about his slow smile and the glow in his eyes made him seem different from the rest of the *hunhuzy*. This difference could also be attributed to his ease with the Russian language, but whatever it was, she was glad. So glad! Illogical to trust him, yet she did, feeling a kinship to him, alone as she was, and a stranger among all the other, sullen bandits.

He smiled broadly at her scrutiny, the first mischievous smile she had seen on his face. "Why do I do it?" He shrugged, broke off a branch of a small fern, and ran it over Svetlana's forearm. It made her shiver.

"Yes, why?" she asked.

"Because . . . I guess because I'm trying to save face before you for having betrayed your trust in me—however innocently. Besides, I don't feel right having you wandering alone in the woods, and my father would forbid you to walk around the clearing where our men come and go all day. You need exercise, and—and we can talk."

"Yes, and I have a lot of questions. For instance, why are your men in such a hurry to stack wood for winter? The summer has just begun, yet it looks as if they're in a frantic haste to pile it up."

"That's right, they *are* in a hurry. Before the winter comes, everyone leaves the camp and goes to towns and villages to live with their families and find work as laborers or farmers. The men take on false names and never let on who they are."

Svetlana remembered her mother's insistence that she would never hire a Chinese cook because he might be a *hunhuz.*

"Then who guards your arsenal and goods during the winter months?"

"One or two men remain in the camp throughout the winter. Usually it's my father, and sometimes I stay with him."

"Just the two of you? How do you manage?"

"We have plenty of food stored for us, and we cook only at night so that the smoke from the fire doesn't betray the whereabouts of our camp. It's not too bad in the late autumn when we can come and go during the day, but once the snow falls, our footprints could lead trespassers to our camp, so then we must become isolated from the rest of the world."

Svetlana was shocked. "It must be a dreadful existence for you."

Li-chun shrugged. "One gets used to the isolation. And solitude is revitalizing. It builds endurance of spirit, strengthens character." He hesitated, then looked pensively into the distance. "Good training for the future."

Something in his last words made her look at him with added interest. "And what do you see for yourself in the future?"

Li-chun sat down on a stump near her. "Someday I'd like to leave the taiga and join Marshal Chang Tso-lin's army."

Svetlana considered the point. "I'd think you would miss the taiga," she said at length. "I always thought that of all the summer resorts I've been to, Laoshan outside of Tsingtao was the most beautiful, but I can see now how one could learn to love the taiga in all its primeval lush beauty."

"There's no doubt that I shall miss my forest, but sacrifices of one kind or another are part of our daily lives," Li-chun said pensively. "In the meantime I hunt and—and help my

father run the camp and see that any bounty is divided prop-
erly to all men according to rank."

"You mean you don't get equal shares?"

"My father gets ten shares of the bounty, and I get five. The
rest of the men get theirs according to the position they occupy in the camp."

Svetlana thought about it for a moment, then said, "That
seems just, all except the bounty itself. It's stolen from hardworking people, isn't it?"

Li-chun frowned. "My father put levies on the neighboring
villages in return for his protection from undisciplined bandits. Otherwise, villagers would be robbed indiscriminately."

What a twisted sense of values, Svetlana thought. And yet
Li-chun didn't find the practice at all unjust, or so it seemed.
Her highly moral, upright Vladimir would have been shocked
at such a philosophy.

Vladimir!

She hadn't thought a lot about him in the last few days. He
must be frantic, too, wondering if she was alive and what was
happening to her. She tried to picture his worried face, but
somehow the image eluded her, for he rarely lost his composure, and it was difficult for her now to imagine him showing
any anxiety. Li-chun's features, on the other hand, spoke far
more explicitly than his frugal words. Although his Chinese
upbringing must have taught him to hide his feelings, his Rus-
sian-Buryat blood betrayed him time and again, and she could
see emotions play on his face. Not so with Vladimir.

Suddenly she caught Li-chun's quizzical look. He was saying something and she wasn't listening. Why in the world was
she comparing these two men? Flustered, she asked, "Did you
say something?"

"Yes. Your thoughts were somewhere else, I could tell by
the look in your eyes. I asked you about your voice. That day
when you were lost, your call for help was like a song. Very
beautiful. Are you a singer?"

Svetlana started. "Not professionally. I don't think my fiancé would approve of my making a career of singing."

"Your fiancé? What does he do?"

"He's an engineer with the railway company."

"Are you getting married soon?"

"We were planning an early-autumn wedding, but now, after the ransom is paid . . . I don't know." Somehow, she didn't want to tell him that her parents might not have enough money to pay for the wedding so soon afterward.

But Li-chun must have guessed. A slow flush colored his handsome face, giving it a vibrant glow. "My father never asks for more than is reasonable," he said quietly, busying his hands with another lacy fern. "May I ask you something, please?"

Svetlana nodded.

"Will you sing a song for me now—only softly, for we mustn't be overheard."

Pleased, she asked, "What would you like me to sing?"

Li-chun's answer was prompt: "A Russian song."

Svetlana looked at him curiously. "You speak Russian almost without an accent, and now you are asking me to sing a Russian song. Why?"

Li-chun told her about his life with the Russian family in Handaohedzi, where he had learned to love Russian music. Svetlana nodded, then said, "I'll sing you a Russian folk song that is well known. It is called 'Scarlet Sarafan.' I don't know if you're familiar with this word, but it is a sleeveless peasant dress worn over an embroidered white blouse. On festive occasions the *sarafan* is usually scarlet."

It was a mournful song of a young girl telling her mother that she was not yet ready to give up her freedom for marriage. Svetlana loved the slow, plaintive melody, and as she sang, her eyes found Li-chun's. Their glances locked, his seeming to touch and probe her very soul. Never before had she been so profoundly aware of another human being. The feeling was so intense that her voice wavered, and embarrassed, she stopped in midphrase. "I'm sorry," she whispered, confused and ill at ease. "I don't know what happened. I haven't practised lately, or—or maybe the cool morning air isn't good for me."

"Thank you for what you have given me," Li-chun said, and took her hand. His touch was like a spark of electricity and she pulled her hand away. What was happening to her? Her heart had jumped at his touch. This was ridiculous.

Quickly she rose and started back toward the camp. Li-chun
followed without a word.

At the edge of the camp's clearing Svetlana paused. A couple of bandits squatted over a large rack of elk antlers, carefully scraping the meat off the frontal bone. Curious as to why
they were struggling to keep the antlers in an upright position,
she asked Li-chun to explain.

"The rack is full of blood right now, and it would collect at
the tips if they let it fall. Then, when it is boiled, the bone
would burst."

"What do you do with it?"

"The velvet of a young elk is very valuable because it serves
great medicinal purposes. It brings us anywhere between two
and four hundred dayans."

"Four hundred dayans! That's a lot of money for you, isn't
it?"

Li-chun smiled. "When you consider that an average Chinese laborer earns somewhere around twelve dayans a month,
it is indeed a lot of money."

Svetlana pondered this information. "So the *hunhuzy* earn
money in honest trade as well," she said quietly, more as a
statement than a question, and Li-chun either didn't hear her
or chose not to answer.

Intrigued by what the two *hunhuzy* were doing, her fears
lulled by Li-chun's presence, Svetlana drew near the two bandits and, fascinated by the antlers, reached out to touch the
velvet. Instantly, one of the bandits jumped up and swore.
With an angry *"Tsu-ba,"* he slapped Svetlana and pushed her
with such force that she lost her balance and would have
fallen had Li-chun not caught her from behind. Li-chun said a
few angry words to the bandit, who growled at him and,
mumbling under his breath, went back to his work.

Terrified, too shocked to cry, she clung to Li-chun. Without
another word he turned and led her away from the bandits. At
the door to the *fanza* he spoke.

"I'm sorry, Svetlana, it was my fault. I should have warned
you. You see, the work the men are doing requires great skill
and they're not used to anyone interfering. Besides, it is most
unfortunate that one of the men there was Chao Chu-lo. He's

mean, and that's why he hit you. I think it's best you stay out of sight for the rest of the day."

After he had left, Svetlana's lips began to tremble. He hadn't even asked if she was hurt. All her fears returned with renewed force. Li-chun might be on her side, but what could he do alone against the rest of the *hunhuzy?* He hadn't reprimanded them enough for hitting her. Why not? Was he that afraid of them? And she'd considered him her friend. . . .

Now, menace hovered around her. She could sense it in the air, feel it in her bones. During the day it seemed to worsen with each passing hour, and at night anxiety disturbed her sleep—anxiety about the long days that were now stretching into weeks, anxiety in the face of the unknown, for it had become more and more difficult for her to find reasons why nothing had been heard from her family. How long would Li-chun's father wait before he hurt her? She hadn't seen him since that first day, but she felt his presence, which seemed to pervade her whole being with fear.

Two days after the incident with the two bandits, Svetlana decided to go for a walk in the woods alone. She felt safer there than in the camp, where she was surrounded by hostile men. Here, among tall evergreens, surrounded by the beauty of the taiga, she could relax a little.

Before she realized it, she came upon the meadow where she had sung for Li-chun. There she paused by the stump on which he had sat listening to her that day. She thought about him now. Although he had been undemanding of her time, his was a disturbing presence with that enigmatic look in his dark, pensive eyes, and his lithe, sinuous body, which moved with such grace and ease.

Today she wanted solitude, that very solitude he had called revitalizing. It was lovely here. The air was perfumed with evergreen freshness, and the peace of the forest seemed filled again with the sounds of yesterday's song.

Li-chun had listened raptly, obviously enjoying it, and had told her so. Vladimir had never asked her to sing for him. He was a practical man, and he talked of a good marriage, of religion, of her wifely duties, of his job. There was nothing wrong in that. He would be a good husband, a loyal one.

But Li-chun had asked her to sing for him.

She moved away from the stump and walked briskly to the edge of the meadow, where she pushed a thicket of ferns aside. Beyond, a birch grove filtered shafts of sun, washing the ground with gold. She stopped.

What was she thinking of, comparing the two men again, as if—as if—She didn't finish the thought. What nonsense. But a pounding started in her chest; her heart raced and raced, too fast. She leaned on the white trunk of the nearest birch and closed her eyes. An image of her mother's weeping face appeared before her mind's eye. Svetlana ached to put her arms around Sonya and tell her that she was unharmed. Tears stung her eyelids, and she blinked to force the image away.

Somewhere near, a woodpecker knocked diligently for a while, then screeched raucously as something interrupted his business. Svetlana looked up at the soaring bird. And as she watched its flight, her gaze was caught by a movement in the burdocks to her right. Curious, she looked at the bushes. The large leaves fluttered, then a darker shadow moved behind them. Was it a marten, or only a squirrel? Svetlana walked over to take a closer look. Stooping over, she looked under the foliage. Two dead martens tied together with a rope lay side by side on the ground. They were dead. She frowned, realizing that someone else, then, had moved in the bushes. She spread the burdock leaves apart and gasped.

A young bandit was squatting beside the animals, and something in the look he gave her made her release the large leaves abruptly. But the bandit rose above them. With panther's stealth he moved noiselessly on his *u-li*. As he reached for her, Svetlana screamed, her voice reverberating through the forest:

"Li-chun! Help!"

With lightning speed the bandit grabbed her by the arm and clasped his hand over her mouth, jerking her head backward. He threaded his other arm through the crook of her elbows and pulled them back. She struggled and kicked, but the man's grip held tight, and the next instant she was thrashing on the ground.

"Molchi! Tebya ubey!"

In spite of the man's pidgin Russian the order to be silent

and the threat to kill were clear. Terrified, Svetlana stopped fighting and stared at the bandit's menacing face. He straddled her, holding her arms down with his knees, then stuffed a rag into her mouth. The pain from his weight on her arms made her whimper, but the bandit ignored her and fumbled with a rope. Li-chun had said that *hunhuzy* never abused women. What kind of a bandit was this, and what was he going to do to her?

Terrified, she turned her head toward the camp and out of the corner of her eye saw Li-chun and three other men run out of the woods. The bandit saw them, too, and dropping the rope, sprinted for cover; but Li-chun and his men had already fanned out, surrounding him. His escape cut off, the bandit stopped, then moved away from where he had left the dead martens.

Svetlana took the dirty rag out of her mouth and sat up. Frightened and shaken by the attack, she was nonetheless amazed to see how instantaneous was the bandit's surrender. Where moments before he had been threatening to kill her, he stood now with head bowed in abject submission. A brief and sharp exchange of words followed, and then Li-chun knelt beside Svetlana.

"Are you hurt?" His voice was so full of anxiety, his eyes so full of concern that she felt a lump rise in her throat, choking her. She wanted to wrap her arms around his neck and be consoled, but instead she bit her lip and shook her head in mute denial.

Gently he helped her to her feet. "Please tell me what happened."

Svetlana found her voice and told him how she had noticed a movement in the burdocks and how she had surprised the bandit.

"What was he doing when you saw him?" Li-chun asked.

"I don't know. When he saw me, he left the two martens in the bushes and attacked me."

"Two martens? Did you say two martens?"

"Yes." She pointed toward the bush. "They should be over there."

In a few brisk steps Li-chun retrieved the martens. At the sight of the animals there was a whistling intake of breath from the other three bandits, and the captured *hunhuz* once again lowered his head. Li-chun examined the martens and handed them to the men. Then he gave a curt order, and the men prodded the bandit with their guns, pushing him forward. As the small group moved toward the camp, Svetlana caught the bandit's quick glance in her direction; and in that split second she saw such animal fear, such despair, that in spite of his attack, pity welled within her.

She turned to Li-chun. "Is it a crime to hunt martens?" she asked.

He shook his head. "Hunting them is no offense. We do it all the time. But stealing them from the camp is a serious crime."

"How do you know that he stole them? Maybe he shot them himself!"

"He didn't say he was going out to hunt. And we would have heard the shots. Besides, why did he attack you?"

The logic of his question was so obvious, Svetlana flushed. "What's going to happen to him now?"

"He will be questioned by judges selected from our camp."

"And what will they do to him?"

"It will depend on his reason for stealing and whether the judges will find that reason sufficient to justify his theft."

"You use big words for such a small theft. What if his reasons aren't good enough? What will his punishment be?"

Li-chun gave her a sidelong glance. "Only one—death."

Svetlana gasped. "You can't mean it! Death for stealing those two small animals?"

"Stealing from the bounty is a grave crime, Svetlana. We live in the taiga and we must abide by her laws. The law of nature is impartial and strict. It makes no compromise. Our judges will either find his reason good enough to set him free, or he will die."

A shiver took hold of Svetlana and she hugged herself. Then she thought of something and stopped. "Li-chun, if I hadn't mentioned the martens—if I hadn't shown you where they were—no one would have known that he had stolen them." She put her hand over her mouth, then grabbed Li-chun by the arm. "Li-chun, it was my fault that the man was caught. You must influence the judges to let him go free.

There must be a way to save the poor man. I can't stand the idea of his losing his life over two small animals. What kind of justice is that?"

"The fact that he was caught through you does not alter his crime, Svetlana. Survival in the taiga is difficult, and her laws are harsh. I'm afraid there is nothing we can do except hope that his reason is valid enough to save his life."

Chapter Seven

At the door to her room Svetlana stood watching Li-chun lead the captured thief to the main entrance of the *fanza* and disappear inside. About ten or twelve bandits followed him. What was going to happen in there? How cruel were those *hunhuzy* who were going to judge the bandit? "The laws of the taiga are strict and impartial," Li-chun had said. But were those judges who held this man's life in their hands as impartial as the laws of nature?

She went into her tiny room and paced the floor. If only there were a door or some kind of an opening through which she could see into the other room! For the first time since her capture she examined the clay wall. Her gaze traveled the length and the height of it and then paused at the pipe that led from the cauldron to the k'ang in the large room. She ran her finger over the uneven opening and found a small space between the pipe and the wall. Dropping to her knees, she pressed an eye to the crack.

To her surprise she could see almost the whole interior of the large room.

Five older men, including Ma Fu-li, sat on the k'ang, and their gazes were centered on the thief, who sat on his haunches in front of the k'ang with his elbows tied behind his back. He seemed a picture of resignation, his eyes lowered and staring at the dirt floor.

The rest of the men squatted on the floor around the prisoner, some smoking, others intent on listening, and only Li-chun stood apart by the door. Ma Fu-li was questioning the thief with sharp, curt phrases, and the man answered in a flat, barely audible voice. In a few minutes Ma Fu-li rose and, picking up a tin can off a shelf, placed it before the judges. He then scooped a handful of black and white beans into the palm of his hand and handed the judges one of each. That done, he picked up the can and held it in front of the elders, who each in turn dropped one in. As each bean hit the bottom of the tin can, it sounded like a hammer stroke in Svetlana's ears.

She closed her eyes. A burning pain clutched her stomach. They were deciding the man's fate with beans. The primitive, unwavering court of the taiga that knew no compromise. If only she hadn't mentioned the dead martens. . . .

She opened her eyes and peered through the opening again. Ma Fu-li had turned over the can, and the beans spilled out on the k'ang's straw mat. Svetlana counted them, then pressed her hands to her chest. Four white ones to one black. Thank God, the judges had found the thief's reasons for taking those two martens valid.

She looked on.

Without a word, Ma Fu-li collected the beans, dropped them back into the can, and replaced it on a shelf at the back of the k'ang. Then he looked at the thief and spoke to him. The man did not reply, his face impassive. *How well they hold their emotions,* Svetlana thought. *I'd think he would smile or bow in gratitude.*

After the beans had been counted, several men left the *fanza* and soon returned bearing plates of hot food, which they placed before the still kneeling thief. His arms were untied and he was motioned to sit on the k'ang. Svetlana watched with interest. There were heaps of meat dumplings and red peppers, mushrooms on rice and turnips, and some other things she could not identify. The men repeatedly offered the thief a drink, which Svetlana guessed to be *hanshin* —that Chinese version of vodka that she had heard about.

The thief took his time eating and drinking, and after he had finished, he was offered an opium pipe. As he puffed on it, a drunken expression appeared on his face and he relaxed among the other men. Svetlana was puzzled by this excessive feasting. Justifiably or not, he had stolen the two martens; why would he be so honored now? She would have to ask Li-chun. And as she thought about him, she noticed that he had disappeared from the *fanza.*

She rose from her knees and ran outside to ask him all about it.

"Li-chun!" she cried, "I saw the whole thing. I'm so glad they let him go free. And those beans . . . how ingenious. I was so happy when I saw four white ones."

Svetlana babbled on and on until she finally realized that Li-chun didn't seem to share her enthusiasm. Disappointed, she stopped. *He's a bandit after all,* she thought. *He can't forgive a thief; he's his father's son. It was probably Ma Fu-li who dropped that one black bean. . . .*

"What's the matter, Li-chun," she said, "aren't you happy with the verdict?" and before he had a chance to reply, she went on: "You certainly do things in a big way. I mean, giving him such a feast afterward."

Suddenly, she thought of something. "What was his reason for stealing?"

"He stole the martens to feed his starving mother. She lost all of her possessions during the big flood in Maoershan, and she would have died if she hadn't been rescued from the roof of her *fanza* by some Russian men."

He said it so quietly, Svetlana had to strain to hear him. Immediately, the scene came to her mind.

"Why, I was there when it happened! My fiancé was the one who directed the rescue."

Li-chun's eyes sparkled with interest. "So it's true, then."

"Did you doubt him?"

"Not really, but you give us proof that he spoke the truth. You see, he's the one who took the ransom note to Maoershan, and while there, he discovered that his mother was sick and starving." He paused, then added quietly, "However, it won't matter now."

Something in the tone of his voice made Svetlana look at him closely. "What do you mean?"

Li-chun hesitated for a few moments. "Svetlana, I'm sorry,

but you misunderstood the whole thing. Don't you know that for the Chinese, white is the color for mourning?"

Slowly, the truth sank in. White for mourning. Four white beans. . . . White for death, not for life. . . . The scene she had just witnessed took on a macabre shading.

"But he stole to keep his mother from starving to death. Wasn't that reason enough?"

Li-chun shook his head. "The elders judged that one marten would have been sufficient to feed his mother. They said it was greed that made him steal two."

"Death for one extra marten. I can't believe it."

The scene in the *fanza* flashed before her mind.

"I don't understand!" she cried. "He was feasted in there after the verdict."

"That's our custom. We feast the condemned man and get him drunk enough to make dying easier."

"And just how is he to die?"

"In the winter he would have had a chance to survive because he would have been taken to the crest of a hill and tied to a tree on the tiger's path. And if the Great Wang didn't find him, his life would have been spared."

"And in the summer?" Svetlana asked, wanting to know yet dreading the answer.

"He will be buried alive."

Nausea churned in her stomach, rose to her throat. "No! I can't believe that. It's barbaric, inhuman!"

"It's expedient."

"Expedient? Why not shoot him?"

"We don't waste ammunition on our criminals."

Frustration, anger, choked Svetlana. "How can you be so—so indifferent? A man is going to die, and you act as though we're discussing an animal that is to be exterminated as a nuisance."

Li-chun's eyes flashed with momentary anger and then his gaze again became veiled and impenetrable. "I have already told you—harsh as they are, the laws of the taiga are never broken. The thief knows this, yet took that risk. That he failed is not the law's fault, but his own."

"But if it weren't for me, he wouldn't have been caught. I

must do something, I can't stand it! Li-chun, help me! I have to talk to your father and explain this to him."

Hysteria was rising within her and she couldn't control it. The stress of the past two weeks, the loneliness, the discomforts, and now this dreadful event, all seemed to come to a head. Without waiting for a reply she turned and rushed toward the main *fanza*.

Li-chun grabbed her arm, trying to stop her, but Svetlana wrenched herself free and ran toward the door.

He followed. Foolish girl—did she think that his father had the final word or the authority to overturn the judges' decision? And certainly, his father was not going to look with favor on any interference, particularly from a Russian captive girl.

He had to stop her.

But Svetlana was already inside, talking rapidly to Ma Fu-li and gesticulating in an attempt to make herself understood.

Out of his mind with drink and opium, the thief had already been taken out and the rest of the men were gone, leaving only Ma Fu-li reclining on the k'ang and puffing on his pipe.

From the expression on his face it was impossible to tell whether he was even aware of Svetlana's presence, but Li-chun knew better. His father's temper was slow to rise, but once aroused, it was fearsome to behold.

Svetlana turned.

"Li-chun!" she cried desperately. "Tell him. Tell your father that I'm responsible . . . that if not for me, the thief would not have been caught . . . and now his mother may die too. Tell him! . . . Does he want to have that innocent life on his conscience as well?"

After Li-chun had translated her words, Ma Fu-li took the pipe slowly out of his mouth. "Tell this impertinent woman that the judges' decision is final. As for the worthless man's mother, the guilt is on *his* conscience, not ours."

When Li-chun told her, Svetlana gasped, then pounded her fists against her thighs. "You can't just sit there in righteous judgment. What if it were *your* mother? Or Li-chun's mother?"

Li-chun hesitated, trying to soften the final words of her

outburst as he translated them to his father, but still, an abrupt change came over Ma Fu-li's face. Rising to his full height, he towered on the k'ang over Svetlana, and pointed to the door.

"*Tsu-ba!* Get out!"

Svetlana looked up at the giant above her and burst into tears. Li-chun grabbed her arm, sure she had forgotten where she was or at whom she was screaming. "Svetlana, stop it! My father is very angry. Go back to your room at once."

"No!"

Ma Fu-li turned to Li-chun. "You were responsible for keeping her under control, but you let her get out of hand. Why?" He waited a few moments for an answer, but Li-chun remained silent. Ma Fu-li's eyes flashed. "Shut her up and come back here. She's become a nuisance, and we'll have to do something about it."

Stupid, stupid female. How utterly stupid of her to bring his father's wrath upon her head. Li-chun pulled her arm, but she fought him, and in his fury he dug his fingers deep, dragging her out of the *fanza*.

Back in her small cell he hurled her down on the straw, all his frustration, anger, and some other emotion he could not readily identify released in that violent gesture.

Although she wasn't hurt as she fell on the soft straw, the look in her eyes, so full of surprise, so deep with pain, shamed him. And with that shame rose a twinge of fear for this girl who was, after all, his responsibility, this girl who had trusted him from the beginning and whose trust he had already betrayed. He couldn't hold that look, couldn't endure the mute accusation. He turned to leave.

"You must obey." He spat the words over his shoulder. "You're foolish to have angered my father. *Stay in!* Do you hear? Stay inside until I come back."

This time she did not protest, and he left. Outside, he leaned against the wall. He couldn't face Ma Fu-li just now. Not yet. He didn't know what his father had in mind; he could only guess.

How long had it been since he'd brought Svetlana into the camp? He counted the time. Two weeks. He was amazed, for it seemed much longer. He had spent a lot of time with her trying to atone for his failure to take her back that same day. Yes. He had spent many hours with this Russian girl, all for that one reason. Was it necessary to justify himself to a mere girl? But then, she was not an ordinary one. During those hours in the woods he had discovered that a man could talk to a woman and find her intelligent and interesting.

No novice in relationships with women, he had found those in Chinese villages subservient and willing enough to satisfy his virile urges, but it had never occurred to him to communicate or converse with them afterward.

Svetlana was different—oh, so different. He told himself every day that each walk they took was purely to keep her rebellious spirit under control and to teach her that open defiance would work against her in his father's camp. But instead, he had talked about many things, answered her questions about the bandits and the taiga, and in turn had asked about her life. When she had sung for him, he had been deeply moved by her beautiful voice, and something she had said about her fiancé made him wonder, with a twinge of resentment, whether the man she was destined to marry would truly appreciate such a gifted woman.

She was his responsibility, and to save face he had to protect her until the ransom was paid. Where had he gone wrong? He thought he knew the girl well enough by now, but he hadn't expected such blind defiance; or was it unabashed courage?

Now he had to face his father and hear what he had to say about Svetlana. Unwittingly, she had touched on the one subject that his father was most sensitive about: Li-chun's mother. Ma Fu-li had never spoken of her to his son, and all his questions during his years of adolescence had met with the same curt answer. "She died giving birth to you. Respect her memory and be an obedient son."

It was a meager answer and as the years passed, Li-chun had stopped asking. But he continued to wonder why his father refused to talk about his mother. Now this Russian girl had brought up the subject that Ma Fu-li had all these years deliberately avoided. No wonder he was angry. The sooner Svetlana was released, the better it would be for all of them. . . . This blond girl with her huge gray eyes that begged for protection. He was beguiled by those eyes and had forgotten to treat her sternly. What was the matter with him? He was his father's son, first and foremost, a Chinese hoping to join the Old Marshal's army, and he should be tough. Had this girl softened him, made him forget his heritage?

Li-chun straightened and resolutely walked back into the *fanza* to face his father.

"I'm displeased with you, my son," Ma Fu-li began. "It was your duty to control this girl and you have failed."

Li-chun bowed to his father. He knew him well. This was no time to argue and fan his already smoldering anger.

"Yes, honored Father, I am guilty. I failed to see the difference between an obedient Chinese woman and a rebellious Russian. I've lived among them and should have learned that."

Ma Fu-li's eyes narrowed. "Do not make me regret your education. I sent you to a Russian school to learn their ways, not to adopt them."

"It was not intentional, Father. I have spoken to her, and she will obey from now on."

"It's been two weeks since the message was delivered, hasn't it?" Ma Fu-li said, reaching for his pipe, and when Li-chun nodded, he added, "My patience is running out."

"Honored father, may I humbly remind you that it was this thief who was ordered to deliver the message. He may have been so concerned about his starving mother that he forgot to pass on the ransom note."

"I don't believe that and neither do you. He couldn't have forgotten that he would receive his share of the ransom."

"The girl's father is in Harbin and there may be some breakdown in communications between him and Maoershan."

That was a lame excuse, and Li-chun knew it. Why was he saying this instead of listening to his father?

Ma Fu-li glared at his son. "Has your association with this Russian woman softened your brain? Beware, Li-chun! I do not tolerate stupidity. I've made a decision. We shall wait one more day, and if by tomorrow night we have had no word from Maoershan, then the following day we will send a messenger with a warning to her parents."

Li-chun knew what this meant—in fact, he had expected it

—yet the spoken words hit him as though he had been cut with a cleaver.

Ma Fu-li's glance seemed to mock him as he said, "They will know that Ma Fu-li is a fair man. The girl has plenty of hair, hasn't she?" and when Li-chun nodded, he went on, "Then a missing ear will be less noticeable than a missing finger."

There was no use saying anything more to his father. From past experience Li-chun knew that further arguments would only hurt Svetlana. He bowed deeply to hide the storm that raged within him, then backed out of his father's presence.

He slipped unnoticed into the woods and walked aimlessly until he came upon the little meadow where the thief had been caught. There he sat down on the moss-covered stump and, resting his hands on his knees, let anguish take over.

The vivid scene of what was to take place the next day—the scene he had witnessed many times before—haunted him.

Svetlana—mutilated.

Time and again he had failed to protect her. And now would come the final insult to his manhood: to be a helpless witness to Svetlana's torture—her futile pleas for mercy, the slicing of her ear, her screams, the ugly bleeding wound, the permanence of her disfigurement. . . .

Yield, obey your elders, respect their age and wisdom. All his life he had been taught these rigid rules, and now, if he suppressed his anger and accepted passively his father's harsh decision, he would fulfill his duty as an obedient son.

But what about his duty to himself?

In the Russian home in Handaohedzi he had been witness to another way of life. There, too, the young obeyed their elders, but not in abject, blind submission.

What tortured emotions, what guilt and moral degradation, would he admit into his conscience by lying to his inner self— that quiet voice within that spoke the truth?

This lovely girl with gentle, trusting eyes, those dainty ears covered by her sheaf of golden hair . . . the softness of her touch; her keen and searching mind that sought to learn about his life, his hopes, his goals. This angel-girl who had trusted him not once but twice, and whom he had twice betrayed . . .

He groaned and covered his face with his hands. Why fool

himself any longer? There was no way to hide. *Face up to it,
Li-chun, face up!*

You love her.

*Yes, you love her with all the futile passion of your miserable
soul. . . .*

How had that love come to possess him so insidiously that
he had denied its presence until a dreadful threat forced him
to admit it? Oh, Svetlana! No more doomed a love could there
be, no more hopeless a future could be imagined. A Russian
girl engaged to marry, and he—a Chinese and a bandit.

How gladly would he tear his heart out and lay it at her
feet. *Take, Svetlana, this foolish heart, this heart of a worthless
bandit who dared to covet you. Take it and laugh at it.*

But she wouldn't laugh, would she? She would look at him
with contempt for having dared to confess his love, or possibly
with hate for having failed to protect her. She would consider
that failure a human weakness, not filial obedience.

And she would be right, of course. But self-accusation now
would lead him nowhere. It was merely a self-indulgence and
would never rid him of his guilt.

There was only one thing to do. Only one action he could
live with—to lead Svetlana out of the forest. Tonight.

The image of Ma Fu-li's wrath rose before him. If he went
through with his plan, he would be defying his father and
depriving the rest of the bandits of their share of the ransom.

The penalty for such a crime was death.

He clenched his fists until they shook. He could escape with
Svetlana, then realize his lifelong ambition of joining the Old
Marshal.

But how could he bring such shame upon his father's head?
His father, who had loved him, reared him, given him education. He—Li-chun, only son of Ma Fu-li . . .

No. He couldn't live with that. After Svetlana was safely
out of the forest, he must return and try to save his own life by
some subterfuge.

He'd think of something.

In the meantime Svetlana's safety had to take priority over
everything else.

He rose. A tiny squirrel dashed across the ground and
scrambled up a tree, startling him. His heart pounded. The

burdocks encircled him, hiding their own secrets well. He looked up. The sky was streaked with gold by the setting sun, and the night would soon descend upon the vast taiga.

Darkness then would be a welcome friend.

Time was short.

Chapter Eight

When Li-chun brought in her evening meal, Svetlana saw immediately that he was still angry, for contrary to the established routine, he didn't talk or ask if she needed anything for the night. In fact, he avoided looking at her altogether and suddenly she wanted to cry. Her mother's favorite saying sounded in her ears: We don't appreciate what we have, and then weep when we lose it. Perhaps she had come to depend too much on Li-chun's company, on his warmth and, especially, on his friendship. Strange, how much it hurt when he refused to look at her or say anything, and she was too proud to start the conversation.

After he'd left, she stared at the food. Cabbage, rice, her favorite black mushrooms, even salt pork. The picture of the condemned man eating his last meal wouldn't go away, and she could hardly bring herself to eat. The gathering dusk added to her gloom, and the black, sooty walls moved closer, pressed upon her, threatened. She swallowed a couple of mouthfuls of rice and pork, and the salty tears along with them. Her fingers shook as she manipulated the chopsticks. She studied them for a few seconds, her mind struggling with her thoughts, then swung her arm and threw the chopsticks across the room with full force. They hit the cauldron and fell to the floor.

She clasped her hands tightly to keep from trembling. She

had angered the mighty Ma Fu-li. Was he going to punish her for her outburst? What would he do to her? She shuddered. Woeful it was to feel abandoned. But wasn't she overreacting? Just because Li-chun no longer seemed friendly, a devastating loneliness had wormed itself into her mind. She thought of their daily walks in the woods, his welcome presence, and suddenly she *had* to talk to him and make him talk to her. Not for another minute would she stay closeted in that dreadful little space with those dreadful sooty walls. And in her desire to see Li-chun at once, to talk to him, she knew with sudden clarity that loneliness had no pride.

The chopsticks still lay where she had flung them. She picked them up and placed them by her tin plate. Then she opened the door and called, "Li-chun! Please, may I see you?"

As though he had been standing around the corner waiting for her call, Li-chun appeared instantly, grabbed her arm, and pulled her inside.

"I told you to stay in," he said quietly, and because this time there was more sadness in his voice than anger, Svetlana smiled at him timidly.

"You're angry with me, Li-chun," she said. "But—but I wanted to tell you that—that I value your friendship."

To her disappointment Li-chun did not answer but, bending over and picking up her shawl, handed it to her. "Wrap it around you for warmth, Svetlana, and don't go to sleep. Eat all your supper. I'll come back for you later." He hesitated only for an instant, then added softly, "I'm taking you back to Maoershan tonight."

Svetlana gasped and pressed her hands to her heart. "Oh, how wonderful!" she cried, and spontaneously clasped his hand in hers. "Thank you, oh, thank you! I know it was you who persuaded your father to let me go. Thank you."

But even as she said this, something intruded into her euphoria. "Tonight," he had said. Why tonight? She frowned and looked at him searchingly.

"Did you say tonight, Li-chun? Why not tomorrow morning, when there is light?"

"Because my father doesn't know about it, Svetlana," he whispered. "He's very angry that the ransom hasn't been paid as yet and his patience has run out. He wants to send a—a warning to your parents. Do you understand what this means?"

He looked at her intently, waiting for an answer, and as she looked back into his eyes, she read the terrible message in them. A fear, like nothing she had experienced before, crawled from the depths of her being to cloud her vision, to choke her.

"Oh, God, what is it to be?" Her voice was hoarse; she shook violently.

For the first time since she'd known him, she saw Li-chun throw his head up defiantly.

"It is *not* going to be. I'm taking you out tonight."

But for Svetlana there was a horrifying fascination in learning what she was about to escape. "Was I to lose my finger or maybe—maybe my ear?" She winced and hid her face in her hands.

Li-chun grabbed her wrists and pulled them away from her face. "I'm not going to tell you anything. The less you know the better. Nothing is going to happen to you, do you understand?"

Suddenly, she screamed: "That's what you said before! I don't believe you!"

With lightning speed he was upon her and clamping her mouth with his hand.

"You impossible woman, stop it at once! Do you want to bring the whole camp in here?"

Then he released her and stared at her for a moment. A muscle twitched below his right eye and his breathing was fast and shallow. With a curt nod he spoke sternly.

"As I said, stay awake. We have to wait until everyone is asleep. Don't make any sound and don't open the door, no matter what you hear outside. Our scouts have sharp ears and the guard on duty is our greatest danger. I'll come for you in due time."

Without giving her a chance to question him further, Li-chun left.

Slowly, deliberately, Svetlana forced herself to sit quietly on the straw, but fear exploded inside her. To be disfigured for life. And why? Because of the whim of a primitive man of the taiga, a man to whom another human life meant little and mutilation even less. She tried to chase away the image of what would take place the next day if their escape attempt failed. But the image, painted by terror, refused to leave her alone.

She was afraid of pain. She had felt it vicariously when Raissa's face was cut, and now she could almost feel the sharp pain from a cut-off ear, or the dreadful agony of a severed finger. How was it done? And what about keeping the wound from becoming infected? What if gangrene set in later in her hand? Oh, God, please, please, don't let this happen!

With an enormous effort of will she channeled her thoughts to her return home, to the end of her ordeal of uncertainty and misery. How was her mother holding up? Had her father come to Maoershan? And Vladimir . . . what had he been doing all this time? Was he frantic about her safety?

She would be so glad to leave this dirty place to which she had been confined for two long weeks, to distance herself from the surly bandits and from everything else connected with the camp.

Even Li-chun.

She sighed. Well, maybe not Li-chun. In spite of his broken promises she would be sorry to say good-bye. After all, it was not his fault that his father had ordered him to keep her in the camp overnight; not his fault that Ma Fu-li had decided to hold her for ransom; and certainly not Li-chun's fault, but hers, that his father had been provoked into losing his patience tonight. She wished Li-chun weren't a *hunhuz*. Under different circumstances they could have been friends. She liked him. But the moment she thought it, she knew it would have been impossible.

No matter that he did not look wholly Chinese, he *was* Chinese and, as such, could never become her friend. Russians did not socialize with Chinese families, and the aloofness was mutual. Business dealings, yes—but social contact? Hardly. Especially not between two young unmarried people of opposite sexes. A slow flush rose to her face. It was warm in the tiny room. If only she could open the door to let in the fresh air. But Li-chun had said not to do that, and this time she would obey.

She sat on the straw, hugging her knees, and listened. Outside, staccato voices died down and the dogs that had been

barking were now silent. In the big *fanza* room she heard
shuffling, murmurs, yawns. Gradually they diminished to an
occasional cough or a sigh, and soon all was quiet.

Minutes crawled. Svetlana's anxiety became unbearable.
What was keeping Li-chun so long? Had something happened
to make the escape impossible, or had he changed his mind?
She dismissed the thought and leaned forward to hear every
tiny sound. Something moved like a whiff of disturbed air, a
sound that was almost nothing; yet now, each disturbance of
this night became a welcome sound.

Unable to sit any longer, she rose and cautiously approached the door. There she waited, barely breathing, fearful
that even her rapid breath might be heard by the patrolling
guard. As she stood there, the door began to swing open
slowly, keeping the rusty hinges from squeaking; silhouetted
against the moonlight, Li-chun slipped in. He lit a match and,
raising it high, looked at her. Svetlana saw his face close before her and was struck anew by his handsome features. In the
glow of a single match too dim to reveal his Chinese clothes,
he looked particularly Russian, and as he handed her a black
cotton gown, she realized with a stab of regret that she was
seeing him for the last time. She had grown accustomed to his
presence beside her, his rare but gentle smile, and she was
surprised that it hurt so much to realize that they were soon to
part.

"Put this gown over your clothes," he whispered. "Your
white dress can easily be spotted in the moonlight."

The match burned out and so, after slipping the gown over
her head, Svetlana groped for Li-chun. He took her hand and
pulled her toward the door. "Stay close behind me and don't
say a word."

For a few moments they stood within the door waiting for
the scout to start his pacing toward the opposite end of the
clearing. Then Li-chun abruptly pulled her out, stepped sideways along the wall of the *fanza*, and moved toward the nearest trees. The guard had reached the end of the clearing and
turned around to pace back toward the *fanza*. Li-chun swung
his arm across Svetlana's chest, pinning her against the wall.
Her pulse pounded so violently in her temples that she was
afraid she would faint. His arm was flung across her bosom,

but Li-chun held himself in a frozen position, and she dared not move. Strangely enough, she was not offended by the gesture. When the guard had turned his back on them again, Li-chun moved stealthily forward, and in a few moments they were in the sanctuary of the forest.

As he led her forward, circling the *fanza* to its western side in a wide arc, she tried to ask if he was sure of his way in the dark, but he placed a finger against her lips. After a brisk walk he stopped and struck a match, lighting a torch. Then, motioning her to silence, he pulled her on. Svetlana followed obediently, allowing him to lead her by the hand, terrified of losing him.

How long would it take to reach the glen in Maoershan? The moon was high but not much light filtered through the shaggy boughs of spruce and pine. Somewhere near an owl hooted, and as Svetlana started, Li-chun's warm hand squeezed hers in reassurance. Every step, every second, took them farther and farther away from the *hunhuzy* camp and its pulsing dangers. No one would discover that she was not in the *fanza* until the next morning, and by then she would be safe with her family and closer to Vladimir. What would he say when he saw her again? Would he hug her immediately, or wait until they were alone?

Her hand was still within the hollow warmth of Li-chun's as he pulled her gently behind him. In a short while she would be saying good-bye to him forever. A small chill shook her body. Forever? Never to see him again? Perhaps he would come to Maoershan passing himself off as a peasant—so many Chinese came and went, and no one need know that he was a *hunhuz*.

Li-chun—a *hunhuz*. It was so incongruous, so impossible to reconcile the image of a cruel, primitive bandit with Li-chun. He was so different from the bandits in Ma Fu-li's camp.

And he had saved her after all.

But why, for heaven's sake, was she worrying about not seeing him again? Suddenly her hand, trapped in his, felt too warm, and she pulled it away. Instantly, he stopped and turned to her.

"Are you tired?" he asked, and lifting the torch, he peered at her closely.

"No, not yet, but"—she groped for words—"but aren't there any wild animals on the prowl at night?"

Li-chun shook his head. "Don't be afraid. I know the taiga well. As I told you before, the animals, as a rule, stay away from the area where humans walk. As long as we stay on the path, we should be safe. Besides, I have my gun just in case."

Svetlana wanted to ask what good his gun would do if a tiger leaped at them, but she thought better of it. There were other things on her mind that needed to be voiced.

"Li-chun!" she said. "What will your father do when he finds out what you've done?"

"He will be angry."

"And?"

"He will scold me."

"And that's all?"

Silence.

"How can you love him after this?"

"My disagreement with my father is temporary, but my respect for him will last forever."

"Why are you doing this, at a grave danger to yourself?"

"You trusted me and I must prove that I am worthy of your trust."

"Why?"

"Because there is no greater duty placed on a friend than confidence."

"And you consider me your friend?"

Silence.

"Answer me, Li-chun!"

"There is wisdom in silence when misfortune cannot be expressed."

"Misfortune? What misfortune?"

"It is a private matter."

Li-chun spread a thick fern and held it back for her with his body. A few minutes later the scratchy bough of a shaggy pine brushed across her face, but she didn't complain. The walk was long, but he said that he knew the way, and she trusted him. The darkness that surrounded them was frightening, but she kept her eyes on Li-chun's back and deliberately avoided looking to either side. The only sound was the owl hooting again as if it were following them along the path.

After a while the path became smoother and the under-brush thinned out. Li-chun walked faster, and she hastened to keep up.

He was risking his father's wrath—and Lord only knew what punishment—to lead her to safety. They would part in a little while, and she would never find out what that terrible *hunhuz* was going to do to Li-chun. Would his father pardon him because he was his son? No, most certainly he would be punished, but how severely? What was the bandits' penalty for disobedience, and for depriving the other men of their share of the ransom?

It was a grave misdeed and she knew he would suffer on her account. He had done this to save her from mutilation.

He cared that much.

Suddenly, the trees thinned and they emerged on the famil-iar glen bathed in the blue light of a full moon. Surprised at how seemingly fast they had reached it, Svetlana stopped. Here was where they would now part. How could she live with the knowledge that he would be hurt because of her? She touched his arm and looked up at him to see his face glowing in the light with warmth and deep sadness. His handsome face, so close and suddenly so dear, overwhelmed her; and there in the glen, at the moment of parting, in a flash of reve-lation, she knew the painful truth at last.

She couldn't even *think* the words.

Her heart had betrayed her. How had it happened? Horri-fied, she clasped her hand over her mouth to stifle a groan. Li-chun grasped her wrist and pulled her to him.

"Here is where we say good-bye, Svetlana. You are safe now."

They stood for a few seconds like this, his hands trembling, squeezing hers, their eyes locked in wordless understanding. Then slowly he released her and stepped back. She couldn't bear it. Her hands reached for him, sliding up his chest and circling his neck of their own volition.

It wasn't happening to her, Svetlana Ozerova, a proper Russian girl. She mustn't think of the futility of it all or of the dreadful pain of rising passion that was not to be appeased. But his arms were suddenly around her and his lips were touching hers. Was this a dream, this thrilling current that coursed through her body, making her gasp? Never, never before had she experienced anything like this.

Though his kiss was slow and gentle, when he stepped back, she could not breathe.

"I hadn't meant for this to happen." His voice was strangled. "Believe me!"

"Why did this happen?"

Li-chun closed his eyes and, frowning, shook his head.

"Tell me, Li-chun!"

He looked at her. "Because—because I love you, Svetlana," he whispered.

Her lips quivered and he lifted her chin. "Did I offend you?"

She shook her head, drinking in his face, his smooth skin, now flushed with emotion. She looked and looked at him, pouring out her love in a caressing, insatiable gaze.

He clasped her shoulders and she could feel his hands shake. Then he pulled her to him, and this time the kiss was deep and long, his mouth on hers in desperate possession. She responded with the reckless freedom of the doomed, pressing herself against him fiercely, wanting to brand in her memory forever this one embrace.

With trembling hands he finally pushed her away.

"There is no future for us, my love. Go!"

Go? This was the final time she'd see him? No! His shining eyes bewitched her, their silent pain reaching to her soul with pleas that his words denied. Wildly, she threw off the black Chinese robe and stood before him in her white dress.

"Li-chun, I love you!"

He backed away and shook his head. "What is love without a goal? Ours is a forbidden love, a hopeless love."

"We have the rest of the night, Li-chun."

"I cannot touch you knowing that you can never be mine to keep."

Tears blurred Svetlana's vision. This was not a *hunhuz* at all, but a special man she loved and was about to lose forever.

Li-chun cupped her chin. "Cry, my love, and let your tears smother our sinful fires. Know that if it is true that a shared suffering is less painful, then you have made it so for me."

She closed her eyes and threw her arms around his neck,

searching for his mouth and clinging, clinging, until he circled her waist with a power that took her breath away. The fire rose within her, threatening to overwhelm her, touching the very soul of her being, and no tears could now extinguish it. It became a consuming drive to know this man in full, if only once—just once—to last forever. And then she was aware that he had forced her hands and lips away and was pushing her violently aside. She lost her balance and fell.

Stunned, hurt, she looked up to see him turn and flee into the forest.

Svetlana collapsed on the soft grass. He had rejected her. She, naive and trusting, had lost her mind and yearned to experience the sublime sensation of being loved by him completely, and he had refused. He didn't love her enough. A bit of affection, a kiss, and a few empty words for the parting— that was all he would give her.

Shadows around her seemed to move like phantoms, swaying in derision. They had hooded faces and a dozen eyes that were watching her rejection. She buried her face in her hands to hide from them.

Li-chun had left her alone in the glen. He had run away. He mocked her. Mocked her!

No!

Svetlana raised her head abruptly. Silly, blind girl. How could she even think that, when he had risked so much for her, perhaps even his life? *Oh, Lord, I know now, I know! Li-chun, Li-chun, you didn't want to touch me because there is no future for us . . . because I must belong to another. But I love you, do you hear? I love you!*

She jumped up and blindly rushed into the forest, running along the path into the blackness of the taiga, without a thought of what she was doing.

"Li-chun!" she cried, "Li-chun! Come back, or I'll follow you into the camp!"

Moving from around a large fern, Li-chun blocked her way. Grabbing her by the arm, he turned her around and pulled her back to the glen. There he stood, towering above her. "What do you think you're doing, you foolish woman? Your cries might be heard. Do you really think you could find your way back into the camp alone? And then what?"

He was angry, oh, so angry, but Svetlana wasn't listening. A blissful smile was twitching her lips as she saw the pain in his eyes, his trembling mouth, and the coursing tears that sparkled in the moonlight.

He was crying.

Crying for her. She reached up and gently, tenderly, touched his tears and kissed them off her fingers. Then she took his hand and placed it on her breast, leaning her head against his shoulder.

"Li-chun, love me, love me now. . . . Don't reject my gift."

What torture! He had fought his love and lost. He was not strong enough to leave her to another man, after all. Such sacrifice was beyond his strength. The moon alone would condone their love—a kind of love that braved conventions and fought to prove itself in insolent defiance. The light above shone silver on the lovers, the satin grass—a welcome bed. A passing breeze caressed the skin, then flew away on waves of rapture. Untouched by human passion, the stately cedars slept.

It was a place in time without a past or future to regret. A time to make a nurtured dream come true, to keep in memory forever. To feed his bursting heart with sustenance from this exquisite moment that now had stopped for him and would be his to cherish. She was so fragile, so delicate, so silken soft and sweet to taste. Yet she had strength and will, this complex girl he loved. He could not get enough of her, this angel he had found and was about to lose.

"My heart, my sweetest love," he murmured, his lips against her tender neck, his hands and mouth afraid to bruise her, yet wild to touch and know each tiny part of her. Oh, he had never meant to hurt, only to protect, her, but now, like a graceful dove rising to the sun, she reached for him, and he was lost . . . lost in seeking, loving, blending. He had never dreamed that such emotion, such yearning, could be his; he—the disciplined, reserved Chinese. Those gray eyes that looked at him awash with tears were driving him mad.

Her hands dug into his back as if afraid to let him go. He himself couldn't bear to part from her. Oh, Svetlana, my

Svetlana! What torment or delight to soar in ecstasy with her, then to burst into a million particles of sweet release. His mind floated for an eternal moment, holding desperately on to this spark in time, this fleeting bliss of union, and then succumbed to the exquisite intimacy of a peaceful aftermath.

Oh, how he wanted to make her permanently his—not in a separate existence, but in a fusion of two souls to make one whole.

The world slept on. In the hush and murmur of the night he cushioned her head on his shoulder and, slipping his hand through her thick loosened hair, soothed and soothed. In the fading moonlight her long dark lashes fluttered and hid the misty eyes that spoke fulfillment. He felt her deep and even breath upon his neck. For a few more precious moments she would be his, and then, when he had gone, she would return to that other life to which he had no claim. What agony to think that time would blur her memory, erase this interlude into oblivion. Already, her soul had flown on wings of slumber, and for him—for him reality, cold and unadorned, beckoned from the taiga. He was a prisoner of his unyielding conscience.

What to do? What subterfuge, what plausible excuse, was there for him to use?

A well-timed, clever lie could save him.

He had no other choice. He would admit his negligence in letting Svetlana escape from the camp, and while the men searched the forest, he would beg his father to let him join the Old Marshal's army. Thus, he would argue, he would redeem his loss of face by proving to his father that he was worthy of his name. It was a dangerous gamble, a risky test of his father's love.

And what if he lost? Then death was better than a guilt-ridden conscience that would torture him for the rest of his life. He *had* to face his father.

And now, the time had come for him to steal away.

He eased Svetlana onto the grass and spread her shawl tenderly across her shoulders. Then, leaning over, he feathered kisses on her forehead—the last farewell.

The silence held, the forest waited.

PART TWO

Illusions

Chapter Nine

Sonya had never received the ransom note. It wasn't until the day before Svetlana's return that the police, searching through the Chinese hamlet again, found an old woman dead in one of the *fanzas;* clutched in her hand was a crumpled ransom note demanding three thousand dayans for Svetlana's safe return. In questioning the villagers the police learned that this was the same woman who had been rescued by the Russians during the flood, and that she had since lived destitute and starving. She had a son in another village who had recently visited her, and in piecing the story together the police concluded that her son was a *hunhuz,* and that the woman must have hesitated to deliver the note for fear of betraying his true identity.

Fully aware of what the *hunhuzy* could do to her daughter if there were a delay in payment, Sonya immediately sent a telegram to Nikolai in Harbin. During the ensuing agonizing wait she had been nearly out of her mind with worry, and so when she saw Svetlana enter the dacha in the early-morning hours with hair disheveled, her once white dress now dirty and stained, Sonya fainted. No one else was in the house and so it was up to Svetlana to look for smelling salts and revive her mother.

Both women wept, one with relief at seeing her daughter alive and unharmed, and the other with conflicting, turbulent emotions that threatened to tear her apart.

Through alternating tears and laughter, almost incoherent, Sonya related how the police had told her that in all probability her daughter had been kidnapped by the *hunhuzy;* how she had immediately sent Raissa back to Harbin for fear that she, too, would be kidnapped; how Nikolai stayed in Harbin, watching over Raissa, ready to withdraw money from the bank to pay the ransom; and, finally, how she had insisted on remaining in Maoershan to wait for some word from the *hunhuzy.* But as the days went on, the police, surprised by the absence of a ransom note, came to the reluctant conclusion that Svetlana was not a victim of human avarice, but an accidental prey to a roaming bear or tiger.

"I refused to believe it. I'm so glad I stayed here!" Sonya cried over and over, hugging her daughter. "Let me look at you, my dear," she said, taking Svetlana's face between her hands. "You've lost weight, you need to rest." Yet at the same time she bombarded her with questions about how she'd been kidnapped and how she'd been treated in the *hunhuzy* camp. Svetlana could not bring herself to tell her mother much about it, except the barest of facts. As Sonya listened to her daughter's story, she clenched her fists and shook them in the air.

"Ah, those savages! First the Rotovs, and now my own daughter abused by these bandits. That *hunhuz* you speak of, he should be the first to have his head cut off and strung up for all to see."

Svetlana flushed. "It wasn't his fault that his father decided to keep me for ransom, Mama. If not for him I wouldn't be here now, and you would have received my cut-off finger or ear instead."

Sonya shuddered and hugged her daughter impulsively. "Oh, my Svetik," she said, "I can't even think of such a possibility. Can't you see? He may have weakened this time, but back in his forest he is still a *hunhuz* and a killer."

"He is *not* a killer! He was gentle and kind to me," Svetlana cried, swallowing tears.

Sonya frowned. "You're gullible and naive. He'll always be a *hunhuz.* I hate them."

"Please, Mama!" Svetlana's voice shook. "Let me rest, take a bath. I—I'm so tired."

Sonya nodded. "Yes, dear, of course. It's just that I'm so

glad to see you, I don't know what I'm saying or doing. I must send a telegram to Papa and Raissa immediately. Your Vladimir will be so happy. He has been keeping vigil with them all this time."

At the mention of Vladimir's name Svetlana felt weak and couldn't wait to leave her mother.

Alone in her room, she slumped in a chair. Loneliness overwhelmed, devastated, her. She ran her hands over her dirty dress, her fingers lingering on the stains from the grass where she and Li-chun had lain together, the places he had touched. Maybe his scent had lingered in the fabric. She lifted the skirt to her face and sniffed, but only the moist fragrance of grass permeated the cloth. How could she bear to have it cleaned? This was her last link with Li-chun. She rose and slowly approached the wardrobe mirror. Had she changed now that she was no longer a virgin? They said that the morning after, the look in the eyes was different. Old wives tales . . . but at the first glance in the mirror she recoiled. There were dark circles under her eyes, and indeed she had lost weight. Her face was covered with dirt smudges, and her hair was a mess. At length she shrugged. After all, it had been two weeks since she'd seen herself in a mirror; a lot of things had happened since then.

For the first time this morning she directed her attention to her body, reviving sensations she had experienced the night before. As she stood looking at herself, she shifted her weight from one leg to another and became aware of a stinging physical discomfort. She closed her eyes tightly. Last night there had been ecstasy in pain, and this was the exquisite legacy of Li-chun's love.

A terrible longing clawed at her. This early morning, bathed in the dawn's pink light in the glen, she had floated for a few seconds in that strange dimension between sleep and wakefulness, sensing Li-chun still by her side. But when she'd awakened and found herself alone, reality had struck with full realization that he was gone from her life forever.

Her home was near, she was free of fear and safe from the *hunhuzy* menace, and she should have gone back to the dacha at once. Instead, she had stayed in the glen, clinging to Li-chun's imaginary presence in the space where he had been and the air that he had breathed. If there were such a thing as an invisible field of energy that emanated from a human being and lingered in the area long after the physical body was gone, then she believed it now—wanted to believe it—and dreaded releasing this nebulous thread to her lost love.

The permanency of their separation! Both of them knew that the formidable obstacles of society's taboos were too great to overcome. There was no hope for them and no future. He was back in the *hunhuzy* camp by now. What was his father going to do to him? What punishment was in store for him? *Oh, God, don't let it be too harsh.* His father must love him enough to be lenient . . . she *had* to believe that.

Facing the wardrobe mirror once more, Svetlana studied herself with detachment. A strange girl stared back at her, a girl with a tragic look, someone who had tasted a brief moment of rapture and was going to pay for it with a lifetime of regret. A lifetime.

Her future with Vladimir.

A knot formed somewhere in her stomach, tightened, wouldn't let go. Vladimir was her future. How could she face him, now that she had known another man? Would she become one of those countless women who marry for any number of reasons except the most important one: romantic love? But love had many faces, and hers was a tragic one. Hopefully, when she saw Vladimir again, the interlude in the taiga would become just that—a romantic interlude to be hidden in memory, and with time—forgotten. And maybe, when Vladimir touched and loved her body, she would feel the same fever that had possessed her in the forest.

Her body. He would know that she had had another man. What could she tell him? That she had given herself to a *hunhuz?* How could she explain that Li-chun was different, that he seemed more Russian than Chinese, that he had protected her and saved her from the ultimate horror, that in fact he had risked his own safety and, possibly his life, and—and that she had been smitten by circumstances? And what would his reaction be? He—the proper, religious Vladimir? She shivered slightly.

No. She couldn't tell him the truth, either before or after the wedding. But that would be dishonest, wouldn't it? Dishonest, yes, but in this case would honesty be the better part of valor? She wanted to marry Vladimir. She had been in love with him before and was sure that when she saw him again, so familiar, so dear, so much her own, she would love him again. So why be foolish and jeopardize her future happiness? Her confession would only cause him heartache and could serve no purpose. No purpose at all—except to clear her conscience. . . .

But there still remained the wedding night. She inhaled deeply and pressed her hands against her stomach to keep it from fluttering. Well, perhaps she could figure out a way to fool him. She would be doing this for his own sake as well as hers.

There was something else. It was hard to admit even to herself, but there it was: though she was ashamed of not entering marriage as a virgin, she was even more ashamed that she did not regret it. That was her private secret. And now she must think only of Vladimir. What was he doing? How worried he must be! She had caused him such grief; she would do her best to make up for it.

Vladimir indeed had been full of anxiety. He had spent every evening during Svetlana's captivity in the Ozerov home in Harbin. The long vigil without a word from the taiga was dreadful, and he couldn't avoid thinking of what might have happened to Svetlana. Had the *hunhuzy* kidnapped her? If so, what had they done to her, and was she even alive? His fiancée must remain unmarred in every way, and the thought of even the tiniest scar on her body upset him.

His parents spent much time in church, requesting *moleben* for Svetlana's health and safety. He went to church, too, not because he believed that much in the power of prayer, but because it was good for his carefully cultivated image of a religious young man of sterling character. And his reputation was very important to him. He had almost tarnished it once, and he would go to great lengths not to let it happen again.

It had been a long time since that shameful episode; his friends' maid had become pregnant and threatened to create a scandal if he didn't marry her. He squirmed, remembering. What a narrow escape that had been. It had taken a lot of persuasion from his parents to convince the simple country girl that the marriage would never work, that it was for her own good to have an abortion by a reputable surgeon, paid for by the Panovs.

Surely he was to have been excused—an impetuous eighteen-year-old on his way to Liège University in Belgium to study engineering. His parents had protected him. His father had chuckled, saying, "Too bad the days of the droit-du-seigneur are over," and his mother had only clucked her tongue indulgently, for her dear Vladimir was now a man and it was too bad that the girl had turned out to be a problem. Vladimir appreciated his parents' support, and ever since that episode he'd feared any breath of scandal becoming attached to his name, vowing that he would never again cause them embarrassment, especially now that he had an enviable position with the railroad.

When he fell in love with Svetlana, he considered it a stroke of good luck, not only because she was beautiful, but because she came from a good family and would be an asset to him in his career. Never mind her fantasy about singing in the opera —he would take care of that after they were married. No wife of his was going to go onstage.

But now he was distraught over her disappearance, agonizing over her safety. Where was his fiancée? At first he feared negative notoriety, but when his friends and acquaintances rallied to his side, he was relieved and was even more pleased by the attention and overt expressions of friendship from his associates at work.

When Raissa returned from Maoershan, frightened but sulking for having her vacation terminated so abruptly, he saw her daily. Together they kept the vigil, whiling the time away by playing cards or listening to gramophone records. Soon she stopped complaining, and Vladimir began to enjoy her company. She had a seductive laugh, and the healed scar did not detract from her dimpled smile—in fact it gave her a fragile and vulnerable look. On many occasions her gaze lingered on him longer than necessary, and once Vladimir caught himself thinking that she, too, could have made him a good wife. Her easy laugh and her gaiety amused and appealed to him.

With the optimism of the very young, Raissa couldn't believe that anything bad was going to happen to her sister, and she refused to go to church to pray for her.

"Nothing will happen to Svetlana," she said flippantly the first time her father admonished her for not attending the services. "She will survive."

Although shocked by her defiance, Vladimir secretly admired her independence of spirit, something he envied but dared not adopt. It was 1922, Harbin was flourishing, and nothing must spoil his promising future.

"Aren't you concerned about Svetlana's safety?" he asked her that evening when they sat in the parlor, keeping company to Nikolai, whose growing anxiety clearly showed in the dark circles under his eyes and in the firm set of his lips.

Raissa raised her eyes slowly and looked at him long and deeply. A tiny smile twitched at the corners of her full mouth, and suddenly Vladimir felt uncomfortable. This girl was decidedly disturbing.

"Of course I am concerned about her," she said at length. "But as I said earlier today, she will survive, and I'm sure that any day now we'll get a ransom note telling us that she is in *hunhuzy* hands."

Nikolai shook his head and frowned. "Whatever you believe, Raissa, an extra prayer and a visit to our church wouldn't hurt. I'm surprised at you!"

Raissa darted him a furtive look and shrugged. "All right, Papa, if it will make you feel better, I'll go to church with you next time."

And then the day came when Sonya's telegram arrived with the ransom demands from the *hunhuzy*. The threat was real, and Vladimir felt duty bound to tell Nikolai that he would be willing to contribute to the demanded sum; but Nikolai wouldn't hear of it.

When another telegram arrived the next day with the good news that Svetlana was back in Maoershan safe and unharmed, Nikolai ordered Sonya and Svetlana to return to Harbin immediately.

Happy that Svetlana was unhurt, Vladimir nonetheless regretted that the solicitous attention of all their friends would now end, and he was a little ashamed of his reaction. He had liked being the center of attention. What was wrong with that?

The rescue in Maoershan during the flood, for instance, was a pleasant memory because it had been his idea and it had made him feel important.

Ah, well, there were other things to think about. In a day or so Svetlana would come home, and he would welcome her for more reasons than one. Raissa's constant proximity and an undefined tension between them had grown into an uncomfortable situation, and it was time he held Svetlana in his arms again, his beautiful Svetlana with her wide, innocent gray eyes and seductive dark lashes, her graceful body and soft inviting lips. Perhaps the wedding could be pushed up a little and they would be married earlier than September.

Why wait?

Chapter Ten

It was called the wedding of the year. The newspapers described in detail the beautiful bride, the elegant groom, the bridesmaids, the clothes the respective parents wore, and the extravagant reception held at the Zhelsob.

Svetlana wanted a big wedding in the large St. Nicholas Cathedral on the Bolshoi Prospekt; she loved that unique landmark of the city designed by St. Petersburg architect Podlevsky and built of wooden logs in the classic Russian style. She wanted a full choir and all the trappings of a Russian ceremony. The more grand and traditional the wedding, the easier it would be, she reasoned, to erase her memories of the taiga, the *hunhuzy* camp, the *fanza*, Ma Fu-li, and . . . Li-chun. From the day she returned to Harbin, she had firmly decided to put the past behind her.

When their train pulled up at the Harbin station, she had been eager to see Vladimir again, stubbornly refusing to admit Li-chun's image into her mind; instead, she forced her thoughts to embrace the imagined figure of her fiancé. At the sight of him, so muscular and well-dressed beside her father, so genuinely happy to see her, a bouquet of roses in his hand, she pressed her hands to her chest to steady the hurried heartbeat. Surely he was the one she had loved all along, so dear and familiar! She rushed forward to embrace him, willing herself to feel the same remembered thrill that she had felt in his arms before he had left Maoershan.

But it was *not* the same.

As his arms circled her waist, his lips brushed briefly over her cheek as if he were embarrassed at the public display of affection. Of course. She had forgotten how reticent Vladimir had been in the past when she had overtly shown tenderness, and how he'd once admitted that he had been brought up never to betray his emotions in the presence of others.

Quickly, she dropped her arms, accepted the flowers with a mumbled "Thank you," and then hugged her father, who held her close and whispered through a nervous laugh, "My dear, sweet child, how glad I am to see you!"

Behind him stood Raissa, chewing on her lips and waiting patiently until her father finally released Svetlana and pushed her toward her sister. The girls hugged each other and then Raissa pulled back and said to her father, "See? What did I tell you? My sister survived. A little thinner, perhaps, but all in one piece."

It broke the awkward moment, and Svetlana hugged her sister again affectionately. "Sorry I spoiled your vacation, *sestryonka,*" she said with a smile, and then turned to her mother, who was beaming happily at everybody.

At home, alone with Vladimir at last, she went easily into his open arms. "Welcome home, my dearest," he said, tightening his embrace. "What a dreadful vigil it has been for me, not knowing what was happening to you. The only comfort I had was the knowledge that *hunhuzy* don't rape kidnapped women. But still, I can imagine how frightened you must have been."

A coolness washed over Svetlana. "I can't talk about it yet," she said. He lifted her chin and smiled, bending close to her face. "I understand, my dear. Let's put the past behind us and look to our future together."

Before she could say anything, he kissed her on the lips, and this time Svetlana tried desperately to recapture the emotion of the past. As she clung to him, an insistent inner voice whispered in her ear, *Don't look back, Svetlana, don't compare, don't remember. Only the future counts now, and your fiancé whom you will love.* Must *love.*

Later, after Vladimir had left and Raissa had excused herself and gone to her room, Nikolai asked Svetlana to tell him exactly what had happened in the taiga. In the warmth of her family dining room, seated near her loving parents, Svetlana at last found it possible to tell the details of her captivity. But as she described her rescue and Li-chun's courage in defying his father's orders, Sonya exploded.

"It was this bandit who was at fault, not his father! After all, he could have taken you out of the forest right away and found some other excuse for the barking dogs. What did you expect the old *hunhuz* to do but to keep you for ransom when his own son delivered you to him on a platter?"

"Mama, I told you, if not for him, I would have been mutilated the next day. He *saved* me, Mama, do you understand? He was wonderful to me." Her voice broke and she coughed to cover up.

Sonya shrugged. "I suppose that even a *hunhuz* might have a momentary twinge of conscience. I thank God you escaped before he changed his mind and brought your ear out of the taiga instead of you." She closed her eyes and shuddered. "Ugh, how I hate them all."

Svetlana's lips trembled and she pressed them shut tightly. Frustrated, angry, she suddenly realized that her father was taking no part in the argument. She turned to him, looking for support, and as their eyes met, she stopped short. His gaze was steady and speculative; something in that pensive look warned her that she was about to betray herself. Alerted, she looked back at her mother, but Sonya was so incensed, so full of hatred for the *hunhuzy*, that she only waved her hand in disgust.

"Someday you'll learn not to be so idealistic. I tell you— that *hunhuz* did you a good turn not because he was so honorable, but for some shady reason of his own, which you will never know. Anyway, it's all over, thank God. I'm going to retire early tonight. I need my rest." With that Sonya rose from the table and left the room.

Svetlana was about to follow when Nikolai placed his hand over hers and said, "Stay here a minute, Svetlana. I want to talk to you."

A spark of fear shot through her as she waited for him to speak.

A bottle of Marnier-Lapostolle cognac stood on the table, and Nikolai poured himself a glass, then twirled the stem, studying the amber liquid. In the awkward silence that followed, a fly buzzed loudly at the other end of the room. A grandfather clock sonorously chimed the half hour past ten.

"Svetlana," Nikolai began, "you know very well the reason behind your mother's hatred of the *hunhuzy*. She will never forget how the Rotovs died or the loss of their baby."

"I know, Papa," Svetlana said quietly. "I've always been appalled by the details of that tragedy, but how long will Mama keep on bringing it up and venting her hatred?"

"It's no use trying to change her mind," he said, taking a sip of the cognac. Then he looked at Svetlana. "Now, about this young *hunhuz* who saved you—what's his name?"

"Li-chun," Svetlana whispered.

"Yes, Li-chun." Nikolai cleared his throat. "I can appreciate your feelings about what he did for you, but, my dear, don't confuse a single act of kindness with the whole character of the man."

"But it wasn't just a single act of kindness, Papa," Svetlana cried, her voice shaking now. "He was considerate and kind and helpful throughout my whole captivity, and—and—"

She couldn't finish the sentence. She didn't know how to defend Li-chun further without betraying her secret, and as she struggled to find the right words, Nikolai raised his head slowly from his glass of cognac and his gaze locked with hers. For a long, devastating moment father and daughter looked at each other without a word. And as Svetlana endured his probing look, she fought without success the hot flush that rose to her face, burning her cheeks, filling her eyes with tears of shame.

It was her father who finally lowered his eyes, and with a deep sigh he patted her hand. "The sooner you forget the whole traumatic episode, the better for you, my child." He looked at her again, this time with what Svetlana thought were understanding and compassion, and added softly, "For many reasons."

Svetlana looked away, and a few moments later her father patted her arm.

"Time is a great healer, my dear. In a few days you will be involved in all the planning and excitement of your wedding preparations. Vladimir has been so faithful during our vigil. He is a good man."

And so it was that everyone agreed to Vladimir's suggestion of an earlier wedding. "Why wait until September?" he argued. "August will be much warmer and we can still get away for our honeymoon without worrying about the cold weather." Thoughtfully, he suggested going west to the romantic resort of Dzhalantun, and Svetlana appreciated his tact.

During the hectic weeks before the wedding Svetlana was determined more than ever to make Vladimir happy, to have a good marriage. Sharing her experiences and thoughts was an important part of that determination, and she decided to tell him as much as she dared about her terror and anxiety while in captivity. But each time she tried, he skillfully changed the subject, leaving her opening phrases hanging in the air. Finally, only days before the ceremony, she said to him, "Vladimir, why don't you want to hear about my kidnapping? I've tried several times to tell you about it, but you won't listen!"

Vladimir frowned and shook his head. "Don't you understand that I *don't want to hear about it?*"

His last phrase was said with such emphasis and anger that she fell silent for a few moments. Then she took a step forward and reached her hands out to him. "I won't talk about it anymore. I just thought you'd want to know."

"And I'm telling you again: I don't want to hear it. Now, do you understand?" There was such anger in his eyes, and something else—was it fear?—that Svetlana was stunned.

Poor, dear Vladimir. He must fear the details of her ordeal. For whatever reason he didn't want her to tell them. Well, so be it. For all his outward self-assurance he was vulnerable after all. Suddenly a wave of such tenderness flooded her that she rushed at him and hugged him.

The past would still haunt her, but it *was* the past, and if it should prove impossible to forget, then at least she must bury it deep in her soul, using the passion as that memory to build a better future.

In the few days preceding the wedding Svetlana indeed lost herself in the flurry of excitement. Her wedding gown, ordered at Churin's, the largest and finest department store in town, was of delicate French georgette with appliquéd rosettes. The skirt was hemmed just above her ankles and fitted to her slender figure in the exclusive salon. The satin shoes were special-ordered to match.

By the eve of her wedding day everything was in readiness, and at Sonya's insistence Svetlana went to bed early. Sleep, however, would not come. She recalled that several months earlier she had dreamed of her wedding night and her honeymoon, glamorizing it in her fantasy as any young girl in love would do. How different reality could prove to be! What would tomorrow bring? She fretted.

So, when her mother came in to bless her—something she hadn't done since Svetlana's adolescence—Svetlana, caught in an unguarded moment, asked her mother if she remembered her feelings and emotional turmoil before her own wedding night.

Sonya sat down on the edge of Svetlana's bed and, taking her hand, patted it affectionately. "I see you've been reading too many romantic novels, my dear. What you've read were fairy tales, I'm sorry to say. I don't want to paint a glamorous picture for you and then have you be disappointed. I'd rather you have a realistic approach to something that is unavoidable and quite disappointing. I told you some time ago what to expect on the physical side, and as to the emotional—well, the thrill and ecstasy are fleeting emotions that rarely occur on the wedding night. It's better that you look forward to future days with your dear husband when you will develop a comfortable, quiet tenderness that will far outlast a momentary passion. I know what I'm saying disappoints you, my child, but don't consume yourself over unattainable dreams that are mostly found in books."

Long after her mother had closed the door behind her, Svetlana stayed awake, wondering what had made her ask that question. Why had she pretended not to know what the first night would be like? Was it because she wanted reassurance from her mother, wanted to hear her say that no matter what, the first loving—and it would be her first with Vladimir —would be a glorious experience? Sonya had disappointed her not so much because of her pragmatic approach to the marriage bed, realistic as it might have been, but because Svetlana discovered that her mother had never experienced what she, Svetlana, had enjoyed with Li-chun.

That night in the forest, in Li-chun's arms, she *had* felt the thrill that her mother relegated to fantasy. Fairy tales and reality did merge, did exist; an unexpected wave of pity for her mother welled within Svetlana. To be married all those years without ever knowing what it was like, this ecstasy of passion —what emptiness marriage must be without such fulfillment! And yet—and yet, her mother did not know what she had been denied, and, not knowing, could never have missed it.

Svetlana turned the light out and huddled with her thoughts under her thin summer blanket. She was home, in Harbin, with her family, where she belonged. But in her future there loomed a challenge. She must learn to love Vladimir with uncompromising passion and never compare that love to her feelings for Li-chun; otherwise she was doomed to suffer.

And what of her love for Li-chun? Maybe she had simply valued his kindness. After all, he had been her savior, protecting her from abuse; he had simply been her refuge from fear. Based on these experiences she mistook her gratitude for love. On sober analysis the answer was logical. Relieved and at peace for the first time in weeks, she fell asleep with a smile on her face.

On her wedding day the hours flew by with a crescendo of activity as the bridesmaids' chatter and laughter filled the house. Raissa, the maid of honor, looked lovely in a salmon-pink chiffon with a satin sash, the scar on her jaw cleverly covered by makeup, her dimpled smile flashing at everyone. And then the best man, Vladimir's colleague Igor Sotin, a stocky man with laughing blue eyes and a shock of blond hair, arrived to let the bride know—according to custom—that the groom was waiting for her in the church. Adhering to tradition, both sets of parents stayed away from the ceremony, and

Svetlana was met at the door to the cathedral by her groom, meticulously dressed in tuxedo and starched wing-collar.

She knew she was beautiful, standing beside Vladimir in the center of the huge St. Nicholas Cathedral, a garland of lilies of the valley intertwined with seed pearls circling her blond chignon, and clouds of gathered veil cascading behind her. They stood in front of the lectern with an icon of St. Nicholas, the patron saint of Harbin. The voices of the twenty-five-member choir soared high in joyous celebration of matrimony, and Svetlana cast sidelong glances at her groom, happy and smiling beside her, convinced that she was falling in love with him all over again.

The priest's gold-embroidered white chasuble, the bejewelled icons, the flickering candles, the fragrance of incense, familiar hymns, all Russian and all so dear—this was her heritage and her life—this was where she belonged. *Nothing* must intrude into this happy and memorable day.

After the wedding the reception was held in the large ballroom of the Zhelsob club, where the newlyweds were toasted with champagne and calls of *"Gorko!"*—the traditional custom of complaining that the wine was "bitter" and asking that the newlyweds sweeten it by kissing. If the kiss were brief or shy, the *"Gorko!"* calls became louder and more insistent. The first kiss that Vladimir gave her was light and feathery, and Svetlana was amused by the reaction of the guests, who vocalized their disappointment and called for more. As glass after glass of champagne took its effect, Vladimir lost his reserve; Svetlana circled his neck and returned his ardent kiss. Eyes closed, she heard a refrain chanting in her brain: *My Vladimir. My Russian man, my husband . . .*

A glow of contentment spread through her, a sense of belonging that was hers to cherish.

A hired orchestra struck up a waltz, and she whirled in his arms to the tune of "Blue Danube," then danced with her father while Vladimir led his mother around the dance floor.

Her mother had thoughtfully ordered her favorite dishes for dinner: pheasant smothered in sour cream, tart cranberry sauce, baked apples, and an ice bombe studded with candied fruit. Veuve Clicquot champagne, choice wines from Rogozinsky's wine cellars, and vodka both from Lazaridi and Antipas distilleries, in fancy cut-glass bottles, flowed freely at the circular dinner tables that were each arranged to seat ten. Svetlana, however, drank little. She was thinking of the night they were to spend at the Hotel Moderne downtown, before they would board the train for Dzalantun in the morning. In a few hours she would leave her family and friends, the laughter, the noise, the music, and be alone with Vladimir.

Suddenly she panicked and looked across the room at her mother. Unaware of her daughter's turmoil, Sonya was beaming with happiness and talking to Vladimir's father, a heavy-set, bearded giant of a man, who was listening to her intently. Svetlana fought an irrepressible urge to run over and bury her face in her mother's lap, as she had done so often when she was hurt as a little girl.

But she was no longer a little girl; she was a married woman with a new husband from whom she had a secret. A secret so important and so disturbing that she couldn't bring herself to think of what would happen if she failed to fool him.

Chapter Eleven

The rooms Vladimir had reserved in the Hotel Moderne were luxurious. Thick Chinese rugs covered the floors—deep rose in the parlor, vivid blue in the bedroom. Heavy brocaded curtains hung over the four-poster bed; a turquoise silk coverlet had been thoughtfully turned back. Svetlana noticed a bottle of Mumm's champagne on the sideboard and, catching her glance, Vladimir turned to it.

"Would you like a glass of champagne now or after you change your clothes?" he asked, not looking at her.

"Now, please," she said, and then thought: *Maybe if I drink a little more, I'll get over my nervousness.*

Although Vladimir carefully worked the cork out of the bottle, it shot across the room, and the bubbly liquid foamed over. Suppressing a nervous giggle, Svetlana moved out of the way, and Vladimir smiled, quickly pouring the two crystal glasses half full. When he clicked his glass against hers, it made a delicate chime. *Fine crystal,* Svetlana thought, and the irrelevant observation startled her. She glanced at the sideboard. The starched crocheted runner was snow white, its edges curled upward to form a wavy ruffle that concealed a silver gallery tray, which held a decanter of burgundy-colored liqueur. Aware that the champagne glass she was holding matched the crystal decanter, she guessed that someone had carefully planned this touch of luxury to create a romantic mood. Ah, but where was hers?

In the sitting area of the large room the ebony chairs with red brocaded cushions looked uncomfortable; who could lounge in those straight-backed thrones with carved dragons for armrests? Her gaze lingered on the dust that had accumulated in the deeply cut grooves. How infinitely more comfortable were the overstuffed plush armchairs in her home.

Why on earth was she concentrating on all the furnishings around her, noticing every unimportant thing?

She looked at Vladimir and caught his intense look. Uncomfortable, she smiled to cover her embarrassment. Raising his glass, he bowed to her slightly. "I toast you, Madame Panova. How does your new name sound?" He looked at her with anticipation.

"Strange, of course, but I like it. Madame Panova," she repeated slowly. "Sounds important. I haven't been a married woman for very long."

Vladimir put down his empty glass and removed his tie. "It's getting warm in here. Perhaps you would like to change?"

Svetlana took the hint and hurriedly left the room. In the bedroom, in front of the floor-length mirror that stood in one corner in a wooden frame, she studied herself for a few moments, reluctant to take off the beautiful ivory linen going-away outfit. She had left her wedding gown in the Zhelsob dressing room and her mother had taken it home. How much care and attention had gone into creating that gown, never, never to be worn again; never again would she look so beautiful, so virginal, swathed in those clouds of veil.

Virginal? The thought had slipped in unintentionally. She flushed. Vladimir was waiting, and she must not test his patience. Reluctantly, she took off her suit and hung it in the wardrobe. By the time she had removed her shiny silk stockings, she was shivering, in spite of the warmth of the room.

Was it guilt or anxiety that made her so apprehensive? After she had slipped a white satin nightgown over her head, she loosened her chignon, letting the blond sheaf of hair cascade down to the middle of her back. Then she turned toward the door.

"You may come in now," she called timidly, unable to bring herself to say that she was ready for him. Vladimir turned the lights out in the parlor and entered the bedroom. For a few moments he stood on the threshold, looking at her.

"It's sinful to be so beautiful, so perfect. You look like a white angel in a halo of gold."

Instinctively, Svetlana touched her hair. *Li-chun had called her an angel too.* "I'm not an angel," she said quickly. "I'm very human, as you will no doubt discover very soon."

The moment she said it, she flushed. What she had meant was that she had her faults and certainly did not want to be idealized, but the moment she uttered the words, she realized the double meaning and looked at him with apprehension. Had he caught the implication? If he had, he concealed it well. Without comment he turned the lamp out and drew the heavy draperies back, allowing the reflection from the streetlights to soften the darkness in the room. *He's doing everything to make it easier for me,* Svetlana thought. Yet, perversely, she was disappointed that he did not take her in his arms right then and kiss her before turning the light out.

Quietly, she slipped into bed and listened. Vladimir moved around, shedding his clothes. In the silence the sounds registered clearly in Svetlana's ears: the coat hung in the wardrobe; the light click of cuff links as he placed them one at a time on the dresser; the rustle of his starched shirt; the thud of dropped shoes. Then lesser sounds, indefinable. He must be taking off his socks now, she guessed. What were his feet like? Were his toes straight and long, or stubby and irregular? Did he keep his toenails clipped? How petty to think such unromantic thoughts at a time like this. What was the matter with her? In a few moments he would climb into bed to claim her as his, and she would submit, eager to please and be pleased.

The bedside lamp went on. He was standing on his side of the bed, looking immaculate in a deep-blue brocaded robe, sashed tightly around his waist.

"Would you like another glass of champagne?" he asked softly, and when she shook her head, he turned the light out and slipped into bed. To her surprise he threw the covers off. In the dim light the outline of her satin-clad body shone in a seductive pose. Quickly she turned to him.

"Are you too warm?" she asked, not knowing what else to say.

"The covers are cumbersome and in the way."

The casual tone of his voice had suddenly changed and Svetlana felt his arms circle her waist and pull her against him. "Don't be so tense, darling," he whispered. "Relax! I'll be very gentle and it shouldn't hurt too much."

She held her breath, and was glad for the darkness. What was she going to say if he guessed? Frantic thoughts shot through her mind, and she was only half conscious of his hands sliding tentatively up and down her body.

She wanted to respond, to be tender and loving and return his caresses, but instead she lay in his arms rigid with anxiety. In a few minutes Vladimir patted her on the shoulder.

"Now, now, darling, it's not going to be as bad as all that. I'm your husband, remember?"

His light touch was lost on Svetlana, and she bit her lip, forcing herself to relax. Hesitantly, she reached for him, moved her hand over the curve of his hip, heard his intake of breath. When his hand slipped under her gown and traced her thigh, however, her skin crawled, and she went rigid again. He placed his knee between her legs and tried to separate them, but she crossed her ankles and tensed.

"For heaven's sake, why can't you relax? I'm not going to *rape* you. Surely you know that much. Hasn't your mother prepared you at all?"

Hot with shame, Svetlana threw her arm impulsively around his neck and pressed herself against him, trying to prevent his hand from going any farther up her leg. Then she whispered "I'm sorry . . . I'm sorry! I'll try. I promise."

And so she did, and in doing so, lay back, closed her eyes, and accepted his caresses without returning them.

The shock came a few minutes later. She was no longer a virgin, was she?—yet she was unprepared for the searing pain that seemed to go on and on. She hadn't expected this, couldn't understand what made the difference between that night in the glen, and this . . .

Perhaps it was just as well that it hurt so much, because she couldn't help but make small whimpering cries, and surely that was what Vladimir expected to hear.

But then it was over. He turned on the light, got up, and came around to her side of the bed, his eyes full of anger and hurt.

"So! I'm not the first man you've had. And I worried about hurting you. The virginal bridal gown, the veil—what a farce."

Svetlana winced. "Please . . . don't!"

"What did you expect me to do? Pretend everything is as it should be? Say nothing? I must be the laughingstock of the town. The bridegroom is the last to find out. Who knows about this?"

"No one, I swear!"

"Except the man himself, right? Handing over damaged goods to the unsuspecting groom and laughing behind his back. Was your lover at the wedding?"

Unable to face him, Svetlana buried her head in the pillow and burst into tears.

"Tears won't help you. I'm asking you again—was he at the wedding?"

Svetlana continued to cry, but he shook her roughly. "Answer me!"

She raised her head. "No."

"Was there more than one, perhaps? Is that it?" Vladimir stepped back. "What a fool I've been. All this acting tonight, moaning as if it really hurt."

"It *did* hurt," Svetlana cried. "It was—I—it happened only once before."

"Only once? Am I supposed to believe it after the way you tried to deceive me?"

"I—I thought of telling you, b-but I was afraid you—you might reject me." She reached her arms to him. "Oh, Vladimir, no matter what you think, I love you!"

"Nice speech. How many times have you rehearsed it?"

He stared at her with such fury that Svetlana cringed and pulled the covers up to her chin. His eyes narrowed, and with one violent movement he threw the coverlet off.

"Spare me your false modesty, my dear. And since you assure me that you love me, you won't mind, will you, if I avail myself of my marital privileges again and dispense with the care I took the first time?"

It was worse the second time. After he had fallen asleep, she stayed awake and shuddered remembering all the places he'd wanted her to touch, and what he'd made her do. Shocked and mortified, she had obeyed and held in her hand the huge rigid thing that was the root of his passion, the thing that pressed and pressed against her groin and sought admittance once again. Vladimir's unrestrained drive seemed to have one purpose—to hurt her as she had hurt him—and she submitted to the ordeal in silence, biting her lip to keep from crying out, until the pain in the lip became stronger than the pain of the assault.

But why think about it now, why dwell on it? she argued fiercely with herself, fighting indignation, ignoring the hurt. She must forget this night, erase it from her memory. But the images filled her mind, burgeoned, then seemed to climb out and hide in the silk draperies, peering at her from the cornices —cyclopsed, leering.

What had she expected? Her husband's meek acceptance of her deceit? He was a bitterly disappointed, humiliated man. How dreadfully it had all turned out. Still, she must not hold tonight's cruel experience against him.

They would have two weeks in Dzhalantun to work things out between them. She would make him forgive her, make him believe that she had tried to spare his pride, that she loved only him, and that she would be a loyal wife.

She *had* to.

But a few tears sneaked out of the corners of her eyes and crawled over her temples to cool her skin and hide in her hair.

Dzhalantun. They called it the Pearl of the East. It was a lovely place. Founded in the valley of the Yalu River under the patronage of the railway-company director, Boris Ostroumov, it was considered one of the most fashionable resorts on the western branch of the railroad. An ample number of tennis courts for the sports minded were scattered throughout the surrounding parks, and hidden gazebos provided ideal hideaways for newlyweds, who were serenaded with romantic music wafting gently from an open-air stand. At night strings of lights stretched along the river, their colors dancing in the prism of the beach waterfall.

A perfect spot for a honeymoon. But in spite of the romantic setting, in spite of Svetlana's efforts to make up to Vladimir, the two weeks proved a fiasco. During the day Vladimir was formal and uncommunicative, spending time on the tennis courts with other vacationers and avoiding being alone with her as much as possible. Only once, early in the week, did he mention their wedding night, and then only to apologize for his behavior. "Abuse" of her, he called it. "You must realize," he said, avoiding her eyes, "that the discovery was so totally unexpected, I lost my head. I promise it will never happen again."

Something in the tone of his voice—sadness or bitterness, she couldn't tell—sent chills through Svetlana. She would rather he had exploded, accused her of deceit again, but in his controlled, civilized words there sounded a determined formality that she instinctively knew would be more difficult to break through. At night he behaved in a similar manner. His approach to lovemaking seemed almost mechanical, calculated to satisfy his physical needs and to make a clumsy attempt to please her—which failed. Not once did he ever use an endearing word.

Frequently, when they were surrounded by other vacationers, Svetlana caught his searching look on her as though he were trying to guess her thoughts. Then, on the last night before they were to return to Harbin, he said, "Svetlana, I know you're trying hard to make a go of our marriage, and I know that we must both try. Divorce is out of the question and would gain us nothing but scandal. So we will make the best of things."

They were sitting in a small gazebo hidden among lilac bushes in the park. Studded with flower beds, the grounds were carefully manicured, and the air was filled with the delicate fragrance of tobacco plants and roses. How different it could have been for them, had their honeymoon not been marred by such a traumatic beginning! Svetlana's mouth tightened as Vladimir continued.

"I have to tell you, though, that I shall never be able to forget that another man had you first. I was brought up to expect the girl I marry to save herself for me. That you failed to adhere to the established code of our society is something beyond my understanding. But, I'll try to adjust to the idea and overcome my resentment. It will take a long time, I'm afraid. The reason I'm bringing this up now is that tomorrow we'll be back in Harbin and I will be plagued by suspicions every time I see anyone, wondering which of our friends and acquaintances sampled you first."

Svetlana rose abruptly. A twitch started below her right eye and she blinked in an effort to stop it.

"I resent your choice of words, Vladimir," she said, struggling for control. "I know it has been difficult for you, but there's no need to be insulting. Lord knows, I've tried hard enough to make it up to you, and I will continue to do so. What else can I do to make you forgive me?"

"I doubt that I'll ever forgive you, Svetlana. Don't expect that. All I can hope for is that I will eventually reach a point where I won't dwell on the past any longer and can bury it as a family skeleton. And I certainly hope that no one in your family knows about this. I don't want any gossip to start."

Suddenly the air seemed stifling to Svetlana and the space in the gazebo too small. Funny that she hadn't noticed before how little room there was to move about. She turned to leave, but Vladimir grabbed her by the arm and pulled her around to face him.

"Svetlana!" His breath quickened. "Who was it?" And when Svetlana, horrified, tried to wrench her arm free, he jerked it. "Tell me! I'd rather know who it was than suspect everyone we see."

With all her strength she pulled herself free and ran down the path toward the river. He did not follow her. There, by the side of the cascading waterfall, she dropped to her knees in the sand, burying her head in her arms. What was she going to do? She knew Vladimir better now. Was he really resentful of the other man, or was he afraid that someone would talk? Whichever it was, she could not tell him the truth, for if it came out, it would devastate him. At whatever cost she must not confess.

Someone tapped her on the shoulder, and she jumped at the touch. Deafened by the rush of the water, she hadn't heard the footsteps behind her. An older woman with bare feet, the hem of her simple cotton dress moist around her ankles, was standing above her.

"Is there anything I can do?" she asked quietly, her face solicitous and a little curious. Svetlana rose from her knees, embarrassed by her display of emotion, and shook her head.

"No, thank you. I—I was just waiting for my headache to go away," she said and, turning toward the park, walked quickly away.

She was not a very good actress, was she? Now there was so much for her to cope with, so much control to exercise. She suspected that most men would prefer not to know the name of the other man, would want to dismiss it from their minds as quickly as possible. Why was Vladimir different? He seemed so concerned with his reputation. How could she assure him that his suspicions of their Russian friends were groundless without divulging Li-chun's identity? It would be beyond his capacity to understand that she had submitted to a Chinese—and a bandit at that.

No one must ever know.

Chapter Twelve

Autumn leaves carpeted the ground of their large fenced-in garden on Pekinskaya Street, only one block from where Svetlana's parents lived. The one-story, gray-stone home belonged to the railway company, and like most of its married employees, Vladimir chose to avail himself of company housing rather than buy his own. The house was large. Surrounded by spacious, fenced-in grounds with a carefully preserved grove of trees, it was set well back from the sidewalk. A glassed-in porch wrapped around it on three sides and in the back was a separate underground ice-cooler, storage shed, and servants' wing that afforded the family complete privacy.

Cold October winds had been blowing from Siberia, whining, whistling, through naked branches. Almost every day sparse drops of rain dappled the sandy ground, filling the air with the smell of resin and wet bark. From a large cedar chest Svetlana had pulled out her autumn coat of fur-trimmed wool.

After the honeymoon was over, she had plunged enthusiastically into decorating her first home. Generous with money, Vladimir nonetheless wanted to see all her bills, and Svetlana chafed from what she felt was his mistrust of her judgment. Once deceived on a major issue, it was as if he could not trust her in other matters either. She tried to show him that she was frugal, and while she bought most of her clothes at Churin's department store, where her wedding dress had been made, she shopped around for best buys in other things. Thus, when she bought another wool coat at the Vinokurov's department store downtown on Mostovaya Street and paid only thirty rubles for it, she thought she'd please Vladimir; instead, he said that he would rather she bought her clothes at Churin's in the Novy Gorod section of town where they lived. She tried to interest him in decorating their house and asked him to go to Vinokurov's with her to see a Chinese rug she liked, but he shook his head.

"Buying household furnishings is a woman's job. I don't want to waste my time shopping. As long as you don't buy a lot of Chinese stuff for the house, it will be all right."

"You don't like Chinese furnishings?"

"We are Russians, living in an essentially Russian city, and I don't see any reason why we should surround ourselves with Chinese pieces. I don't mind an occasional silk hanging—they are artistic and add to the decor of the room—but the black Chinese furniture with carved dragons is extremely uncomfortable. Besides, the day may well come when we'll all return to Russia, and we should remain as Russian as possible."

Taken aback, Svetlana looked at him for a moment. "What are you talking about? As long as the Bolsheviks are in power, we can never go back."

"The Bolsheviks made a clean sweep at the top during the Revolution, and now, as the years go by, they may well simmer down and lean toward a more democratic type of government. Life under the tsars was anything but a bed of roses."

"You talk like a twentieth-century Decembrist. I had no idea you felt this way. Do your parents share your thoughts?"

"They think Tsar-Batyushka was a saint and could do no wrong, so there's no use discussing it with them. Harbin is their Russia." Vladimir frowned. "How can we forget that we are the so-called guests of the Chinese government? We, the people of a great country, are reduced to accepting charity from the Asians. I find this demeaning."

Svetlana was dismayed. Not only her mother, but now her husband, was basically anti-Chinese. That generous country had given them shelter, had allowed them to build their own city and practically govern themselves without interfering, accepted their alien culture, permitted them to live as they pleased, and here was her husband expressing anti-Chinese sentiments. How ungrateful!

Unpleasant it was to dwell on their differences, and down deep she was glad that he came home late and retired early, so that their time alone was short. Vladimir was dedicated to his work, and his only recreation consisted of the tennis he played at the English club on Bolshoi Prospekt, a few blocks from their house. But when winter came, she knew he would want to ice-skate, and she was glad that at least they shared the love of that sport.

At night his demands on her were always in the dark after they went to bed, and Svetlana preferred it that way. No embarrassing eye contact with his silent accusation reminding her—as if she could forget—that he had not forgiven her. But time was on her side and she would be patient. Sooner or later his memory would dim, and the closeness she hoped for would be established. She had to believe that.

In the meantime her love of singing and her desire to continue her training had not abated. In fact, it was her escape from the ever-present, nagging feeling that sooner or later Vladimir would bring up her deceit again. To avoid thinking about it, she spent hours practicing her vocal lessons at the upright piano Vladimir had bought her. Although he could well afford it on his five-thousand-a-year salary, she nonetheless valued his generosity, for she knew he did not take her singing seriously.

At the music school, one of the many friends she had made was a young tenor, Kyril Volin, with whom she practised operatic duets. Not until after she was married did Svetlana discover quite by accident that he had no family and lived in a rented attic room in a downtown hotel. The last time she had gone to her lesson, she had asked him on an impulse to come to dinner, and he had accepted.

In order not to embarrass him with an elaborate meal, Svetlana had instructed the cook to prepare ground beef and rice cabbage rolls in tomato sauce. After they had eaten and the dishes were cleared by the maid, Svetlana went to the piano and opened the sheet music she had bought specially for tonight. Vladimir, who had been quiet throughout the meal, walked over and glanced at the music.

"I don't remember you singing anything from the *Queen of Spades* before. Where did you get it?" he asked, picking up the sheet music and leafing through it perfunctorily.

"I got it yesterday at Vakhrushev's on Diagonalnaya Street," Svetlana replied.

Vladimir looked at her. "Since when have you been tackling such difficult arias as the 'Why These Tears'?"

Kyril answered for Svetlana. "I'm afraid it was my fault. I think Svetlana's voice is so good that I told her it wouldn't hurt to sing a big aria once in a while even if our teachers would say that we're reaching beyond our capabilities." He smiled apologetically and sat down at the piano to accompany Svetlana.

Vladimir's face showed little emotion while Svetlana sang the aria, in which Lisa, the heroine of the opera, questions herself as to why she should be crying on the day of her engagement. Svetlana kept up with Kyril's accompaniment, enormously pleased by his approving look.

When she had finished, she turned to Vladimir only to catch him watching them both with narrowed eyes. Those looks of his, so penetrating, so full of hidden suspicion, made her uneasy.

"How about a duet now?" Kyril asked, seemingly oblivious of Vladimir's silent scrutiny.

"What would you like to sing?" she asked, reaching for the sheaf of music on top of the piano.

Kyril leafed through them. "How about this one?" he asked, handing her a love duet from the first act of *Madama Butterfly*. Svetlana hesitated. "I'm not sure I can manage this one," she said, giving Vladimir a sidelong glance, but Vladimir sat impassive, waiting.

"Nonsense. You've just handled the *Queen of Spades* aria beautifully. Besides, your husband is our only audience, and if we make a mistake, well, he will understand, won't you?" Kyril said, turning to Vladimir, who was pouring himself a glass of brandy.

"Even if you made a mistake, I wouldn't know it. I'm not much on opera. I think Svetlana would do better to stay with lighter music than attempt operatic arias."

Kyril shot him a quick glance. "If we fear failure and don't take risks, we will never achieve anything."

They sang the duet with the full emotional impact it demanded, holding hands and looking into each other's eyes, and at one point Kyril placed his arm around Svetlana's shoulders. In this passionate avowal of love Kyril's voice blended beautifully with hers.

Vladimir's applause was so mild, so inadequate to the beauty of the music and their voices, that Svetlana was angry; Kyril, on the other hand, nodded to Vladimir good humoredly and said, "I guess we didn't please you all that much, eh?"

Vladimir, who had finished his brandy and was pouring himself another, shrugged. "As I said before, I don't understand operatic music, but it sounded fine to me. Now, how about something light? Something from *The Merry Widow* or *The Gypsy Baron?*"

Piqued, Svetlana closed the music and replaced it on the top of the piano. "I haven't studied those as yet. It will have to wait."

After Kyril had left and the servants had retired to their quarters, Svetlana looked at Vladimir.

"I don't understand why you are so against my singing operatic arias. It is good training, and the more difficult they are, the easier it will be for me later to learn the lighter ones. I think you could have shown a little more enthusiasm, especially since Kyril does have a magnificent voice and is being groomed for a professional career."

"And I suppose you would like the same to happen to you, is that it?"

"I haven't given it much thought," Svetlana replied evasively. "After all, I have a long way to go before that could happen. I'm only a beginner."

Vladimir downed his brandy, rose, refilled his glass, and walked over to the piano. There he looked through the music again. "I see that all of these are romantic arias and duets. How long have you and Kyril been singing together?"

Carefully, Svetlana replaced the lid of the piano. "We started our lessons at the same time, but he is far ahead of me, I'm afraid. He spends many more hours practicing."

"And just how do you know that?" His words were slurred, and Svetlana, taken by surprise, stumbled over her response.

"I—I don't know what you mean. I just assume that he does, because he seems to know more arias and doesn't hesitate over difficult passages, all of which indicates much practice."

"Is that why he takes the liberty of wrapping his arm around you and looking into your eyes as if he possessed you?"

"Now, really, Vladimir! You've had too much to drink tonight. We're taught at school that besides the beauty of the voice, the quality that separates an ordinary singer from a great one is the ability to act, to involve the audience in the dramatic impact of the opera. So it's natural for us to learn to act out the emotional content of the given aria or duet as the case may be." Svetlana looked at Vladimir for a moment, then added, "Frankly, I don't understand why you are so against my studying voice. When you bought me this piano, I thought you had changed your mind and would approve of my studies."

"I don't mind your studies. It gives you something to occupy your time. But I do object to your getting so serious about it, and I don't like your being pawed by Kyril."

Exasperated, Svetlana said, "I've just explained that to you. How long are you going to be suspicious of every man we see?"

She was immediately sorry to have touched on the very subject she had tried to avoid ever since they'd returned from their honeymoon. But Vladimir's lingering looks when they were in the company of other young men, his brooding moods, were telling on her nerves. Suddenly, she hadn't been able to restrain herself from blurting the words out.

"I can't help it," he said, his eyes bleary, his face flushed. "Every time I see you talking to another man, I am wondering if he's the one. Can't you understand"—his voice suddenly shook—"how humiliating it is for me to know that among our friends there is a man who had you before I did, a man who looks at me and knows me for a dupe?"

"Then tell me what I can do to help you get over it."

"Tell me the name of the man and—and I'll never mention it again."

"You're asking the impossible. I can't tell you!" Svetlana cried.

Vladimir looked at her with pain in his eyes. "After tonight, I don't think you need to tell me. The intimacy with which Kyril held you during your duet was more than just dramatic acting. Only a man who has been intimate with a woman would hold her with such familiarity."

"You're wrong. Wrong! Kyril is only a classmate, a friend. God, how can I stop you being obsessed by this?"

"I told you—tell me who it is. If it isn't Kyril, then who?" Suddenly, he grabbed her by the forearm and squeezed hard. "Answer me! Who? I've got to know!"

"It isn't anyone you know, Vladimir. I swear it! Isn't that enough? Please don't ask me any more."

"If it isn't anyone I know, then where did you meet him? Where does he live?"

He was still holding on to her forearm and was hurting her. Svetlana tried to get free, but he twisted her arm instead. "I said, tell me who it is and how is it that I don't know him?"

Svetlana fought again to free herself but he held tight. "Let me go, you're hurting me!"

"Not until you tell me. I'm tired of guessing games." He raised his voice. "I want to know. Now! Who is he?"

"He—he's not in Harbin."

"Then where?"

Svetlana had dropped to her knees under the pressure of his grasp, and now she started to cry. "Please, don't make me tell you. Oh, please!"

"I'm asking once again, where is the man?"

"Oh, God! In—in the taiga."

Slowly, Vladimir released her, and she crouched on the floor, rubbing her forearm. He squinted, shaking his head in confusion.

"In the taiga?" he repeated, not comprehending.

She nodded.

"You don't mean the Chinese bandit who kidnapped you?" His voice was incredulous.

Svetlana nodded again.

"A *hunhuz?* My God! *Hunhuzy* don't rape kidnapped women. What kind of a bandit would do this? Why didn't you tell me that you had been raped?"

But Svetlana only bowed her head and continued to cry.

"And I wasted all this time feeling humiliated and suspecting all our friends." Vladimir replaced the music and helped Svetlana rise. "I—I'm sorry you were raped. Truly sorry. But I must confess, I'm relieved that it wasn't anyone among our Russian acquaintances."

There was nothing more she could say to him. How could she? He was actually relieved in assuming that she had been raped rather than having given in willingly to someone he knew. The relief he felt at not having been humiliated evidently far outweighed any concern for her traumatic experience. How selfish of him. And the devil of it was that she could not, dared not, confront him with this accusation. She was treading on dangerous ground and she knew it.

Suddenly, Vladimir thought of something. "Is this why the *hunhuz* brought you out of the forest? A pang of conscience, perhaps?" And when Svetlana did not answer, he swayed on his feet for a few moments and then went on. "His head should be dangling from a stake somewhere, and the ravens should pluck his eyes out. And even that would be too good for him."

With a violent movement Vladimir swept the sheaf of music from the piano top to the floor. "My wife raped by a Chinaman. A savage! A criminal!"

Svetlana pressed her hands against her ears to keep from hearing insults heaped on Li-chun.

Vladimir pulled her hands away and shook her. "We'll get him yet. We'll string him up for all to see. The bastard!" His face was contorted, and his breath was heavy with liquor.

Svetlana winced and turned her face away. "You're drunk. I've never seen you drunk. You're revolting. Let me go!"

But Vladimir tightened his grip on her. "So I'm drunk. Do you blame me? My wife defiled by a bandit. Sullied. The dirty, dirty bastard! The scum!"

That was too much. The foul breath, the wild unfocused eyes, the verbal abuse—it was all too much. The desire to hurt him became overwhelming. Nothing mattered at the moment but to hurt him.

All caution aside, Svetlana cried: "No! Don't you call him a scum. He's not a bastard. He's not! I—he—he didn't—"

"What are you saying? The man raped you and you're defending him?"

"He—he didn't rape me!"

"What do you mean?"

"I—I mean—it—it wasn't a rape."

"Whaaat? What are you telling me? You don't mean that you submitted to him *willingly?*"

Miserably, Svetlana nodded.

A vein bulged on Vladimir's temple and his face turned dark red. He clenched his fists and shook them at her. "What kind of woman are you, to submit to a man before marriage— and not only a Chinaman, but a *hunhuz?*" His voice shook, and he shoved her aside so hard that she lost her balance and grabbed at the tabletop to keep from falling.

Vladimir breathed heavily. "You submitted to the lowest of the low. I say—scum!"

"He's not the lowest of the low. He was educated in a Russian school and speaks Russian as well as you and I."

"Oh, I see. And that makes it acceptable for you to sleep with a foul *hunhuz?*"

"Don't insult him!"

"And I'll say what I want! He's a *Phazan* and a criminal who took advantage of a helpless victim. Death is too good for him!"

"I've told you before—he was kind to me, and—and—"

"And so in gratitude you slept with him? Please spare me from having to hear the details."

Common sense told her to accept Vladimir's abuse against Li-chun and be silent. But she couldn't. Let him know the truth. Let him be humiliated.

"It wasn't gratitude, Vladimir." Her voice broke.

"Then what?"

"I—I cared for him."

"What?"

Svetlana straightened and looked him directly in the eyes, and saw the shock there.

"You heard me," she said deliberately. "I *cared* for him. But you wouldn't understand, of course. You're only concerned with your reputation, your own colossal egoism, and how to protect yourself from humiliation and ridicule."

"Well! I had no idea I had married a tramp."

"Your insults are beneath your dignity. I'm not a tramp. I promised to be a loyal wife to you and I intend to keep that promise whether you believe it or not. The past is gone and I want to bury it as quickly as possible. Now do you understand?"

Vladimir opened his mouth, closed it, pressed his lips tight, then shook his head as if refusing to accept all that he had just heard.

"I don't know how I'll ever bring myself to touch you again," he said, and stalked out of the room.

Svetlana gathered up the sheets of music scattered on the floor and stood by the piano, holding them in her shaking hands. What an enormous relief it was to have told the truth at last, to have unburdened the secret that had hung like the sword of Damocles over her head. And although the truth had had a devastating effect on Vladimir, it had served a purpose. It had removed the suspicions that were poisoning his mind.

But in the long run had she done the wisest thing? What if Li-chun made good his wish to leave the taiga and join Chang Tso-lin's army? If so, there was a good chance they would meet again, for the Old Marshal's lieutenants often came to Harbin to gather information about the railroad and its activities.

She must not think of such a possibility. "Fear has huge eyes," her mother often told her when she was a little girl, and she was now imagining things. Her chances of meeting Li-chun again were remote and she shouldn't think about it.

What had Vladimir said before he left the room? *I don't know if I'll ever be able to touch you again.* Surely he didn't mean it. He had spoken in anger. More than ever she wanted to make a fresh start, now that the truth was out and there was no suspicion hanging between them any longer. She would continue to be a good wife, and maybe there would be a child. Yes, a baby would be a healing influence, the deepest bond imaginable. Of course!

She nodded at her thought and started tidying the sheet music on top of the piano, though it needed no tidying.

Chapter Thirteen

After that disastrous evening when Svetlana's confession had been wrenched out of her, Vladimir did not touch her for days. He worked late hours and when he did come home, he avoided looking at her. Later, in the bedroom, under the pretext of being tired, he went straight to sleep.

At first, relieved that there were no more accusations from him, Svetlana plunged deeper into her studies, practicing her vocal lessons and visiting her parents in her spare time. But as the days dragged on, the estrangement deepened. A furrow appeared on Vladimir's forehead and there were lines of stress around his mouth. She knew how deeply his pride had been hurt, and she wanted to comfort him but didn't know how to approach him. Worst of all there was no one to whom she could turn for advice. She couldn't ask her mother how to break the impasse in her marriage without divulging the cause behind it. Sonya would surely want to know, and if she told her—Svetlana shuddered at the thought of her reaction if she should learn about Li-chun. Her father suspected something, but surely not the truth.

So, she was alone with her problem. Aware that their estrangement was her fault, she desperately wanted his reassurance, his affection, but instead, he was withdrawn and aloof. Somehow she had to break the tension; but how? Who could tell her? Surely not his parents, especially his mother, so prim and proper, so critical of social graces. Fortunately, they lived in Modyagow, and since that section of town was many blocks away and much too far to reach on foot, Svetlana used the distance as an excuse for not visiting them more often.

In the middle of November the skating rink was opened, and on Sunday, when Vladimir could not use his work as an excuse, Svetlana urged him to go skating with her. It was the first time since their marriage that Vladimir seemed to have forgotten his resentment. He gave in totally to the enjoyment of his favorite sport. The air was crisp, the snow sparkled in the sun, and the rink was full of vigorous, happy skaters. Svetlana and Vladimir glided hand in hand around the rink, then watched each other do a figure eight in one corner reserved for practice. Vladimir, caught up in the sport, helped her improve the difficult exercise. She was pleased and congratulated herself for having thought of this outing, already planning her strategy for the rest of the day.

That night after dinner, their faces glowing from the exercise and the frosty air, they sat in their living room, Svetlana with a cup of tea and Vladimir sipping brandy.

"I'm so glad the skating rink is open for the season," Svetlana said, putting down her cup on the low coffee table in front of her. "There's something so invigorating about our winters that one's body feels bursting with energy. I love the still air, the hush of nature, the blanket of snow. Everything looks so fresh and clean."

Vladimir smiled, twirling the stem of his glass. "Yes, we have that in common; I, too, love the winter and the skating. And speaking of skating, you're quite good at figures. It takes discipline to make the figure eight on one leg."

"I prefer dancing, though. It's more fun. How old were you when you started skating?"

"I think I was about eight."

"So was I. I remember how proud I was when my child's skates with those triple blades at the heel were replaced by regular skates." Svetlana laughed, remembering. "I felt so grown up." She turned to Vladimir. "You know, I think we ought to start our child on regular skates right from the beginning."

Vladimir raised an eyebrow. "Our child?"

Svetlana nodded. "I want a child so much, dear, don't you?"

After a brief pause, he nodded. "Yes, of course I do, and— and I'm glad you want to have a child. I don't know why, but for some reason I thought you didn't."

Svetlana moved closer and, circling his neck, kissed him on the cheek, then impulsively showered his face and neck with quick, feathery kisses. In a moment she felt his arm circle her waist and draw her to him, and as he did, she found his mouth and kissed him with a long, determined kiss.

The ice was broken. How foolish of her to have waited this long! After all, his pride had been hurt, and she should have made the first move long before this. As though he had been waiting for her to reaffirm her love, his passion for her now seemed free of anger, and Svetlana responded willingly, driven by her determination to make the marriage work. She had broken the first barrier, had gotten him to react to her for the first time without bitterness. It wasn't hard to convince herself that her own fulfillment would come in due time.

For now, there were no more secrets between them, and things could only improve from now on. She wanted a child. A wonderful little baby would help bridge any gulf that might still exist between them. She wanted that baby desperately.

There *was* a baby. A healthy, kicking little boy whom they named Georgy. Born on Tuesday, the twenty-eighth of August, 1923, he was quickly called Georgik by his aunt, Raissa, whom Svetlana had asked to be his godmother, and the name stuck. Svetlana was immensely gratified to see her husband beaming, proud to be a father, yet a nasty suspicion spoiled the pleasure: was he so happy only because his child was a son to carry on the family name? Ashamed of these thoughts at a time when she should have felt unmarred happiness, Svetlana chased the thoughts away and enjoyed the attention showered upon her by both sets of parents. Even Vera, always so critical, had fussed over her, shaking her head disapprovingly when Svetlana left her bed before the customary ten days had passed.

"But I feel completely well, Maman," she said to her

mother-in-law, "and I really think it will make me weaker if I stay in bed any longer."

"Why the hurry? Vladimir's hired an experienced nurse for Georgik, and the servants know their business in running the house. Besides, I can always stop by to check on things, if you want any help."

God forbid, Svetlana thought. *With that kind of help I'll get sick again.* Aloud she thanked Vera and assured her she was feeling just fine but would certainly call on her if she needed anything. She didn't say, of course, that it would be more practical to call on her own mother; Sonya lived only a block away and could come over anytime.

Pampered by family and servants, Svetlana enjoyed a few days of leisure before returning to the music school. She had progressed enough so that she was now being asked to perform at school concerts, and even at parties their friends always asked her to sing. With tacit acceptance of her hobby, as he insisted on calling it, Vladimir no longer voiced his objection, but Svetlana felt his disapproval and it somewhat tarnished the thrill of knowing how much pleasure she was giving to her audiences.

But now she had another member of the family for whom to sing. Her Georgik. What a pleasure it was to sing him her favorite Lermontov lullaby. Rocking him in her arms, she watched his eyes focus on her and then the lids become heavy and finally close to her song:

> *Sleep, my lovely child,*
> *Lullaby!*
> *Quietly shines the clear moon*
> *Into your cradle.*

To all outward appearances her life was idyllic. "Some people have it all," her friend Nina Serova said to her shortly after Georgik was born. "Beauty, talent, a handsome and well-to-do husband, and now a healthy, adorable baby. And look at me, still a spinster."

Svetlana smiled at the good-natured statement, but after her friend had left, she sat down in her parlor and thought about her life. Did she really have it all? She looked around. Everything in the parlor was to her taste: the deep-blue Chinese rugs, (Vladimir's only concession to having anything Chinese in the house), the expensive walnut furniture, the overstuffed chairs, the crystal, even a silver samovar. Their home was spacious, the servants well trained, Vladimir's job assured. And in addition to all the material comforts, she had something special that an average wife did not possess: a God-given talent, a beautiful soprano voice. She was popular and they were in demand at parties. And above all she had the joy of her life—Georgik.

Yes, Georgik. The months slipped by through the winter and spring, and by the time early summer had arrived, he was struggling to walk, holding on to chairs and tables. Pleased with himself, he grinned at anyone who watched. Svetlana was pleased with him, too, and was amused to see how Vladimir struggled to conceal the enormous pride he felt in his little boy. "He's made the normal progress for a child. I'm certainly glad he is growing up to be a strong boy," he had said, and Svetlana chuckled inwardly at his beaming face that belied his words.

From that day on she shared with Vladimir every little incident in Georgik's life. Sonya, of course, was a doting grandmother, but Vera always managed to find something to criticize in her grandchild's upbringing.

Although Svetlana's days were filled with activities, she had come to dread the quiet evenings at home, when they were not going out at night.

She listened dutifully to Vladimir's recitation of the day's events at work, so predictable, so monotonous, that she could almost guess what he would say next, and in turn, after telling him about Georgik, she tried to find something to say about *her* activities during the day. Her singing progress was always met with stony silence, and it was only when she spoke of Georgik that her husband smiled and nodded indulgently.

More and more Svetlana felt that she was living with a stranger. Try as she might, there was a barrier within him, a point beyond which he did not admit anyone, least of all his wife. The external veneer was obvious: she had learned how important were outward appearances to him and how he went to great lengths to present to the world the image of a happily married couple. All his overt gestures of affection were made in the presence of family or friends, never in the privacy of their bedroom.

There, his lovemaking was always the same, predictable, monotonous, without romance. The fulfillment she had been hoping for never came, and after she had recuperated from Georgik's birth, she had run out of excuses. Bitterly she thought that her mother's warning about her wedding night had extended into her whole married life.

And as she dwelt on it, to her dismay the image of Li-chun and his love came back to her with a clarity so vivid, so acute, that her hands shook and she nearly dropped a crystal decanter she was moving from the sideboard to the table. She put it down and sat in the nearest chair, shocked by the intrusion of Li-chun's image into her thoughts, stunned by her reaction to it.

After that sudden memory, others followed. Soon they had become cruel companions, torturing her with yearnings of unfulfilled passion. And the more she told herself that hers was a hopeless yearning, the more she longed for Li-chun. It wasn't even clear to her what she was yearning for. Even if such a miracle were possible and she were to see him again, what good would that do except create a more painful longing never to be satisfied, a dream never to come true?

Someone had once told her that Russians reveled in tragedy, that a Russian woman was never content unless she was shedding copious tears for the good of her soul. Well, she had cause to shed not only copious, but hopeless, tears over a brief love she had known and lost forever. In the predictable routine of her loveless marriage, she now derived a certain perverse sense of satisfaction from seeing herself as a tragic figure.

Then, one night in early September, she was told that she had been selected to sing at a concert in the Zhelsob, at the performance planned for the following month. Her lesson was late that day and she could hardly wait to tell Vladimir about it. At home, however, she found her parents and her sister sitting around the dining table, engaged in a spirited discussion with Vladimir.

Nikolai was alternately taking off and replacing his pincenez, a sure sign that he was nervous. "I'm concerned about what the Soviets will do when their treaty with Peking goes into effect next month," he said, shaking his head and looking at no one in particular.

Vladimir shrugged. "I don't know why you worry about it. After all, it will be a joint management of the railway company only as far as the commercial venture is concerned, and the Chinese will have more control in all other matters."

Sonya nodded. "Vladimir is right, Nikolai. Surely you haven't forgotten that General Horvath acted on his own when he gave up the extraterritorial rights in order to prevent the Soviets from coming into Manchuria. I'm sure that the Peking government knows what it's doing in allowing the joint management now."

"I know all that, but what worries me is that the next step will be a complete takeover of the railroad, and it will happen before the trusting Chinese realize it. We were told that Russia spent two hundred sixty million gold rubles in the first twenty years developing the Manchurian area and building up Harbin. I'm sure the Soviets haven't forgotten that and will want it back."

"Don't forget that this is still Manchuria," Vladimir said. "Marshal Chang Tso-lin is watching vigilantly, I assure you, from his palace in Mukden."

Nikolai looked dubious. "That's just it. The Old Marshal is in Mukden, and the railway management is here, in Harbin. Even though he insisted on a separate Mukden Agreement, he can't be both places at the same time."

"He must have his spies everywhere. All you have to remember are the days when he controlled the Peking government: the moment he got wind that he had no chance against the combined forces of feuding warlords, he withdrew into the safety of Manchuria, and now he's virtually our dictator. He's shrewd, that one."

Sonya frowned. "I don't understand where his loyalties lie. At one time he courted the Russians, and now he seems to be collaborating with the Japanese."

Nikolai removed his pince-nez and rubbed them carefully with his handkerchief. "He is Chinese first and foremost. He may seem friendly with the Japanese, but I'm sure he is pursuing his own ends. I only fear that the Soviets will outsmart him."

"Well, let's look at it positively," Vladimir said with a smile. "After all, it's been seven years since the 1917 revolution, and surely not all Soviets today are as bad as the Bolsheviks during the Red Terror."

Nikolai clipped his pince-nez firmly on the bridge of his nose, then studied Vladimir with deliberate scrutiny.

"Are you telling me," he said slowly, "that you would prefer Soviet administration of the railroad to that of the Chinese?"

"I'm only saying that I don't trust the Chinese."

"We've had no trouble working for them these past few years."

Svetlana, who had quietly slipped into a chair between her mother and Raissa, now turned to her sister. "Why so quiet tonight, my dear?" she asked, trying to change the subject. Appalled as she had been by Vladimir's words, she suspected that he did not favor the Soviets as much as he hated everything connected with the Chinese. And of course, she knew the reason.

"I get tired of all these political discussions. They are so boring," Raissa said pouting. "Why don't we talk about something else?"

Sonya, obviously glad for the diversion, glanced at her wristwatch. "My goodness, it's late, we have to go home."

But Svetlana raised her hand. "Wait! I have something exciting to tell you all. I've been asked to sing at the Zhelsob at the next concert."

"My dear child, that's wonderful!" Sonya smiled and hugged her daughter. "We're so proud of you. Come over to the house tomorrow and tell us all the details. But right now we really must go."

As Nikolai and Sonya rose to leave, Raissa lingered behind. "You go ahead, I'll stay for a few more minutes," she said.

Svetlana saw her parents to the door, and when she reentered the dining room, Raissa and Vladimir were discussing the current plays performed at the drama theater in town.

". . . They're going to have a new production of

Turgenev's *A Nest of Gentlefolk,"* Raissa was saying. "I plan to go, for I've never seen it."

Svetlana noticed that Vladimir was all attention and was looking at Raissa with keen interest. *He's never this interested in anything I have to say,* she thought more with curiosity than resentment.

"I'd think they would stage Griboyedov's *Woe from Wit* or Fonvisin's *The Minor,"* Vladimir said. "Those are much more enjoyable, because they have a lighter touch."

Raissa shrugged. "Well, you didn't seem to object to the staging of Chekhov's *Cherry Orchard,* or *The Three Sisters."*

"That's exactly why I think a change of pace would be good."

Svetlana listened, watching her sister, surprised by her sudden maturity. At eighteen Raissa had developed into a voluptuous young woman with sparkling eyes and a ready smile, interested in the theater and frequenting student halls, where she was popular among young people of both sexes. Svetlana was pleased that her sister had strong family feelings, for she often stopped by to see them or to play with little Georgik, and Svetlana was grateful when Raissa's cheerful presence broke the monotony of a dull evening at home.

But tonight Svetlana turned impatiently to Vladimir. "Aren't you pleased with my exciting news?" she asked.

Vladimir looked at her disapprovingly. "I thought it was understood a long time ago, Svetlana, that you were never going to perform in a public place."

"But it's a concert at the Zhelsob! You and I met the night I sang there, remember?"

"That was different. It was a dance and you were asked informally to sing a couple of songs. No wife of mine is going to appear onstage like some professional singer or—or something."

"Surely you're not serious, Vladimir. I'm going to be one of several singers, and everyone knows that I don't need the money and that I'm only doing it for the love of art."

"Are you sure it's only for the love of art," Raissa said smoothly, "and not for accolades from your adoring public?"

Piqued by her sister's unexpected barb, Svetlana flared.

"And what's wrong about wanting to receive acknowledgment from the audience? It is more than I get at home."

Vladimir narrowed his eyes. "Seems to me you receive plenty of applause from your family and friends when you sing to us at parties."

"But I want broader exposure."

"Exactly. And the more applause you get, the more acknowledgment you will want, and from a wider audience."

"You're being unfair. I've studied long and hard and I have a voice to share with the public. Why should I be denied that?"

"You're not being denied that. You sing for us often and well, but unless you were a singer of prima donna quality, I don't see why you need be so ambitious."

"Are you saying that my voice isn't good enough to perform before a wider audience?"

"You're deliberately twisting my words, Svetlana. All I'm saying is that I don't want you to perform onstage, that's all."

Raissa rose, circled her hand slowly around Vladimir's neck, and kissed him lightly on the forehead. "I don't want to be involved in a family squabble. I'll be leaving now. Let me know if you and Svetlana want to go to the theater with me." She slipped her hand from his neck and lifted a strand of hair off his forehead, smoothing it back. Then a slow smile spread over her face. Her eyes twinkled. "I had no idea you were such a spirited man, dear brother-in-law. I like that. I think my sister needs to be reined in occasionally."

Svetlana was stunned. Whose side was her sister on? And as she looked at her, too surprised to speak, she watched her husband and Raissa exchange a quick smile and make a silent eye contact that was held for a second longer than necessary.

Why, Raissa was flirting with Vladimir! Hadn't she enough young men ringing her doorbell? She was popular among her peers. Why this? And to take sides with Vladimir against her own sister—that was disloyal. Svetlana nodded briefly to Raissa when she left the room, followed by Vladimir.

Certainly, she couldn't reproach Vladimir with her own sister's foolish behavior. She would only come through as a jealous wife striking back at him for forbidding her to appear in concert. But she was nevertheless disgusted by Raissa's flirtatious behavior.

The concert was scheduled for October. She would pursue the point and bring all her feminine wiles into play to win Vladimir's approval. Without it the thrill of the performance would be marred.

When Vladimir came back into the room, he motioned toward the door through which Raissa had left. "Your sister is interested in literature, and she likes the theater as a spectator and not as a performer. Why do you have to channel your interests into something so unbecoming to a respectable married woman?"

"I don't understand your reasoning at all, Vladimir. There's absolutely nothing wrong in my singing onstage, and I shall never understand your objections."

"Don't make me say things I'll regret later," he answered testily. "Since you don't seem to understand my feelings, then suffice it to say that I firmly oppose your ambition. You should turn to literature instead. We would have something to talk about then."

He turned and left the room. Their relationship wasn't improving the way she had planned. No matter how she tried, Vladimir continued to find fault with her.

To top it all now, he was even allowing his hatred of everything Chinese to influence him to take a favorable attitude toward the Soviets. Marshal Chang Tso-lin was shrewd, Vladimir had said. Well, perhaps he would be shrewd enough to have many of his men stationed in Harbin watching the Soviets when the joint management went into effect.

A gnawing started in her stomach. Whenever the Old Marshal's name was mentioned, another name echoed in her ears. Where was Li-chun? Had he ever realized his dream and joined Chang Tso-lin's army?

For a long while Svetlana sat at the table, toying with a spoon, unaware of the passage of time, until she heard Georgik fret in his nursery. Relieved to channel her attention away from her confusing thoughts, she rose and went to her child's room. She would sing to Georgik. A song always lifted her spirits, made her forget her worries. Besides, Georgik loved her singing.

Chapter Fourteen

Ever since general Dmitri Horvath, the retired officer of the
tsarist army and general manager of the Chinese Eastern Railway at the time of the Russian Revolution of 1917, had had
the courage to risk independent action by returning the railway to the Chinese government in order to prevent the extraterritorial rights from falling into Bolshevik hands, the Russian emigrés had enjoyed peaceful working conditions under
the Chinese. But Russia wanted her extraterritorial rights
back, and after negotiations with the Chinese government a
treaty was signed, and on October 3, 1924, the Sino-Soviet
management of the Chinese Eastern Railroad went into effect.

The agreement stipulated that this was to be a joint commercial venture. Apprehension, however, at what new regula-
tions the Soviets might introduce pervaded the Harbin offices,
filling the White Russian employees with dread. They couldn't
believe that the Soviets would limit their activities to com-
merce alone. "They have had their eye on Manchuria for a
long time," some said. "Give them a hand, and they'll bite the
whole arm off," others predicted. But what was there to do?
Harbin was the only place left in the world, they felt, that was
still like the old Russia they had known, and it was inconceiv-
able to panic prematurely and flee again. And where would
they go? Whatever the Soviets had up their sleeve, there

would be plenty of time to act later. After all, the government was still Chinese.

Two hundred and fifty miles south of Harbin, along the Japanese-controlled South Manchurian Railway, was the city of Mukden, Marshal Chang Tso-lin's headquarters. Today, an aura of tension hovered in his spacious office, where the Old Marshal stood waiting for his trusted aide. A slightly built, wiry man with delicate features and a benign smile that belied his shrewd and ambitious character, Chang Tso-lin looked younger than his fifty-one years. Beneath his soft-spoken and humorous personality lurked a ruthless and cruel streak and a disregard for human life that had earned him the nickname of the Manchurian Tiger.

Dressed in a long black silk gown and matching skullcap with a single large pearl, he stood in the middle of his huge reception hall, which was filled with black teak furniture. His glance traveled idly over two stuffed tigers, silk rugs, bronzes, scroll hangings, the jade and porcelain jars that decorated the room. He had come a long way from his humble peasant beginning, his family so poor that when he was ten years old and his father died in a friend's house, it was that friend who had paid for the funeral.

Cunning and astute, he had risen to the top, had achieved his autonomy, and it seemed to him now that he should be able to enjoy his position. In his private life he was blessed with a large family: five obedient wives, several concubines, children and grandchildren. But in the public sphere, he was not so lucky.

Somehow, his problems were never single. With the continuing threat from the other two warlords—the scholarly Wu Pei-fu, who now controlled Peking, and Feng Yu-hsiang, the "Christian General," who accepted support from the Soviets and controlled the area in the northwestern part of Manchuria —he had to be constantly on guard against treachery.

And of course there was always Chiang Kai-shek in the south.

Antagonism existed among his own men as well. He regretted the many rivalries that had developed in his army since he had reorganized it and embarked on a program to modernize the old techniques of administration and warfare. Of necessity he had accepted new men—for the most part graduates of the Japanese Military Academy—and soon there were two cliques, the "new" and the "old." Well, he had more confidence in the old group, men who had been with him throughout his rise to power. Never mind their so-called outmoded ways of thinking—he trusted them. In the new clique his elder son's friend, Kuo Sung-ling, was a case in point. There was nothing that he could definitely accuse him of, but his sixth sense told him not to trust the man.

Chang Tso-lin sighed. Maybe he was becoming too suspicious, too mistrustful of everybody. He pursed his lips. After all, he himself had been accused of collaborating with an alien force ever since he had been captured, and his life spared, by the Japanese during the Russo-Japanese war. Well, he had no alternative but to keep his relationship with the Japanese in delicate balance. It was an uneasy alliance. His regime in Mukden performed all the functions of an independent state, and Mukden flourished. He was proud of it. There were spinning mills, an arsenal, a mint, municipal light and telephone plants, all well run. Yet he was never allowed to forget that the Japanese holdings, which consisted of the leased Kwantung Territory in Manchuria, including Port Arthur and Dairen, also reached north to Mukden and even to Changchun. The area was administered by a governor, appointed by the Japanese, who controlled taxation and police as well as public utilities.

He chafed at having to cooperate with the Japanese. How satisfying it had been to have the Soviet representative, Nikolai Kuznetsov, agree to recognize his government as autonomous during the signing of the Mukden–Soviet agreement on September twentieth!

The problem now was that the Soviets would be sharing the railroad administrative offices in Harbin, while his headquarters was two hundred and fifty miles away in Mukden. He needed to have a qualified and trusted man in Harbin to keep an eye on the Russians. And he knew just the man for the job.

A rustling sound interrupted his thoughts. He turned around and nodded to the young man who had entered quietly and now stood respectfully before him. The Marshal tucked his hands in his sleeves and studied his aide for a few moments. He was tall, with thick dark hair and light skin, and though he was dressed in the gray uniform of the Fengtien army, his features readily betrayed a mixture of European blood. Yes, the Marshal decided, he would do very well.

"How long have you been with me, Ma Li-chun?"

"A little over two years."

The Marshal smiled. "And you've done well in so short a time."

"Under your tutelage the task of learning has been a great honor."

Yes, indeed, the Old Marshal thought, *I singled you out because you speak fluent Russian and I knew you would be useful to me.*

"You have learned fast," he said, "and I am well pleased. And now I have a new and important assignment for you. You are to go to Harbin, where I have arranged an administrative position for you in the Chinese Eastern Railway offices. I don't want this joint commercial venture to turn into a Soviet-dominated railway, or have them spread their political influence throughout the country."

A flutter of eyelids was the only sign of emotion from the younger man. Chang Tso-lin interpreted it as a pleased reaction.

"You will have to wear civilian clothes to draw as little attention to yourself as possible. I want you to keep your eyes and ears open and immediately report to me anything that sounds suspicious. Although I know it is not customary to mix with the Russians, don't isolate yourself from them. With the joint administration, you're bound to have opportunities to attend their social functions, and with your fluency in their language, it shouldn't be difficult. In particular keep an eye on their administrator, Ivanov."

Chang Tso-lin paused, his mouth twitching under his thick, drooping moustache. "Li-chun, we both come from modest backgrounds, and I admire your ambition. I've treated you well, even offered you one of my concubines—whom, surprisingly, you have refused. Perhaps now, in Harbin, a Russian girl will be more to your liking. Feel free to enjoy yourself."

Li-chun bowed low. "The primary purpose of this unworthy soldier will be to serve you, honorable Marshal, and I shall do my best to deserve your trust."

"You have already done that, and I have complete faith that you will not fail me. Go now, and get ready for your new assignment."

Li-chun had, indeed, done well in the two years since he had left his father's enclave in the taiga, and the passage of time had somewhat dulled the painful memories of his precipitous departure. It had been a traumatic experience that left him with regret and shame for having deceived his father; yet he was grateful for the ultimate outcome.

That night, after he had left Svetlana asleep in the glen, he had returned to the camp and the next morning reported her escape to Ma Fu-li. His father's rage was fearsome. He accused his son of incompetency, of failing in his duty to guard the captive.

While the rest of the men scattered through the forest looking for the fugitive, Li-chun, acting contrite and humble, meekly admitted his negligence and, taking advantage of his father's anger, begged to leave the camp and join Marshal Chang Tso-lin's army.

"I must prove worthy to be your son, Father. I have to atone for the loss of face. Please let me go."

His initial anger spent, Ma Fu-li studied his son in silence for a long time. Li-chun endured his scrutiny without flinching.

Had his father guessed the truth? He would never know, for without waiting to find out whether Svetlana would be found in the forest, Ma Fu-li ordered him to leave immediately, thus sparing him any punishment. His love for his son, then, had proved stronger than his sense of taiga justice, for Li-chun knew that it took tremendous courage to skirt the primitive law. He was deeply indebted to his father and felt badly for having secretly betrayed his trust. As he was readying himself to leave, Ma Fu-li said, "No one escapes from Ma Fu-li's camp without my revenge. If the girl is dead, the time will come when my wrath will fall upon the family."

His father's parting words pursued him all the way to Mukden. When Chang Tso-lin learned who Li-chun's father was, he questioned him at length about his background, nodding with satisfaction on hearing about the young man's education.

He took to Li-chun and gave him quarters nearby in the vast complex of his compound, assigning his chauffeur to teach him to drive a car. Li-chun applied himself diligently, and although it wasn't easy to master the Marshal's fleet of cars—Cadillacs, Pierce-Arrows, Packards—master them he did.

He was not paid a regular salary, but once a month the Marshal's treasurer came in and poured some gold coins at the foot of the k'ang where he slept on a tiger skin. Although Li-chun thought this method of payment unusual, he accepted it without question. Before long Chang Tso-lin had brought him into his office and made him his aide.

He treated Li-chun as his own son, but only once did he lower his guard and talk about his own youth, his humble beginnings in the village of Haich'eng in Fengtien Province, where he had lived as a boy. He never told him whether he had actually been a bandit himself, but he admitted that he missed his older brother, Chang Tso-fu, who had been executed as one. Li-chun listened politely but never told him of his real reasons for leaving his father and the taiga.

And then one night the Old Marshal sent him one of his concubines. It wasn't quite true that he had refused her. It would take him a long time to overcome his longing for Svetlana, but he knew that eventually he would have to lead the normal life of a young and virile man. Surely he couldn't remain celibate for the rest of his life, nurturing his body and soul on a past dream. Yet, when the concubine, her face white with powder, her lips painted bright carmine, entered his room, he was embarrassed and politely declined her services. The determined girl, however, did not take no for an answer. Trained to please a man, she had been ordered to accommodate the Marshal's new aide, and she knew how to accomplish it. Slowly, she approached him and proceeded to play on his senses, her movements calculated to entice and arouse, her hands and mouth touching him with an intimacy and audacity that at first shocked him, then rendered him helpless and willing to succumb to her sexual expertise.

Later, after his passion had been appeased, he stayed awake

a long time, fighting to dismiss from his mind the fiery longing for Svetlana—a longing well suppressed until then, suddenly revitalized by the sensuality of an experienced concubine.

And now, with his new position in Harbin, he was almost certain he would see Svetlana again. How could it be otherwise? She was the daughter of a railway company employee, and her husband, if she had indeed married him, was an engineer with the same company. But to refuse the assignment would show a weakness of character, and what possible explanation could he give to the Marshal? Chang Tso-lin's approval had always been of paramount importance, and he would not jeopardize his trust.

The Marshal had become his father-figure, for communications with his own father had grown brief and rare. Neither wished to compromise the other's position. But from the few words that were passed on to Li-chun, he knew that although Ma Fu-li was basically proud of him, he had never forgotten the loss of face he had suffered when Svetlana escaped from his camp without the ransom having been paid. One day Ma Fu-li intended to avenge himself on the Ozerovs. All Li-chun could hope was that Svetlana and her family would never return to Maoershan; though the *hunhuzy* vengeance sometimes reached its hand into Harbin proper, he doubted that Ma Fu-li would risk that.

The next day after he received his new orders, Li-chun purchased his first European clothes: a dark-brown suit with a tie to match, and a white shirt. He was surprised to see how European clothes made him look more Russian than Chinese. For a long time he had suspected that his mother must have been more Russian than Buryat; now he was more sure than ever.

After getting his final instructions from Chang Tso-lin, he left for Harbin, his excitement growing as the train passed Changchun and sped through the flatlands toward the city he had dreamed of for so long. When the locomotive pulled into the Harbin station and came to a stop, Li-chun couldn't wait to get off. He carried his bag into the station building and was amazed to find a Russian Orthodox shrine with an icon of St. Nicholas in one corner of the large waiting room. Once outside, he saw only Russian droshky drivers and heard more

Russian speech than Chinese. Atop a hill in the distance a Russian wooden cathedral dominated the skyline. Long-forgotten feelings of nostalgia for the village where he had lived as a boy surfaced in him. He was overcome.

He took a droshky to the address given him in the Chinese Foudzyadyan section of town, but he found it to be a slum area. After spending the night in the Grand Hotel near the railway station, he was directed to the five-story apartment house on the corner of Strelkovaya and Pochtovaya Streets in Novy Gorod section of town, and there he rented a small flat. He was glad to discover that it was not far from the railway company offices, only about seven blocks away. The next day he reported to his Chinese superior.

His duty was to check the cash flow from commercial transportation. The work was simple to learn, as Chang Tso-lin had seen to it that Li-chun had had training in basic bookkeeping. Spying on the Russians was not a job he relished, and he hoped there would be nothing going on to justify the Old Marshal's suspicions. Unfortunately, ever since the Russo-Japanese war of 1904 Chang Tso-lin had nurtured a constant suspicion of the Russians, both White and Red. Although the Russian side of the railway company was now entirely under Soviet control, there were many White Russian employees, and certainly the majority of Russian residents in Harbin were Whites.

At night, in the privacy of his bedroom, Li-chun wondered what had happened to Svetlana, where she lived and if indeed she had married. He hoped so, for if she were single, the temptation to see her would be strong. What was she like now? Did she still look like an angel with that haunting, vulnerable face that had taken his breath away? Did she ever think of him?

Why torture himself with these thoughts? He would not ask about her, he would not try to find out where she lived. But . . . what if he met her at a social gathering, at a concert perhaps, or in someone's home? He had no answer. It would be best if he didn't meet her at all.

If he did see her again, he would keep his emotions under control, he would not give himself away. But what about her? Whatever her feelings for him now—and she might well be ashamed of that interlude in the glen—she would be unprepared for the encounter and might betray herself on seeing him.

She must have matured, must be more beautiful than ever. Now that he was so close, he longed to see her; and although he knew he must not, he wished he could, if only for a brief moment. What would she say? What would he say?

And so he dreamed and fantasized.

Chapter Fifteen

For the first time since their marriage Svetlana defied Vladimir's wishes. After all, she was not starting a professional career but had merely responded to an invitation to appear in a concert at the Zhelsob club. Sponsored by the railway company with a dinner party to follow, it could hardly be termed a professional appearance, so what was wrong with her accepting the invitation? Vladimir was becoming rigid and uncompromising, and she had to do something about it, or her marriage would become unbearable.

She chose two arias—the tender one from the first act of Verdi's *La Traviata,* in which Violetta learns the meaning of true love, and the letter-writing scene from Tchaikovsky's *Eugene Onegin.* Before her solo numbers, however, she was to sing a duet with Kyril Volin. After some discussion they settled on the one they had sung so well together in practice—the impassioned love duet from the first act of *Madama Butterfly.*

Although she knew the music well, she practiced hour after hour at home, perfecting her phrasing and nuances.

The concert was scheduled for the end of October, and as the time drew near, Svetlana decided to spend several additional hours at the music school at night; there she had the added help of her teacher, who would devote extra time to her after regular classes.

Convinced at last that Svetlana was determined to go

through with the concert, Vladimir acquiesced with reluctance and showed his disapproval in moody silence. When she began to go out at night, he questioned the necessity for so much practice, but after she had explained why, he shrugged and said, "Suit yourself, but after this concert is over, I want to be sure you don't accept any professional engagements."

One night, as she was about to leave, Raissa came by for a visit. Svetlana looked at her pensively. Her little sister had certainly grown up. Having finished gymnasium this year, she had started at the Polytechnic Institute, studying physics and chemistry. When Svetlana had asked her why she'd chosen the sciences, Raissa shrugged and answered flippantly: "Oh, I don't know! Maybe eventually I'll become a pharmacist." Then she had run her finger over the scar on her jaw and added a little too casually, "I *have* to do something more practical than singing, for I don't have a pretty face to show off onstage."

Svetlana flushed at the none-too-subtle reference to the accident on the skating rink. Somehow, Raissa always managed to remind her that the scar on her face was Svetlana's fault.

At eighteen Raissa was conscious of changing styles, wore skirts that had risen to midcalf, and had cut her hair short in a bob.

"Why don't you cut your hair, Svetlana?" she had asked her sister shortly after this style became popular. "You look so old fashioned with your long hair!"

But Svetlana didn't want to change. Aware of her classical features, she knew that her long hair would survive the current fad and give her a distinct style of her own.

With the passing of time Svetlana had begun to find little in common with her younger sister, and now, as she watched her bright smile, she wished she had her lighthearted approach to life. She kissed Raissa and waved in the direction of the dining room, where Vladimir was reading the paper, then left for the music school.

Raissa hung her autumn coat on the hall tree and looked at herself in the mirror there. The more her mother tried to reassure her that the scar was barely noticeable, the greater was Raissa's conviction that she was disfigured. Her glance traveled to the rigid keloid outlining her jaw and giving her face an asymmetrical shape. Reason told her that Svetlana felt badly about the accident, but subconscious resentment grew against her older sister, who seemed to have everything she lacked. She pushed her hair off her forehead and went to the dining room.

Vladimir looked up and smiled. Her heart pounded. It was always the same. Each time she saw him, her body reacted to her hidden emotions. Only recently had she finally admitted to herself that she was desperately, hopelessly, in love with her sister's husband. And *had* been ever since she had met him. If only she had been a few years older when they met, she instead of Svetlana would have won him and married him. Her sister had never shown affection or warmth toward Vladimir. She was cold and didn't appreciate him. Well, one of these days . . .

Raissa didn't finish her thought, for Vladimir put down his paper and rose.

"What a pleasant surprise!" he said, taking her hand in his and looking into her eyes. Raissa's bobbed hair bounced in careful disarray, and as he continued to look at her, her eyes sparkled with mischief. Vladimir's smile broadened. This girl had a carefree air about her that infected those with whom she came in contact, creating an atmosphere of gaiety and informality that was so lacking in Svetlana. But more than that she had an uncanny way of making him feel important.

He offered her a chair, thinking that the straight shift dress of pale-green wool—one that could make other women look shapeless—on her evoked a suggestion of hidden sensuality. He sat down beside her and forced himself to look back at the newspaper.

"Where's my sister going?" Raissa asked gaily, pouring herself a cup of tea from the silver samovar on the dining table.

"She's practicing at the music school every night now before the concert. I'll be glad when that's over."

Raissa threw him a sidelong glance. "You don't approve of her singing, do you?"

Vladimir bristled. "That's not exactly the right way to put it. I don't disapprove of her *singing*. But I do disapprove strongly of her aiming toward a professional career."

"Why do you object?"

"Because I find it improper for a woman of our social standing to be singing onstage and earning money when it isn't necessary. I provide for her more than adequately."

"That's not the point, Vladik."

Vladimir looked up sharply at the endearing name she had used, and he found Raissa smiling. "Money doesn't come into it. As long as I can remember, Svetlana has wanted to sing professionally. Don't you see, that's the ultimate recognition."

Vladimir frowned. "I certainly didn't realize she was so determined to sing onstage. I wish I had known it earlier."

"And if you had, what would you have done? Refused to marry her?"

Audacious girl, to ask that; yet somehow, he didn't hold it against her.

"I don't know, I probably would have given her an ultimatum," he said vaguely.

Raissa placed her hand on his. The touch was gentle and warm.

"I like you very much, Vladik," she said softly.

The temperature in the room had suddenly turned warm. Vladimir looked at the grandfather clock as it struck eight, and busily he pulled the chain from his waistcoat to check his watch. "You remember my friend Igor Sotin? He was best man at my wedding. He's coming over tonight for a game of cards. Would you like to join us?"

Raissa pulled her hand away, gulped the last of her tea, and rose. "No. Cards bore me. I'll be running along home to study. I may drop in tomorrow."

"Svetlana will be out again. She said she'd be gone every night before the blasted concert."

Raissa shrugged. "So what? I'll come to see *you* instead. We have much in common, you and I." With a quick movement she bent over and kissed him lightly on the forehead. "See you!"

The next evening Raissa came wearing a cocoa-colored dress of crepe de chine with a deeply cut neckline, and on each subsequent night she appeared in a different outfit. Toward the end of the week Vladimir came to anticipate her visits, and no longer objected to Svetlana's absences. In fact, he was eager for her to leave.

One night, after Vladimir had hung Raissa's coat on the hall tree she said, "I forgot to ask you, how was your game with Igor Sotin the other night?"

"Fine. We played until Svetlana came home. I won. Igor's mind was miles away. By the way, he saw you leave the house."

"So? Is there anything wrong with him seeing your wife's sister come for a visit?"

"No, but he's aware that Svetlana is not home these evenings."

"Oh, Vladimir, stop being such a prude. Your house is full of people—the servants in their quarters, and Georgik with his nurse in the nursery. What harm is there in my coming by? Besides, I enjoy your company more than that of all the students at the Polytechnic Institute put together. They are such bores. All they talk about are their current assignments and sports."

"It's still improper for you to be here while Svetlana is not at home, Raissa. The servants have their quarters in a separate part of the house, and once their chores are done for the evening, they never come back in. As for the nurse, she retires early and we don't see her until the next morning. For all intents and purposes we are alone in the house, and Igor knows it."

"Are you afraid of me, then?"

"You're the most exasperating girl I know. I'm not afraid of you, but I don't want tongues to wag."

"And what if they do? It will only add spice to our lives."

"You can't mean it."

"Try me!"

Raissa leaned over Vladimir, rubbed her cheek against his, wrapped her arm around his neck, and then slid her soft, full lips over his mouth. When she finally pulled away, she whispered, "I'm in love with you, Vladik. Have been for a long time."

Before Vladimir could collect himself, she had tightened her grip around his neck and kissed him again, this time with a probing, searching kiss.

Svetlana had never kissed him like this, had never shown such ardor. To be the object of desire for this young girl was a heady feeling, and doing something forbidden added to the exciting sensation. Why not? Sure, it was wrong—she was his wife's sister—but, hell, Svetlana had wronged him, had come to him after already having been used by another man—and a Chinese at that; he shivered a little at the thought. He could not forget that she had deprived him of the joy of that first, special initiation.

As for Raissa, he had not started this, and as long as she was in love with him and seemed willing—no, eager—for his response . . . yes, why not?

He pulled her down on his lap and kissed her hard on the mouth. She responded passionately and Vladimir knew he was lost.

He took her into the bedroom and locked the door. And what if Svetlana came home early? His pulse quickened. Let her! Let her discover what it was like to be wronged. The thought taunted, titillated. He almost wished she would come home early. Guilty herself, she wouldn't dare to create a scandal.

Feverishly, he watched as Raissa stripped to her garter belt and her bra and then stretched kittenishly on the bed. For a moment Vladimir stood over her, mesmerized. She was voluptuous, even plump. Not at all slender like Svetlana, whose ribs he could feel under his fingers. Unable to contain himself, he pulled the straps of her bra down and with a quick movement tore it off, releasing her entire body to his hungry eyes.

The sight intoxicated him, sent his pulse racing, and he reached for her with impatient hands. He had never experienced such acute passion as he felt now for this girl, who was pressing her body tightly against his; he had never felt such desire, never realized how pleasurable it was to caress the soft, soft flesh, to bury his face in its warmth, and to enjoy her reaction to his fondling.

Where Svetlana had always been silent during their lovemaking, Raissa murmured endearments in his ear, responded to each new caress with tiny gasping moans. It was too much for a man. He was only human.

"I so wanted you to be the first, Vladik. Only you!" Raissa whispered, looking up at him with eyes clouded with passion. Vladimir, aroused to an unbearable pitch in his lust for this sensuous yet virginal girl, gave in to the wild pleasure of experiencing at last what he thought had been denied him forever.

As the day of her performance approached, Svetlana's excitement grew. Aware that at a concert she wouldn't have the staging props of an opera, she planned her attire carefully, grateful for Vladimir's unfailing generosity. Whatever his motives, he wanted her to wear expensive and stylish clothes. At Churin's department store she had found the latest imports from Paris and selected an elegant blue silk dress by Worth. Sleeveless, with thin shoulder straps, it hung straight to the hip, then flared into handkerchief points that swirled gracefully around her midcalf. A single choker of pearls with matching teardrop earrings completed her outfit. She decided not to braid her hair but, parting it in the middle, pulled it back off her face and twisted it into a figure-eight chignon at the nape of her neck. The mirror told her that she was stunningly beautiful, and she longed for a compliment, or at least an approving look, from Vladimir, but none came. His glance swept over her from head to foot, and without comment he helped her with her beaver coat.

Once backstage, however, she forgot her disappointment and was swept into the excitement of the coming performance. Her parents appeared to give her encouragement, Sonya looking much younger than her forty-three years with a sleek, marceled hairdo and a shingled neckline, and a pleated black dress that minimized her plump figure.

"We're so proud of you!" she said, kissing Svetlana on the cheek. Nikolai patted her on the shoulder and then ushered his wife back into the auditorium. *Tactful, sensitive Papa,* Svetlana thought. *He knows I need to be alone right now.* Then, peeking through the heavy curtain, she looked at the orchestra seats. Raissa and Vladimir were already seated as Sonya and Nikolai joined them in the third row of the huge concert hall. Svetlana was sorry that Vladimir's parents were not there, but Arseny was sick with a bad cold and Vera never went to any performances without him.

The horseshoe balcony was filled with both Russian and Chinese spectators, and it seemed impossible to Svetlana that this hall, large enough to accommodate over a thousand people, should be full tonight. All white with sculpted çeiling and sparkling chandeliers, it was offset by a blue curtain with the railway company's emblem embroidered in gold. The festive atmosphere palpitated in the air, and Svetlana felt the excitement rising within her.

"Nervous?"

Svetlana started and turned around to face a smiling Kyril Volin, handsome in his tuxedo, his dark eyes sparkling with humor.

Svetlana laughed self-consciously: "A little—aren't you?"

Kyril shrugged and patted her hand. "I'd worry if we *weren't* nervous. Remember, a healthy amount of tension is good for the performer."

She looked at him gratefully, glad that they were to sing the duet first, before their solos.

It was a glorious experience. Unsure at first, her voice soon soared during the duet, and by the time she had finished her own aria from *La Traviata,* she knew she had won the audience.

She had left Tatiana's letter-writing aria for the last, and as she started to sing, the vast hall and the people in their seats gradually faded away. Magically, she became Pushkin's Tatiana, in love with Eugene Onegin and writing him a confession of her love. With the first famous words:

> *I'm writing you,*
> *What more can I say?*
> *I know it is now in your power*
> *To punish me with your disdain,*

she had lost herself.

In all her singing performances she had never been so emotionally involved with a song as she was at that moment, pouring out her hidden love publicly, still unaware how closely she had merged herself with Pushkin's heroine, until she could no longer distinguish between her own and Tatiana's hopeless love.

When she finally came to the last note, it took her a few moments to return to the present. There was a momentary hush, and then the audience was on its feet, giving her a standing ovation with repeated shouts of "Bravo!" and *"Bis!"* for an encore.

In a daze she had to force herself to acknowledge everyone gathered around her: beaming parents, who hugged her, Raissa, who gave her a peck on the cheek, and even Vladimir, who kissed her hand and smiled with satisfaction at their friends crowding around them.

Then, through the fog of euphoria, Svetlana saw Igor Sotin tap Vladimir on the shoulder, saw him speaking to him briefly and then turning away.

"You were terrific, Svetlana. I'm so proud of you!"

Kyril Volin's voice made her turn around. She smiled. "Thank you, Kyril. You know how I value your opinion, and besides, a compliment from such a magnificent tenor as yourself is very flattering."

"Well, then, our admiration is mutual. Aha! Here comes our teacher. Let's see what *she* says."

Madame Teshina, a large woman of undetermined age, pushed her hefty bulk through the crowd and hugged Svetlana. "I have nothing but praise, my dear," she said, and then winked at Kyril. "You did a fine job, too, but I'm afraid the evening belongs to Svetlana."

Kyril bowed gallantly. "I agree completely, for I'm an ardent admirer of Svetlana. It was a privilege to sing with her."

Madame Teshina patted Svetlana on the arm. "You have a great future ahead of you, my dear."

"The credit goes to you, Madame Teshina," Svetlana said modestly, happiness rising within her.

Someone grasped her arm from behind. "My dear," Vladimir said, "Igor has brought over one of our Chinese colleagues who wishes to meet you and pay his respects."

Svetlana turned around and smiled at a rotund Chinese official dressed in a dark-blue suit.

"May I present Mr. Liu Tsu-min of the Chinese Eastern Railway," Igor said, and Svetlana inclined her head.

"How do you do, Mr. Liu," she said pleasantly.

"Unfortunately, Mr. Liu does not speak Russian, but he brought his associate to interpret for him." Igor nodded toward a much taller man who moved forward from behind Mr. Liu.

"May I present Mr. Ma Li-chun."

The ceiling above her tilted, floated in a circular motion. She could feel the blood drain from her face, and she knew if she closed her eyes, she would faint. With supreme effort she forced her gaze to meet Li-chun's, and for an infinitesimal moment she was back in the forest glen. The smell of the dew-washed grass, the pine-scented air, the fragrance of his skin . . . she sensed them all again, acutely, vividly, with stabbing pain and a dreadful revelation that nothing had changed within her since that fateful night.

Had Vladimir noticed anything? He must not see her confusion, must not suspect. Abruptly, she lowered her gaze and gave Li-chun her hand. He bent over and kissed it lightly. *He's following our Russian customs, why?* she thought, weak from the touch of his lips.

Dressed in a brown suit of European cut, he was well groomed and looked less Chinese than ever before. He looked more mature than he had two years ago in the taiga, but as he spoke, his voice had the same lilting quality she remembered.

"Mr. Liu wishes to convey his felicitations to you on your successful performance, and to tell you that he enjoyed the arias you sang tonight."

"Please tell Mr. Liu that I am flattered." Her voice was barely audible as dizziness overcame her. People crowded around her; voices blurred and grew into a steady hum. *Please, dear Lord, don't let me faint,* she prayed, looking about her for her father and not seeing him in the milling crowd.

Nikolai, who had moved away to talk to his friends, was threading his way toward his daughter when he saw the two Chinese men. He had seen the rotund Chinese official before, but it was the tall young man next to him who attracted his attention. Something about the set of his broad shoulders and the way he turned his head to listen to those around him triggered a forgotten memory that disappeared before he could identify it. Why did he look familiar? The thought tugged at Nikolai's brain for a second as he came near enough to hear the introductions.

Ma Li-chun. He had heard the name. Quickly, he looked at Svetlana. If moments before he hadn't been sure who Li-chun was, his daughter's face now told him everything he needed to know. He was stunned. He had had no idea how deep her involvement with the bandit had been. Strange, that he thought Li-chun familiar before he knew who he was, as if he had seen him before. Well, Svetlana had once described him in detail.

His heart turned over. He must take her away before Vladimir noticed anything. He approached her from behind and slipped a supporting arm around her waist.

"Will Mr. Liu and Mr. Ma please excuse me if I take my daughter into the restaurant? She hasn't eaten since before the concert, and I suspect she must feel faint by now from all the excitement." Nikolai turned to Vladimir. "You won't mind, will you, if I steal your wife for a few minutes and have her to myself?"

Vladimir bowed silently and turned to the two Chinese men with a polite smile as Nikolai led Svetlana toward the door.

Li-chun watched them walk away, barely able to concentrate on what Mr. Liu Tsu-min wanted him to translate to Svetlana's husband. . . . *This was the lucky man who possessed Svetlana.*

Before the concert, when he and Liu Tsu-min had settled into their seats and opened their programs, Svetlana Panova's name had leaped out at him. Could there be two Svetlanas in Harbin, each with a soprano voice? It was not a common name. He was sure it was she, and when her number came, he thought he was prepared. But as she walked onstage with Kyril Volin, she took his breath away. No longer the young girl he remembered, she was a stunning, sophisticated woman, more beautiful than ever.

And married.

After his arrival in Harbin, he had discovered that a few Chinese businessmen were married to Russian women, but those marriages were exceptions to the rule, and he knew it would be difficult to win her family's approval even if Svetlana herself still loved him.

This way he was safe from temptation. The mind was glad, but, oh, the heart could not be tamed. It raced and mocked his common sense and rationalizations. He would not speak to her, would not seek her out in the crowd. But he had forgotten that he was not alone, that Liu Tsu-min would want to meet the beautiful singer and pay his respects. And as they worked their way toward her through the crowd, he caught a glimpse of the nape of her neck, saw the same downy wisps of blond hair below her chignon—the lovely hair that he had kissed that night in the glen—and he remembered achingly its softness, the warmth of her skin, the perfume of her mouth.

What was he thinking? She belonged to another man now and was probably ashamed of her youthful indiscretion.

And then the introductions, her hand, those same gray eyes, but now so full of shock and pain. . . . His heart stood still. Those large, lovely eyes—they told him all he wished to know.

At the buffet Svetlana accepted a sandwich from her father with shaking hands. Nikolai patted her hand. "Take it easy, my dear child. No one noticed anything, I'm sure."

Svetlana stared at her father with wide-open eyes, afraid to blink and spill the gathering tears. How had he guessed? Was her shock that obvious? Had Vladimir . . . ? And as she continued to stare, her chin starting to quiver, Nikolai nodded as if in answer to her mute question.

"Ma Li-chun. I think I'm the only one to whom you mentioned his name, or at least I'm the only one who still remembers it."

Nikolai paused, then went on: "He's not all Chinese, is he?"

Svetlana was reluctant to talk about him now. "No," she whispered with an effort, "his mother was part Buryat and part Russian."

"Your secret is safe with me, Svetlana," Nikolai said softly. "I'm not going to ask any more questions. My dear, you need nourishment, and—and strength. Whatever past ghosts may haunt you, keep reminding yourself that you're now a wife and mother. It may help. Now eat, for after a while we *must* rejoin them."

Before Svetlana had finished eating, however, Sonya, Igor Sotin with Mr. Liu and Li-chun, and Vladimir with Raissa on his arm, all came into the restaurant.

"I'm going to the powder room, Papa," Svetlana said quickly, and moved away from the buffet.

She had to be alone for a few minutes, to collect herself, put on a mask of reserve, act the contented married woman she knew now she could never be. After she had powdered her face and repaired the smudges left by the unwanted tears that had spilled over, she crossed the vestibule connecting the restaurant to the concert hall and went to the other side of the building, losing herself among strangers, relieved to be away from her friends and family.

Now that they had met again, all her unanswered questions surfaced. What had happened to him after she had left the taiga? Why was he in Harbin? How long would he be here? Surely they could meet somewhere just once and talk about these things. What could be wrong in wanting to know about his life during the past two years? After all, he had saved her from a dreadful experience, and it was only natural for her to be interested in her benefactor. Her interest had nothing to do with her avowals of loyalty to Vladimir; she would continue to remain loyal to her husband. She couldn't, she wouldn't, betray him twice, but . . . she *had* to talk to Li-chun.

She paused in front of a window, turning her back to the bright lights and the people, trying to lose herself in the darkness outside, but instead, she saw the sparkling chandeliers, the strolling guests, and her own reflection in the glass. She—the new, successful singer, the sensation of tonight's performance, standing here alone, an agonized, tormented figure. And then, as she continued to look into the window, there appeared Li-chun's reflection as he came and stood watching her in silence.

Without turning she spoke. "Oh, why, why, did you come here? Didn't you know that sooner or later we would meet?"

"I'm under Marshal Chang Tso-lin's orders to work for the railway company. I couldn't refuse."

She turned around and gave him a tiny smile. "So your secret wish came true. I'm glad for you."

He didn't answer, only looked at her, his eyes intent and shining. An awkward silence grew between them. The air was charged with humming sounds, dissolving voices, bridging thoughts. She ached to touch him, dared not.

He reached toward her arm, paused in midair, then changed his mind, withdrew.

"My dear!" His voice was low and caressing, like the gentle wind in the taiga. "My dearest one, what now?"

"I don't know. We have to talk, I have to tell you—things . . . but where? Not here, in front of everyone."

"I live alone in a flat on Pochtovaya and Strelkovaya. Here's the address." He put a crumpled piece of paper in her hand, then turned abruptly, as if afraid she would refuse it, and vanished in the crowd.

Chapter Sixteen

Svetlana had no trouble finding Li-chun's flat, for it was in a well-known apartment building. He opened the door almost immediately and without a word stood aside to let her in. She didn't offer to shake hands; it would be unbearable to touch him.

Hesitantly, she walked into the living room, which was as unadorned and without identity as most furnished rooms, and a thought crossed her mind that he had lived too long in the forest, and that someone should help him personalize this place. On the small table by the sofa he had placed a pot of tea and a dish of mint cookies.

He took her coat and gloves from her, and she stood uncertainly before him, for some reason feeling exposed, though her gray wool dress was demure enough, with a high neckline, only a long strand of pearls relieving its simplicity. The roomy folds of her autumn coat had given her security, but in this elegant dress there seemed no place for her to hide. Why on earth should she feel that way? After all, he couldn't possibly read her thoughts or hear her wildly beating heart.

He seemed afraid to talk, but silently motioned her to the sofa. She sat awkwardly on the edge, her body tense, ready to leap at the first sign of danger. What danger? She had rehearsed a dozen times what she would ask him, how she would behave, how soon she would leave.

190

"A cup of tea?" he asked finally, avoiding her eyes.

"Yes, please," she said.

"Two sugars?"

"Yes, thank you."

"Lemon?"

She nodded. *He remembers how I like my tea. He's telling me he hasn't forgotten that he couldn't provide any lemon for me in the taiga.*

He pushed the plate of cookies toward her. "I bought these at Mars's—I was told they were good."

"Yes, Mars is the best place in town for sweets."

She took the cookie without moving her elbow away from her body. She was trembling so!

After taking a bite she said, "These are delicious. Won't you have one too?"

He poured himself a glass of tea—she noted that he was using a Russian glass-holder—and bit into the cookie.

"Yes, they *are* good," he said.

We're walking a tightrope. I came to ask him about his life, and here we are using inanities to pass the time.

She drank her tea, put down the cup, and clasped her hands tightly on her knees.

"I told Vladimir I was going shopping, so I must be home in time for supper," she said, glancing at the round clock ticking loudly on the sideboard. It was only three o'clock. How stupid to have said that. Surely it wouldn't take four hours to find out about his life. She glanced at him, blushing.

Li-chun nodded solemnly. "I understand."

If only he would take the initiative in the conversation and tell her what had happened to him after she left the taiga, it would be so much easier. But Li-chun said nothing and waited for her to begin.

"I came because—I mean, I want so much to know what happened to you after—after—" Terrified, she didn't know how to finish her sentence.

"After I returned to the camp," he finished, and she nodded gratefully, feeling her face grow hot again.

"I told my father that you had escaped and that I was to blame for my negligence. He sent the men into the forest immediately to look for you." He paused and smiled. "But of course I knew they wouldn't find you."

"Were you—were you punished?"

Li-chun shook his head. "No, I—"

"Oh, I'm so glad!" she interrupted, pressing her hands against her heart. "So, so glad! I was tortured by the thought that you'd be punished, and—and not knowing what the punishment would be . . ." she shuddered and let the sentence trail.

"I'm sorry you worried for nothing. You see, I knew that I couldn't escape punishment once the men returned empty handed, so I asked my father to let me leave and join Marshal Chang Tso-lin's army. I told him that I'd serve honorably in the army and make him proud of me."

"And he agreed?"

"Yes. Once he made his decision, he ordered me to leave immediately, and we both knew why. He wanted me gone when the men returned." Li-chun paused, then added, "I owe a lot to my father."

"But—but he couldn't have known that the men wouldn't find me!"

"My father has developed an instinct for such things. He is wise, and—and I think he suspected the truth."

Now his eyes shifted from his hands, came around, fastened on hers, and held.

"Not much escapes my father," he added softly.

"I worried so . . . I didn't even know if you were alive."

"And I thought you must have forgotten all about me or perhaps even felt ashamed of—of having known me."

Svetlana averted her eyes. "I felt responsible for your fate."

"I see. Well, you can rest easy now. But as far as you are concerned, my father is not going to forget his loss of face. I urge you never to go near Maoershan again."

Instantly, she shot a frightened look at him. "You mean he would kidnap me again?"

Li-chun shook his head. "I can't speak for my father, but why tempt fate? There are many other places to take a vacation."

She nodded. "I understand. And I'm grateful that you didn't suffer on my account."

"I suffered no punishment at all," he said, and then added softly, "at least not physically."

Svetlana looked away. As long as they talked about his activities, she felt safe. He wouldn't—he shouldn't—say anything about his feelings for her—what was in his heart. She mustn't hear it; she was afraid to hear it. So afraid! She was married now, had a child . . . he knew that. Maybe he didn't know about Georgik. Then she should tell him about her son; it would be easy to talk about her Georgik. . . .

"Did you know that I have a little boy?" she asked smiling, eager to tell him.

He nodded. "Yes, someone said at the concert that you had a year-old son. What's his name?"

"Georgy. We call him Georgik."

"Motherhood, especially of a son, is the highest achievement of happiness among Chinese women."

"It wouldn't have made any difference to me. I would have loved a little girl as well."

The tremor had eased, and she unclasped her hands, then lifted her cup. "May I have another cup, please?"

He filled it, added the two cubes of sugar and the slice of lemon, and handed it back to her.

"You live in a different world from mine," he said. "Girl babies are a burden among our peasants. Sometimes they're sold to a rich merchant, and sometimes—sometimes they are drowned at birth."

Svetlana nodded. "I know. I have heard. It's horrible! But you—you're no longer a bandit, are you? You must be happy in your new career. Tell me about it."

Li-chun shrugged. "There isn't much to tell. I was Marshal Chang Tso-lin's chauffeur, and after a while he made me his aide. Now he has sent me here to work with the railway and see that—that there are no problems."

"Do you like the Old Marshal?"

Li-chun nodded. "Very much. He's a great leader."

"Have you heard from your father?"

"Yes, but not often. It's best that no one knows where I come from. Here, I live alone and keep much to myself."

"It must be lonely. You should make friends among your Chinese associates and their families."

"Yes, they have been kind to me."

"Will you ever return to your life in the taiga?"

"No. I shall never go back there. I like my new life and the freedom it gives me to plan my own future."

"And what are your plans?"

Li-chun shrugged, then after a moment's silence said, "I was surprised to find a few of my associates married to Russian women."

She shifted uncomfortably in her seat. They were treading on dangerous ground. Why had he said that?

"I know," she said at length, not looking at him, "but it doesn't happen too often, and of course, mixed marriages do present difficulties."

"Prejudice dies hard, but if love is strong enough, the marriage can be the better for it."

Li-chun put down his cup and suddenly took her hand in his. She tried to pull away, but he held it gently but firmly.

"It's no use, Svetlana. We're both avoiding our problem and we should face it together. Hiding from the truth will only make it harder to deal with."

Svetlana looked down at her hand, still entrapped in his. "I don't know what you're talking about," she said softly.

"Oh, yes, you do. I could read it on your face the moment we met at the Zhelsob. As for me, I have never forgotten you. Lord knows, I tried. Actually, I almost convinced myself that I had gotten over you, and I believed it until I saw you walk onstage; and then I knew. . . ."

"You mustn't say these things to me, you know I'm married now. But—but even if I were free, there still wouldn't have been any future for us. I mean—"

Li-chun's eyes narrowed. "You mean because I am Chinese and you are Russian. Is that why?"

Svetlana flushed and pulled her hand away. "There are so many things . . . we come from such different backgrounds, our families . . . oh, why are we saying this to each other? It's so futile, so painful!"

"Yes, very painful, and because it is, we *must* talk about it."

"Please, don't!"

"You came here today. Why did you come?"

"I—I wanted to—to know what has happened to you in the

past two years. I *had* to find out if you had suffered on my account."

When he didn't answer, she cried desperately, "Don't you see?"

"Yes, I do, but not what you're telling me."

He was stripping her of her defenses, exposing the truth she refused to face. She rose quickly.

"I have to go now. I shouldn't have come here."

Li-chun rose too. "We must never see each other again."

She glanced at him quickly. "That's not possible. You're with the railway company now. We're bound to run into each other."

"I meant privately. Like this."

She lowered her gaze, picked up her purse and coat. "Good-bye, then, Li-chun." Her voice shook.

"Farewells are bitter," he said quietly, "so full of anguish and despair. Let's just say, until we meet again."

Without a word she gave him her hand, and he took it and held it tightly. "The image of your face—do you know that I see it in my sleep?"

She tried to move, to pull her hand away. That was all it took to ignite a smoldering fire, to explode a force too powerful for them to fight.

How was it that she suddenly found herself encircled in his arms? So unexpected was his reaction, she dropped her purse and coat and pressed her forehead against his cheek.

"Oh, Li-chun, Li-chun," she moaned, "why torture ourselves, why pretend it is so easy to say good-bye?"

"I am not pretending, Svetlana. *You* are. I thought I was strong and could let you leave with a civilized handshake. We're fooling ourselves. I can't let you go, can't bear the thought of seeing you again in public, exchanging banal phrases, regretting forever having this moment slip out of my grasp. How would I live with that? It would haunt me forever."

He buried his face in her neck, slipped his hand across the back of her head and up through her hair.

"Oh, my dearest, I love you!"

Svetlana put her hands against his chest, tried to push him away. "Li-chun—we mustn't—I can't—oh, please!"

But Li-chun pulled her back into his arms, found her lips, and silenced the words that she was duty bound to utter.

Two years. Two years of trying to forget him—of deceiving herself that she had—all that was now wiped out in one passionate, insistent kiss.

Vladimir! The name, not the image, of her husband crossed her mind fleetingly, guiltily, and then was drowned in the wonderful power of Li-chun's embrace. And as she responded to his kiss, hungrily pressing her mouth against his, drinking in his essence, she forgot her guilt and that other world that was her duty, and gave in to this man whom she loved tragically, beyond hope, beyond reason.

Later she would reason, but now Li-chun was her life and her world. She would give her all to him. This once. Just this once, without thought or regret, she would submit gladly, passionately, to his demands.

And what demands they were! His loving was a poem, a slow, deliciously slow, progression from a gentle coaxing of his hands upon her skin, his mouth upon her lips—firm and probing—to greater depths of urgency in his quest for union. Each tiny fraction of her being thrilled with finely tuned responses to his unhurried rise to passion.

Aware of his desire to please her, of his restraint in his own need, she touched him with her hands and lips and loved the feel of him. How different their lovemaking was now from what it had been that reckless night in the forest glen! This time it was deliberate and tender, an impulse to taste and savor, a chance to breathe his fragrance and hold it in to last a lifetime. The years had nurtured her desire, and now she knew that her fulfillment need not be a fleeting spark, but in its slow ascent would become acute and unforgettable.

"Li-chun, Li-chun!" she cried, and gave in to a body song of arms and legs and total pleasure. She pressed herself against his chest to feel the whole of him at once, to mold her memory of joining into a lasting joy. And when the moment came, that special moment of exquisite ecstasy, she fought to hold it in suspension, and lost it to a dreamy afterglow of passion.

For a while the silence hummed and sang.

But then, one by one, the minutes slipped away and stole the sated bliss. The dream dissolved into the clarity of reason.

Oh, how she resented the intrusion of her thoughts whispering cruelly to her that this was not to be again—that today was their final time, the only time to love like this!

And through it all the guilt returned and lingered.

His fingers moved like feathers at her neck. His eyes were watchful—his dark and tilted eyes. She turned away. Li-chun was now free of the *hunhuzy* stigma. And free to choose a wife with honor and respect. A chill swept through the room. She shivered. Was it the sober presence of reality that had come to claim its due?

"One final favor," he said. "Tell me that you love me!"

She stirred, tried to get up, but he held her tight.

"I love you," she said, her voice shaking.

Li-chun kissed her tenderly on the forehead. "Thank you," he whispered.

Desperately, fiercely, she clung to him again for a brief moment, then wrenched herself free. "But, oh, how I resent the fate that made me love you!" she cried. "It's such a tyrant and we are its pawns. You've come back into my life, Li-chun, and I feel weak and guilty. You shouldn't love me."

"Don't say that. True love is the one thing in life that is without blemish. Look inside yourself; look well, and see why I love you."

She clung to his words long after she had left him.

Chapter Seventeen

It had been snowing all afternoon, the first snowfall this year, and although it was only November fourth, it felt like deep winter. Vladimir squirmed inside his heavy winter coat. His sealskin hat had earflaps, but he was too proud to lower them and lifted his fur collar instead. Blast the wind! He sank his head into his shoulders, then dug his hands deep into the pockets. Dim in the dusk, the streetlights were barely visible through the snowflakes, and the overall grayness of the late afternoon only deepened his irritation.

He walked home slowly. There was no hurry. Svetlana had told him that she would be shopping late, and he had a lot to think about. Without consulting her, without telling his parents or Raissa, he had made a momentous decision. Now, right or wrong, there was no turning back.

After all these years he should have known better than to share his news with his parents this afternoon. What right had they to sit in judgment of his decisions, to be so righteous, so disapproving? You'd think he was still a teenager, incapable of making up his own mind.

His mother had been delighted to have him drop in on his way home from the office, and she'd given him an exuberant hug. Her fragrance of Guerlain's L'Heure Bleue was as strong as ever, and it submerged him in the nostalgia of his childhood.

Vera immediately ordered the maid to fix tea and bring out sweet bread with his favorite poppy-seed filling, then called his father out of his study.

"Papa has just come home from the office and will be glad to see you. You don't spoil us too often lately with your visits," she said, placing an empty glass in a silver holder in front of him.

Arseny Panov walked in smiling, his large frame now padded with excess flesh. He shook hands heartily with his son and sat down, a look of expectancy on his face. Vladimir looked at him attentively. Strange, that he hadn't noticed before how his father had aged during the past couple of years. There were deep furrows in his high forehead, and his brown beard had grayed considerably. His mother's plump face, on the other hand, was still smooth, and he suspected that the reason she kept her weight was to avoid wrinkles.

The tea served, his father spooned the raspberry jam into his glass, then asked: "To what do we owe this pleasant surprise, Vladimir?"

His mother put down her cup, folded her arms, and waited.

Vladimir bit into the bread and chewed it carefully to gain time, for he knew it wouldn't be easy to choose the right words for what he was about to say. The whole town had been buzzing with the news that the Soviet manager of the railroad, Ivanov, had made it clear that unless all Russian employees took out Soviet citizenship, they would lose their jobs. Vladimir was delighted. He welcomed the opportunity to relinquish the hateful status of an emigré without a country, to become a citizen of Russia. Never mind that the Chinese authorities had come forth with a counteroffer of Chinese citizenship. *He* chose to become a Soviet citizen.

But how to tell this to his parents now, to explain his desire to be under the protection of Mother Russia? He cleared his throat.

"I came to talk to you about the new ruling of the railway company," he said.

Arseny raised his brows in surprise. "What about it? Thank God for the Chinese authorities who came to the rescue. Now most of you who work for the railway company will be Chinese citizens."

Vera, who had been silent, now leaned forward slowly and looked at her son.

"Surely you've taken the Chinese citizenship, haven't you?"

"We all seem to forget that we are Russians, not Chinese, and should be loyal to our motherland," Vladimir answered.

Arseny looked at his son sharply. "Are you telling us that you've taken out Soviet citizenship?"

"Yes, I have."

Vera gasped and Arseny hit the table with his fist. "Are you out of your mind? The Bolsheviks have filled your brain with giblets and you've listened to them. I'm ashamed of you, Vladimir!"

"Oh, how could you?" Vera added angrily. "Have you forgotten that your father is a deacon at the church, and we are respected citizens here? Now you're going to shame us!"

"Citizens of what?" Vladimir asked heatedly, looking from one parent to the other. "Of a government that has been annihilated? You all live in the past. And you, Mama"—he pointed an accusing finger—"as long as I can remember, you've never been particularly enamored of the monarchy. What made you suddenly change your mind now?"

"We're not talking about the monarchy!" Vera cried. "We're talking about your swearing allegiance to the Bolsheviks!"

"And I am talking about your clinging to the fantasy that Tsar-Batyushka is going to rise like the phoenix from the ashes and save you all."

"I won't permit you to speak disrespectfully of our martyred tsar, Vladimir," Arseny said, his voice shaking with anger. "I would never be a subject of our country's communist government."

"And I think it is ludicrous to take out Chinese citizenship solely to keep our jobs on the railroad."

"I don't think it is ludicrous at all. As a matter of fact, I consider it a stroke of good luck."

"My affection lies with Russia, not with China," Vladimir replied doggedly.

"You've been antagonistic toward the Chinese ever since Svetlana's abduction," Vera said. "Is that what is influencing you? Surely you can't hold the deed of a certain criminal element against the whole country."

"That has nothing to do with my decision," Vladimir snapped.

He hadn't meant to raise his voice, hadn't intended to lose his composure. *Stubborn old people. They get set in their ways and nothing can change their outlook. Well, so be it.*

He looked at his watch. "I have to go home now. As for what I've done, you'll find that I'm not the only one who has decided on Soviet citizenship. My friend Igor Sotin has done the same. Don't forget that we live in Harbin, and we don't have to return to Russia."

"As a subject of the Soviet Union you will have to obey your government's orders," Arseny said, his voice flat and tinged with sadness.

"Oh, Papa, stop being such a pessimist. True, there were excesses during the Revolution, but tell me what country didn't have them? Take the French and their revolution—it will be the same with ours—things will smooth over and return to normal, if they haven't already. The Soviets I've met here are civilized people, and they're *Russian* first and foremost. I feel far greater affinity toward them than to the Chinese."

Arseny crossed himself several times. "Misguided and trusting young man! I shall pray and ask our priest to serve a *moleben* for you. Let's hope that you shall never regret your decision."

Vladimir threw up his hands in frustration and rose to leave.

Outside, he had taken a droshky, for he hadn't felt like walking home all the way from Modyagow, but the fresh snow made the roads slippery and the horse could not pull the droshky uphill. The coachman spread his hands. "Sorry, *barin,* I wasn't prepared for the snow and I haven't got my sleigh yet."

It took him forty-five minutes to reach Bolshoi Prospekt, and by then he was so cold, he didn't care how he looked, so he pulled the earflaps over his ears.

There was still Svetlana to be faced. He didn't think her reaction would be as strong as his parents' had been. Of late she seemed so preoccupied with her singing lessons and the care of little Georgik that their communication had been re-

duced to daily minutiae. He was glad, though, that she was a
conscientious mother. He couldn't stand it to be otherwise.
Georgik was his whole life now, his adored son. After a busy
day at the office it was his outlet to come home and romp on
the floor of his son's nursery. What other relaxation did he
have? He felt his face grow warm in spite of the biting wind.

Raissa.

Their love affair was a passionate one. Acutely conscious of
their betrayal of Svetlana, they met at the bachelor flat of Igor
Sotin, their trysts both poignant and titillating. There was nowhere else they could meet secretly, and in desperation he had
risked confiding in his friend. To his surprise Igor had chuckled.

"You're such a prude, Vladimir," he had said, his blue eyes
twinkling with mischief. "One would think you're committing
a serious crime. As a matter of fact I'm relieved to discover
that you're human after all. What's a little affair on the side,
eh?" He winked and slapped him on the back. "I'll be delighted to give you a second key, and all you have to do is tell
me when I should work late at the office."

Vladimir was both shocked and relieved by his friend's reaction and wondered what the seemingly broad-minded Igor
would have said had he known with whom Vladimir was
spending his stolen hours.

As for Raissa, she had cried in his arms several times, seeking consolation for what she was doing.

"I feel so ashamed when I think of Svetlana, but when I'm
with you, I forget all about my guilt. I'm helpless in your
arms. I love you, Vladimir. I think I've loved you longer than
Svetlana has."

He listened in silence, flattered by her avowal of love, vastly
gratified to have her devotion and to have been the first and
only man she had known. Though there was no future to their
relationship, and Raissa's love for him was surely futile, passion did not reason.

How satisfying it was to spend a few clandestine hours with
a woman whose body he enjoyed without being burdened by
love. He felt no guilt. Raissa gave him relief from his frustra-
tions. Why shouldn't he take it after what Svetlana had done
to him?

Svetlana. He still loved her with a bitter and angry love, though he didn't think he would ever forgive her for having given herself willingly to a Chinese bandit. If ever anyone found out about it . . . he shuddered at the thought, dreading the scandal, the shame of it all. But then, why dwell on such thoughts when the possibility of the truth coming to light was completely nil?

Right now he had to think how to break the news of his plan to adopt Soviet citizenship.

He turned the corner of Pekinskaya Street and in a few minutes was home.

Georgik's nanny, Agrafena, a middle-aged woman of such voluminous proportions that she waddled rather than walked, handed the child to him immediately. Plump and of cheerful disposition, the child wrapped his chubby arms around his father's neck and cooed. This was Vladimir's favorite time of the day, when he bounced Georgik on his knee and laughed with him. How wonderful it was to have a son, a boy whom he would raise to be proud of his heritage, proud to be a Russian.

Svetlana entered the parlor a few minutes later and stood watching them at the door; Vladimir was surprised to find that she had preceded him home. He took Georgik's hand and waved it at Svetlana. "Won't he make a wonderful Russian citizen?" he asked, not looking at his wife.

"Russian citizen?" Svetlana repeated, frowning.

"Yes."

"I don't understand, Vladimir. You know very well there is no such thing for us as Russian citizenship."

"Of course there is. What about Comrade Ivanov's announcement?"

"But the Chinese authorities made a counteroffer."

"Well, it seems foolish to accept that, since our heritage is Russian. What's the difference, Soviet or not, as long as we continue to live in China?"

He raised his head and looked at Svetlana.

She paled. "Are you telling me that you've decided to become a Soviet citizen?"

"I most certainly have, and I'm proud to be one."

He said it with an assurance he didn't feel, but the more he

spoke—without apology, as if it were the most logical solution
—the less, he hoped, Svetlana would argue.

"I can't believe you're serious, Vladimir."

"I would hardly joke about this."

"How could you decide this without first consulting me?
I'm your *wife,* and I have a right to know when you're considering such a drastic step."

"I don't see anything drastic about it. Had I refused the
citizenship and lost my job, then you would have had a right
to be upset."

"You could have taken the Chinese offer. I'm sure most of
the people we know have done just that."

"I could never be a loyal Chinese subject, and to take it
only to save my job would have been dishonest."

"And why *couldn't* you have been a loyal Chinese citizen?
This country has been kind to us."

"I don't want to continue this discussion. My decision is
final." He looked at her, then added, "I'm sorry you're upset."

"How do you think your parents will take this news?"

"They already know about it. I went to see them from the
office."

"And what did they say?"

Irritated, Vladimir shrugged and handed Georgik to
Svetlana. The child had suddenly become restless in his arms.

"What did your parents say?" Svetlana repeated.

"Well, you know how old fashioned they are and how they
cling to an extinct regime. I tell you, they live in the past. In
the meantime they're stateless, without a country, beholden to
an alien government that is giving them shelter, God only
knows for how long. I didn't expect them to approve of my
decision, but I had certainly hoped you would come around to
my way of thinking."

"I have a feeling, Vladimir, that you chose the Soviet citizenship only to avoid becoming a Chinese citizen, not because
you're so pro-Russian."

"That's not true!" Vladimir suddenly shouted. "How dare
you accuse me of this?"

"You needn't shout. And I have to tell you that I shall
never come around to your way of thinking. I'm ashamed of

your decision, and I'm glad I don't have to become a Soviet citizen too."

Hugging Georgik tightly in her arms, Svetlana turned and left the room.

In the ensuing weeks the two never broached the subject again. It would be futile to start another argument, Svetlana reasoned. What good would a quarrel do except widen the rift? And it was important for her not to do that, especially now, when she wanted so much to maintain a friendly relationship between them. All she could hope for was that Vladimir would never be ordered by the Soviet government to immigrate to Russia.

Inevitably her thoughts turned to Li-chun. So determined had she been to remain faithful to Vladimir—already once betrayed—that she had overestimated her power of resistance to Li-chun. Of small consolation was the certainty that *this* time Vladimir wouldn't find out about it. Keeping her own emotions in check was the hardest thing of all.

Memories of Li-chun haunted her. So tall, so noble in bearing, yet so gentle and understanding . . . She had succumbed easily after having convinced herself of her immunity to his love. But once in his arms, how was it possible to think rationally? Images of that one afternoon tantalized, tortured, her. How was it that those sweet moments had become such cruel memories? How was she to live with them?

Oh, the mortal despair, the cruelty of his absence—was this her destiny, then, to suffer from the past? She thought about it. No. She would find strength—she must—to put her conflict to use by channeling her energies elsewhere. She had done it before and she could do it again.

Winter came, dressing the city in white, gifting Harbin with turquoise skies and crisp, still air, sending the hushed wind to ruffle the sun-sparkled snowflakes that clothed the naked branches.

Skating on HOTKS rink, sledding on the river Sungari that hugged the downtown Pristan, revived Svetlana's spirits, especially since she and Vladimir were now able to take their Georgik with them.

But as March came around and the sun stepped up its warming rays, the snow melted and icicles hung from the eaves, the sidewalks started to dry from the slush, and Svetlana became restless again. At home she couldn't help noticing the flirtation between Vladimir and her sister. While she suspected that Vladimir did it to pique her, she felt sorry for Raissa—who must have been flattered by the attentions of an older man—yet hurt by her disloyalty.

Saddened, she took stock of her life. Georgik was her joy, but she also had something else: her voice. After years of training she wasn't about to give up singing. But how far should she pursue it, aware as she was that any ambition would be against Vladimir's wishes? Did she really want to make it a full-time career? She had to admit, the idea no longer appealed to her. So, after some soul searching, she decided to accept all the invitations to sing that she liked, without signing any contracts for long-term commitments. As for Li-chun, either fate had helped her out, or he had made a point of avoiding her, for she had not seen him at any of the social functions since her October performance.

In June she took Georgik to Dzhalantun for the summer, vowing never again to return to the eastern side of Harbin, where memories were bittersweet. The child brightened her days. At almost two years old he had been forming short sentences for some time now, referring to himself in the third person and carrying on a one-way nonstop conversation with himself. Most of the time it began with: "Georgik wants . . ." and Svetlana had to exercise all her willpower not to give in to the little rascal, especially when, on seeing any small package, he would take hold of it, nod his blond head, and ask with pleading eyes, "Georgik's present?"

When she returned to Harbin in September, rested and tanned, she continued to sing, grateful that Vladimir no longer said anything at all about it and seemed more and more preoccupied with his work.

In December of 1925 she heard about the revolt within Marshal Chang Tso-lin's army, organized by one of his trusted men, General Kuo Sung-ling, a friend of his own son. It was said that Kuo had demanded Chang Tso-lin's retirement in favor of his son, but because Kuo had aligned himself with General Feng Yu-hsiang, who was sponsored by the Russians, the Japanese came to Chang Tso-lin's aid and the revolt was crushed. One day Svetlana's Chinese cook, a slender, self-effacing young man, told them in an awed voice that government proclamations had been posted throughout the country promising an award of eight hundred thousand dayans for the capture of Kuo, or eighty thousand for his head.

Then, at the end of December, the cook shuffled into the parlor with mincing steps. *"Barynia,"* he said, "General Kuo and his wife tried to flee in disguise, but they were captured and shot. Their bodies were displayed in a Mukden public square."

Svetlana shuddered. "Why the wife also?"

The cook lowered his gaze. "She was his *wife, barynia,"* he replied simply. Svetlana nodded dismissal and then sat motionless, thinking. Her thoughts flew to Li-chun. How had he reacted to this news? Was he as horrified as she? Probably not. Having been raised with the primitive and harsh laws of the taiga, he would feel that the ignominious deaths of the guilty would be only natural. But why display them in a public square, why desecrate the bodies? That, too, was commonplace. She was glad that Li-chun was working in Harbin and had not been involved in the incident in Mukden.

Once again she was grateful for the security of her marriage, and she realized that her love for Li-chun need not be tested as it might have been had she been free to marry him. Would she have been strong enough then, much as she loved him, to defy conventions and her family, all she held dear, to build happiness on love alone? She wasn't sure. In spite of Li-chun's education and adolescent years with a Russian family, he was still Chinese and an ex-bandit.

The yearning to see him started anew, as it did every time she thought about him. Perhaps if she knew he had left Harbin, she would not think about him, would not long for him, so much, as she longed now to touch his smooth, handsome face, to press against his slim, hard body and listen to his caressing voice. . . . She knew with certainty that if they met again, she would still be unable to resist him.

PART THREE

The Decision

Chapter Eighteen

By the month of June the streets of Harbin were usually masked with wind-blown dust from the Gobi Desert. This year of 1927 was no exception; the gritty film covered the city with a sandy mantle. Households were sent into a frenzy of activity in order to leave town and spend the summer in one of the many resorts along the eastern or western branches of the railway.

On a Monday afternoon after work, Li-chun, too, thought of his long-delayed vacation, while he walked aimlessly through the city garden in the old section of Harbin, watching the Chinese peddlers roam the streets. Industrious bunch, those. They entered courtyards, knocked on doors, selling their wares or buying empty bottles of any size or shape. A tinker with a complete workshop hanging from a yoke on his shoulders singsonged his skills in pidgin Russian, offering to repair a leaky tin pot or a copper kettle; as he shuffled past Li-chun, his weather-beaten face crinkled into an obsequious smile. Another peddler in faded blue pants and shirt, a cone-shaped straw hat shielding him from the sun, sharpened knives at the edge of the garden, the high-pitched noise scraping Li-chun's nerves. Whether carrying their loads from house to house taking mincing steps in their pointed cloth shoes, or bargaining over prices with prospective customers, they breathed vitality and good humor. The sight depressed Li-chun. Turning abruptly, he walked deeper into the garden, sat down on a shady wooden bench behind a gazebo, and watched children play in a nearby sandpile. Their young voices soothed him.

The last three years had been difficult. Ever since Svetlana's visit to his flat he had been determined never to see her again, and studiously avoided making friends with the Russians, refusing to patronize the Zhelsob club—to the surprise of his colleagues, who consistently invited him there. Why take an unnecessary risk of running into her at a social function, he reasoned, and inviting pain that had no cure? Sooner or later the memories would dim.

Thus the mind agreed, but the heart argued. At night in his bed—in the same room and in the same bed in which he had loved Svetlana—these intangible memories became real, taunting his virile body with imagery that bathed his skin with perspiration and stiffened his muscles. How he ached to fill his arms once more with her softness and never let her go! At times in the darkness he actually grasped at the air, so sure was he that she was there, and then cursed himself for having given in to his fantasy.

In desperation he went to a bordello and sought a Chinese rather than a Russian girl in a deliberate attempt to suppress any thought of Svetlana. But the experience only exacerbated his loneliness, underscoring a love that transcended the physical. How foolish to think that physical release would be enough to allow him to forget her.

Winters in particular depressed him. He didn't know how to enjoy the wintertime recreation that seemed to be so pleasing to the Russians. His memories of the winter months in the taiga were grim, and he wanted no part of the freezing outdoors. Once or twice, under pressure from his colleagues, he ventured down to the Sungari and joined them in sledding on the hunting lodge's ice hill.

But most of the time he spent his leisure hours going to the nearby Oriant cinema to see a Clara Bow or a Harold Lloyd film in an effort to escape from reality for a few hours. At home he read Dostoyevsky, Turgenev, and Tolstoy, steeping himself in the romantic era of the past century. But he also read the works of Confucius and Lao-tsu, studying their philosophies and trying to educate himself beyond the Russian school he had attended. Turgenev's novel *Fathers and Sons* haunted him. The gulf between generations depicted in the novel made him think of his own defiance of his father and his betrayal of filial obedience, the very obedience that had been instilled in him since birth. Could such a betrayal be forgiven, prompted as it had been by his innate sense of justice—or was that only a rationalization to salve his conscience?

From time to time secret messages were passed to him about his father's health. He was ailing; Li-chun thought of going to see him but in the end rejected the idea. It would be unwise to let anyone find out that he still had connections with the bandits; moreover, he would certainly be risking his own safety by returning to his father's enclave, where ruthless and cruel men—like Chao Chu-lo, who had once slapped Svetlana—were still among the outlaws.

What else was there to do? He began to frequent St. Nicholas Cathedral on the square where Bolshoi and Vokzalny Prospekts met. The beauty of the Russian Orthodox services impressed him. The solemn liturgy, the pageantry, the glorious chant of the choir, all appealed to his sense of mysticism.

He also turned to his work. In hopes that hard work would leave no time for brooding, he plunged deeper into his assignments. As time went on, he found himself obliged to send Chang Tso-lin alarming reports of the expanding Soviet influence in Harbin. Late in 1925 he learned that Ivanov, the Soviet general manager of the Chinese Eastern Railway Company, had tried to stop transportation of Chinese military forces unless immediate cash payment was made. Although Li-chun knew that some action would have to be taken, he was stunned when on January 21, 1926, the Old Marshal arrested Ivanov, along with a few key Soviet officials, and put them in jail. Li-chun was present when the arrests were made, and although he realized that this was an arbitrary move to demolish spreading Soviet interests in Manchuria, he felt indirectly responsible.

"On what grounds are you arresting us?" Ivanov asked Li-chun's superior indignantly, and the Chinese official, without bothering to avail himself of Li-chun's excellent Russian, shrugged and replied in pidgin Russian: *"Vasha posidi, nasha podumai*—You sit a while, and we shall think."

For the first time in his life Li-chun, shocked by Chang Tso-lin's action, was embarrassed for his compatriots.

It didn't take long for Moscow to respond with a threat of military action if the prisoners weren't released immediately, and, to Li-chun's vast relief, Chang Tso-lin was forced to acquiesce.

More and more Li-chun was torn between two loyalties: one to his heritage as a Chinese citizen and his love for his father, and the other—his emotional attachment to everything Russian, an attachment nurtured as a youngster from the day he'd first gone to live with a Russian family.

He felt isolated, existing in a no-man's-land of emotions, belonging to no one.

He yearned to get away from Harbin and its painful memories, and after the Ivanov incident he was glad for the excuse to make occasional trips to Mukden to report his on-scene findings. Of late he availed himself of this opportunity at every turn, hoping that the Old Marshal would transfer him from Harbin and give him another assignment. But no such order came.

When at last the sun softened the bitter temperatures and melted the snow, turning it into rivulets of gurgling water that flowed cheerfully in the gutters, Li-chun's spirits rose. He walked long miles through the city, the warming winds a caress on his face. Let the Russians complain about the slush—*he* was delighted to see the birth of a new spring.

Then, as the sidewalks dried and the flower vendors placed buckets of violets and lilies of the valley along the curbs, he decided that with the advent of summer, he would take his vacation and go far away from Harbin and the railway company. He had heard that south of the Manchurian border, near the seaport of Tsingtao, in the rugged mountain resort of Laoshan, one could commune with his soul undisturbed; there one's companions were mountain peaks, crystal water pools, and cascading falls. Wasn't it time to put in for his vacation and plan his trip?

Instead, the long-hoped-for summons came. He was ordered to Peking, where the Marshal was now virtually in con-

trol of that government. Relieved, he went to Peking with the
hope that a happier future was in store for him, that the old
Russian cliche—*out of sight, out of heart*—would work in his
case. But when he got there, the capital of Northern China
overwhelmed him.

For the next ten months he struggled to adjust to the city's
noise and mass of humanity, which was so foreign to him after
the peace of the taiga and the relative serenity of Harbin's
streets. Here, the broad Hatamen Street teemed with people:
the jostling coolies threaded through the throng of people
with a singsong of "Hey-ho!" as they carried baskets full of
produce dangling from the ends of a pole slung over their
shoulders, or pushed a one-wheeled cart loaded with vegeta-
bles and an occasional child; dozens of little urchins in padded
cotton pants with slit bottoms made a nuisance of themselves,
darting in and out among milling pedestrians.

Li-chun averted his eyes from the professional beggars who
sat on the dirty sidewalks, exposing their dust-crusted, oozing
sores to attract pity. One day he watched a Manchu lady
emerge from a sedan chair in a peacock-blue silk embroidered
gown with a matching fanned headdress. Her face white with
powder, her lips painted in a small crimson circle, she walked
ponderously on her pedestal shoes toward a gate. He had
never expected to see such a garish woman except on picture
postcards.

Never in his life had he seen so many people in one place,
and suddenly he felt as a foreigner among them. Why did he
feel so strangely alienated? After all, he *was* Chinese.

Whenever he could, he escaped into the Foreign Legation,
which was separated from the rest of the city by a stone wall.
Here the tree-lined streets reminded him a little of Harbin
with their well-kept gardens and handsome buildings. A German hospital behind an iron-grilled fence with brick posts sat
deeply recessed from the sidewalk, its garden serene and quiet,
and as he strolled along Canal Street, passing the British embassy and the neighboring palatial Soviet embassy, Li-chun
was glad that he no longer had to spy on the Soviets and was
limited to his work at the Presidential Palace. There he did his
bookkeeping conscientiously and stayed out of politics.

After work he frequently visited the gardens of the Forbidden City, hidden from the outside world by a high wall, where the emperors of the past had walked along brightly painted pillared walkways that protected them from the rain. Sometimes he spent hours admiring the priceless treasures at the Palace of Empresses, where jade and ivory had been carved into toys for the royal children, and where the artisans' imagination had known no limits in creating intricate bibelots. He stood fascinated before a miniature clock hidden among the jade leaves of a gold tree, or tried to fathom the value of a four-foot block of precious jade.

Outside these palaces Li-chun kept to the broad streets and avoided the narrow maze of alleys called *houtungs* that checkered the city with their clay walls, behind which families had their dwellings and courtyards, and in whose labyrinths an unwary traveler could get easily lost. To him this was a foreign land he neither liked nor understood, and gradually, insidiously, the longing for Manchuria consumed him.

His roots were there, and it was time to think of his future. He was already twenty-six years old and still without a family. Here, in Peking, an entirely Chinese environment had proved more alien to him than the Russian ambience of Harbin. Suddenly, the idea of marrying a Russian no longer threatened to be a painful reminder of Svetlana. On the contrary, as long as he could not have her, then perhaps another Russian girl *would* bring him a measure of happiness.

But how could he possibly approach the Marshal with a request to return to Harbin after he had hinted for months that he wanted a transfer?

Then, early in March, he heard that Marshal Chang Tso-lin had detained a Soviet vessel, *Pamyat Lenina,* on its way to Hankow, and had seized its intelligence documents. But it wasn't until April fifth, when the Old Marshal had called him into his office, that Li-chun learned how damaging were those documents to the Soviet cause.

In facing Chang Tso-lin, who sat in a large ebony throne, it struck Li-chun how diminutive and delicate the Old Marshal seemed, and how tragic for those who underestimated the steel that was hidden beneath that fragile exterior.

Attended by a secretary who sat behind a large desk studying a sheaf of papers before him, and a husky guard, immobile as a statue, standing by the door, the Marshal presented an imperious figure.

He now tapped his finger on the carved arm of his throne. "Li-chun," he said, "I sense you dislike any armed action, but tomorrow I shall need your help during the raid I have ordered on the Soviet embassy."

"A raid on the Soviet embassy?" Li-chun repeated, stupefied. "But that's illegal!" The words slipped out before he could restrain himself. No subordinate had ever dared question the Marshal before, and out of the corner of his eye Li-chun saw a startled movement from the secretary, who looked up sharply.

The Marshal's lips tightened. "You should be censured. However, I'll overlook your impertinence this time. I need your knowledge of Russian during the raid tomorrow. I'm convinced that we shall find incriminating documents relating to Soviet espionage and communist efforts in our country."

The Marshal paused, then added evenly, "Sometimes it is imperative to practice illegality in order to oppose illegality."

For a long time afterward Li-chun tried to erase from his memory the day of the raid, April 6, 1927. Accompanied by Chang Tso-lin's men and the Peking municipal police, Li-chun ransacked the embassy and seized a vast number of documents. While he was collecting the papers, the other raiders searched the premises and arrested nineteen Chinese communists, including their leader, Li Ta-chao, who had taken refuge in the Soviet compound.

True to the Marshal's suspicions one of the documents that Li-chun brought back with him was a detailed plan for the communist takeover of China.

A few days later the Marshal waved the papers before Li-chun. "In the future you shall obey my orders without comment!" Then, taking a closer look at him, the Marshal asked, "Are you ill?"

Li-chun, who had learned earlier in the day that the arrested men had been strangled, and thought it had been done without the Marshal's orders, replied, "No, honorable Marshal, I am not ill. I have just heard that the prisoners were strangled."

"You have a queasy stomach, Li-chun," the Marshal said

evenly. "Evidently the thought of executions makes you squirm; that's too bad. You disappoint me. I don't like to be surrounded by weak men."

Li-chun chafed at the insult, especially since it was delivered in the presence of other subordinates in the room.

"I don't object to executions when they are carried out on orders," he said quietly.

Chang Tso-lin jerked his head up and stared at Li-chun, who was a head taller than he.

"I see!" he said, his voice rising. "And you think these were *not* my orders?"

Li-chun felt a flush rise to his face. How foolish to antagonize the Old Marshal! What had happened to his discipline, the years of self-control practiced in the taiga? He lowered his gaze and bowed slowly. "I was not aware that this was done on the honorable Marshal's orders. Perhaps I could best serve the Marshal back in my familiar territory in Harbin."

Li-chun did not realize how timely was his mention of Harbin, for Chang Tso-lin remained silent for a few seconds and then said, "Yes, I agree. That's where you're the most useful to me . . . among the Russians."

The subtly deprecating remark did not escape Li-chun, but he was so glad to have caught the Marshal off guard and to have extracted an order from him to return to Harbin, that the insult hardly hurt.

In less than a week he arrived in Harbin and rented a flat in the same building on Pochtovaya Street. How different it seemed on his return! It was home, and he felt as if he belonged in the city.

Now, nine weeks later, sitting on a bench in the garden, he suddenly realized that this time he should be able to get his vacation in Laoshan.

The wind was picking up and he could taste the dust in it. Slowly he rose and went back to his flat. He'd hardly been there five minutes before the bell rang and someone pounded impatiently on the door. Taken by surprise—for he had few visitors—Li-chun went to open the door.

Pale, her eyes wide with anguish, Svetlana burst into the room. Li-chun swiftly closed the door behind her.

"Svetlana, what is it?" he said, grasping her hands.

Svetlana's lips quivered. "Georgik was kidnapped yesterday morning! We've notified the police, but I thought that you—you'd know how to find out faster who took him."

She wrung her hands and looked at Li-chun with pleading eyes. "Oh, Li-chun, I'm so frightened! I keep thinking"—her voice broke for a moment—"I keep thinking, what if—what if it's your father? Could he have done this for revenge? Oh God, what's going to happen to my Georgik?"

Li-chun tightened his lips and led her to a chair.

"I'll do what I can. Now, sit down and tell me how it happened."

Chapter Nineteen

The day before, Raissa had telephoned in the morning asking if she could take Georgik for a walk in the Pitomnik—the city arboretum. Igor Sotin had asked her out, she explained, and since she knew it was Agrafena's day off, she thought she'd give Svetlana and Vladimir a chance to go to church without having to leave Georgik in the care of the maid.

In reality Raissa had an ulterior motive. Of late Igor Sotin had begun courting her, and Raissa, having run out of excuses to refuse his invitations, didn't want to be alone with him in the Pitomnik. Georgik, with his insatiable curiosity about everything and his constant, unpunctuated chatter, would keep the conversation away from personal themes, she reasoned. Recently, it had become an awkward situation.

If not for Vladimir, who encouraged her seeing Igor, she would have let Igor know long ago that she was not interested in him. As it was, she often wondered what he would say if he knew that it was she who used his modest flat for her trysts with Vladimir, and that she knew and disliked his personal habits. As a matter of fact she felt that his tidiness bordered on fetish.

At the foot of his brass bed a Chinese camphor chest of carved wood was covered with a starched white runner on top of which a brush, a shoe horn, and a pair of gaiters were always lined up in the same position, as if every time he used

220

them he counted the centimeters in either direction. Never mind that the mattress on the bed sagged or that the enamel in the bathroom sink was chipped. Tidiness, evidently, was more important to him than comfort and repair.

One wall was covered with picture cutouts from magazines and newspapers, the sepia ones and the black-and-white arranged not according to subject matter, but to preserve the color groupings. A small Soviet flag with its hammer and sickle pointing upward was glued to the wall below the pictures. There was no sign of a cross or an icon anywhere in the room.

On the dresser near the door a row of colored tops from his discarded tooth-powder containers were arranged in studied geometrical pattern. Now, really! She'd giggled the first time she saw them and, glancing at Vladimir, twirled her finger at her temple to indicate Igor's eccentricity.

Vladimir failed to see the humor.

"I wish I were this tidy," he had said rather testily. "I for one am always misplacing the top to *my* tooth-powder container."

Raissa had noticed that of late Vladimir had become irritable and impatient with her. Was the guilt of the last three years getting to him? Or was there another reason? She didn't want to ask. She had adjusted to living with her guilt, so why couldn't he?

In the beginning of their love affair she had been disturbed by conflicting emotions. On one hand there was the guilt of sibling betrayal, of having fallen in love with her sister's husband, of having sacrificed her virginity to a married man. On the other hand there was the intensity of their sexual encounters, with the added titillation of secret meetings, and, finally, the satisfaction—yes, the shameful satisfaction—of knowing that she was filling a void that Vladimir must have felt in his marriage to Svetlana. And there was something else: the smug feeling of triumph that in spite of the disfiguring scar on her face, for which she could never forgive her sister, she was the one who pleased Vladimir.

Early in their affair she had feared pregnancy, but after Vladimir assured her that he would prevent it from happening, Raissa had shut her mind to the future and lived from one rendezvous to another. As the months turned into years, the acute sense of her guilt and shame had dulled into an uneasy acceptance of the situation, and finally she'd justified her behavior by the self-serving conviction that Svetlana did not love Vladimir as much as she did.

Vladimir's recent irritability with her could well be explained by his fear of being discovered.

"We must always be cautious, Raissa," he had said to her a few weeks earlier. "After all this time it is easy to become careless when we arrange our meetings."

She was sure this was why he had been insisting that she be seen in Igor's company. As for Igor, there was another thing that bothered her. Whenever they were together, he seemed compelled to justify his Soviet citizenship by telling her of all the improvements in Russia that were written up in the left-wing newspaper, *Novosti Zhizni.*

Today was no exception, and to Raissa's annoyance Igor embarked on his favorite subject.

"Stalin is after the peasants, you know. They've been lazy and slovenly for centuries, and now, to improve agriculture, he's organizing them into collective farms, or *kolkhozy,* as they're called. Wait and see! Before long Russia's economy will soar."

Raissa couldn't resist a barb. "A veritable heaven, right?"

Igor bristled and for a few minutes said nothing, twirling a broken twig in his hands.

The sun was warm. A Chinese vendor, carrying a basket of flowers, shuffled slowly by. Occasionally, he dipped into it, brought out a small bunch of violets, and offered it to a passerby, intoning with a broad smile, "Smells good! Sell cheap!"

Another vendor sold candied crab apples strung on long straws that were fanned out in front of him. Children nagged their parents to buy them the treat, and Raissa wondered if Svetlana ever allowed Georgik to have one. Georgik, who had been playing with the other children, ran over with his favorite stuffed bear, Mishka, clutched under his arm.

"Tyotya Raissa," he said tugging at her skirt and looking up with his round gray eyes that looked so much like Svetlana's, "why do swallows dive?"

Glad for diversion from Igor's dialogue, Raissa ruffled her

nephew's silky hair. She felt very mature when he called her *"tyotya"*—auntie. She adored him.

"Because," she said, "when the swallows dive close to the ground, it is going to rain."

Georgik digested the information, then asked, "Why don't the other birds dive also?"

Raissa looked up and pointed to the sky. "Look up, quick, see that hawk in the sky?"

Taking Georgik's arm, she turned him around, but by then the hawk had disappeared behind a tree. Georgik looked back at Raissa accusingly. "Georgik doesn't see anything in the sky, Tyotya Raissa."

Raissa smiled. "We missed him, didn't we?"

Georgik studied her pensively, then suddenly wheeled around and, pointing to the sky, cried: "Tyotya, Tyotya, look! There's a big falcon up there!"

Raissa looked up into an empty sky.

"I don't see any falcon, Georgik," she said.

Georgik nodded solemnly. "See? Just like Georgik didn't see the hawk."

Igor bent over the child. "How old are you, Georgik?"

The little boy fanned out four of his fingers. Raissa laughed. "Not yet, Georgik. Not until August."

Igor shook his head. "My, he's precocious for his age."

Raissa laughed. "He certainly got even with me!"

As Georgik ran back to the children, Igor returned to his favorite theme.

"The trouble with all of us here," he said, "is that we've closed our minds completely to the possibility that the Soviet government may do better than the tsars did in the past."

Raissa shot him a sidelong glance. His hair was disheveled and needed to be cut, and his blond eyebrows had shot up in awkward concentration and eagerness to prove his point.

"Then why are you sitting here, arguing with me," she said sweetly, "instead of planning to emigrate to the Soviet paradise you are so convinced will come about in Russia?"

"You see? You're immediately taking extremes and refusing to accept any positive statement about Russia."

Irritated, Raissa raised her voice. "Don't say *Russia!* That word encompasses the whole country and its people—they haven't changed. Only the *government* has. And you haven't answered my question: Why aren't you planning to emigrate to the Soviet paradise?"

Igor shrugged and pursed his lips. "I'm watching the developments there closely. Who knows, I may just do that." *And I certainly hope you do,* Raissa thought. *Good riddance it would be.*

Aloud she said, "Let's change the subject, shall we? Look at those candied crab apples. I adore them. Let's buy a few and give one to Georgik. I know he'd love it."

Igor rose and bought two straws of strung up crab apples. He gave one to Raissa and then, pulling off the top crab apple, turned to where Georgik was playing with the children. Then he looked back at Raissa.

"Where's Georgik?" he asked, looking at her with mild surprise.

Raissa leaned forward to look behind Igor. The children were still there, but Georgik and his toy Mishka were gone.

Raissa smiled and shook her head. "That little rascal. First he pretends there's a falcon in the sky, now he's hiding from me himself." She rose and walked over to where Georgik had been playing a few minutes before. "Georgik! Where are you? Come on out, I have a treat for you!"

Georgik didn't answer. A couple of vendors were still milling nearby and a few mothers were chatting on the bench. Now one of them looked up.

"Have you seen my nephew?" Raissa asked her.

The woman raised her brows. "Which one was your nephew?" she asked.

"The gray-eyed blond boy in a white shirt and dark-blue pants!"

The woman nodded. "Oh, *that* one!" She chuckled and shook her head. "Yes, I saw him talking to a Chinese coolie. A friendly little fellow, isn't he? He talks to everyone. Anyway, the coolie took him by the hand and led him away. Is he your family servant?"

Raissa grabbed her head with both hands. "Oh, my God, no! Why would a servant lead him away when he was with me?"

The woman shrugged. "I heard him say that the boy's mother wanted him home."

Frantic, Raissa turned on Igor. "It's your fault! If you hadn't started on your ridiculous diatribe about Russia—" She didn't finish her sentence but rushed around the corner of the path, looking behind and under the bushes, calling for Georgik, and knowing all along with a sinking feeling that it was a futile search, that she was wasting time, and that Georgik had been kidnapped while in her care; but she *had* to search for him, and maybe, just maybe, he would answer and run to her with a big smile and arms outstretched, asking her another "why" question about anything and everything.

But Georgik was not there.

Igor grabbed her by the arm. "Don't waste time, Raissa. Let's look on the street. Maybe we'll see something there. Hurry!"

They ran up to Modyagowskaya Street and then along Girinskaya to Sadovaya, asking the passing droshky drivers if they had seen a Chinese coolie leading a Russian boy by the hand. No one had seen the child. . . . Georgik had disappeared.

A weakness spread through her limbs, her legs gave way, and she sank to her knees right there, on a granite slab of the sidewalk, and covered her face with her hands.

Igor pulled her up. "Raissa, this isn't going to bring Georgik back. We must hurry to the house and notify the police." He turned and hailed a passing droshky. After helping a distraught Raissa into the cab, he gave the coachman the address, climbed in beside her, and put his arm around her shoulders.

All the way home Raissa kept repeating: "How did this happen—in broad daylight with people around? I heard him talking to the children all the time! How did this happen?"

At the house Svetlana and Vladimir had just returned from church with Sonya and Nikolai and were sitting in the parlor. Stumbling over her words, Raissa spurted out the dreadful news.

Stunned into momentary shock, Sonya was the first to react. "What did I tell you?" she screamed. "Sooner or later that *hunhuz* would return! He did it, he's the one, I know it, I know it!"

Nikolai took one look at Svetlana's ashen face and shook his wife by the shoulders. "Stop it, Sonya, do you hear me? Stop it this minute!" Then, turning to Vladimir, who stood rocking back and forth on his heels, his fists clenched so tightly that his whole body trembled, Nikolai said firmly, "We mustn't waste another minute. Call the police, Vladimir. Let them know what happened, and don't forget to describe Georgik."

Vladimir's gaze roamed wildly over the shocked group, and Nikolai realized that the distraught young father had not even heard him. Releasing Sonya's arm, he went to the telephone.

The police said that they would do what they could, but if it was indeed a kidnapping, it wouldn't be until a ransom note arrived that they would know what clue to follow.

In the meantime the vigil began.

Svetlana's mind swam, drowned in terror, guilt, suspicions. She saw that Vladimir was devastated, his face ashen, and because of her own anguish, was grateful that he had not seconded Sonya's conviction that it was the work of the *hunhuzy* and a specific bandit at that. He must have wanted, and probably yearned, to add his own bitter slander against the unnamed *hunhuz,* yet he remained silent, avoiding her glance. She could hardly expect him to console her, himself distraught and in need of the solace that neither seemed able to offer the other.

She looked at Raissa, who sat in the corner of the room rubbing her hands nervously, chewing her lips and blinking in an obvious effort to fight back tears. Although she felt momentarily sorry for her sister, for she knew how she loved her little nephew, she couldn't help but blame her for her negligence. What else could it have been? One had to keep a child constantly within sight, especially Georgik—her gregarious, friendly son who talked to anyone on the street, who raised his big trusting eyes and smiled at strangers. Raissa had known that. In spite of Igor's chivalrous effort to take the blame for distracting Raissa's attention, it still had been *her* responsibility to watch Georgik.

The endless hours of agony crawled toward evening, then

crept with malicious slowness through the night. In bed under the covers Svetlana reached over to touch Vladimir, but feeling him stiffen, she withdrew. The grandfather clock in the hallway chimed twice, then three times.

Little Georgik. Where was he? Had he cried himself to sleep, calling for his mama? Was he tucked into someone's bed? Had the kidnapping really been engineered by Ma Fu-li, exercising his long-delayed vengeance? Was he cruel enough to use an innocent child as revenge to get back at the family for her escape? Or was this the work of someone else?

They were all wrong, her parents and Vladimir and even Raissa; they didn't say so, but they were all thinking that it was the work of the bandit who had brought her out of the forest.

No. Not all of them, not her father. He knew who Li-chun was, knew that he was now in Harbin, working for the railway company. Her dear, understanding father had guessed about Li-chun long ago, although even he couldn't know the whole of it. . . .

She was convinced that this crime was the work of Ma Fu-li. She and Vladimir were not rich. No, her child had been taken for more than mercenary reasons. The thought of Georgik in the hands of that vindictive bandit, hidden away in the distant taiga, was almost more than she could bear. The ache . . . oh, how she ached to hold her son in her arms again!

Lying there in the darkness, staring at the carved wood footboard that shone crimson in the glow of the icon's vigil light, her thoughts raced. Tomorrow she would wait until Li-chun came home from the office, and then she would go to him. He would know what to do—if indeed it was the work of the *hunhuzy*—where to go, whom to contact, faster than would the police. What did the police know about the intricacies of this particular kidnapping? Nothing. But Li-chun would find out, and if by chance it wasn't his father who had taken Georgik, then perhaps through the network of his informants, he could find her son and get him back.

Tomorrow. Where was the welcome dawn?

Five days. Six. Then seven and eight since she had gone to Li-chun. She had panicked when she discovered that he had moved, and so was relieved to learn that he still lived in the same building. Since then, there had been no ransom note and no word from Li-chun. He had promised to do what he could. Where was he? What was he doing?

Waiting, wondering . . . Was there a worse torture than not knowing what was happening to your child? The anguish would not go away.

Raissa had obtained a prescription for Veronal and brought it to Svetlana so she could sleep at night. But the sedative only filled her with nightmares, made her thrash and disturb Vladimir, the dark circles under whose eyes betrayed his suffering in spite of his outward self-control. Bathed in cold perspiration, Svetlana awoke every night gasping for breath, her stomach tight with paralyzing anxiety.

On the afternoon of the eighth day, after Vladimir had returned from work, she ventured outdoors away from the telephone and sat down on the slatted wooden bench on the sidewalk near her house. Behind her, their deep garden nurtured tuberoses, white and purple lilacs, asters in season. An espaliered jasmine screened the windows from the neighbors' view, and a birch cast speckled shadows over the sandy earth.

The wind that was gusting earlier had subsided, and the day sparkled with the morning's raindrops that still glistened on the leaves, mirroring the sun in sparkling prisms. Svetlana leaned back against the fence with half-closed eyes, loath to shut out the busyness of the June afternoon. She watched the street, the industry of an army of ants marching past her at the edge of the gutter, and listened to the sounds around her, trying to direct her mind away from Georgik.

The sun, brushing lightly over her face, was warm; she sat motionless, her hands clasped tightly in her lap, her mind, weary of stress, trying to drift with the pulse of the day. She looked up. The silvery leaves of a nearby birch shimmered in the sun. The hawk soared high, its forked wings keeling toward earth.

The air was fresh. A gentle breeze brought the pungent scent of a passing horse on Bolshoi Prospekt. She heard the droshky wheels and the urging on of the coachman, the rhythmic clipclop of hooves. Familiar sounds, so soothing before, were now annoying.

Eight days. No answer for eight days. A deep aching pain started up in Svetlana's chest, grew, and squeezed her heart. Georgik, where was her Georgik?

The sun had crawled behind a passing cloud and a cool whiff of air touched her face. She rose abruptly and went home.

Somehow she couldn't summon any energy into her movements after she entered the house and walked slowly toward the parlor. At the door she heard Vladimir's angry voice coming from the bedroom. Puzzled, she stopped and listened.

". . . I told you yesterday," Vladimir was saying, "it's all over between us. . . . No! Georgik's abduction has nothing to do with it. . . ." His voice was irritable, impatient. For a few moments there was silence, and when Vladimir spoke again, Svetlana realized that he was talking to someone on the telephone.

"It's time to end our affair. Otherwise, there's no future for you. . . . You need to settle your own life. . . . Yes, that's how I feel about it. . . . You should consider Igor Sotin. . . . He's an appropriate suitor for you . . . he's a good man and would make you a good husband. . . . Listen to me . . . I tell you, he doesn't know! . . . I've always warned him when to stay away from his flat. . . ."

There was a pause, and then Vladimir said sharply: "No! Georgik's return will not change my mind. I mean it, Raissa, this is final."

At the mention of Raissa's name the room swam before Svetlana's eyes. She leaned against the door to keep from falling. Then, feeling sick, she closed it quickly and rushed outside. There she ran across the street into the garden square. Her clenched fists thrust inside her skirt pockets, she paced the narrow lane to the opposite side of the block, then turned around and retraced her steps.

The garden around her appeared deserted. She sat down on a wooden bench and, closing her eyes, shaded them with her hand.

If she sat quietly and didn't move, the nausea would go away and she could then think. Why was it suddenly so cold?

The air must have turned chilly, for it was sending tremorlike
ripples through her limbs. What an effort to get the air in and
out of her lungs!

*Vladimir and her sister . . . in Igor's flat. . . . How—how
despicable. . . .* But, oh, it was difficult to breathe! She
grasped the bench on each side of her and leaned forward.

Vladimir and Raissa . . . a double betrayal: her husband's
infidelity with her own sister. Svetlana crossed her arms and
clasped her shoulders, rubbing them up and down.

Her little sister. Why? What had she ever done to Raissa to
deserve her betrayal? Suddenly, she stopped rubbing her arms
and her hands fell limply into her lap. Surely Raissa couldn't
hate her for that accident on the ice rink five years ago? No.
She could hardly believe that. Precocious Raissa had just let
her flirtation go too far. Her twinkling eyes whenever she
looked at Vladimir, the hugging, and the rippling laughter—
Svetlana had seen them all, but never dreamed, never suspected, it would lead to this. Raissa must have fallen in love
with Vladimir and he had taken advantage of her.

Svetlana clenched her fists. Vladimir was getting back at
her, unable to forget what she had done. She was sorry about
that. But how dare he carry on a clandestine affair with his
wife's sister?

What now? What, if anything, should she do now? Divorce?
That would gain her nothing. From what Vladimir had said
on the telephone, it was all over. It would serve no purpose to
disclose that she knew about them. Besides, she could hardly
stand the thought of a confrontation now. . . . Why must
she find out about it at this time?

The anger. The hurt. She wasn't even sure which was
greater. And all this time she had felt so guilty for having
gone to Li-chun's flat three years ago. Since then she had kept
away from him; she'd gone three long years without having
seen or touched him, while all along Vladimir and Raissa—
She was choking. How could she bear to face them?

A dangerous thought crept in. *If only Li-chun weren't what
he was . . .*

"*Madama, svezhy sieryen*—fresh lilacs," intoned a peddler
in his memorized pidgin Russian.

Svetlana raised her head and focused on the white lilacs.

Holding the bouquet in front of her, the peddler waited expectantly. On an impulse she bought the small bunch and buried her face in its fragrance.

Thoughts clamored, pounded, in her head. She shifted uncomfortably, then looked around her. What in the world was she doing out here? She looked up. The leaves of a nearby oak were dark and motionless. A few rooks blinked at her through an alder whose branches brushed the sky with lacy fingers. At her feet a mound of sand lay snugly against one leg of the bench where she was sitting, ants scurrying around building it up, grain by grain. Everything was quiet, and nature dozed in the sleepy afternoon. The silence pressed, whispered admonition. She was a trespasser here, daring to intrude upon the languid rest of the summer garden. Once more she buried her face in the lilacs. Then, as she looked up, she saw a young couple strolling toward her from the opposite side of the square, their arms entwined, the girl's head resting against the man's shoulder.

Her heart drumming painfully in her chest, Svetlana rose and threw the bouquet on the bench behind her. She was a fool to have felt guilty toward Vladimir, to have denied herself the happiness of *that other*. . . .

Li-chun. Where was he now? And why wasn't there a ransom note? Li-chun would know. He would find her Georgik for her. He would bring him back to her safely. She was sure of that. And afterward she would go to his flat to thank him . . . this time without any guilt.

Chapter Twenty

Frightened by the presence of an intruder, the magpies scrambled high into the branches of the forest pines and spruce, chattering excitedly from the safety of their haven. The taiga rustled and buzzed with midday sounds of life. At the base of a tall cedar a squirrel sat on its hind legs holding a nut in its paws, watching with curiosity as the man moved stealthily through the underbrush, a rifle slung over his shoulder, a knife and looped rope at the side of his belt. Convinced that the man paid no attention to little animals, the squirrel lost interest and, twitching its whiskered nose, went back to the business of cracking the nutshell.

Crouching behind a large burdock, the man listened carefully, his finely attuned ear identifying each new sound. So far, no problems. After five years' absence from his father's enclave Li-chun was pleased at how easily he was able to orient himself once again in the taiga. His early training was serving him well. He shouldn't have been surprised. After all, cities and people change, but the taiga remains the same. He felt very much at home in this dense forest. In spite of the time he had lived with the Russian family in Handaohedzi and his recent years in the city, the pull of the taiga was still strong. He shook his head and adjusted his rifle. Who *was* he, then? When with the Chinese, he longed to be with the Russians, and when surrounded by Russians, he missed the serenity of the forest. Well, this was no time to analyze his feelings. Caution and single-mindedness of purpose were what he needed in order to succeed in what he had decided to do.

When, a week earlier, Svetlana had told him how Georgik was kidnapped, he wondered immediately if it were his father's work, for he had suspected all along that Ma Fu-li would not rest until he had avenged himself.

He did not confirm Svetlana's suspicions, however, but after she had left him, he contacted the man in Foudzyadyan who through the years had kept him well informed of his father's health and activities. The next evening, as he was waiting in his flat, the information came back that Georgik was indeed in the hands of Ma Fu-li.

Li-chun sat down on his sofa to ponder the situation. He knew his father well; the ransom note would be delayed so that the anxiety placed on the family would be at least as great as the loss of face his father had suffered on their account when Svetlana had escaped.

The sensible thing to do, then, would be to leave Georgik in the hands of Ma Fu-li until the ransom was paid and the child returned safely to his family. But when it came to Svetlana, Li-chun was not sensible. Besides, he could not guarantee that in his drive for vengeance, Ma Fu-li might not decide to harm Georgik anyway and send the child's finger or ear to the parents. So, the child had to be rescued as soon as possible.

There was no doubt in Li-chun's mind that he was the only person likely to succeed in rescuing the boy from Ma Fu-li's camp. He knew the location of the enclave and was thoroughly familiar with his father's habits and the band's daily routine. The danger lay in being seen and recognized by any member of the band. It was imperative to plan his moves thoughtfully and not to overlook any minor detail. The slightest oversight might make a difference between life and death, for not only could it endanger little Georgik's life but his own as well.

An unwanted thought worked itself into his brain. He must risk his life for another man's child—the man who claimed Svetlana as his own, and whom she did not love. The man who shared her bed. . . . Abruptly, Li-chun rose and walked over to the window.

The street below was deserted. He rarely saw a rickshaw coolie padding by or heard a trotting droshky horse. It was a quiet residential area; he had chosen it because of its seclusion. Now, with no distractions, he could think.

How painful to harbor jealousy. To resent a man who had a right to Svetlana, a right that he, Li-chun, could never have. He hit his fist against the frame of the window. Fate had been cruel to him, hadn't it? He had no right to love Svetlana. But the fact was that he did. And loving her beyond all reason, he had been deeply affected by her plea and by the anguish in her eyes. "Find my Georgik!" she had implored.

The child was hers, and that was what he had to think about while making his plans. He had thought of everything. Before Svetlana left his flat, he had asked her to tell him about Georgik's habits, his toys, his personality. He had learned that his favorite toy was Mishka, a stuffed bear, that he frequently carried on animated conversations with himself and Mishka, and that he had had the bear with him when he was kidnapped.

The distance from Harbin added to the problem. There was also the question of his clothes. He would attract no attention riding the train to Maoershan in Chinese clothes, but what about the return trip with Georgik? A Chinese man accompanying a Russian boy would be noticed by the train conductor, and he couldn't risk being identified. He must take his European suit with him and change before boarding the train on the return trip with Georgik. Once again he thanked his luck for his fluency in Russian, for to his superiors, he was now on vacation in Laoshan, and it wouldn't do at all for him to be seen in a different part of the country—and with a little Russian boy at that.

With all the details painstakingly worked out, Li-chun left for Maoershan. Once there, he hired a horse, for after he got Georgik out of the camp, he would need to get away as fast as possible. Everything depended on good timing and his inborn instinct to sense danger.

Early the next morning he set out toward his father's enclave. As he penetrated the first thicket of firs, he reined in his horse. He had forgotten how strong was the fragrance of evergreens, how somber and stately the towering spruce. Cool air enveloped him, making him shiver, both from the imaginary chill and the awareness—no, the certainty—that in a few minutes he would reach the familiar glen. Chase away the bittersweet memories; foolish to indulge in their taunting imagery.

Yet he was unable to restrain himself from glancing at the tiny meadow dotted with field flowers, now sprinkled generously with morning dew; the same velvet patch of grass where he had loved Svetlana for the first time. Clutching the reins spasmodically, he hurried the horse across the glen and reentered the forest. There he hid his western suit under a fern and disappeared into the thickness of the taiga.

He had calculated that the best time of day to rescue Georgik would be midmorning, when the camp was lightly guarded by one or two bandits left behind while the rest scattered to do their hunting. It was fortunate that most of the time they hunted to the north and east of the camp, toward the deep interior of the forest, and he would be in little danger of running into them in his approach from the west.

As he drew closer to the enclave, a storm of emotions flooded Li-chun. Memories of years past tumbled before his mind's eye in a kaleidoscope of brilliant shards, threatening to overwhelm him with their vivid scenes of pain and pleasure.

He stopped to collect himself, to wipe out the intruding thoughts. Where was his discipline? It would be weakness to give in to sentiment, but then, how did he expect to return to the taiga and not be affected by it? Most of his childhood and youth had been spent here. He knew every bush, every secret path, every tree, along his way. Svetlana had been here with him. They had walked and talked together. And she had sung for him in that beautiful pure voice of hers. Memories. It was impossible to think that he could live here again in this primitive, forbidding place. But the taiga whispered . . . softly whispered, tugged, and lured.

Not far from the clearing he dismounted, tied the horse to a tree, and cautiously moved on. A sudden sharp sound near the tree sent him hiding in the underbrush. Crouching behind a burdock, he watched a squirrel cracking a nutshell.

His greatest danger now was from the dogs. Their barking would reveal his presence. Familiar smells assailed his nostrils: cabbage, garlic, burning wood. A few more steps and he saw the outlines of the *fanza*. Teased by the tantalizing smells of food, the dogs were barking and seemed unaware of his approach. Li-chun moved slowly, each foot carefully planted on the path to avoid snapping twigs that would alert the dogs.

He heard voices and listened. The words carried clearly through the trees, and as Li-chun squatted in the underbrush behind the *fanza*, he recognized one of the voices. It was Chao Chu-lo. The image of the bandit slapping and shoving Svetlana away from the deer rack intruded into Li-chun's mind. His hand tightened on the handle of his knife as he listened to the two men discuss the daily bounty and the food they had for Ma Fu-li. From their conversation Li-chun gathered that his father was now spending most of his time in the *fanza*, no longer participating in the *hunhuzy* raids.

Li-chun's chest tightened. He was but a few paces from his father. Only the wall of the *fanza* and the stacked wood beside it separated them. He remembered him as a strong, powerful man. Was he ravaged by disease now, had he become aged and frail before his time? Did he long to see his son, too proud to ask for him? One wall separated them, yet he would leave without seeing his father.

"Mishka, Mishka! Be careful!" a child's voice called in Russian.

Georgik.

Li-chun strained to understand his words. Georgik was carrying on a conversation with his Mishka and an invisible friend. Li-chun smiled with satisfaction. The child's continuous chatter was a blessing. Flattening himself on the ground, Li-chun crawled toward the side of the *fanza* where he had heard Georgik's voice. After reaching the end of the wall Li-chun peeked around the corner. The little boy was indeed playing with his stuffed bear. His face dirty and smudged with recent tears, he nonetheless had stopped crying and had encircled himself with wooden sticks, leaving an opening at one side, and was now ordering his Mishka to stay in his house, otherwise the bad man would get him.

The bandits had constructed a paling fence to keep the child from straying out into the woods. There was a gate at the side of the *fanza* and another one that led into the clearing. Staying close to the ground, Li-chun moved farther out from behind the back wall and looked at the clearing, where he saw the two men working at the cauldron. Aside from the two ponies tied at the far end and three dogs lying beside them, the place seemed deserted.

Good. The dogs were close to the cooking food and their continual barking should not alert the two men. The aroma of the cooking cabbage made him hungry. He had forgotten that he hadn't eaten that morning, and he watched as the men added pieces of meat into the suspended iron pot, stirring the food with a long spoon.

While the men seemed preoccupied with their work, Li-chun acted quickly. In a few steps he reached the open gate of the paling fence and called quietly: "Georgik! Georgik, come here!"

The child raised his head, obviously surprised to hear good Russian.

"Who are you?" he asked raising his voice, and then, without waiting for an answer, pursed his lips and shook his head. "I don't want to!"

Li-chun was about to answer, but Chao Chu-lo, too, had heard the child's raised voice.

Swearing, the bandit walked over to the fence and opened another gate from the side of the clearing.

"Tebya shto nado—what do you want?" he said gruffly in pidgin Russian, then grabbed the child by the shoulder and shook him. Georgik's mouth began to tremble, and his eyes filled with tears. "Nothing! Nothing!" he cried. Chao Chu-lo shoved him down. "Then play quietly. Don't raise your voice, do you hear?"

Georgik nodded, the corners of his mouth turned down, and tears rolled down his cheeks, making rivulets through the grime. He clutched Mishka to his chest and whimpered. There he sat, watching Chao Chu-lo move out of the enclosure and close the gate behind him, after shaking his fist at the little boy.

Li-chun could barely contain himself. The bastard! The cruel, nasty bastard to rough up a child like that. The others were kinder, they liked children and treated them with care, especially boy-children. Chao Chu-lo had always been an angry man, full of hate and envy. Li-chun had never been able to understand why his father kept him in his camp. Ma Fu-li had once said that Chao Chu-lo was daring and fearless during their raids, so maybe that was why he tolerated him. Right now, however, Li-chun wanted to strangle the man for making Svetlana's son cry. He clenched his fists until his hands shook and waited until the bandit had returned to his chores.

In a few moments Li-chun heard the younger man say, "Looks like the fire is going out. I'll get some more wood."

Li-chun glanced at the stack of wood piled high against the back wall of the *fanza*. Quickly, he slipped his rifle off his shoulder, placed it on the ground, and waited. A moment later the young bandit appeared from around the corner and reached for the wood. When his arms were full, Li-chun sprang from his hiding place in the underbrush and, before the bandit could turn around, gave him a sharp blow on the neck, knocking him out with the edge of his hand and kicking him at the same time. Kneeling beside him, Li-chun deftly roped his elbows together behind his back, tied his ankles, then gagged and blindfolded him with pieces of cloth he carried in his pocket. With his rifle back over his shoulder Li-chun turned toward the enclosure, where Georgik was still whimpering, too frightened even to talk to his Mishka.

"Georgik!" Li-chun tried again. "Come here. I'll take you to your mama."

At the mention of his mother Georgik stopped sniffling and looked at Li-chun. After a moment he shook his head. "No! The bad man will catch and hurt Georgik again."

"He didn't hurt you now."

"He beat me. It still hurts."

"He won't catch you, Georgik. I want to take you back to your mama."

Georgik thought for a second, then dropped his Mishka and stared at Li-chun.

"Promise?" he asked hopefully.

"I promise," Li-chun answered.

Georgik jumped up and ran toward Li-chun.

"I want my mama, I want to go home to Mama!" he cried.

Li-chun grabbed Georgik by the arm and, pulling him behind the *fanza*, put his hand over the boy's mouth. "Shhhh! Don't let that man hear you!" Then, shaking his finger in front of the boy's face, he said, "We'll go see your mama right away, only you must be very, very quiet. Do you hear?"

The child looked at Li-chun with eyes full of eagerness, and nodded. Then he sniffled and said, "You're not like that bad man. You're different. You talk like my mama and papa and Tyotya Raissa. Where is Mama?"

Li-chun moved quickly, pulling Georgik behind him, but the child suddenly stopped. "I forgot my Mishka. I'll be right back!"

Li-chun held him tight. "No, Georgik, we must go, do you understand?"

Georgik shook his head stubbornly and fought to free himself from Li-chun's grip. "I want my Mishka. The bad man will hurt him."

But Li-chun held on, and Georgik cried: "Mishka is my friend! I must take him with me!"

Instantly, Li-chun released him, and as Georgik ran back to get his toy, he leaned against the wall of the *fanza* almost afraid to breathe, hoping against hope that Chao Chu-lo would ignore the boy's cries this time. But the bandit was back in the enclosure in seconds.

"What's going on?" Chao Chu-lo shouted angrily, and slapped Georgik across the face. Georgik screamed and, with lightning speed, picked Mishka off the ground and ran for the side gate toward Li-chun. But Chao Chu-lo moved faster and caught him by the collar.

"What did you want out there?" he shouted, throwing him to the ground. As Georgik started to cry with hiccuping gasps, Chao Chu-lo looked suspiciously beyond the side gate, then slammed it shut behind him and headed toward the back of the *fanza*.

Li-chun, who had been watching from around the corner, now stepped quickly behind the pile of wood. There, he pulled his knife out and slipped his rifle off his shoulder again, hoping to strike Chao Chu-lo on the neck with his hand and knock him out before the bandit got a chance to see him.

But Li-chun had forgotten the bandit's keenly developed

sense of danger, and as he swung his arm, Chao Chu-lo turned and saw the quick movement from the corner of his eye. With the agility of a panther he jumped out of Li-chun's range and wheeled to face him.

Stunned by recognition, he stared at Li-chun for a moment, then sucked in his breath through clenched teeth.

"You!" he hissed.

This was what Li-chun had feared most. His father would learn who had stolen Georgik from his camp. If ever Ma Fu-li had suspected his son's part in Svetlana's escape, now he would be sure. A double loss of face.

No. He couldn't do this to his father.

Suddenly, Chao Chu-lo saw the unconscious bandit on the ground. His eyes narrowed.

"Ta Ma-de!" he swore, spitting on the ground. "You're not going to get away with this!"

A smirk twisted his mouth, and his look was so full of malice that there was no doubt as to his intentions.

Li-chun reacted instantly. With his knife raised for a strike he jumped at the bandit. Chao Chu-lo grabbed Li-chun's wrist in midair, but with a quick movement of his foot Li-chun tripped his adversary, flinging himself down on top of him. Placed at a disadvantage, Chao Chu-lo struggled to roll over, but Li-chun immobilized the bandit's free arm with his knee, then pressed the thumb of his left hand on Chao Chu-lo's windpipe. In a few seconds the bandit's arm weakened, and Li-chun wrenched his wrist free. With a quick thrust he stabbed Chao Chu-lo in the chest.

He waited a few seconds to make sure the man was dead, then wiped the blade on Chao Chu-lo's shirt and, after a moment's hesitation, turned him over on his stomach. No need to expose the little boy to the sight of death.

As he rose to his feet, the younger man groaned. In a few moments he would regain consciousness and try to free himself. Li-chun didn't want to hit him again.

Now there was no time to lose. Quickly, he moved around the corner.

"Hurry, Georgik!" Li-chun whispered. "We must go. Your mama is waiting for you at home."

This time Georgik grabbed his Mishka and ran into Li-chun's arms. To keep the child from seeing the two bandits Li-chun pressed Georgik's face against his shoulder and ran a short distance into the brush to where he had left his horse. Once there, he lifted Georgik onto it, then mounted behind him and headed toward Maoershan, choosing a circuitous route to avoid running into any bandits returning to camp.

But he hadn't counted on the Russian hunters who might be in the forest, and before long he heard voices speaking Russian. As they drew closer, Li-chun dismounted quickly and hid Georgik in the bushes. "You must be very quiet now, Georgik," he admonished him and the little boy, his eyes wide with fear, nodded.

Moments later two Russian men came out from around a large burdock and stopped. Noticing Li-chun's rifle, they asked, "Have you been hunting too?" and when Li-chun nodded, they guffawed. "Looks like you haven't shot anything yet, huh? Maybe we'll have better luck."

With that they waved and went on. With a sigh of relief Li-chun pulled Georgik out and lifted him back onto his horse. For the rest of the ride, Li-chun held the little boy tightly around the waist.

At the edge of the forest Li-chun dismounted and lifted Georgik off the saddle. Lowering him gently to the ground, he said, "Wait here, Georgik. I have to change clothes."

The child watched as Li-chun discarded his Chinese garb and put on the suit he had hidden in the shrubbery. Then Georgik asked, "Why are you changing clothes?"

Li-chun thought quickly. "Because they got dirty in the forest," he said.

Georgik hugged his Mishka and continued to watch Li-chun. "Are you Russian?"

"No, I'm Chinese."

Georgik shook his head. "You look different in these clothes."

"It only seems so because I put on this suit."

The little boy studied him with his candid, serious eyes, then announced, "Georgik likes you better this way. You speak like my papa, not like that bad Chinese man. What's your name?"

The last thing Li-chun wanted to do was to tell his name to Georgik.

"Just call me Dyadya-Uncle."

"Dyadya what?" he persisted.

In desperation Li-chun said the first name that came to mind: "Dyadya Wu."

Georgik nodded solemnly, then added, "Dyadya Wu, you don't look Chinese."

"Very well," Li-chun said with a smile. "Have it your way. Let's pretend during our train ride that I am Russian, and you can then call me Dyadya Vanya."

Georgik nodded. "I'll call you Dyadya Vanya now."

Li-chun took the child's hand and the two walked toward Maoershan, leading the horse behind them.

On the train to Harbin, Georgik snuggled up to Li-chun and promptly fell asleep against his arm. Carefully, Li-chun looked at the little boy, and the child's dark long lashes and his blond hair reminded him so much of Svetlana that his heart turned over. How wonderful that he was able to get the boy out of the forest and to safety. Ah, but to see Svetlana's happy and relieved face when she took her child into her arms!

When they arrived in Harbin, Li-chun avoided the busy Vokzalny Prospekt to minimize chances of being recognized, and took a side street to his flat.

Once inside, he heated some tea and gave Georgik a cookie. Then he placed the exhausted boy on the couch, tucked a blanket around him, and called Svetlana.

Chapter Twenty-one

When Svetlana heard Li-chun's voice on the phone, she clutched the receiver and thanked God that Vladimir was not yet home. Tears of overwhelming relief poured down her face as she listened, nodding into the mouthpiece and not comprehending anything Li-chun said except that her Georgik was safe, with him, in his flat.

Since she had been more and more in demand lately to sing at concerts, her name and face were now easily recognized in Harbin. It wouldn't do to be seen today entering Li-chun's flat, so to cover her distinctive hairstyle, she put on a hat, grateful for its modern shape with the rim resting low on her forehead. It wasn't for herself that she took these precautions; at all costs she wanted to keep Li-chun's name from being involved in Georgik's kidnapping.

Pushing the hat firmly down on her head, she rushed out of the house. In spite of her eagerness to see Georgik she avoided the shortcut across the thoroughfare cathedral square where she could easily have run into friends, and took a longer way, crossing Bolshoi Prospekt to Pochtovaya.

Breathless, she knocked on his door, and when Li-chun answered, she pushed past him and scooped Georgik into her embrace. The little boy wrapped his arms around her neck. As she showered his face with kisses, he kept repeating over and over, "Mama, Mama, Mama," until she finally shushed him and, with one more hug, put him down on the floor.

All the while Li-chun stood patiently aside and smiled at her with pleasure. She turned to him. That dear, beloved face. Oh, how she longed to touch him, to embrace him, again! Her body moved of its own volition—she did not order it to move —but her feet made a step toward him, then another; her hand reached out and gently, shyly, touched his arm.

"How can I ever thank you?" she wanted to say, but the words were strangled and she had to clear her throat and say them again in a whisper.

Li-chun shook his head. "I did what I had to do, Svetlana. I was the only person who could have succeeded."

Svetlana looked at him. "Then it was—it was—" She hesitated, glanced at Georgik, then back at Li-chun.

He nodded. "Yes, it was. I suspected as much when you first came to me, but wasn't sure until I checked. That's why you received no ransom note. Ma Fu-li was waiting deliberately to make you suffer. It was his way of avenging his loss of face."

"He certainly did that," Svetlana said, wincing, then added after a pause, "What are you going to say about your absence from the office?"

Li-chun smiled. "A fortunate quirk of fate. I had taken two weeks off to go on vacation. My superiors think I'm in Laoshan now."

At the mention of Laoshan, Svetlana started. "When I was a child, I spent a summer there with my family," she said. "I'm sorry that your vacation has been ruined."

"Not at all. I plan to extend it and will leave in a day or so. I'll inform the office that I've been ill and couldn't go until now."

Svetlana looked away, afraid he would read her thoughts. Li-chun was going to Laoshan—that beautiful, remote place deep in the mountainous country inland from Tsingtao. The first time she had mentioned it to Vladimir, he had refused to consider going there, for it would have taken too much time from his work, he said; and he *was* so wrapped up in his work now.

Suddenly, a daring idea took shape in her mind. Yes. Why

not? And as she thought about it, her heart fluttered with excitement like a restless bird.

Georgik tugged at her skirt. "Mama, I want to go home now," he whined.

Svetlana stooped over her son. "Are you tired, *synochek?*" and when he nodded, Li-chun picked him up and smiled at him. "We had a long day, didn't we? But your mama will be pleased to hear that you were a *very* good boy."

Georgik stopped whining, grinned, and wrapped his arms around Li-chun's neck. Then, leaning closer to him, he planted a smacking kiss on his cheek.

"I like you, Dyadya Vanya," he said looking deeply into his eyes. "You must come to see us."

Svetlana raised her eyebrows. "Dyadya Vanya?" she said with a smile.

Li-chun nodded solemnly. "I told Georgik that my name was Dyadya Wu, but once I changed into my suit, I said that he could call me Dyadya Vanya."

Their gaze locked and Svetlana understood. Watching Li-chun and her son together, her throat constricted. Her child in Li-chun's arms . . .

As she prepared to leave, Li-chun said quietly, "Svetlana, please spread the word that your family paid the ransom to get Georgik back. This will make my father believe that the child was stolen from him by a rival band." He paused, then added, "Otherwise he will guess the truth."

So, Svetlana thought, *he still cares enough not to want to hurt his father.* Impulsively, she touched his arm. "Don't worry. I'll find a way to convince my family that the man who brought Georgik back had his reasons for wanting it that way."

"Thank you," Li-chun said simply, then added, "When the police question you, you can say that one of the terms of ransom was to keep the payment secret from them."

"I'm the one who can never thank you enough for what you've done," she said, her voice shaking. Then she added quickly, "I hope you have a nice vacation."

On the way home Georgik kept talking about the bad man and his Mishka, but Svetlana wasn't listening. She was still in Li-chun's flat. Li-chun had made friends with Georgik. . . .

He had held the child so gently . . . had looked so lovingly at him. . . . Georgik had kissed him. . . . Georgik in Li-chun's arms . . .

She couldn't get the image out of her mind.

At the house Vladimir swept Georgik into his arms and heaved with dry sobs, repeating over and over, "Oh, thank God, thank God!"

Svetlana winced at this display of emotion from her husband and couldn't understand why it affected her so adversely. When he was finally able to listen, she told him her prepared story.

"I had a telephone call telling me to meet someone at the corner of Tsentralnaya and Sadovaya," she said, "and when I got there, I saw a coolie holding Georgik by the hand. He asked me to tell everyone that we had paid ransom to get Georgik back. He explained that he stole Georgik from the *hunhuzy* as a personal vendetta and didn't want them to suspect that he was the one who had done it. He wanted them to think that Georgik was stolen by a rival band and that we paid ransom to them."

And that's part of the truth, Svetlana thought, then added: "And he threatened reprisals if we don't follow his instructions."

Vladimir was so overwhelmed by happiness at having his son back that he accepted her story without comment, and Svetlana wondered if he had really listened to it.

A little later her parents arrived, and when they saw Georgik, they laughed and kissed and hugged the child until the tired Georgik, overcome by the multitude of the day's impressions, started to cry.

Immediately, Sonya said, "What did I tell you? Look how thin he is! Lord only knows what those *hunhuzy* have done to the child."

Herself overwrought with emotion, Svetlana lost her temper. "Stop it, Mama!" she cried, her voice breaking. "Do you hear? Stop it!"

Sonya raised one brow. "Well! Why are you so defensive? You've had nothing but trouble from the *hunhuzy.* Now tell us how you got Georgik back."

Svetlana took a deep breath. Whether they believed her story or not, at least they had no way of proving it false.

"Sounds suspicious to me," Sonya grumbled after Svetlana had repeated her story, "but I guess we shouldn't complain, as long as Georgik is home."

Nikolai patted his wife on the hand. "Yes, my dear, and that's exactly what we shall do. And we'll tell the police to drop the case, since we supposedly have paid the ransom and want no future reprisals. Now, let's change the subject."

Sonya sighed. "I guess I've been upset by too many things lately," she said. "First Georgik, and now Raissa."

"What's wrong with Raissa?" Svetlana asked without looking at Vladimir.

Sonya shook her head. "I don't know. She's not herself lately. At first I thought she felt guilty about Georgik's kidnapping, but not only does she cry . . . she seems—" Sonya hesitated searching for words—"withdrawn, even depressed. She wouldn't even come here with us to see Georgik. I'm worried about her."

Nikolai frowned. "I wonder what's wrong with her?"

Sonya turned to Svetlana. "Sometimes children won't talk to their parents as readily as they will to a sister. Svetlana, I wish you'd talk to her, see if you can find out what's causing all this."

Svetlana paled. *How could I possibly talk to her?*

"I think now that Georgik is back, we ought to give her a little time, Mama," she said at length. "We all need to recover from this ordeal."

Vladimir cleared his throat. "I agree. We should leave Raissa to herself for a while. I'm sure she'll bounce back into her usual good spirits before long. This awful vigil has taken a toll on all of us."

"Yes, indeed it has," Nikolai said, then looked at Svetlana. "It upsets me to see you so thin, my dear."

Svetlana shrugged. "Georgik and I hadn't even had our vacation this year before this dreadful experience happened."

"I think it would be good for you to get out of the city for a while," Nikolai said quietly, and then looked at Vladimir. "Don't you agree?"

Vladimir nodded and turned to Svetlana. "Where would you like to go?"

"Laoshan!" Svetlana said impulsively, then bit her lip. Why had she blurted this out? And as the thoughts swirled in her mind, Sonya nodded.

"Wise choice, my dear," she said. "Why not get away from the Manchurian resorts, far away from bad memories? The sea in Tsingtao is warm and soothing, and you may find that you'll want to stay there a few days before going on to Laoshan. But I have a suggestion. Don't take Georgik with you. Leave him home, with us."

"No!"

Svetlana's cry was so frantic that Sonya raised her hand. "Believe me, he'll be safe now with all of us watching. I'm sure Agrafena will be glad to have him all to herself, and on her day off we'll take good care of our grandchild, I promise you."

Svetlana shook her head vehemently. "No, no, I tell you— no! How can you even think that I could leave my child behind just after I got him back?"

"You need a real rest, and with Georgik along, you won't take your eyes off him for a second. Don't you see, my dear? What you need is to be away from all responsibilities."

"I can't think about myself at a time like this. I can't bear the thought of parting from him even for a minute, and you're talking about my rest? I'd worry about him all the time I'd be away."

Sonya shook her head. "And what makes you think Georgik would be safer with you than with all of us? Away from home you'd be the only one watching the child, a much riskier situation than if he stays home and is watched constantly by the family."

Svetlana's anger evaporated. Her mother was right. Why hadn't she thought of it that way? Alone in the rugged mountains of Laoshan she would be poor protection for her child. Well, then, if that was the case, she wouldn't go anywhere.

And so it was that she won the argument and stayed home with Georgik. But the whole next day she was irritable and snapped at everyone, including her precious child. When she raised her voice at Georgik, he burst into tears and ran out of the room crying for Agrafena.

Everyone irritated her: the slow-moving Agrafena, who looked at her accusingly when she came in to gather Georgik in her arms and soothe his crying; the cook who came to ask about the week's menu; the well-meaning friends who telephoned to talk about Georgik. Imaginary pressures mounted, and when Nikolai and Sonya came by in the late afternoon to see how things were going, Svetlana suddenly sat down at the table and without any reason at all, burst into tears.

At this Vladimir had had enough. "That does it, Svetlana! Don't you see how overwrought you are? You're not going to be any good around Georgik. He needs to be back in a normal atmosphere, free of tears and tension. You desperately need to get away for a rest."

With an effort Svetlana controlled her weeping. Yes. Little Georgik was traumatized and needed to be handled with patience, not snapped at irritably.

"I guess you're right," she agreed reluctantly. "I'll go away for a few days, but you all must promise not to let Georgik out of your sight even for a single minute."

The train ride along the South Manchurian Railway from Harbin to Dairen was restful, and Svetlana had time to think. Sitting in a comfortable, velvet-upholstered compartment, she watched the rolling flatlands float by, grateful for the freedom from worries. She smiled. Good-hearted, affectionate Agrafena. When told that Svetlana was leaving, she wouldn't hear of taking a day off in her absence.

"I don't need it," she said. "I won't let Georgik out of my sight while you're gone, Svetlana Nikolaevna. Your parents are kind to offer, but Georgik will be more comfortable with me," she ended firmly, and that was that. Svetlana was relieved. Common sense told her that her mother was right in saying that Georgik was safest at home.

As she looked out the train window, her thoughts inexorably turned to Li-chun. She was drawn to him—what was the old cliché?—like a moth to the flame. After what she had learned about Vladimir and Raissa, she no longer felt guilty about seeing Li-chun. Especially now, when she wanted so much to express her gratitude to him for what he had done. She also needed to learn the details of the rescue.

Was that all she wanted? Why fool herself? She wanted to be in his arms, to be alone with him for more than a few hours at a time, to spend a whole day with him—and, yes, a whole night. Ahh, what joy it would be not to worry about rushing home! The thought of spending a few days of vacation with him sent a flush to her face, set her heart to racing. She closed her eyes.

Oh, my dear, my true love!

In Dairen she stayed in the Yamato Hotel on the spacious plaza with streets radiating from it like spokes on a wheel. The square, geometrically landscaped with shrubbery, was meticulously kept. How tidy were the Japanese!

Although built by the Russians at the turn of the century, Dairen had been in Japanese hands ever since the war of 1904, when the Russians ceded to the Japanese their lease of the Liaotung Peninsula and the possession of the South Manchurian Railway as far north as Changchun.

In the afternoon she went to the neighboring resort of Hoshigaura. She had heard that the Japanese were especially protective of their children; nevertheless, it surprised her to see adults yield their seats to children on the tramway, for since early childhood she had been taught to give up seats to those older than herself.

The air in Hoshigaura was cool and damp as she walked on the pebbly beach, watching the children splash in the water. Georgik would have had such fun here, she thought, and immediately chastised herself for dwelling on her guilt for leaving him behind. After all, he was surely safer at home, and she needed this rest to revitalize her energy, so drained by her recent anguish.

To stop thinking about her child she looked away from the children toward a few Japanese men and women walking along the beach. The women wore modest bathing suits or kimonos, but each man had nothing on but a loincloth pulled snugly between his legs and roped to the waistband in the back.

Shocked, she returned to the hotel; she felt much more at home among the Chinese. In a few days she would see Li-chun. Laoshan was small, and it would not take her long to find out where he was staying. Beyond that she would let things fall as they may. But she knew . . . oh, she knew that the thought, so casually stated by the mind, could not fool the heart. It quickened her breath, made her flush with embarrassment at her own duplicity. Whom was she fooling? She *yearned* to be alone with Li-chun, *longed* to be in his arms, *ached* for his loving.

The next day she boarded the ship for Tsingtao, praying that the Yellow Sea would be placid enough not to make her seasick, and to her enormous relief the frequently rough waters cooperated.

The first thing Svetlana saw as the boat entered the Tsingtao Harbor was the Catholic cathedral, its two spires dominating the view from the highest hill. It stood adjacent to the Holy Ghost Convent of the Franciscan Missionaries of Mary. Although she had seen Tsingtao when she was a child, Svetlana had forgotten how picturesque it was, and now she was struck by the sight before her.

Built mostly by the Germans, the city was spread out over gently rolling hills dotted with red roofs of freshly painted houses that seemed to hide in the profusion of shrubbery and scrub pines.

The undulating shoreline offered a wealth of sandy inlets, and one only needed to decide where to rent the summer dacha in order to be near one of the three most popular beaches: the long Strand Beach, nearest to downtown; the German Beach farther up on the other side of the jutting peninsula; or farther still, the exclusive American Beach, where the majority of foreigners had their private bungalows.

Svetlana checked into a hotel at the end of Strand Beach, then walked along the quay to the German Beach, favored mostly by Russian vacationers because it was not as crowded as the Strand.

A small gray-stone castle, enclosed by an iron grilled fence with stone pillars, stood on a bluff at the far end, lording it over the sea-washed rocks. Fenced, shaded cottages nestled on higher ground above the wide stretch of sand. A narrow, crooked path led to the nearest bluff, where a single gazebo with a cone-shaped thatched roof dominated the view.

Svetlana sat down on a boulder near the gazebo, wrapped her arms around her knees, and watched the breakers foam around the rocks below, her eyes following the waves as the emerald water sparkled, rippling out into a mirror smoothness at the horizon. The sun was low in the late afternoon, and where the sky met the sea, silhouetted ships steamed by in placid tandem.

She could not remember ever being so completely alone, away from home and family. It took time to clear her mind of the people who had filled it for so long. Vladimir. Raissa. Her parents. She thought only of her little boy, who was now returned to her and was safe at home. It was such a relief to have no one to claim her time, now so totally peaceful. And it was a surprise to discover that she didn't feel lonely. In fact, it felt wonderful to think only of herself, of her own needs, of the world around her, and the pleasures it promised to bring.

What luxury to indulge in self-centered thoughts, to listen to the plaintive cries of sea gulls swooping past her, to surrender to the hypnotic rhythm of the surging tide!

No one disturbed her solitude. She sat a long time, her chin resting on her knees, her mind lulled by the murmur of the sea. A fresh breeze picked up from the water with its strong sea aroma, and Svetlana's arms felt cool. When the sun touched the horizon, she rose and walked back to the hotel.

The following day she left for Laoshan with a rented automobile and driver. Deep inland at the end of the road she transferred to a sedan chair that would carry her the last few miles of her journey.

She hadn't remembered how rugged the terrain was. As a child she had been more fascinated by the sedan chair and the steady trot of the two coolies in their broad-rimmed, cone-shaped straw hats, than by the surrounding scenery. Now she was awed by the majesty of the towering precipices on both sides and by the narrow gorge through which the coolies picked their way cautiously along the winding sandy path.

It was hot, and she was grateful that the cane back of her bamboo chair allowed the breeze to get through. By the time she had reached a small plateau on the west side of the narrow gorge, it was late afternoon. A large wooden house stood at the edge of the bluff, with a row of log cabins in the back. The place was owned by a Russian couple, the Potapovs, whose main house had a spacious communal dining room overlooking the deep valley below.

Tired, but with a feeling of exhilaration, Svetlana unpacked her suitcase, hung her clothes in a rickety wardrobe, and walked outside. The sun was about to set behind the tallest peak, its slanted shafts painting the cliffs an amber hue. The floor of the valley was already shadowed. Fresh, crisp air, fragrant with pine, wrapped itself around her, pleasantly cooling her sun-warmed skin.

The Potapov family consisted of a middle-aged couple and their spinster daughter of indeterminate age, who greeted her warmly and urged her into the dining room, where five other guests were already eating. The smell of roasted leg of lamb and freshly baked bread made Svetlana realize how hungry she was.

She sat down to eat at a small table by the window. The view was spectacular. What better place, after the turbulence of the last two weeks, than the seclusion of this lovely mountain resort in which to place her thoughts and emotions in proper perspective?

Swimming in mountain pools, sunning, walking in the wilderness of Laoshan, she'd be completely undisturbed by human travail, far from her complex family problems. How lovely!

And she would be with Li-chun. No excuses, no hiding, this time. She was far from home, no one knew her here, and if anyone raised an eyebrow about her keeping company with a Chinese man—so be it. Chances of word getting back to Harbin were unlikely, for most of the vacationers here were from Shanghai and Tientsin, not from Manchuria.

Tomorrow she would look for him. Her excitement grew.

Then . . . a familiar voice asked, "May I join you?"

Li-chun! Her heart leaped, pounded in her chest. She had known he was somewhere in Laoshan. But here, in the same house? Of course. She might have guessed that he, too, would seek out the best and most comfortable dacha. And there were so few in this remote place.

She nodded, not trusting herself to talk just yet. If only her foolish heart would stop beating so fast!

She looked up and gave him her hand.

He kissed it, held it a fraction longer than was customary, then sat down opposite her.

Oh, God, he looked so handsome! His lean, muscular body, his sparkling dark eyes, his shiny thick hair.

"What an unexpected pleasure, Svetlana. I am completely surprised. Are you alone?"

"Yes," she said softly.

He studied her intently for a few moments, his mouth soft with a tender smile, his eyes full of unconcealed love. She flushed, her spirit soaring, her heart begging to burst out.

Talk hummed around her. She did not listen. His eyes held hers. They had such a look. . . . Without a doubt it said, *Here, you're mine.* . . .

He asked quietly, "Why?"

Svetlana lowered her eyes, then slowly raised them again and met his gaze.

"Do you need to ask?"

Chapter Twenty-two

The next morning they asked Mrs. Potapov to fix them a picnic lunch and, when it was ready, took off for a day in the wilderness.

Down in the valley the brilliant shafts of sunlight had worked themselves into narrow ravines on the eastern side of the mountains, where huge boulders crowded precipitously above sapphire pools, and the cascading waters tumbled over glistening rocks. They found a secluded spot and spread their blanket under the shade of a nearby oak. As Svetlana reached for the food basket, Li-chun put his hand on hers.

"It's not good to swim on a full stomach," he said, smiling. "Let's go in first."

They stripped to their swimsuits and walked over to the pool. On their left a smooth boulder hung over the water with the shale above forming a dark crevice. The elongated narrow entrance was dark and irresistibly inviting. Svetlana climbed on the bottom rock.

Li-chun propped his fists on his hips and looked up. "Explorer, huh?" he said, laughing softly. "You make quite a picture up there. What do you see?"

Sheepishly, Svetlana shrugged. "Nothing. It's too narrow for me to crawl in. Besides, I may not get out." She looked down into the pool and suddenly felt dizzy. "I'm more concerned about how I'm going to get down from here."

Li-chun waded into the pool, then swam to the base of the boulder. "Slide down the rock and I'll catch you in the water," he called to her.

Svetlana edged herself carefully forward and, shutting her eyes tight, slipped down, feet first. As soon as her legs hit the water, Li-chun's arms slid up her thighs and encircled her waist. She sank below the surface, but he pulled her up and held her until she stopped gasping and shivering from the cold water. Then she wriggled out of his embrace and swam across the deep pool to where a few small boulders created a narrow flow of rapids. She pulled herself onto them and lay back against the rocks, letting the foam roll over her body. Li-chun was saying something to her, but she couldn't hear him over the rushing water. After she pointed to her ears to indicate she couldn't hear, he climbed out and grasped her arm.

"You look like a nymph. A golden nymph!"

Svetlana tossed her head. She had loosened her chignon, and her blond hair hung around her shoulders in long, wet strands. She laughed.

"The water is so cold, I hardly qualify."

"Then come over here and dry out. The sun is glorious today," Li-chun said.

With his hand steadying her, she pulled herself out of the water and stood facing him.

For a moment neither spoke. The rush of rapids and the warbling of birds echoed and bounced off the sheer cliffs with a deafening sound. Svetlana wanted to move, to say something, but no words came. The air shimmered between them, and as she looked at his face, her glance dropped down to his shoulders. The water droplets on his chest glistened in the sun and quivered from his quick breathing, then dropped off, leaving his skin smooth and shining. She leaned over and kissed off a few remaining drops—a feathery touch, a fleeting contact, but enough to send an electric current that surged through her with unexpected intensity.

With a sharp intake of breath Li-chun grasped her wrist and, without a word, led her off the rock and around the large cavernous boulder; then he pulled her down onto the blanket.

Kneeling beside her, he cupped her face in both his palms. "Oh, my dearest," he whispered, leaning over and kissing her wet eyelids tenderly. "I struggled to destroy my love for you and found myself a hypocrite. How could I ever have thought that I could keep my word never to see you again?" He looked at her in wonder. "Never to touch you again?"

He was trembling. She looked into his eyes and saw a stunning force of passion clouding his gaze. She wrapped her arms around him and found his mouth to silence words she feared to hear. This was the time to flee from painful thoughts into the world of sharpened senses—the smell of sun-kissed skin, the sound of quickened breath, the flavor of a kiss, the touch of love.

There would be no holding back with what the hands and mouth so yearned to do. In this wild, enchanted time they would let untamed desires take over and grant a glimpse of Eden. Their singular, suspended Eden. She circled his neck, then clutched at his back, impatient, longing.

He eased the pressure on her lips. "My love, this day is ours. I want to nurture each moment of our time together, for here—you're mine. Let me show you the ways of love. . . ."

She sensed a deeper meaning in his words, a promise of a new fulfillment as yet untried.

And soon she knew. Was it a kiss or a caress? What matter? A silken touch that gently pressed and moved, consumed and thrilled, an intimate communion of such private worship that her mind, abashed at first, could not resist. Her spirit rose into a new dimension to float in total helplessness. So unexpected, unimagined, and supreme this was, she reveled in complete surrender.

This tender man with fierce desires who loved her thus with long, exquisite joining, what kind of love would he expect from her, what could she give him in return? And as she thought these thoughts, he raised his head and said: "Oh, my dear, how long I dreamed of loving you like this!"

Her body moved in silent acquiescence to give him what she knew he wanted. The feel of him! The smooth, unblemished skin, the muscles trembling at her touch . . . his quickened breath, the tense, expectant face . . . this strong, courageous man was hers—her captive for the moment, this long, unending moment that would be hers to cherish and prolong in memory.

And then, driven beyond endurance and restraint, a wild and reckless man emerged to claim his right to her.

The noonday sun had moved to bless this union of unbridled love; to witness human splendor in the meadow.

The quiet moments kept the pleasure alive. Side by side they lay, reluctant to disrupt the gentle river of contentment. Her cheek was cushioned by his shoulder, his mouth against her forehead. She touched her lips against his neck and kissed its throbbing pulse.

After a while he moved, raised his head, and smiled at her.

"Isn't there a Russian saying—One doesn't feed a nightingale with fables?" he asked, sitting up and reaching for the food basket.

Svetlana laughed. "I had forgotten it! Mama used to say that to me when I would refuse to eat dinner and beg her to tell me a story."

"Well, let's see what the Potapovs have fixed for us."

Svetlana slipped on her chemise, unwrapped an open-faced sandwich of buttered sesame bread generously spread with red caviar, and, after biting off a small piece, lifted it to Li-chun's mouth. He kissed the spot where her mouth had been, then took a generous bite of the sandwich. As she smiled at his gesture, he reached into the basket and pulled out a sandwich with a garlic tea sausage and another with liver pâté, and he let her take a bite first. They played this silent game of feeding each other with dill pickles and marinated mushrooms, opened a bottle of red wine, and sipped it from two metal cups provided with the Thermos of hot tea.

Oh, how good everything tasted in the fresh air!

"I hadn't realized how hungry I was," Li-chun said with a chuckle. "I see that you were hungry too," he added, nodding at the second helping of mushrooms that Svetlana was reaching for. She tilted her head. "Must be the fresh air that's giving us the appetite."

Li-chun's mouth quivered with a suppressed smile. "Are you sure it's only the air?"

Svetlana flushed and busied her hands with the top of the Thermos. "Would you like some tea now with these sweet rolls and black currant jam?" she asked.

Li-chun nodded. "Yes, thank you."

Then, as he accepted the cup from her hands, he said, "You know, Svetlana, the grief that haunts me is the futility of my love for you now. It is all in the timing. If only I had been older when we met. . . ."

She looked at him without comprehending, and he went on: "Don't you see? Our love was so hopeless when we first met in the taiga. I was an outlaw living in primitive conditions—a hunted bandit. What could I have offered you? But if I'd been older and already in the service of the Marshal as I am now, I could have honorably asked for your hand and provided a decent life for you."

Svetlana looked away and busied herself with another cup of tea. "Why torture yourself with unfulfilled dreams?" she said quietly. "We can't turn the clock back."

Li-chun took her hand and held it. "But we can turn the clock forward."

"What do you mean?"

"I mean that you are married to Vladimir and I am alone, and that's how the future will be unless we do something about it."

Svetlana looked at him sharply. "What are you saying?"

"It is possible, you know, to change our future."

He paused, took a sip of his tea, then asked quietly, "Tell me, what is Vladimir like?"

"He's a hardworking man. A generous provider and a devoted father."

"Do you love him at all?"

"He's my *husband!*"

"You haven't answered my question."

"Oh, Li-chun, please don't! It's so painful for me to talk about it."

"And so, you've given me the answer."

He took the cup out of her hand, grasped both her hands in his, and looked intently into her eyes. "Svetlana, my dearest, I've lived in Harbin long enough to observe several mixed marriages. Granted, there are not many Russian women who have the courage to follow their hearts, but these marriages *are* accepted in society. I know!"

Svetlana looked down at her hands held captive in his. She

pulled them away, picked up her cup again, and took a gulp of tea, then circled the rim of the cup with her finger.

"Maybe they're tolerated by society, but not by their own families. And in my case there would be the added scandal of a divorce."

The moment she said it, she could see Li-chun's face flush. *"Added* scandal?" he said with an emphasis on the first word. "You consider it scandalous, then, for a Russian girl to marry a Chinese?"

"Li-chun, please! Not I—my *family* would. All I'm saying is that I couldn't go against my parents and divorce Vladimir. I—I also have Georgik to consider."

A lame excuse, for in truth she was relieved she was married and thus spared the difficult decision of marrying a Chinese man. The mere thought of opposing her family and facing their friends' reactions made her shiver.

Li-chun was watching her. "I see," he said. "I have been fooled by your love. Forgive me for even considering the possibility of a marriage. I was misled into false hope." His voice was bitter, and as he rose, she looked at him pleadingly, not knowing what to say or how to justify herself. But he turned away and leaned on the trunk of the tree.

She rose and walked toward him, but dared not touch him.

"Li-chun, please try to understand. There would be so many obstacles, so many problems to solve. My family would be alienated from us. I never told you this, but my parents' friends and their child were killed by the *hunhuzy* twenty-seven years ago, and my mother has never forgotten the tragedy. You and I would be living in an island surrounded by stormy waters. What peace could we have?"

He wheeled to face her and she was shocked to see the fierce anger in his eyes.

"Svetlana, I can overcome loss of face, even accept the truth that you don't love me as much as I thought, but I cannot stand here listening to your litany of obstacles and remain silent. It all amounts to one painful fact: your love is not strong enough. You must remember, I am no longer a bandit." He paused, then added coldly, "Only a Chinese."

"But I do love you, Li-chun!" she said, thinking how un-Chinese he looked with a lock of hair falling on his forehead, his wide-open eyes so Caucasian at that moment. "You don't understand. There are Chinese who don't want anything to do with us Russians either. There is prejudice on both sides."

"I know that too. But that doesn't make it right, does it? Strong and true love is uncompromising. It can stand against all obstacles and survive."

Svetlana winced. "Oh, how painful it is, how dreadful! All I can say to you is that I love only you, and I shall never love anyone else."

She looked up at him pleadingly. "Oh, please, Li-chun, don't look at me with such disdain, such anger. I can't bear it!"

For a while Li-chun did not touch her. The sound of cascading water continued to fill her ears, and a cold spray, carried on a sudden rush of air, made her shiver.

"Well, Svetlana," he said at last, "you can hardly blame me for being hurt. It will take a while for me to accept your decision." He turned away and squinted in the sun, watching the foaming rapids. Then he looked at her again with a sad smile. "In the meantime we might as well enjoy the rest of our days in Laoshan. We have so few of them."

He walked over to the edge of the pool and looked into the water. In the silence that followed, Svetlana agonized over the right words and found none. After a few minutes he looked at her again.

"I guess I knew all along that I was dreaming an impossible dream, and there were times when I envied those who do not feel intense emotions. But, my dear, when I speak to you of love"—he spread his hands in a helpless gesture—"at such a moment it is impossible for me to understand the empty peace of those who love no one."

His voice shook as he took her in his arms and said, "Ah, but how can I deny myself the ecstasy of making you mine even if only for a brief time?"

There was such passion in his voice that Svetlana hugged him fiercely.

"I love you, Li-chun, I do love you!" she said, pressing her face against his chest.

He held her for a moment, then pushed her gently away. A sudden smile illuminated his features.

"I think I'll take another swim before we return to the house," he said, and, turning toward the pool, dived in.

Svetlana dived after him, surfacing by his side. Again the cold water took her breath away, and for a few moments she thrashed around, wiping her face and pushing back her wet hair. Then she turned to face Li-chun and wrapped her arms around his neck. Weightless in the pool, they touched and moved in slow motion against each other. The rippling water, disturbed by the slippery friction of their bodies, tickled the skin and stirred the blood. Suddenly, she felt Li-chun's muscles tighten and in the next instant he plunged his mouth into the hollow of her neck with a passionate, drawing kiss. His arm around her waist, he pulled her firmly toward the shore. Once they were on dry ground, in the shelter of an overhanging rock, he reached for her with frenzied impatience, his arms and legs roping around her in a frenetic search for union. No tenderness this time. No gentle kiss. Only anger and frustration and the passion to possess.

And she understood then that this union, however brief, however fleeting, he was taking in lieu of the permanent gift of herself.

That evening she couldn't bear to face him in front of other guests in the dining room. Some things were beyond one's ability to hide. She feigned a headache and asked to have a tray brought to her room. After she had eaten, she waited until darkness fell, then walked out and stood by the edge of the bluff in the moonless night.

Prejudice dies hard, Li-chun had said to her once. He had learned of her family's prejudice this afternoon and had bristled at the humiliation. And she loved him deeply, passionately, with a kind of love she could never feel for Vladimir nor for any other man; of this she was sure. How shameful that such a love was still not strong enough to overcome her fear of arguments, of disapproval, of the bitter accusations from her mother, if she were to divorce Vladimir and marry Li-chun. How could she do that to her mother, who hated the *hunhuzy* with a justifiable passion?

But were these the real reasons? She shuddered and hugged herself.

How foolish to be dishonest when alone, in the solitude of

the night. Why not admit the truth? Shame was like a shadow —a haunting specter of the soul. Hers was devastating. Painful it was to wrench it out. Painful, like a malignant growth. Her parents, her friends, Vladimir, her child . . . She had used all of them as excuses to cover up the real reason. Oh, it hurt to admit it even to herself! But there it was: she herself could not completely accept the idea of being married to Li-chun. Every time she would go into the Zhelsob club, or appear onstage, she would imagine people whispering behind her back, pointing their finger at her as the one who had divorced her Russian husband and chosen instead to marry a Chinese. Maybe they'd even despise her for leaving such a seemingly loyal, devoted husband at that. Loyal! If they only knew the truth! She shivered in the cool darkness.

But that didn't change anything. While she could understand Li-chun's thoughts about a divorce, it wasn't fair of him to voice them to her. *She* was the one who should have brought it up if she truly wanted this, not he. Now he felt that her love was not as great as his—and perhaps he was right. Though he had risked his life for her twice, she had repaid him by revealing her own lack of courage.

In the end he had forgiven her, had loved her again with a passion born of desperation. Now she would always be ashamed of her cowardice—yes, cowardice. No other word could better describe her fear of society's and her family's disapproval.

So, she had chosen to reject Li-chun's offer, and in doing so had condemned herself to living—or rather existing—with a man she no longer loved, a man who was unfaithful, and whose political views were repugnant to her. A life of deceit. A sham. And the devil of it was that society—and even her family—could accept and forgive Vladimir's infidelity more readily than if *she* were to defy their conventions.

What was there to do? She closed her eyes for a few moments. Maybe she wasn't being totally fair to Vladimir. He had his ideals, his convictions. He considered himself a disappointed man, a cheated man, and perhaps he had been driven into the affair with Raissa by what he thought was his wife's betrayal and her lack of affection. After all, in his own way he

tried to be a good husband, devoted to the family, generous.
And he adored Georgik.

She shook her head. Why say all this to herself? It didn't
change anything. Her heart belonged to Li-chun, and always
would. Only one path remained. She would savor the crumbs
of her love and see Li-chun as often as possible. The future as
a whole loomed painfully, but if she thought of a day at a time
—maybe . . .

*Don't think of it, Svetlana, enjoy the rest of your vacation.
Love Li-chun. He's yours right now.*

There were only five days left. Every morning they disappeared into the wilderness, swam, sunned, loved, and slept in
each other's arms under the sky. He taught her the names of
various flowers and trees as they walked in the valley, and she
sang for him and saw his eyes light with pleasure and wonder
as her pure soprano echoed among the cliffs. She told him
how much she loved poetry and was delighted with the slight
lilt of his Russian words as he recited her favorite poems of
Pushkin and Lermontov.

They talked about happy things, shared memories from
their childhoods, and painted their love with graceful words.
But the words were tinged with sorrow, the kisses flavored
with regret.

And then the last day arrived—a brilliant day with the air
windless and the birds hidden in the leafy branches of a tree.
The sun burned their skin, and the fire from the sky joined
their inner fires.

In the murmur and the rush of flowing water they cooled
themselves in silence, clinging to each other and to the hours
that slipped away. Relentless time marched on.

In the melancholy of the final moments there were no
words to say.

No solace.

Chapter Twenty-three

Li-chun left first. Svetlana didn't want to say good-bye. "It's silly," she said rather shortly. "Aren't we going to see each other soon? I'll call you after I return to Harbin, and—and I hope you have a good trip home." She tried to make her voice sound crisp and confident, but it rang false in her ears. Li-chun only nodded, turned on his heel, and climbed into the waiting sedan chair.

Oh, the fierce intensity of parting! Svetlana watched the coolies as they carried him down into the valley, straining to keep him in sight until they disappeared behind the bend of the valley floor. Then she slowly returned to her room.

In the remaining days she shunned human contact and the beehive activity of the dining room during mealtime. Her room was hot, and a troublesome fly droned above her head. Outside, the strident cry of cicadas rang painfully in her ears.

What was she doing there, alone in Laoshan, torturing herself with the lonely void left by Li-chun? The daily busyness of family routine would be good for her now; preferable to staying here alone and longing for her love. At home Georgik would occupy her waking hours with touching affection. Suddenly she longed to see him, to hold his solid little body in her arms again. Her spare time would be devoted to her singing. She had already been scheduled for three more concerts in the autumn, and before them she would need further coaching.

She also needed the reassurance that she was right in her decision not to wound her parents, not to traumatize little Georgik by a divorce. Her own doubts were secondary. Surely.

After the joy of seeing Georgik things at home were not peaceful. Sullen and irritable, Vladimir showed no appreciable pleasure at seeing her. "Your mother wants to talk to you," he said bluntly over dinner the first night.

"Oh? What about?" Svetlana asked, and when he hesitated, she went on, "How is Raissa?"

"I think that's what Sonya wants to talk to you about," he replied, burying himself in the newspaper.

"Is Raissa still depressed?"

The newspaper rustled in Vladimir's hands. "How would I know? She hasn't been around lately," he answered testily, and Svetlana realized that she must resist taunting him, great as the temptation was. It would serve no purpose except to cause more tension between them.

The next morning Sonya came to see her after Vladimir had gone to work. She seemed relieved to see Svetlana again, and hugged her longer than usual. "I'm so glad you're back, my dear. I need you!"

"What is it, Mother? You looked worried."

Sonya accepted a cup of coffee, pushed a silver filigreed basket of poppy-seed bread away, and settled back in her chair. This was unlike Sonya, Svetlana thought, for her mother had always loved her midmorning refreshments.

"I'm dreadfully worried about Raissa," she began. "I thought she'd snap out of whatever was bothering her, but she seems worse. In the morning her eyes are red from crying and bleary from lack of sleep. She is so depressed, she hardly touches any food. You should see her—a mere shadow of herself. Most of her days she spends curled up on her bed staring at the wall, and she has stopped socializing entirely. She refuses to see Igor Sotin, and so he stopped coming around. I guess he thinks she wants to break off their relationship." Sonya frowned. "Silly girl. Good men are hard to come by nowadays, and he would have been a good match. She's no beauty, and unfortunately, that scar on her face doesn't appeal to young men who see her for the first time. So what does she want out of life?"

Svetlana bristled. "Mama! How unkind! I think Raissa is quite pretty. And also, she has sex appeal. The scar certainly didn't prevent Igor Sotin from falling in love with her."

"I know, I know, that's why I'm saying she is foolish to reject him. Anyway, I can't talk to her, and your father has had no luck either. As I said before you left for Laoshan, I think she'd talk to you, if she will talk to anyone. There's nothing we can do unless we know what's troubling her. Go see her, Svetlana. Try your best to draw her out, find out what it is that's causing her deep depression."

"Have you considered taking her to Dr. Bodrin? A professional—and a stranger—may be the one to whom she would talk more readily than to me, Mama. You know very well that members of the family are often the last to know how to help one of their own."

"No! I don't want any scandal in town. Someone may see us going into the psychiatrist's office and jump to the wrong conclusions. You know how rumors start, and then it's impossible to dispel them. Besides, I did ask Raissa if she would like to see a doctor, and she flatly refused."

"I'll try, Mama, but I don't know if I can do any more than you have," Svetlana said reluctantly, painfully aware of the problem that she would face when she confronted her sister.

After Sonya had left, Svetlana decided to see Raissa that afternoon, for putting off an unpleasant encounter, she decided, was far worse than getting it over with. As she stepped out of her house, she remembered the Veronal tablets that Raissa had brought her during Georgik's kidnapping. She went back to the bedroom and picked up the almost untouched bottle of sleeping pills and put it in her purse. As she walked to her parents' house, she mused over her lack of bitterness over Raissa's betrayal. She blamed Vladimir entirely, and in fact felt sorry for her sister. Was it because she herself was guilty of infidelity and her heart belonged to another?

But she was not so naive as to think her conversation with Raissa was going to be easy, for there still remained a touch of anger at her sister's audacity and breach of loyalty. Raissa, however, evidently needed help badly. Her own resentment had to be pocketed for a while; she would do whatever she could—if Raissa would accept her help.

At the house Sonya rose from her chair in the parlor and in a purposefully loud voice announced, "How nice of you to drop by, Svetlana. I'm sorry I have to leave on an errand, but I'm sure Raissa will be glad to see you. Have a nice visit, you two."

Svetlana nodded her understanding and knocked on Raissa's bedroom door. After a long time the door opened, and without a word Raissa stepped aside to let Svetlana in.

Svetlana studied her. *This is going to be more difficult than I thought,* she realized, shocked by the change in her sister. Pale, with dark circles under her eyes, Raissa looked older than her twenty-one years. She had lost weight and her cheeks were sunken, accentuating the scar on her jaw. Impulsively, Svetlana reached for Raissa's hand and took it between her palms. It was cold.

"Raechka," Svetlana said, "talk to me, tell me what's wrong."

But Raissa sat down on the edge of her bed and, staring at the window with a fixed and unseeing look, withdrew her hand. She said nothing.

Svetlana pulled up a chair and sat down near the bed. "You've lost too much weight, and I can see by the look in your eyes that you're not sleeping at night," she said, taking the bottle of Veronal out of her purse and shaking out a pill. "Take this pill in the evening and see if it won't break the vicious cycle of your insomnia."

Raissa followed her sister's movements as Svetlana placed the bottle on the nightstand and held the pill out on the palm of her hand. When Raissa failed to respond, Svetlana took her sister's face between her hands and said, "Are you still fretting over Georgik's kidnapping?" When Raissa did not answer, Svetlana went on, "Surely you know that our anxiety over Georgik is behind us? Look at me, I'm his mother, and I left him at home with Agrafena and went off on a vacation by myself. You should see him now. Agrafena took even better care of him than I would. He gained weight in my absence and apparently was as cheerful as he has always been. What more proof do you want that I am no longer worried?"

As she talked, Svetlana noticed that Raissa's glance flickered with a trace of animation and she moved her hand slightly as though to dismiss the problem.

Svetlana shook her arm. "Raissa, can't you say *anything*, for goodness sake?"

Raissa lowered her gaze and stared at the floor. "I'm glad Georgik is well," she said without inflection.

Slowly, Svetlana sat back. An unpleasant thought filled her mind. *It isn't Georgik at all. She hasn't thought about Georgik.* It wasn't guilt about the kidnapping that was bothering her sister. Svetlana sat up straight and moved to the edge of the chair.

Vladimir. It was Vladimir her sister was still grieving over; she couldn't get over his rejection. Raissa really loved him. She actually *loved* him! For a few minutes Svetlana studied the abject face of her sister. Vladimir was the one who had ended their affair. He wasn't worth this kind of anguish. Somehow she had to break through Raissa's withdrawal, bring on tears, make her weep the hurt out. And one way to do this was to risk adding to her shame by confronting her.

Svetlana rose.

"Raissa," she said quietly, "I *know* what is bothering you. I've known all along."

When Raissa still did not respond, Svetlana lost her patience. She raised her voice. "Do you hear? Do you understand what I am saying to you? I *know* what happened."

Raissa frowned; a flicker of fear flashed in her eyes and quickly died out. She seemed to reject the threatening thought.

Exasperated, Svetlana tried again. "I *know* about you and Vladimir. I've known for some time now. You see, I overheard his telephone conversation with you that day when he told you it was all over."

Suddenly, Raissa's lips began to quiver. Slowly, piteously, she collapsed on the bed, burying her face deep in the pillow, and heaved with gasping sobs.

Svetlana touched her shoulder. "Raechka, please, look at me! I want you to know that I don't hold it against you anymore. I've forgiven you, and I think I can even understand how it happened. I—I still love you, do you hear?"

But Raissa continued to sob, clutching the pillow and not letting Svetlana turn her over.

"I've just told you that I still love you, dear. I want you to put it behind you. There are eligible, worthy men around, and you will get over this."

As Raissa continued to weep, Svetlana raised her voice: "For heaven's sake, Raissa, you can at least tell me you're grateful I came to see you and that I've forgiven you."

Raissa's sobs became louder. Through hiccuping gasps she whimpered, her voice muffled by the pillow, "Oh, go away! Please, please go away! I can't bear to face you, can't bear it . . . oh, I can't bear it!"

Svetlana stood over Raissa for a few minutes, listening to her sobs. Perhaps her sister needed this time alone for the quiet catharsis of tears.

Saddened, she turned and left the room.

The telephone rang shrilly at eleven o'clock that night and Svetlana, who had just climbed into bed beside a sleeping Vladimir, jumped out and ran to answer it. Sonya's voice was hysterical, incoherent. "Raissa . . . I went in to her room to see if she had eaten any of her dinner. . . . I can't rouse her, she's unconscious! Nikolai called the doctor. . . . Oh, God, what's happened to her?"

"We'll be right over, Mama!" Svetlana said, and raced to wake Vladimir. He flushed a dull red when she said she wanted him to come with her. While he was dressing, she opened her purse and looked for the Veronal bottle. It wasn't there. She tried to recall the details of her visit to Raissa that afternoon. She remembered placing the bottle on the night-stand while she was offering the pill to Raissa, but she couldn't recall putting the bottle back in her purse. . . . Svetlana's hands shook as she snapped her purse shut.

At her parents' home they found Nikolai pacing the dining room floor.

"Talk to Papa," Svetlana said curtly to Vladimir, and rushed to Raissa's bedroom. Sonya was kneeling beside the unconscious girl, talking and slapping her cheeks.

"I tried the spirits of ammonia, but she doesn't react at all. Oh, God, is she going to die?"

Svetlana pushed past her mother and opened the drawer of the nightstand. The bottle of Veronal was lying on its side, empty. She ran back to the dining room.

"Call the ambulance at once," she ordered Vladimir. "Raissa took an overdose of Veronal. We can't wait for the doctor to arrive. Every second counts."

At the Tsentralnaya Bolnitsa they paced the waiting-room floor for several hours, not knowing whether Raissa would live. Vladimir ignored Svetlana's pointed glances, unaware of the accusation behind them, and showered attention on distraught Sonya and Nikolai.

The vigil was long, but Raissa lived. The time between the ingestion of pills and the pumping of her stomach had been short enough to prevent lethal absorption. Relieved and exhausted, the family returned to their respective homes to await Raissa's recovery.

Shattered by the experience, Svetlana stayed home during the ensuing days, practicing her singing, caring for and playing with her little son, and venturing outdoors only with Agrafena and Georgik. For she *did* feel guilty about what had happened. If she hadn't forgotten those pills . . . But then, how could she have thought that Raissa would try to take her own life? Still, in a way, she felt responsible.

She did not call Li-chun or go to see him. Somehow, she was afraid that the lovely, dreamlike quality of their time together in Laoshan would be destroyed if she went to his flat again so soon. She needed time to put distance between that precious dream and her daily life, before she faced the reality of their relationship and allowed her love to become guilty of subtle indiscretions.

Right now she hoped to help her sister rebuild her life. Raissa was kept in the hospital for a couple of weeks, and after she returned home, she did not go to see her older sister. Svetlana understood. According to Sonya's reports Raissa had plunged anew into her studies in spite of the summer recess at school.

Then, one day, Vladimir came home agitated. After dinner, when they were alone in the room, he said, "Igor Sotin hasn't been to work for a few days. I thought he was ill, but today he came in and said he was leaving."

Svetlana raised her brows and waited.

Vladimir paused for effect, then continued: "He is emigrating to the Soviet Union."

"Oh? Where is he going to settle?" Svetlana asked, then corrected herself. "Or rather, where are they sending him?"

Vladimir let the sarcasm pass. "He was told he would be sent to Moscow."

"I wonder. . . . It will be interesting to see the postmark on his first letter, provided we get a letter at all."

"Igor has the courage of his convictions," Vladimir said defensively. "He was assured of an excellent position in the capital. So you see, I am not the only one who feels that Russia can't be as bad as you all think."

There was a wistful note in his voice. Svetlana looked up sharply. "Don't tell me *you* are considering doing the same?"

"How could I, with a wife who doesn't even have a Soviet passport?" Vladimir said. "I must say it looks more and more attractive to me. I only wish you weren't so blindly influenced by your parents—and mine."

Svetlana shrugged and did not answer. There was no point in continuing the discussion, for it would only lead to rancor.

The next afternoon Raissa at last came to see Svetlana. She still looked thin, but the color had returned to her cheeks and her eyes no longer looked listless and dull. When Svetlana moved toward her with outstretched arms, Raissa backed away. Svetlana stopped and silently offered her a chair, but her sister shook her head. With an effort she cleared her throat and carefully placed a wrapped gift on the table.

"This is a little toy for Georgik. He likes to twirl tops, and this is a colorful one," she said without a smile.

"Thank you," Svetlana replied. "I'm sure Georgik will love it. Why won't you sit down?"

Raissa shook her head again and stood rigidly in the center of the room.

"Svetlana," she said with an effort, "I—I'm ashamed to face you. Nonetheless I found courage to come here. I felt I owed you that much." Her voice was strained, as if she were delivering a memorized speech. "I—I came to tell you that I'm sorry for having hurt you. I've decided to leave Harbin. I can't stay here and continue seeing you and—and Vladimir.

And to avoid you would be impossible. Sooner or later Mama and Papa would wonder."

"But where will you go?"

"I have it all worked out. I'm going to Shanghai. I'll finish my pharmaceutical training there. I told Mama and Papa that I wanted to build a career of my own and"—she smiled ruefully—"my plans happen to coincide with Igor Sotin's decision to emigrate to Russia. They think I'm heartbroken over that."

"Aren't you afraid to be alone in a strange city?" Svetlana asked with alarm. "Can you leave everything familiar behind? You'll be on your own!"

"It will be far better than staying here and living with an impossible situation," Raissa answered quietly.

Suddenly, Svetlana felt an overwhelming compassion for her sister, and with it memories of their childhood came flooding back. "I hope you understand what you're doing. You don't know anyone in Shanghai."

"No, but friends at school have given me addresses of their relatives and friends who have been living there for quite some time."

"Oh, my dear! You have courage to do this." Svetlana moved toward her again, but Raissa backed away.

"Raissa!" Svetlana said. "Let's try to put the past behind us."

"No. Please don't! It took a lot to pull myself together and —and to admit that I've hurt you, that I've all but ruined my life. I can't face you again—ever—without shame. Perhaps it would have been easier if you hadn't been so kind. I've cried all my tears out. Please don't ask the impossible. If you touch me—if you hug me—I—I'm afraid I'll break down again. This way it's easier for me to say how sorry I am. Can you understand that?" She twisted her lips in a sardonic smile. "Call it my penance, if you wish."

"I understand," Svetlana said quietly, "and I'm glad you're strong enough to make the break and want to start your life afresh. Oh, it's all so sad, Raissa! Please write to us."

As Raissa nodded and turned to leave, Svetlana instinctively reached out to touch her but caught her hand in midair and slowly lowered it.

As the door was about to shut behind Raissa, Svetlana called out after her, "I love you, little *sestryonka!*"

But the door had slammed shut and she wasn't sure if Raissa heard.

Chapter Twenty-four

Once back in Harbin, Li-chun found himself relieved that Svetlana had stayed on in Laoshan. He wasn't sure he could face her right away now that he knew she would never divorce Vladimir. As a Chinese he should have been more understanding of her filial obedience, her abhorrence of the idea of hurting her parents. After all, he himself had been taught those values since childhood. Surely it was a noble deed to sacrifice one's love in order to avoid shaming one's parents and hurting their pride.

Then why did he feel resentful? The question irked him. Was it because in his case he had found the strength to defy his father? But then, he had been spared the difficult test of living among his people, who would condemn him for his actions, and surely his father had never found out who had rescued Georgik.

It was different with Svetlana, and it was wrong of him to forget that, for she would have had to remain among her friends and face her parents.

But what about the mixed marriages he had seen? Those couples seemed well adjusted. Sooner or later her parents would have had to accept her decision. And if there were to be another child . . . He closed his eyes and inhaled deeply. His child.

No, he was not going to give up so easily. A plan found its

way into his mind. He would start attending all social functions where he might see Svetlana, go to all her performances, keep her love for him alive, provoke her restlessness and then . . . maybe . . .

He slept well that night, and when he awoke the next morning, the world looked less bleak than it had the day before.

But at work his superior, Liu Tsu-min, called him into his office and informed him that he had been summoned to Mukden.

"Mukden?" Li-chun repeated, surprised. "But Marshal Chang Tso-lin is now in Peking. Who is summoning me?"

Liu Tsu-min busied himself with a sheaf of papers on his desk and didn't look up.

"A Captain Yoshida," he replied in a flat tone.

Japanese. He was being summoned by the Japanese. While the Soviet influence in Manchuria was an ongoing threat, the Japanese presence and growing control were very real and unsettling.

"I'll leave tomorrow," he said, wondering why someone in Mukden had suddenly remembered his existence. And why the summons?

Captain Yoshida, a short and slender man, studied Li-chun with a shrewd, and what seemed a crafty, look.

"Our command," Captain Yoshida began, carefully enunciating his words, "is concerned with the latest developments in China. The Nationalists have advanced into Honan and are now in a position to threaten Shantung. Unified under Chiang Kai-shek, they would be a great threat to Marshal Chang Tso-lin in Peking. As you probably know, our Premier General Tanaka wishes for the Marshal to concentrate on keeping his position here in Manchuria. We've been advising him to return to Mukden and abandon his adventures in China proper."

Li-chun bristled at the deprecating word but remained silent and studied the Japanese officer, who had assumed an erect, pompous pose in front of him. *What you really mean,* Li-chun thought, *is that the Old Marshal is too far away for you to control him.*

"If the Marshal stays in Peking much longer," Captain

Yoshida went on, "he'll be defeated. You've been the Marshal's aide. He trusted you enough to send you on a delicate assignment to Harbin."

It was not a question, and Li-chun listened without comment.

"Go to Peking with our memorandum and persuade him to return here," Captain Yoshida said. "We feel he'll consider our message more favorably if it is delivered by you. We are assuring him of all our support once he is back in Mukden."

Li-chun's first loyalty was to the Old Marshal, in spite of the distance that had grown between them ever since that incident in the Soviet embassy, but he couldn't help agreeing with Captain Yoshida that Chang Tso-lin had overestimated his power in China and was now losing ground. Although it was distasteful for Li-chun to be an emissary of the Japanese, he had no alternative but to obey.

When he arrived in Peking, he found that the situation was indeed deteriorating; yet the Marshal stubbornly refused to heed the warning and withdraw his army to Manchuria. He kept Li-chun by his side in his old capacity as an aide, and still Li-chun expected that any day now the Marshal would agree to return to Mukden. So sure was Li-chun of this, that he continued to pay rent on his flat in Harbin.

But it took until the following May for the old warlord to conclude that unless he took his units back to Manchuria, his defeat was imminent. So later that month he finally sent Li-chun back to Mukden to prepare the way for his return and to see that the security along both the South Manchurian Railway and the Peking–Mukden tracks was adequate.

Finally, on Sunday, June 3, 1928, Marshal Chang Tso-lin left for Manchuria.

Meanwhile in Mukden, Li-chun had run into unexpected opposition from the Japanese command, who would not allow Chang's troops to guard the railway. Although his request to place fifty military police and mounted guards for approximately three miles along the approaches to the city was granted because of the danger of sabotage, the Japanese refused permission to position Chinese police where the Peking–Mukden line passed under the South Manchurian Railway viaduct. They reinforced their own guards, however, and

tightened security measures under the bridge along the Peking–Mukden right of way, thus excluding Chinese police
from all points of the intersection.

Uneasy about this development, Li-chun awaited the Old
Marshal's arrival on the morning of June fourth.

*During the night of June third a group of men dressed in
dark clothing appeared at the crossing of the Peking–Mukden
and the South Manchurian railways. They carried square-
shaped explosives, electric wire, and detonators. Their work was
concentrated on the South Manchurian viaduct above the Peking–Mukden tracks. It took them several hours to finish their
labor, and then they left as quietly and as stealthily as they had
appeared. An hour later a convoy of Japanese soldiers brought
three Chinese men to the tracks and bayoneted two of them at
the crossing. During the struggle the third man escaped into the
darkness and fled.*

Early in the morning of June fourth Li-chun stood at the
Mukden station waiting for the Marshal's arrival. An honor
guard was positioned on the platform, and an air of expectancy hung in the air. Then, at five-thirty A.M., a thunderous
explosion sounded in the distance. Li-chun started. Where
had it come from? He had seen to it that the Chinese guarded
the approach to Mukden. Except—his pulse quickened and a
sick feeling tightened his stomach—except the crossing of the
Peking–Mukden and South Manchurian tracks.

He rushed out of the station, but in the ensuing confusion it
took him a while to find an automobile. When at last he arrived on the scene and jumped out, he was stunned by the
sight before him.

The accident had taken place at the spot where the South
Manchurian Railway between Mukden and Changchun
crossed on a viaduct the Peking–Mukden railway between
Huangkutun and Mukden City station.

Quickly Li-chun scanned the train, looking for the Marshal's car. The rear of the eighth car, number eighty, was on
fire. It was Peking–Mukden Railway's private car for Marshal
Chang Tso-lin, and Li-chun had no trouble identifying it. The
top of the car was blown off, but the lower part was still intact

and stood upright in spite of the fact that the first six cars had overturned. The explosion, then, must have happened on the viaduct above.

Dazed, he stopped for a moment, trying to absorb the extent of the disaster, oblivious of the Japanese guards and Chinese police working feverishly around him to remove the wounded from the derailed cars. Then he hurried forward, passing two dead Chinese men lying by the embankment, stepping over debris, and maneuvering his way among the throng of people toward car number eighty. But before he reached it, Major Giga, the Marshal's Japanese military advisor, appeared by his side. Visibly shaken, the man pulled Li-chun away from the train.

"Where's the Marshal? Is he hurt?" Li-chun asked anxiously.

"The Marshal was taken to his mansion in a Ford automobile," Major Giga replied. "But General Wu Chun-sheng has been taken in a carriage to a hospital." He averted his eyes from Li-chun's searching look. "They're both badly wounded, but the Marshal insisted on being taken to his home," he added, then pointed to his leg. "I'm lucky. I was in the same car when it happened, and I have only this bruise."

Li-chun was silent. All he could think of was that both the Marshal and his close associate, General Wu Chun-sheng, were wounded badly enough to be immediately taken away from the scene of disaster.

"Was anyone killed beside these two?" he asked, pointing to the dead Chinese men.

"No one else, to my knowledge."

Li-chun took a closer look at the dead men, then raised his head slowly. "Looks like these men were bayoneted. Who are they?"

Major Giga shrugged. "I don't know, I haven't seen them before."

"You said you were in the Marshal's car. Were you with him when it exploded?" he asked.

Major Giga nodded.

"Please tell me what happened," Li-chun said.

"We were sitting in the observation area of the car," Major Giga told him. "It was cold, and General Wu suggested that the Marshal put his coat on. Then, just as the Marshal stood up, there was this deafening explosion and seconds later we heard a terrible crash." Major Giga pointed to the steel spans of the South Manchurian Railway viaduct that had fallen on the train. "We were all thrown about. The Marshal fell. He—he was bleeding heavily from a chest wound." Major Giga shook his head. "A dreadful catastrophe!"

Shuddering slightly, the major nodded and walked away.

Li-chun studied the scene of the disaster. The steel bridges were of heavy construction, their three spans supported by two piers in the middle and buttresses at each end. These were of granite masonry, and the piers had been reinforced by concrete that must have measured about six feet across. Whoever planned the accident had known that it would require a lot of explosives and several hours of work to secure them to the viaduct. And close to the viaduct, near the base of the South Manchurian Railway embankment, there were several railway sleeper cars surrounded by barbed wire entanglements and serving as blockhouses for the Japanese guards.

The whole area had been guarded entirely by the Japanese. Li-chun looked pensively at the two dead Chinese men. Were they being used as decoys?

It was too frightening a thought and he didn't want to guess the answer. Turning abruptly, he boarded his automobile and raced back to the Marshal's mansion.

Li-chun stayed in the mansion's reception room waiting for word on the Marshal's condition. An air of tension pervaded the great hall as aides and servants and medical personnel rushed back and forth.

Li-chun waited. At ten o'clock in the morning he was told that Marshal Chang Tso-lin had died.

Who had masterminded the plan? The Japanese? It seemed unlikely, since the Old Marshal¹was returning to Manchuria to cooperate with Japan, unless—unless the more radical group of the Japanese military had taken things into their own hands. Suddenly, Li-chun remembered hearing about a speech made by Colonel Kawamoto, a senior staff officer of the Kwantung Army, at the Yamato Hotel in Dairen. He had publicly declared for the overthrow of Marshal Chang Tso-lin, calling him an obstacle to Japan's policy in Manchuria. At the time this speech was repeated to Li-chun by his superior in Harbin, he had thought it the rhetoric of a single radical officer; but now he was not so sure.

Distraught, apprehensive, not knowing what to think, Li-chun decided to leave Mukden. The Marshal's oldest son, Chang Hsueh-liang, would no doubt be stepping into his father's place now, and he had his own aides. Li-chun did not stay to pay his respects, for some sixth sense urged him to go back to Harbin immediately.

When Svetlana heard the news of Marshal Chang Tso-lin's assassination, her first thought was of Li-chun. Had he been with the Marshal on the train? And if not, where was he now? Her anxiety was such that it took tremendous effort to conceal it from Vladimir and the rest of the family. Several times a day she telephoned his flat and let it ring longer than usual. The monotonous ringing sounded in her ears, and during the brief silences she prayed frantically that he would answer, her thoughts racing to outrun the next ring, willing it to be the last, and then listening with disappointment to yet another precise and impersonal ring. . . .

Surely there was a simple explanation; a dozen reasons why he could have been delayed in Mukden. So her thoughts ran, and her indomitable hope continued to deny a tragedy.

In the end it was Li-chun who called her, and she wanted to drop everything and rush out to see him, for she knew that he had admired the Old Marshal and would be devastated by his death.

That afternoon it started to rain; nevertheless she decided not to wait but to slip out of the house before Vladimir came home. It was easier to leave without having to give him excuses as to where she was going.

Now that Li-chun had returned to Harbin, though, she would rarely have to worry about devising a plausible reason for her absence. Her continual rehearsals and coaching lessons would be a good cover-up for her late home arrival. Of course Vladimir could easily check by telephoning the studio, but somehow it no longer was important to keep him free of suspicion. In some perverted way Vladimir's affair with Raissa freed her from guilt and salved her conscience.

Of late her husband had become more and more pensive and withdrawn. After many months of silence he had received his first letter from Igor Sotin. His friend wrote glowingly about his new life in Moscow and how happy he was to be in his motherland. The last word was underlined.

"See? What did I tell you?" Vladimir said triumphantly. "They *did* keep their promise to send him to Moscow." And when Svetlana only shrugged and said nothing, he added wistfully, "How wonderful it must be to live among your own people, in a truly Russian city, and—"

"In the Soviet paradise," Svetlana finished for him. "We're all aware that letters are censored before they are allowed to leave the country, so we'll never know the truth. And just why did it take him so long to write his first letter? Where was he until now?"

"Oh, it's no use talking to you. I can't believe how biased you are," Vladimir snapped, ending the conversation.

That had been a few weeks ago, and since then the distance between them had grown. They were polite to each other and cool, and his demands on her at night were rare.

The long months of Li-chun's absence from Harbin had been torturous. His letters from Peking had been passed to her surreptitiously by a silent rickshaw coolie who seemed to be aware of the times she left the house alone.

Li-chun had written of his love and his impatience to see her again when he returned to Harbin. Of his work or what kept him in Peking he had written nothing, and she guessed that he did not want to mention sensitive political issues in a letter that would pass through several hands before reaching her. In his last message, however, he'd announced that he was going to Mukden and then to Harbin, but could not write more because he was leaving Peking in a hurry.

What a glorious relief to have heard his voice at last! She smiled now as she hurried to his flat. By the time she reached it, her patent leather Bata shoes were spotted with raindrops. She wiped them with her handkerchief and rang the bell.

Li-chun opened the door immediately, as though he had been expecting her. Svetlana wrapped her arms around him and felt his heart pounding against her. *Oh, my dear, my dear! All these months, and now* . . . She hugged him and he found her mouth in a long and hungry kiss. They stood in a tight embrace for a long time, each loath to be the first to break away. Finally, she moved back slightly and studied his face with tenderness. How drawn he looked, how sad. Yet another emotion burned through the sadness in his eyes. Anxiety? Fear?

"I came as soon as I could," she said. "How difficult it must be for you. And how sad it is to meet like this after all these months. I've missed you so much!"

"And I missed you. You must know that from my letters. It was worse for me, for I knew you couldn't risk writing to me."

Svetlana nodded, then said, "The Marshal's death . . . how tragic for Manchuria! Who's behind all this?"

"I doubt we'll ever know the truth," Li-chun replied quietly. "He had so many enemies. And General Wu Chun-sheng died too."

"But who gains the most by his death?" And when Li-chun didn't answer, she asked, "Do you suppose the Japanese are involved in this?"

Slowly he turned his head away. "I don't know."

"Li-chun! Your mind is somewhere else. What is it?"

"I'm just wondering on whom the real culprits are going to pin the crime."

Something in his voice made her shiver a little. "Li-chun, my dear, don't think such dreadful thoughts."

He turned and took her gently in his arms, then pressed his face against her hair.

"I'm sorry, dearest. My mind is really wandering today. A messenger came yesterday to tell me my father is dying and wants to see me. I've been wrestling with my conscience all night, and this morning I decided to go into the taiga to see him."

Shocked, Svetlana grabbed his hands. "Oh, please, don't go! Don't take such a risk. I'm so afraid for you! Think how dangerous it was when you went in to get Georgik. Don't test your fate now."

"I'll be going at my father's request this time, and I should be guaranteed safe passage."

"How do you know that your father isn't already dead and you're being lured into a trap? Your father may have *wanted* to believe in your innocence, but others in the camp may not have been so willing to accept your explanation of my escape."

Li-chun looked at her pensively. "I don't think I could live with my guilt if I found out that my father had indeed summoned me on his deathbed and I failed to obey him again."

Svetlana frowned. "Everyone who has been close to the Old Marshal will be under suspicion now, won't they?" she said. "What if someone recognizes you in Maoershan and reports to the police that you are not only a former bandit, but that you went back into the taiga? They'll conclude that you still have dealings with the *hunhuzy*. And if, as you say, the real culprits are looking for someone to pin the crime on, this will give them an excuse to say that for some personal grudge you did the job."

He shrugged. "I have to take that risk. Besides, chances of my being recognized in Maoershan are remote."

He took her by the shoulders and shook her slightly.

"Don't you understand, it may be my father's last wish! I can't dismiss it lightly."

Svetlana sighed and, after a pause, nodded slowly. "No, I suppose not," she said quietly. "I know in my heart that you're right, but, oh, I'm so worried about your safety."

He smiled ruefully. "I promise to be careful, dearest. And thank you for coming over. I should be back in a few days, and then we'll see each other again. I love you so much."

She went into his arms briefly and, sensing his need to be alone, left him.

Chapter Twenty-five

Once again he rented a horse in Maoershan and entered the forest. Quickly he crossed the glen, without pausing this time to relive the sweet moments of love.

This time he was expected, and when the taiga cedars closed in on him, several bandits on horseback emerged from their hideouts in the dense burdocks and silently escorted him to his father's enclave. On the clearing he dismounted and waited until the men took his horse and withdrew, leaving him to enter the *fanza* alone.

He had forgotten how grim and dirty the interior was. The shaggy strands of soot seemed to have multiplied in the rafters, and the stale odors of opium pipe and garlic and rancid fat assailed his nostrils. The light was dim and it took him a few moments to adjust to the darkness.

A reclining figure on the k'ang moved and leaned up on one elbow. Li-chun closed his eyes momentarily to conceal his shock. His father had aged almost beyond recognition. The defiant and feared chieftain was now an emaciated old man with a shaking head and tremulous hands. Only a flicker of the old fierceness remained in the pain-filled eyes.

Slowly, Ma Fu-li beckoned to his son with his bony hand. As Li-chun approached, his father was seized by a paroxysm of coughing. Li-chun waited until the spell was over, then bowed low in obeisance.

"I received your message, honored Father, and came as soon as I could," he said.

Ma Fu-li squinted. "Come closer, my son," he said, and Li-chun was further shocked by the feeble sound of his voice. As Li-chun reached the k'ang and knelt, Ma Fu-li looked at him eagerly, scanning his freshly pressed clothes, his neat appearance. Then the older man nodded approvingly. "You look well, Li-chun. Strong, matured. Just as I had hoped you'd be." For a moment Ma Fu-li closed his eyes. "My efforts were not in vain." There was a pause, and then he seemed to think of something. "Why aren't you in uniform?"

When Li-chun explained that his job in Harbin required him to wear civilian clothes, Ma Fu-li reflected for a moment as though it was difficult for him to digest the information, then smiled his first, shaky smile. "Now that the Old Marshal is dead, you're going to be a great warlord yourself. Your time is coming, I know it."

Li-chun wanted to tell him that the Marshal's oldest son, Chang Hsueh-liang, would take his father's place, that he himself was disillusioned by the constant feuding among warlords, and he had no desire to serve the Marshal's son. All these things and more he wanted to tell his father. But he knew he couldn't disappoint a dying man, so he lowered his head and remained silent.

"I called you here, my son, to tell you something, because—because I'll be joining my ancestors soon, and—and—"

Li-chun looked up at his father abruptly. "What's wrong with you, my Father?" he asked.

Ma Fu-li thumped his chest with his fist. "It is here, the pain. For a long time now it has been growing worse."

"What medicines have you tried?"

"I've tried many remedies. Nothing helps. . . . I've inhaled garlic fumes from a bottle of extract every day for months . . . drunk boiled garlic in tea." Ma Fu-li paused, gasping for breath. After a few moments he went on. "I suppose I am still alive because I've been taking ginseng powder for strength. But all this has only lengthened my suffering, not helped me."

"You're strong, my Father. You will live a long time yet," Li-chun said, aware that his voice sounded false.

Ma Fu-li frowned. "Your words do not please me, my son. They cover the truth. I *know* this old body is worn out. There's not much time left. That's why I summoned you here. I want to tell you—I *must* tell you something before I die."

Ma Fu-li pointed to a lacquered box at the foot of the k'ang. Li-chun looked down and, from the picture of a Russian fairy tale on its lid, now scratched and dirty with age, recognized it at once as one of the Russian boxes he had seen in Handaohedzi when he lived with the Russian family, and later, in the stores in Harbin. Curious, he picked it up and handed it to his father.

Ma Fu-li shook his head. "Look inside, my son," he said, refusing to take the box.

Li-chun opened it. A piece of amber on a gold chain lay on top of a letter written in Russian. The edges were yellowed and the writing tidy and feminine. Li-chun touched the stone and looked at his father. "Is this a Russian talisman of some sort?" he asked. "I know that the Russians are very fond of amber."

"No. It's a woman's necklace. But look under it. Read the letter."

Li-chun unfolded the sheet of paper. The salutation was smeared and he could not read to whom it was addressed. But the rest of it was clear. A woman was writing to a friend about the expected birth of her child.

> . . . If it's a boy, my dear, and I feel it *will* be a son, we shall call him Gennady. He will be Gennady Rotov. I feel the child moving. It won't be long now, for it has been almost nine months. . . .

Li-chun frowned. What was this all about? He looked up. "Who wrote this letter, my Father?"

Ma Fu-li sighed and closed his eyes. When he opened them again, they were shining with moisture. "Li-chun," he said, his voice shaking, "a trusted friend translated this letter to me years ago. It was written by your mother. The child she was carrying *was* a boy, and you are that child. Your real name is Gennady Rotov, and your father was Oleg Rotov."

As Li-chun listened in shock, Ma Fu-li told him about the

incident of his birth and his parents' deaths, sparing no details and making no excuses for his decision to take the newborn boy-child and raise him as his own.

"I had no reason to kill your mother, Li-chun. You know I don't kill women unnecessarily. But she attacked me when she saw that your father was dead. . . . All I did was throw her off."

A coughing spell interrupted Ma Fu-li's words. He stopped to catch his breath, then continued. "She fell, and by the time I came out of the *fanza,* she was dead. . . . From the looks of her she probably bled to death after childbirth." He fell silent, then looked at Li-chun searchingly. "I had lost my own son earlier, and when I found you on the k'ang, I saw this as a sign from the gods."

Ma Fu-li paused, exhausted by his long speech. "This is why I sent you to live with a Russian family and go to a Russian school . . . not only for your great future, but also because I wanted you to know your real heritage as well as your adoptive one."

Ma Fu-li shifted laboriously on the k'ang. "I did my best in raising you to be a good man . . . a great man," he said. "By blood you are Russian, but I raised you to be Chinese . . . and I know I succeeded." A note of desperation had crept into Ma Fu-li's last words, as though by voicing them he needed to reassure himself about something that had worried him for a long time.

Stunned, Li-chun sat on his haunches, unable to give his father the consolation that he was seeking. A multitude of thoughts fought for priority in his head, and he was so overwhelmed, he could not say a word. The silence between them stretched on, and Li-chun became aware of the buzzing, annoying sound of a wheeling fly. It broke into his thoughts, brought him up short, made him look at his father. His *father?* Li-chun studied the emaciated face before him, and for the first time in his life he saw an almost pleading look in Ma Fu-li's face.

Yes. This *was* his father. He had known no other, and no matter what he had learned today, this was the man whom he must honor. Li-chun bowed low before the sick man.

"I thank you, honored Father, for telling me of my birth. It explains many things to me now."

Indeed. It also removed many obstacles, would help to solve his problems. He kept his eyes downcast, trying to conceal the thrill of this knowledge from Ma Fu-li.

"Never forget that you were born in China and brought up among Chinese people. Serve your country well!"

Ma Fu-li's voice weakened and he fell back on the k'ang. Li-chun looked up. A stranger lay before him, and he realized that the chasm that had grown between them over the years was too great to bridge, even on Ma Fu-li's deathbed. Saddened, he took the dying man's shriveled hand and touched his forehead to it.

"I shall never forget what you have told me, my Father," he said.

Ma Fu-li's eyelids fluttered as he waved his hand, dismissing Li-chun. "Go now, Li-chun. Take the box with you and tell none of my men of what you have just learned." His look was clouded with pain and his voice faltered when he added, "My son! . . . honor my memory."

Li-chun rose, bowed, and, clutching the precious box to his chest, backed out of the *fanza.*

Outside, he took deep gulps of fresh air, fighting to control his racing heart. Russian. He was Russian! He looked around him. Russian? But this was the place where he had spent many years of his youth with his father; the warm summer months when his father had taken him hunting and taught him many things. This was the place where he had first known Svetlana and had fallen in love with her. Those were bitter-sweet memories, and nostalgia knocked at his heart. He had to restrain his desire to walk in the surrounding woods, to linger in the clearing. It would be a foolish thing to do. There before him a group of bandits stood watching his every move in hostile silence.

He threw a last lingering look at the *fanza.* His dying father was behind those walls and he would never see him again; the father who had raised him, who was proud of him, and whose trust in the end he had betrayed. A dull ache filled his chest. He could have chosen to stay and succeed Ma Fu-li, but he no longer belonged in the taiga and had never wanted to remain with the bandits. Another man would now take his father's place; Li-chun did not want to know his name.

As slowly as he could, he walked over to his stallion, untied it, and after nodding briefly to the men, mounted and rode away.

Alone in the forest he allowed his sorrow to give way to the excitement of what his father had just told him. Ah, if only he could embrace the world, hug the ancient cedars, talk to the darting squirrels, and proclaim to the sky above what he had just learned!

He should be grieving, shouldn't he? He felt sadness, regret, compassion, but not grief. How could he grieve when everything inside him rejoiced? Should he act a bereaved son and weep with forced tears like the hired mourners at a Chinese funeral? He wouldn't even be able to come back for his father's burial after his death. It would be too dangerous to risk returning to the taiga yet another time, for then he would no longer be under his father's protection. One look at the bandits' sullen faces had told him that he was not a welcome guest. No. He had to break with his past once and for all.

He looked up. This taiga, this familiar taiga, with its ancient firs and cedars that witnessed nature's work, stood unmoved, serene. Yes. The forest sheds no tears, and he would now leave it forever.

He felt immensely relieved. Svetlana . . . his happiness with her was no longer out of the realm of possibility. His golden angel. Would she laugh or cry on learning that the greatest barrier to their love had now been removed? They would marry after her divorce from Vladimir became final, and theirs would not be a mixed marriage. He threw his head back and smiled.

Never particularly religious, he had nevertheless enjoyed attending Russian churches in Harbin. Now he had a right—no, an obligation—to become a Christian and to be baptized in the Russian Orthodox faith.

He could hardly wait to return to Harbin. With the Old Marshal now dead, he had no qualms about resigning from the army and keeping his position with the railway company as a civilian.

The lovely blond girl he had first met in the very taiga that he was now crossing would soon be his. At long last, *truly* his. What sublime happiness! He was ashamed of being so overjoyed when his father lay dying, and so soon after Marshal Chang Tso-lin's murder. After all, he owed a lot to the Marshal too. But the Marshal was dead, and he had paid his last respects to his father. And he was alive; oh, so very much alive and yearning to claim his love on equal ground now. Was that so wrong? He was young, and for the first time his future loomed unblemished.

As his horse stepped out into the glen, Li-chun reigned in the animal, dismounted, and tied it to a tree. Then he walked over to the familiar spot and, looking down at the meadow, smiled. How wonderful to be able to pause here and remember the lovely hours in Svetlana's arms, this time without pain or regret. For the first time he could indulge in reliving, without anguish, the ecstasy of that moonlit night. What happiness!

He lowered himself to the ground and stretched out in sheer exuberance that begged expression. Leaning on one hand, he moved the palm of the other over the soft grass, caressing it with vivid memories of that first passion.

It wasn't necessary for Svetlana to tell him that she was unhappy with Vladimir. He knew—and, knowing, was glad of it, for then the divorce would not be too traumatic for her. Unfortunate that she had to go through it at all, but then he would reward her with his care and love and make her forget all the unhappiness of the past years. And God willing, they would have a child of their own. As for Georgik, he already loved the child. Suddenly, Li-chun stopped stroking the grass. What if Vladimir decided to fight for the custody of the child? Surely he couldn't be that selfish. The child belonged with his mother.

Li-chun looked at the sky. The day was ending, and the taiga chill would soon enter the glen. It was time to leave and return the horse. He rose and untied him and then, with a last look at the glen that held such deep sentiment for him, mounted and started for Maoershan, entering the forest on its western side.

Deep in his thoughts, he followed the familiar path and soon emerged from the taiga to see the Maoershan cottages, the river, and . . . the police waiting for him at the edge of the forest.

Chapter Twenty-six

The *Zarya* carried the story on its front page. The headline read AIDE TO MARSHAL CHANG TSO-LIN ARRESTED AND CHARGED WITH COMPLICITY IN ASSASSINATION OF MARSHAL. The story disclosed that one Ma Li-chun, who had been employed by the Chinese Eastern Railway Company, had been revealed as a former *hunhuz*. He had been arrested in Maoershan, where he had gone to visit his father, an outlaw chieftain. Those close to Marshal Chang Tso-lin stated that the Marshal had been displeased with his aide in the past and on several occasions had voiced his disappointment. The report went on to say that on the night of June third Ma Li-chun had been seen on the viaduct at the site of the explosion where the two railway lines crossed each other.

As Svetlana read the article, which spared no details, the room blackened before her and she had to sit down to keep from fainting.

Perhaps if she had insisted more forcefully that he stay away from his father's enclave, he would have listened to her. But even as she thought this, she knew it wasn't likely. And now he was in terrible danger, arrested on false charges—for surely they *were* false. Li-chun had suspected the crime might be pinned on an innocent person. Of course he could exonerate himself, prove that he had not been involved in the plot. How could he have been? He had been in Mukden only a few days and would have had no time to plan the assassination. Besides, what reason would he have had to want the Marshal's death? None at all.

Her anxious thoughts ran on, arguing with one another. What did she know about Chinese courts and their system of justice? She had never been exposed to them. Would there be a trial—and if so, how fair could it be? Another worry surfaced. What about witnesses to prove his innocence, to give him an alibi for the night of the train explosion?

She went about her daily chores automatically. Little Georgik tugged at her skirt and looked up at her with his large gray eyes. He chattered constantly. He had learned to say longer sentences, had reached the stage of placing "why" in front of every question. Today she found that his curiosity exhausted her. Finally she called Agrafena in.

"Please keep Georgik away from me for a couple of days, Agrafena. I think I'm coming down with a cold," she lied, watching the disapproving and suspicious look on the woman's face.

That done, she must deal now with Vladimir. How would it be possible for her to hear talk about the assassination and accompanying details—for surely it would be the topic of every household's conversation—and appear disinterested? And would Vladimir connect the name of Ma Li-chun with the Chinese interpreter he had met only once four years ago? She hoped not.

But Vladimir did indeed remember Li-chun. "Isn't that the tall Chinese who interpreted for the official from the railway company after your performance at the Zhelsob?" And when Svetlana nodded, he added, "Yes, I remember him. He spoke excellent Russian and didn't look entirely Chinese."

Vladimir glanced at the article again. "So! It turns out he's a former *hunhuz,*" he read on, then added flatly, "From somewhere near Maoershan. . . ." He narrowed his eyes but did not look at Svetlana. "Well, if that's the case, then the police may be on the right track. I don't know what he had to gain by the Marshal's murder, but he could have been hired by the assassins for a bribe too attractive to turn down."

Svetlana bit her lip and watched his movements as he pushed his chair back from the table, rose, and stretched. "I

don't know about you, but I am going to turn in early tonight.
Care to join me?"

Svetlana flushed. Anything but *that* tonight. She shook her
head. "I'm not feeling too well. I think I'm coming down with
a cold, so I'll stay up and have some tea with cognac," she
said, following through on the story she had told Agrafena.

She sat alone late into the night, her thoughts circling
around Li-chun. At last, unable to stifle her anxiety, she went
to bed. "Mornings are wiser than evenings," her mother used
to say. Maybe tomorrow's issue of the *Zarya* would have better news.

But the next day's newspaper report was even worse. Li-
chun had no witnesses to give him an alibi. His assurances
that he was a loyal aide to Marshal Chang Tso-lin met with
the denigrating comments—what could one expect from a former *hunhuz* who hadn't broken his ties with the band? Things
didn't look good for Ma Li-chun, the paper reported, and
there was widespread belief that at the forthcoming trial he
would be proven guilty.

The paper shook in Svetlana's hands as she stared at the
article. Printed words blurred on the page, then came into
focus again only to stare back at her with mockery. Li-chun
found guilty of murder . . .

Her imagination ran wild. Somewhere outside of Harbin
people would find a *hunhuz* head impaled on a stake and
would point to it as an example of *hunhuzy* justice, saying that
it should have been Li-chun's head instead.

Without warning, bile rose to her throat and she raced to
the bathroom, where she lost her meal. Shaking, weak, she
returned to stare at the paper again. She hadn't dressed all
day, and now her slippered feet moved under the table. Back
and forth, toe to toe, heel to heel. No one questioned her
strange behavior—she had a cold, hadn't she?—and the well-
trained servants moved quietly around her.

One question drummed dully in her brain. What could she
do to help him? Surely there must be something that could be
done to prove his innocence. The alternative was too terrible
to contemplate.

Perhaps there *was* a way. An alibi. He needed someone to
come forward and claim he had not been near the railway

crossing the night of the explosion. An idea began forming in her mind. She had to save him from conviction and from—in no way could she bring herself to finish the thought. In the face of such a devastating possibility her fears of parental disapproval suddenly had become minor. She had thought her love for Li-chun was not strong enough to overcome public opinion. What about now?

Before she could honestly answer this question, the doorbell rang, she heard muffled voices in the hallway, and moments later her father entered the room. She rushed at him, circled his neck, and clung to him desperately.

"Papa, Papa! Oh, I'm so glad you came. So glad!"

He hugged her, then pushed her back a little and took her chin into his hand, looking into her face. "My dear child, tearing yourself apart is not going to help. Let's talk."

He led her to a love seat in the small parlor off the dining room, sat her down, took her hand in his, then said, "Now, tell me about it."

But Svetlana choked on her words, fought tears, and shook her head.

Nikolai waited for a few moments, then said quietly, "Svetlana, give your sorrow words. The grief that doesn't speak out can break your heart. Do you hear me, child?" And when Svetlana's lips quivered, he went on: "Well, then, let me tell you what I know. This Ma Li-chun, this *hunhuz* they arrested, he's the same man we met at the Zhelsob, right?" When Svetlana nodded, he continued: "One look at you confirms what I suspected all along. You love him. But, my dear, not all of us are privileged to marry those whom we truly love, and I had hoped that over the years you would forget Li-chun and learn to love Vladimir. You must have thought you loved him at one time."

Nikolai paused and sighed. "I can see now that I was mistaken. I know how difficult it must be for you, my dear, if you still care for him, but with the turn of events, perhaps it's all happening for the best. With his continual presence in Harbin you could hardly have forgotten him, but now you may be able to wipe the futile dream from your heart."

Quietly, piteously, Svetlana began to cry. "You don't understand, Papa," she whispered, not looking at him. "You don't know the rest of it." With a sudden flow of tears the dam broke and she poured out her anguish. She told him of her love affair, her first submission to Li-chun in the glen, Vladimir's anger, Li-chun's rescue of Georgik, her tryst in Laoshan. Finally, she spoke of her last visit to his flat when he told her he was going to see his father, and of her fear of his exposure as a *hunhuz*. One thing she withheld from her father: she didn't tell him about Vladimir's affair with Raissa.

If Nikolai was shocked, he did not show it, though a couple of times he took off his pince-nez and rubbed the bridge of his nose. He listened to her until she had finished her story, then sat for a while looking at his hands and blinking his eyes as if he were trying to come to terms with what he had just learned. At last he nodded, then looked up and met Svetlana's gaze.

"I can't condone your actions in the past; still, what's done is done," he said at last. "But now, you must remember that your first loyalty is to your husband. Don't hurt him any further by revealing who Li-chun is. He loves you and he's been faithful to you all this time. Don't betray him again."

"Faithful! He—he hasn't been faithful, Papa. He's betrayed me too. I didn't want to tell you this, but he had an affair. I found out about it quite by accident."

Nikolai winced. "My God! With whom?"

Svetlana bit her lip and averted her gaze. "Someone I know very well, Papa. That's why things could never be right in our marriage. There's too much bitterness between us." She shook her head. "Please don't ask any more questions."

Nikolai narrowed his eyes and shook his head slowly. After a few moments he picked up Svetlana's hand and kissed it. "My dear, you must let your conscience guide you now."

"What should I do, Papa?"

"You can't hide from a problem, child. Face it."

"But how?"

"Sometimes you have to take great risks in life." Nikolai looked at her with great tenderness and what seemed to Svetlana compassion, then added, "Whatever you decide to do, my dear, know that at least one member of your family will support you."

When Svetlana realized what her father was trying to tell

her, she put her arms around him and pressed her forehead into his shoulder. For a long while she continued to cling to him. It wasn't necessary to say anything. He understood. He was her wonderful, loving Papa.

After he'd left, she sat for a long time, thinking. Li-chun had to be cleared of the charges. One thing and one thing only mattered—to save him.

Suddenly, a long-denied truth, like the petals of a sun-kissed flower, unfolded in the brilliant flash of revelation. She loved him beyond reason; loved him beyond prejudice and public opinion, beyond the scandal that her actions would bring. And only when she was about to lose him had she come to understand all this. Shame, bitter, galling shame spread through her. What delusions had she lived under all this time? That she could spend the rest of her life with Vladimir and steal secret moments of love with Li-chun?

And now there was a possibility that her making a statement might not save him. It would be her word against theirs. But try she must.

Li-chun needed an alibi. The question now remained, how to provide one. He had been in Mukden the night before the assassination. That was a confirmed fact, and she couldn't say that he had been with her in Harbin. There was only one thing to do. She would have to say she had traveled secretly to meet him in Mukden and was with him that fatal night. Vladimir would, of course, know she was lying. But by the time he learned of her statement, he wouldn't dare to repudiate it, for he would be mortified by her actions and wouldn't want to make a public statement. It would only add to the scandal, and he had always been so afraid of scandal.

She shuddered at the thought of having to tell Vladimir the truth about Li-chun. But she wouldn't say anything to him until after she had gone to the courthouse and told her story. Then, when she came home, and before the newspapers printed her story, she would prepare Vladimir. . . .

That night she tossed in bed, unable to sleep, rehearsing the speech she would give in the courthouse chambers, afraid of being trapped by some question she could not readily answer. Toward dawn she dozed and dreamed that the officials were listening to her with sneers on their faces, pointing their fingers at her, even to the point of calling her a whore whose word could not be taken seriously. She awakened bathed in perspiration, her heart pounding painfully, her body weak and shaking.

After a hot bath she collected herself enough to dress carefully in a summer suit of pale-blue shantung silk, swept her blond hair off her face into a chignon at the nape of her neck, and, afraid to lose courage, hurried out of the house.

At the entrance to the courthouse she slowed down. Each move brought her closer and closer to the irrevocable step she was about to take. She was going to tear her life apart, but the thought of changing her mind was unacceptable.

She smoothed the silk of her slim skirt, lifted her head, and walked in. A thin Chinese receptionist looked up, folded his hands, and waited for her to speak. Summoning courage, she told him that she wished to make a deposition. He inclined his head and without a word rose and left her alone. Before long she was shown into a large chamber, where a Chinese clerk and an interpreter looked her over curiously. She held on to the well-worn bentwood chair to hide her trembling, then lowered herself slowly into it.

The Chinese clerk nodded and said something to the interpreter.

"You are to state your name and address and the purpose of your visit," the interpreter translated in a monotone.

Speaking slowly to keep from stumbling over words, Svetlana did as she was told, and after the clerk had recorded the statement, she proceeded to tell her story: She and Li-chun had been lovers for some time. . . . They hadn't seen each other while he was in Peking, and so when she heard that he was returning to Mukden, she went there to meet him. . . . On the night of June third she was with him the whole night.

After her statement was recorded and she left the chamber, the interpreter, a tall, broad-shouldered young man, followed her into the corridor. When they were out of anyone's hearing, he looked around, then said quietly to her, "Ma Li-chun is not accused of planting the explosives himself. He has been arrested on charges of complicity in the plot. The fact that he was with you the night of June third does not exonerate him from the crime."

"But the newspapers said he is supposed to have been one of the Chinese men seen on the viaduct that night!" Svetlana said, her voice shaking.

"The journalists do not always report accurately. Even if it is proven that he was not at the crossing the night of the explosion, his acquittal cannot be based on that fact alone."

"You mean my deposition makes no difference?" Svetlana asked, trying to hold down a wave of hysteria.

"It is possible that your testimony at the trial will be accepted, but the basic accusation of his complicity still remains."

Svetlana clasped her hands together so hard they shook. "My statement, then, is worthless!"

The interpreter shrugged and looked at her with compassion. "Not necessarily, madam."

The words rang in Svetlana's ears as she walked home slowly, unsteady from lack of sleep, shaken by the strain of the last two days. The revelation that her painful sacrifice might have been in vain pursued her relentlessly. What bitter irony to think that the ordeal was not yet over and she might have to testify at the trial anyway! She leaned against a picket fence bordering the sidewalk and held on to it for a few moments. The reporters would splash the story on the front page of tomorrow's paper. They wouldn't pass up such a juicy bit of scandal. She could see the headline now: RUSSIAN WIFE OF ENGINEER SPENT NIGHT BEFORE ASSASSINATION WITH ACCUSED HUNHUZ.

There was yet the dreadful confrontation with Vladimir to endure, and it had to be done that day, before the sensational news hit the papers. What would his reaction be? Anger, insults, deprecation? No matter.

The only thing that mattered now was that she had failed to guarantee Li-chun's acquittal. How naive of her to think that her word would be sufficient to exonerate him. But hadn't the newspaper led her to believe that the only thing lacking was his alibi for that night of June third?

As for Vladimir . . . well, perhaps it was just as well for

the truth to come out. There would no longer be any subterfuge in their relationship.

But the scene at home was worse than she had imagined. After dinner, when Georgik had been put to bed and Agrafena and the servants had gone to their rooms, Svetlana braced herself for the confrontation and poured the whole story out to Vladimir from the very beginning in the taiga to the last day's events. Sparing him nothing, she spoke quickly, barely pausing for breath, afraid he would start shouting and not let her finish.

"I couldn't help falling in love with him, Vladimir. Whatever you say now doesn't really make any difference, because I shall always love him no matter what happens. I married you because that was expected of me by my parents, by society at large. I want you to know that I did love you before I met Li-chun, and after we were married, I truly hoped to forget the past and be a good wife to you. You see, I knew that my love for Li-chun was hopeless, for at that time he was an outlaw and the obstacles were impossible to overcome. But all that has changed now. I know this is hurting you, but I had to make a choice between inviting scandal or doing nothing to save Li-chun."

Her voice shook at this point, but one thing she could not bring herself to tell Vladimir: her failure to save Li-chun with her alibi.

All the time she spoke, she never took her eyes away from his, wanting to tell him everything, wanting to make him hurt as much as he had hurt her in the past. And as she talked, she watched the change come over his face. She had expected fury, angry retorts, insults like the ones she had endured on their wedding night and in the first weeks of their marriage. Instead, she was shocked by what she saw. Vladimir's face was suffused with color, and he sat rigidly in his armchair, grasping it with his hands so hard that his knuckles were white. As she met his gaze, she was suddenly pained to see his eyes cloud with humiliation and fill with tears. As she looked at him, he slumped in his chair and buried his face in his arms.

Svetlana had never seen a man weep this way before. The tears she had seen on Li-chun's face that beautiful night in the

forest were nothing compared to this devastating sight. What
had she done? With all his faults, Vladimir *was* her husband,
and in her own heartache she hadn't thought how great a
shock her confession would be to him. She moved forward
and hesitantly put her hand on his shoulder.

"Please, Vladimir, stop! Believe me, in spite of all the bitterness between us, I'm truly sorry to have hurt you; I—I didn't
think you'd react like this."

He raised his head and threw her hand off. After fumbling
for a handkerchief in his pocket, he wiped his face, rose, and
faced her.

"What did you expect?" With reddened eyes he swept the
room as though seeing it for the first time. "I tried so hard
. . . so hard! I wanted to be respected in the community, to
salvage what I could in my family life. I knew you didn't love
me—how could you, after what you had confessed? But I
thought you'd forget him, learn to be content in our life together. I never denied you anything." He slammed his fist on
the table. "I was a good husband and father! I love our Georgik. . . . Oh, God, he has to live with this scandal now for
the rest of his life. What can we tell him when he's old enough
to understand? . . . This sordid affair . . . And how can we
continue to live in Harbin and see all our friends as though
nothing has happened?" His voice rose. "Did you think about
it before you let your passion rule your head? What happened
to your common sense? Or don't you have any? Have you no
decency left in you, no sense of obligation toward the people
involved?"

He clasped his head in his hands. "My God, my God! I
can't face my parents, my friends, my associates at work."

Having expected to spite him for what he had done to
Raissa, Svetlana instead was filled with pity.

"Vladimir," she said quietly, moving toward him, "I can't
undo what I've done, but at least believe me when I say that I
am sorry . . . so very sorry!"

Suddenly, Vladimir moved away, looking at her as though
he were seeing her for the first time. There was such anger,
such disgust, in his face, that she stepped back quickly.

"Don't you touch me! Do you hear? Don't touch me again.
All your words are a farce. You can afford to be contrite now

that you've done what you wanted to do. You've destroyed me. Have you thought what this will do to my parents? Have you thought about *them?* Have you? Answer me!"

Now she saw him as the man she had known all these years, and her pity evaporated as quickly as it had started. But before she had a chance to answer, his mouth twisted and he went on: "And what do you expect *your* parents to think of their daughter who has cuckolded her husband and who sleeps with a *hunhuz?* You're a hypocrite!"

Red circles floated before her eyes, clouding her vision. How dare he! Of all people, how dare he talk to her like that?

"Hypocrite? You dare call *me* a hypocrite?" Rigidly, she pointed her finger at him. "What about you and *your* affair with my own sister? What do you think *your* parents would say to that?"

If words could slap, hers surely did then. Vladimir paled. For a few moments he was at a loss for words, then he seemed to force them out: "How did you know?"

His voice was hoarse, and as Svetlana looked at him, she suddenly felt weary of this argument. *What's the use?* she thought.

"Never mind how I found out," she said evenly. "The fact remains that you have no right to accuse me of the very thing you yourself are guilty of. I may have fallen in love with a bandit, but what *you* did is despicable. You're always worried about public opinion, yet you seduced your wife's sister and carried on an affair with her. Thank God, she's happy in Shanghai. I fell in love, but you—you were guided by lust!"

Vladimir pressed his fists to his forehead and muttered under his breath, "I can't face anyone. I can't face the whole of Harbin." Abruptly, he turned and strode out of the room without looking at Svetlana.

Chapter Twenty-seven

The following day the newspaper carried the usual daily news, social events, and a small notice about Ma Li-chun's forthcoming trial. Anxiously, Svetlana scanned the entire paper page by page, but there was not a word about her deposition. At first she was flooded with enormous relief, but as she thought about it, she wondered if her statement had been judged invalid for use in the trial. She longed to see Li-chun in prison, but she knew that he would try to dissuade her from sacrificing her reputation on the witness stand. She decided that she would wait a day or two to see if she might still receive a summons to appear as a witness at the trial. If not, she would go see him anyway.

Although she could not guess the reason for the newspaper's silence, she was at least grateful that Vladimir had been spared humiliation. Now it wouldn't be so difficult to face him when he returned from work. Surely he would be somewhat relieved.

At the office Vladimir flushed with shame as he greeted his colleagues and went to his desk. He sat shuffling papers, unable to concentrate on his work. Although he was relieved that no mention had been made in the newspaper about Svetlana, he now felt a more subtle, more insidious, anxiety that reminded him of the early days of his marriage when he had seen Svetlana's lover in every man's face. He wondered how quickly the news would leak out and the rumors start around town. Which of his friends would learn first of his humiliation and look at him with disdain and pity?

How could Svetlana do this to him, and then turn the tables and accuse him of his affair with Raissa? He regretted that she had found out about it, but what if she'd been aware that it was Raissa who had thrown herself at him in the first place? Anyway, wasn't the whole affair indirectly Svetlana's fault? Had she been a loving wife, he would never have looked at Raissa with anything but brotherly affection. But he had been vulnerable then. He was not to blame. Besides, it was *he* who had ended the affair. Now he wished he had never met either of the Ozerov sisters.

"Daydreaming, Panov?"

Vladimir started and looked up. Lev Petrov stood before him, smiling. Short and rotund with a receding blond hairline, he was one of the Soviet engineers who had joined the office shortly after the treaty of 1924.

Vladimir looked up and shook his head.

Lev waved a letter in the air. "Look what I've got! A letter from Igor Sotin. Wasn't he a friend of yours?" When Vladimir nodded, he continued, "Well, he's singing praises about life in Moscow."

Vladimir spent the rest of his hours in the office thinking about what Lev had said. Igor Sotin would not have written a second letter full of enthusiasm for his life if he weren't sincere about it. Suddenly, Vladimir's heart filled with such envy, his eyes burned. His close friend was already there, established and enjoying life. To live in Moscow where everyone on the streets was Russian . . . to enjoy his heritage denied him since birth . . . to be rid of the Chinese influence and all things Chinese . . .

Ever since he attained adulthood, Harbin had held nothing but bad memories for him. The near scandal with that maid when he was young, and his subsequent fear of disgrace, had haunted him for years. Then, just as he thought he had found happiness and a good, respectable marriage, he had discovered that his young bride had betrayed him with another man, and

a *hunhuz* at that! The mere thought of Svetlana in the arms of
a *hunhuz* revolted him.

Lord knows, he had tried to forgive her, had tried to make
the best of it—at least in the eyes of society. The one bright
spot in his life was little Georgik, and he adored him. Then,
the affair with Raissa. That was an interlude he hadn't been
strong enough to resist. And now, what was there for him in
the future? Facing public ridicule, however surreptitious, was
unbearable even to think about. The guesswork, the suspicion
of who might know . . .

With his head lowered over his papers so that he wouldn't
have to see who went past his desk, Vladimir counted the
hours until the office day would end.

Svetlana never got the chance to visit Li-chun in prison. She
waited for the summons to court for two days, picking up
each day's newspaper with shaking hands, her heart pounding
so hard that she could hardly control her breathing. And each
day there was nothing in the paper about her deposition. The
suspense was dreadful. Then suddenly, on the third day, the
telephone rang in the middle of the day, and she heard Li-
chun's voice on the other end. Li-chun! She clutched the receiver, barely able to understand what he was saying.

"I've been released, Svetlana. I'm home. There's something
very important I must tell you. When can you come?"

"Right away. I'll be there right away!" she cried through
tears and laughter. After hanging up the receiver, she grabbed
her purse, and, with a quick "Don't prepare tea for me" to the
maid, ran out of the house.

She was in his arms before she was quite through the door.
He pressed her to him fiercely, showering her face with kisses,
running his hands over her hair, her face, and her neck, then
holding her away from him as though he had forgotten what
she looked like.

"My dearest, I've been told what you tried to do for me. I
know what it must have cost you, and I am deeply grateful.
What dreadful irony for you to find out that your sacrifice was
not enough to acquit me! I knew the interpreter from long
ago. He was a *hunhuz* at one time. He told me that he was
able to withhold your deposition from the records, and unless

it was vital to my freedom, he planned to destroy it." Li-chun held her tightly by the shoulders. "Dearest, our secret is safe. I'm only sorry you had to go through it at all."

"But I didn't know that it wouldn't be made public," Svetlana said. "I thought the scandal would break in the newspaper the next day and so I *had* to tell Vladimir about it. I couldn't let him learn it from the paper."

Li-chun shook his head and held her close. "Oh, my dear, sweet angel! How dreadful for you. I'm sorry."

Svetlana pulled back. "Let's not talk about that now. Tell me how you were freed."

Li-chun spread his hands and shrugged. "Suddenly, without any explanation, an official order came from the Mukden to release me. The interpreter told me unofficially that there had been not two but three men at the scene of the explosion, and that they were supposed to have been stabbed by the Japanese and then blamed for planting the explosives. The third man escaped and reportedly his story reached Mukden authorities. . . . I don't know what else they learned to convince them that I was innocent, but whatever it was, I am deeply thankful I was exonerated and my life spared."

"But who framed you? Were the Japanese the real murderers?" Svetlana asked.

"We may never learn. The delicate question of whether the Japanese in Mukden were involved remains unanswered. The investigation will continue, of course, but how long it will take, or whether the truth will ever come out, remains to be seen."

Enormously relieved, Svetlana reached for Li-chun and stroked his face. "What happiness! It minimizes my own problems. Even though my alibi for you was not the one that freed you, it all seems worthwhile."

Li-chun smiled. "And now, I have something else to tell you." He took her hand and led her to the sofa, where he picked up the lacquered box and handed it to her.

"Open it," he said quietly.

Puzzled, Svetlana opened the box and took out an amber necklace. It looked old, and the golden stone felt smooth to her touch. She looked at Li-chun questioningly.

He nodded toward the box. "There's a letter inside. Read it."

Svetlana unfolded the yellowed fragile paper and started to read, but when she came to the name *Rotov,* she gasped. "Li-chun! Where did you get this? Rotov was the name of my parents' friends, the ones who were killed by the *hunhuzy.*"

For a few moments Li-chun stared at Svetlana, and she saw color rise to his face. Then he took her hands in his and held them tightly. ."My dearest, when I went to see my father, he gave me this box. He told me that I am Gennady Rotov, son of Oleg Rotov." Li-chun then repeated what Ma Fu-li had told him about his birth and abduction.

When he finished, Svetlana was crying. Such happy, wonderful tears she had never shed in her entire life. She tried to smile and even laugh, but the tears would not stop. She could actually feel the physical release of all the painful dross in her heart that had been accumulating over the past few years. She would never suffer it again. Never, never again.

Finally, she was able to whisper, "Gennady . . . you are Gennady. I can't believe it. Such happiness, such complete happiness! Oh, I can't wait to see my mother's face."

"What about your father?"

"He knows about you, Li-chun. He guessed a long time ago about us, and he understands. He'll be happy to learn all this. But it's my mother who hates all *hunhuzy* because they killed your parents and, presumably, their infant child. Oh, wait until I tell her who you really are!"

"It may be difficult for her at first, but I think when you show her the necklace, she may remember my mother—so strange to call her my mother. . . ." He smiled shyly. "Anyway, she may remember her wearing it when they were in Harbin together."

He took her in his arms, and she kissed him; a deep, hungry kiss it was, and she savored its taste as if she were kissing him for the first time. He sensed her need and responded with his own deep hunger. What happened then was a fury of emotions. He carried her into his bedroom, where a fugue of unabashed love swept them into each other's arms without restraint, all barriers removed at last.

What time flew by on wings of abandon was filled with a

kind of happiness she had never known. Her arms around him, she smiled with pleasure and held him to herself long after the last moments of loving were over. What a marvelous feeling to drift on this softness, this warmth of a peaceful aftermath of union. . . .

No more anxiety, no more guilt or fear of family disapproval. No more obstacles. She shifted uncomfortably, released Li-chun from her embrace, and rose.

No more obstacles. Save one. Vladimir.

Vladimir would object to a divorce, another scandal for him to weather. More fear of public opinion. And although divorces happened every day, she knew her father-in-law would be a strong influence on Vladimir.

She could hear him now: "Divorce is out of the question. The son of a deacon at St. Nicholas Cathedral agreeing to a divorce? Never!"

Well, she would insist on a divorce, threaten to move out of the house and thereby cause even greater scandal.

"Where are your thoughts, dearest?" Li-chun asked softly, kissing her forehead and her eyelids. "You left me for a while, didn't you?"

"I'm thinking of what I have to do now."

"And that is?"

"I'm going to ask Vladimir for a divorce. It won't be easy to make him agree, but—"

Li-chun smothered her words with kisses.

After a while she pulled away. "But first, I want to tell my parents about you. On a day like this I don't want to think of confronting Vladimir. I want to make it a totally happy day."

"Do you think your mother will accept me?" he asked.

"How can she not accept you? You're Russian, and you are the child of her best friend, whom she mourned all these years. It may take her a while to get over her shock, but think of the eventual happiness we shall bring her. And as for my father—I have no worries there at all. Oh, Li-chun, I can't wait to tell them!"

"Li-chun? You're still calling me Li-chun?" he teased. "Have you forgotten so quickly that my name is Gennady?"

Svetlana shook her head. "You'll always be Li-chun to me. Everyone else will call you Gennady Olegovich now—a mouthful for the Chinese! But to me, you are my own Li-chun."

Chapter Twenty-eight

Nikolai and Sonya were reading the paper in their parlor when Svetlana entered the room. Nikolai rose to greet her.

Svetlana kissed her parents, then sat down and looked at her mother. "Mama, I have something wonderful to tell you. This will come as a shock, but, oh, such exciting news! It's about the Rotovs. Their baby survived."

Sonya gasped. "My God!"

"The *hunhuz* chieftain," Svetlana went on, "didn't kill the newborn child that day during the raid, but took the boy into the taiga and raised him as his own."

Sonya shook her head. "I can't believe it! Who told you this?"

Without a word Svetlana opened the lacquered box and pulled the letter out. "Here," she said, handing it to her mother, "read it and see if you don't recognize the handwriting. Although the name is smeared at the top, I'm sure it was addressed to you."

Svetlana watched the pain on her mother's face as she read the letter, and when Sonya raised her eyes, they were filled with tears. "Where did it come from?" she asked in a choked voice. "This *is* Anya's handwriting, but—but I don't understand! . . ."

"The letter and this box were given to Li-chun by his father, Ma Fu-li, the tall *hunhuz* who raided the village where the Rotovs lived."

"Li-chun?" Sonya frowned. "Are you talking about the *hunhuz* who was arrested for Marshal Chang Tso-lin's murder? The one we met at your concert several years ago?"

Svetlana bristled. "He was arrested on *suspicion* of murder, Mama, and he has since been exonerated and released. What I'm trying to tell you is that Li-chun is Anya Rotov's son, Gennady, and—"

"What?" Sonya interrupted, shaking her head in disbelief.

"Yes, Mama, Li-chun is Anya Rotov's son. I've always thought he looked more Buryat and Russian than Chinese. Didn't you notice it when you met him at the Zhelsob?"

"What do you mean, 'always thought so'?" Sonya said indignantly. "You speak as if you've known him for a long time." Suddenly, she raised her voice. "What's this all about? You're not telling me everything!"

Svetlana glanced at her father, who smiled and nodded to her in silent exchange of their shared secret.

"Mama," Svetlana said, "Li-chun is the one who brought me out of the forest when I was kept for ransom by his father. And—and we've loved each other for a long time, but—"

Sonya half rose from her chair. "Whaaat? He's the one! He's responsible for that terrible experience! My God! You're a wife and a mother, and you dare to tell me you're in love with this *hunhuz?* You disgrace Vladimir's good name. And now you say he's Anya's son? Don't tell me fairy tales. I don't believe you."

Nikolai placed a restraining hand on Sonya's arm and pulled her down. "Sonya, calm down. Hear Svetlana out." His face was beaming, and Svetlana wanted to hug him. Then she pulled out the amber necklace and handed it to her mother. "If Anya's letter doesn't convince you, maybe this will. Have you seen this before?"

Sonya paled and her hands trembled as she reached for the necklace. "Where did you get this?" she whispered.

"Li-chun's father kept it all these years. He had no reason to save it or to tell all this to Li-chun unless it was the truth."

Carefully, tenderly, Sonya stroked the amber stone. "This

was *my* necklace. I brought it from Moscow." Her lips quivered. "When Anya was leaving Harbin, I gave it to her."

Sonya looked at Svetlana, and then at Nikolai. With a strangled sob she put the back of her hand against her mouth and dashed out of the room.

Nikolai shook his head. "Forgive her. It is such a shock after all these years. She has hated the *hunhuzy* for so long. . . . First the Rotovs were killed, then you were kept for ransom, and then little Georgik was kidnapped. And now suddenly she has to come to terms with the fact that the very *hunhuz* she hated is her friend's son—and that you love him. All this is too much. Give her a little time. But at least let me tell you how pleased *I* am to learn that Li-chun is in reality a Rotov."

It didn't escape Svetlana that her tactful father didn't actually say he was glad Li-chun was not Chinese.

After a pause Nikolai asked, "And now, what are your plans, my dear?"

Svetlana raised her head and thrust her chin forward. "I can't stay married to Vladimir, Papa. I want a divorce. Surely you must understand that. He already knows about Li-chun. I told him after I made my deposition at the courthouse, because I thought it would be printed in the paper and I wanted him to be prepared."

"What about Georgik?" Nikolai asked quietly.

Svetlana instinctively clutched the lacquered box. "Georgik already knows and likes Li-chun. Remember, it was Li-chun who brought him back to us."

Nikolai shook his head. "I didn't mean that. I'm wondering if Vladimir will want to fight for custody of the child, since you're the one who is asking for a divorce."

Svetlana shook her head in mute denial. "No. He won't dare!" she cried, a chill sweeping over her.

Nikolai nodded. "Let's hope he doesn't."

But Vladimir did object. Georgik was his sunshine, and the child brought the only happiness to his otherwise frustrated life. Georgik was *his* son, and he didn't want to give him up.

"Why do you want a divorce? To shame me and my parents further? Haven't you done enough already?" he shouted, and when Svetlana didn't answer, his eyes narrowed. "I see. You want to marry that *hunhuz!*"

"He's not a *hunhuz.* I told you—he's a Rotov. I want a divorce because you and I can't live together after all that has gone between us. We've both been unhappy, you can't deny it. So why not admit that our marriage has failed?"

Everything Svetlana said made sense, and he knew it was all over between them, but he couldn't accept the truth.

"How could you?" he said, his voice shaking with emotion, "You and the *hunhuz* . . . how humiliating. And now you'll cause even more scandal with a divorce."

"An amicable divorce doesn't cause a scandal. Only if you contest it could it possibly become sensational."

Vladimir clenched his fists until they shook. Then he forced the words out. "Very well. Have it your way. But I won't give up Georgik. You can't take everything away. My son stays with me, and the judge will uphold me when I tell him about your past."

"I wouldn't be so sure."

Svetlana's voice was level, and Vladimir looked at her sharply. "What do you mean?"

"I wonder what the judge will decide when I tell him that my husband seduced my own sister."

Vladimir's anger evaporated as if from a punctured balloon. She would win. At his expense she would win, willing to let his affair with Raissa become public knowledge. He was half a head taller than she, but it was she who stood towering above him now. She had stripped him of his pride, his pretense at happiness.

The world crumbled around him, closed in, and he could see no escape from the very phantom he feared the most: ridicule. If only he could hide from his conscious mind and escape into oblivion!

He became excruciatingly aware of her presence, and couldn't tolerate another second of it. There wasn't enough air for both of them in the room. He was choking. A low hum started in his ears—the ring of silence after the bitter words. He wished she would leave him alone with his misery, but she stood there with her hands folded in front of her, waiting. Patiently waiting.

"I'll think about it," he forced himself to say and, turning sharply on his heel, stalked out of the room.

He didn't remember how or why he found himself in his office after hours that same day, but his desk was still cluttered with work and he was grateful for the distraction it would give him.

As he sat in his chair, trying to concentrate, Lev Petrov walked in carrying a sheaf of papers. On seeing Vladimir he stopped in the middle of the room.

"Well! I didn't expect you here after hours. It's usually we bachelors who work late," he said with a chuckle.

When Vladimir gave him a weary look, Lev asked, "Is there anything wrong?"

Vladimir shook his head and didn't answer. Lev studied him for a few moments, then turned to go, but at the door he hesitated and looked back. "By the way, I've served my time in Harbin and will be going home soon."

Vladimir looked up sharply. "I didn't know you were leaving Harbin. Where's your home?"

"I'm from Saratov on the Volga. Your Sungari here can't begin to compare to our Volga. Well, anyway, I'm counting the days; it won't be long now."

He left the room whistling the *Internationale*. Vladimir sat at his desk, his hands in his lap, just as he had been when Lev came in.

Suddenly an idea that had clung to the periphery of his consciousness asserted itself. An idea he would have rejected only a few days ago, and which now appeared like a gift from heaven.

Leave everything behind and go to Russia . . . a new life, a rebirth. Things couldn't be as bad as the White Russian paranoia described it. Igor Sotin attested to that. Now he, too, could leave Harbin without regrets. He and Svetlana had grown far apart and she was right, there was too much bitterness between them to salvage the marriage. His parents would be upset, but he had nothing in common with them anymore —they were rigid in their religion, narrow in their political views. They would worry about what he would find in Russia once he took that irrevocable step, but he would prove them wrong and in time they would get over their shock. Yes, what a relief it would be to escape from his shame!

He would have only one heartache. Georgik. His son. His only child. But for Georgik's sake he must leave him behind. Appealing as his motherland seemed, still, there remained an uncertainty as to where he would be sent and what his home life would be like. Much as it galled him to admit it, Georgik was better off remaining in his mother's care, with both sets of grandparents to love and care for him, secure in familiar surroundings. He had to make this sacrifice for the good of his son. Suddenly, he remembered what Svetlana had said: "Amicable divorces don't cause scandals." Yes, they would have an amicable divorce and he would leave without any gossip.

He *was* a Soviet citizen now, going to Russia, and maybe, just maybe, he would be envied secretly in some quarters for his decision to regain his motherland while those others were still refugees without their country.

As he raced home, he wasn't aware that he had a smile on his face until he realized that passersby were looking at him and smiling back.

To prepare Georgik for his departure, Vladimir moved to his parents' house, for although they were shocked by his decision to emigrate to Russia, they wanted to have him with them for as long as possible before he left. Svetlana filed for divorce, and while Vladimir waited for it to become final, he visited his son for an hour every third day. Georgik missed him, cried, and had tantrums, and, with the simple logic of a five-year-old, asked, "Why can't I see Papa every afternoon?" When Svetlana explained that Papa didn't live with them anymore, Georgik demanded to know why.

Svetlana worried about her son, hoping that the traumatic period of adjustment would eventually dim in his memory. She turned to Li-chun and asked him to spend more time with Georgik.

Ten days after Svetlana had told her mother who Li-chun was, Sonya asked her to bring him over. Now, sitting at the table and pouring tea from the samovar, Sonya carried on a polite conversation, stealing searching glances at Li-chun while he was not looking at her. In spite of Nikolai's bemused smile and the warmth with which he engaged Li-chun in conversation, Svetlana was annoyed that it was taking her mother this long to come around.

As Sonya poured another glass of tea and handed it to Li-chun, their hands touched. Suddenly the glass began to shake in her hand and the tea spilled on the white cloth. Quickly, Li-chun took it out of her hand and thanked her.

Sonya put her hand on his arm. "Let me look at you closely, Li-chun. Turn your head, will you?" she said pleadingly. As Li-chun obliged and cocked his head sideways, Sonya gasped and nodded her head rapidly as if in answer to her own question.

"Anya used to turn her head exactly as you did just then. And your eyes have that same shape that she laughed about. *My Buryat blood,* she used to say. But you also have something of Oleg in you. He, too, was tall and held himself very erect, as you do."

Nikolai clapped his hands. "That's it! Now I realize what it was that looked familiar when I first saw you at the Zhelsob concert."

Sonya smiled and shook her head. "Forgive me for taking this long to recognize you in my heart. It was such a shock. I still can hardly believe it!"

Li-chun took her hand and, after a slight hesitation, bent over and kissed it. "I understand. I have a hard time believing it myself. I must ask you most humbly to tell me all you can about my parents, so I may know them through you."

Nikolai laughed softly. "Well, to begin with, you must unlearn your formal way of speaking. You needn't ask 'most humbly' for anything anymore. I realize that it will take time for you to adjust to these changes. And as for us, we have to learn to call you Gennady now."

Li-chun smiled and nodded. "I'm resigning from the army and I'll continue to work for the railway company as a civilian. My colleagues, too, will have to learn my new name."

Nikolai turned to Svetlana. "My dear, I haven't seen you this radiant in many years."

Svetlana smiled and kissed her father. Then she hugged her mother, who still sat staring at Li-chun with a look of wonder and newly found affection. Sonya came alive then. With a quick movement she removed the amber necklace from her neck and put it over Svetlana's head.

"It is yours, my dear. It rightfully belongs to you, for had Anya been alive, she would have wanted you to have it. It is part of our Russian heritage now."

Svetlana couldn't speak. She bent over again and kissed her mother, then turned to Li-chun.

"It's getting late. We have to go home."

At the gate to her garden Svetlana paused. "Won't you come in and—and stay?" she asked shyly.

Li-chun hesitated only a second, then shook his head. "No, dearest," he said firmly. "It is still *your* home, and I will not stay overnight until I am master of the house. Now"—he bent over her and smiled—"will you come with me to *my* house?"

It was her turn to shake her head. "Not tonight, my love. I've been gone all afternoon, and Georgik needs me."

He nodded. "I understand. There's much for both of us to learn! Adjustments are not easy. But we have our love, and that's the most important thing, isn't it?"

Without a word she lifted her face to him and he kissed her with the tenderness she knew so well. In the softened air of the late afternoon the lovers clung to each other in total commitment.

A setting sun combed the trees in the little square across the street and bathed the garden in an amber light. A swallow darted past them, then disappeared behind the trees. A few sparrows gossiped, cocking their heads at the two people locked in an embrace.

In the approaching twilight the clear air sang.